OF
BLOOD
AND
DECEIT

OF
BLOOD
AND
DECEIT

RACHEL A. COLLETT

OF BLOOD AND DECEIT

Copyright © 2019 by Rachel Collett

Cover design by ©Jennifer Zemanek/Seedlings Design Studio.
www.seedlingsonline.com

Published by Rachel Collett
www.rachelcollett.com

ISBN-13: 978-1798876572

To my husband, Dan:

you are my real-life, dark and brooding love interest,

and you always will be.

CONTENTS

1

ROYAL PRISONER

RUSTED CUFFS BIT INTO THE FLESH of my ankles, shooting sharp pains up bruised legs. My heart pounded and my head throbbed as I shuffled down the cell corridor in a red, shapeless prison gown. Red signified female, though I hardly felt like one anymore.

Once a week. Just once a week, we could escape our hell on earth and breathe the air outside of the piss-saturated, rat-infested walls of our confinement. Ten cells a day were given their freedom for an hour. That was what the king of Anolyn granted, which was kind compared to what my uncle would have allowed.

I paced my steps and thoughts, hiding my excitement from the guards who unshackled the manacles from my bare feet. The cement stairs were ice cold. As we climbed in single file, the wind blew through the cracks of the prison doors.

Then they were thrown wide. Light poured in, blinding me.

Water fell from a bloated sky. The wind chilled my wet skin, and goosebumps shivered down my back, but I didn't care. The rain was a blessing. It was the only shower I had had since being captured by Riaan's men. I lifted my face to the heavens of Anolyn, letting it wash away months of dirt and grime.

An automatic grunt bubbled from my lips as Lucan shoved past to go sulk in the corner of the arena with the other prisoners, his broad shoulders and large biceps too big for the prison garb given to him. A mop of dishwater blond hair hung down his pale face. Under the protection of a large oak, he scowled at me. Another reason why I was thankful for the rain. He would leave me alone for once.

Retracing the muddied circle entrenched in the ground from countless other prisoners, I walked my laps alone, lifting my shackled hands as high in front of me as I could to stretch sore muscles. I almost looked tan, but it was only dirt that darkened my skin.

This was my tenth walk, my first given to me after healing from a severe beating by an overzealous guard upon my arrival. In his defense, I deserved it. He would never regrow the ear that now rotted in the dense soil of Varian Forest.

It had been approximately three months since my capture, and I was nowhere nearer to escape. Not that I was trying. Riaan's prison was luxury compared to what awaited me when my uncle reclaimed me. Death came to those who he deemed a traitor—and I was a traitor.

I rolled my neck, feeling the tight strain of my skin and the burn mark from my uncle. The scar stretched from just beneath my ear to right above my collarbone—a reminder of a past treachery, and only one of many. Blood or not, he did not tolerate dissidence.

The sound of hooves arrested my attention as a man on his horse cantered into the arena. The prison guard whistled—a signal that our recess was over early. My shoulders hunched as I walked back, the muddy ground squishing between my toes. The rain grew heavier. By the time the last man entered the prison doors, I couldn't see a foot in front of my face.

Which was why I ran headlong into the horse's ass... and his black steed.

Letting out a surprised curse, I pushed away, but kept my head down.

The man brushed at the watery filth left behind on the sleeve of his black uniform and tsked. "That's not very becoming of a lady."

My face burned, but I swallowed my sarcastic reply. I had never been a lady. Born as a girl, I was already thought weak. Second-rate. Seventeen years of fighting proved I was anything but. Now I accepted the truth that I was a woman, but a lady? No. That station only came with additional costs. Costs I was unwilling to pay. But if I wanted to remain hidden, I needed to pretend for the time being.

"Nothing?" His deep voice was gruff and unnervingly calm. I didn't like it.

His very presence radiated authority. His eyes bore through my face as he stood silently watching me, waiting for me to say something imprudent—to fall into some unknown trap.

I mumbled my apologies and prayed to be excused. Rain dripped from my dirt-crusted hairline, down my face, and onto my soiled feet, but still the man stayed where he was. The mud coated his once nicely polished boots and I fought the growing temptation to look up. Enlightenment could sometimes be deadly.

"Sir." A panicked guard rushed from the prison doors, grabbing me roughly by the arm.

Despite the pain, relief flooded through me. I was happily ready to be dragged back to my cell.

"Bring her to my office," the man said.

The guard stuttered, surprised. "Sir?

"Now." Then he spun on his heel and led his horse away to the stables. He vanished through the downpour.

My heart dropped.

"What did you do?"

Before I could respond to the infuriated guard, he knocked me to the ground with a solid backhand to the face. Shock and then anger surged, but within seconds, two guards rushed me and I had barely enough time to block my face from a kick—missing the one to my side. The air knocked from me, my lungs seized in pain, then another blow to my head—

ဆဝင

I came to when my legs crumpled on a hard floor. Wet, weak and annoyed, I allowed the cold of the concrete to seep into my skin, glad to feel something other than my throbbing body. I pushed my hands against the ground, rising partway.

At first hazy, my gaze darted about an expansive and impeccably clean room. A huge stone fireplace blazed, warm and alive. A window was cracked open to allow a small breeze from outside, although the rain still poured in sheets.

The smell of freshly baked bread wafted through the air, seizing almost every sense. A crystal goblet, a smaller wooden cup, and a platter with half a loaf of steaming bread teased from the top of an ornate wooden desk that faced the door. My stomach growled pitifully, but I forced myself to ignore the irritating hunger.

Masses of papers and folders littered the top of the desk. Books were scattered about the room, stacked upon the floor and lined within rows of a private library. The owner of this receiving room was important. Advisor to the king? The king's commander?

"What is this?" His voice was instantly recognizable and so were his boots now cleaned from the mud.

I inhaled a ragged breath as the guards gripped my arms and dragged me to my feet. I swayed on the spot but managed to stay upright.

Three guards stood at attention behind me. The one from the prison spoke. "The prisoner, sir."

Clean and dry in new black pants and a white shirt unbuttoned at the top, the man with the impossibly deep voice finished drying his thick black hair cropped tight on the sides, then tossed the towel to the ground. He ran his fingers through the tresses, calming the damp mess.

I cursed beneath my breath.

The King's brother. Prince Castiel Anouk of Anolyn, known for his cunning in battle. I had yet to face the renowned warrior. Something within warned me that I never wanted to.

The room went silent. His piercing blue eyes scanned my appearance, then that of the guards. "It's Lieutenant Scores, correct?"

Scores nodded. "Yes, sir."

The prince scrutinized each guard from top to bottom. "I don't see a mark upon anyone else. Did she attack you?"

Scores's head twitched. "No, sir."

He crossed his arms over his chest. "She must have attacked someone. Why else would you have beaten her to a pulp?"

The two other guards gawked at each other, their faces pale.

"You—you requested the prisoner be brought to you," Scores said.

Another moment of silence, then, "And so you *beat* her?"

"I thought she had offended—"

Quicker than lightning, the prince thrust forward his hand. The lieutenant, as if seized by the throat, lifted into the air, although no physical contact was made. Power radiated the room, and I cringed.

A magician. A hiss issued from my lips as magic pulsed through the air. I took an automatic step back, my adrenaline firing, but could not look away. How much could he sense?

Muscles rippled in his jaw. Anger infused the prince's words. "If I'd been offended, I wouldn't need someone like you to do my dirty work for me, would I?"

Then the energy released, and Scores crashed to the ground. He wrapped a hand around his neck and coughed, his voice rasped. "No, sir. Forgive me, sir."

The prince whipped around. "Captain!"

Not even a second passed before the large oak door opened. The man—if you could call him that—must have been listening from outside, awaiting his orders. A beast of hulking muscles and ink, he entered the room, making the space a little too crowded. I instinctively took another step back.

A magician and a giant.

He smirked, catching the movement. His eyes pinned me to the spot, stopping any further retreat. Blood drew to my cheeks. Shaved close on the sides and back like his prince, his blond hair pulled tight into a pony-tail, exposing a high forehead and severely cut jawline. A tattoo crawled down the side of his neck and disappeared beneath his black, leather jerkin.

"Yes, sir," the giant said. His voice rumbled within his throat.

"Mikael, Lieutenant Scores is relieved from duty."

Scores stuttered. "But—but, sir!"

"Make sure he's reassigned somewhere far away, with no option for promotion. Find an appropriate replacement among your men. And send for Sameen."

Mikael stifled a laughed. "Yes, sir. Come with me, Scores."

Scores's mouth opened and closed like a fish, the blood draining from his face.

"You're all dismissed," the prince said, his tone an icy warning.

Bowing, Scores and his men trailed after Mikael.

The prince considered me from across the room, then walked to his desk, giving me the ability to study him unabashed. He was young. Probably no more than twenty. And he was handsome. No, that was the wrong word. He was breathtaking—which meant only one thing: he was dangerous.

He drank from a crystal goblet. The skin of his throat and hands were favorably tanned, unlike so many of the nobles of my kingdom. Eira's harsh climates kept most indoors. Even those with dark skin paled in the lack of sun.

His gaze found mine before I could lower my eyes to my hands. Did he expect me to speak? I clamped my mouth even tighter.

He set his cup down with a clank. Then, producing a knife from the holster at his belt, he sliced a chunk of bread from the loaf, but he did not eat. "Please," he said, gesturing to a chair on the other side of his desk. I did not move until he put away his blade.

The prince noticed.

Even though my legs shook with fatigue I wavered, wary to sit across from a being that was both a prince and a magician. I perched at the edge of my seat, ready to make my escape if necessary. My gaze flashed to the cracked window.

Prince Castiel's head tipped to one side as he inspected me, curiosity brimming in those strange blue eyes. Unexpectedly conscious of my appearance, I pawed at my dark hair, but gave up when my fingers caught in a tangled, greasy mess. I peered down at my ragged prison gown, bruised ankles, and dirty, black-encrusted toenails.

"You must be hungry," he said, gesturing to the bread. "Go ahead."

I didn't wait for another invitation. I snatched the cut piece and took a bite. The king of Anolyn didn't starve his prisoners like Eira's did, but this wasn't stale or full of weevils, and my taste buds zinged to the mouthwatering flavor. For the briefest moment, I wondered if I should be worried it was poisoned, but the next bite smothered the fear. It was the best tasting thing I had ever had and well worth dying for.

"Careful," the prince cautioned. "You don't want to make yourself sick."

I swallowed, chewing slower.

Again, he watched me, waiting until I finished the last bite. My eyes dropped to the remaining loaf, but he pulled the plate out of reach. "You can have the rest later." He leaned back, resting his chin on steepled fingers. "You've created quite a stir as of late, did you know that?"

My head shot up and my heart quickened, but I didn't answer.

One eyebrow raised. "We've been waiting for some time for you to make your move, but three months and... absolutely nothing." He sighed again, then picked up a folder from his desk, searching through the contents. "You've only ever been seen in battle, so you were almost unrecognizable without your usual attire."

My voice rasped. "Please, Your Highness—"

"So, you know who I am?" He picked up another folder and thumbed past a few pages. Heat rose to my face as I speculated just what condemning documents he was searching through.

I swallowed. "Of course. All your loyal subjects do. You are Prince Castiel Anouk of Anolyn."

"And so that is who you are? A loyal subject?"

"Of course, Your Highness."

He paused, stroking the line of his sharp chin with his fingers. "That's an interesting lie. But I'm pleased you know who I am. It makes things a lot easier. "His eyes narrowed as he considered me. "I couldn't believe it at first. The Scourge of Men right here in my very own home. I wonder if you think I should be honored."

I barely contained my surprise. "There is no such person, and even if there was, that title is not mine."

His tone was like ice. "Why did you attack a soldier?

"He attacked me."

"You failed to provide any sort of identification."

"I didn't know I needed any. "I could feel his fingers tighten around my throat like a vise, but knew it was just my imagination.

His fist slammed on the top of his desk. I hid a responding jolt, my insides lurching.

"Anyone traveling outside of their community where they will not be recognized must have the proper paperwork." His face softened. A smile tipped one side of his mouth. "But it's alright. That has been rectified."

He selected a page from his folder then lightly tossed it away. It fluttered to the table top in front of me and I froze. My mouth opened, but nothing came out. "There's your paperwork." He smiled. "Now that we both know each other, you can stop the charade, Your Highness."

I licked my dry lips. "My lord, please,"

"Princess Ilianna Drakara, daughter to the fallen Prince Toma, and the only living relative to King Johan Drakara. You have been offered as a mate to my brother, which is why he sent us this lovely depiction of you to persuade him into matrimony, along with lists describing your many attributes." One brow ticked high on a smooth forehead. "I must say I was impressed to hear you are such a fine dancer on top of being a fearless warrior."

My face flushed an even deeper shade of red. It took everything I had not to grab the papers from his hands.

"Despite the months of grime, your likeness is uncanny. I have to say: your eyes are much more unsettling in person." He gestured to the picture. "They're almost transparent. Perhaps silver. Even still, I assume you resemble your mother more. Besides the hair color, I see nothing of Toma or Johan in you, although, not much is known of the woman who bore you."

My mouth clamped shut with an audible click. My mother was a peasant woman. Unworthy of a prince, she sufficed as a mistress and Toma had taken her to his bed. Unfortunately, she soon became pregnant, then died giving birth to me. After my father's death, my uncle took me under his wing, but he never let me forget my lineage. I never spoke of my mother. No one did.

A smug smile lifted the corners of his mouth. "If you wanted the crown so badly, did you really think encroaching upon our dungeons would gain my brother's attention?"

Rage infused my tone. "How dare you—"

"Or were you going for pity with this look?" His gazed lowered to my clenched fists.

I gave up all pretenses, realizing they were useless. "I didn't want *any* attention at all, *Your Highness.*"

"Then why did you come?"

"I didn't come to your kingdom to stay, but to pass through. It was your men that stopped me."

He closed the file with a snap. The hard lines of his face deepened as he regarded me. "Passage amid our two kingdoms has been forbidden for many years, Princess, due to the wars fought against your uncle to keep our lands safe from his greed."

The muscles between my brows pinched, but I kept my voice as even as possible. "The war is over. Peace has been established. Our roads should be reopened to allow safe passage."

He leaned forward, pressing his hands against the top of his desk. "Did Johan tell you that? Neither kingdom has seen peace since before the demon wars, over twenty years ago. Treaties have just begun. Your uncle's offering of his only blood relation was a way of beginning that treaty."

"I—" I couldn't form the appropriate sentence. "I was not aware of any offering…" At least any offer that had been *made*. As far as I knew, he had only mentioned the idea to me the day of my escape. That was the very reason I had fled my kingdom, but I would never have run *toward* a country we still were at war with. It made no sense.

"And why would you want to leave your country?" the prince pressed.

I swallowed. "My reasons are my own." Phantom pain slid through the burn at my neck, touching upon the others that would stay unseen.

"They must not have been that important. You barely put up a fight. Only an ear was lost before you gave up. That's nothing for you."

Tired of this interrogation, I slid on a fake smile. It was the face I displayed when necessary. A mask to hide what weakness lay beneath. "I didn't want to be recognized."

"That's right. Because Eira's Demon Daughter would be recognized within my kingdom. How old were you when you started fighting for king and country? Fifteen? Sixteen?"

I was twelve, not that I would tell him.

He continued. "Your name is one of legends."

"Legends can be deceiving. I do not own that ridiculous title." Or at least I didn't want it. I didn't want any of it. "Surely you must know there's no such person. Just stories spread to incite fear among the enemy."

"Stories spawn from somewhere, Princess." He threw down another piece of paper. A sketch. And I froze.

"As you see, not everyone who has seen your face has died. This was created by someone who saw you and lived to tell the tale."

The blood drained from my already paled cheeks. I stared at a terrifying sketch of me—or what appeared to be me—in full battle gear. Flames haloed my body in a harrowing depiction of what I believed was my inner beast. How the artist managed to draw such amazing detail was beyond understanding. Only one had ever called me the Demon Daughter of Eira to my face, and I had killed him. Is that what I really looked like? Who else knew?

He smiled wickedly, exposing a perfect set of white teeth. "Obviously, the artist leans toward the dramatic, but it's close enough."

I glared, my mind spinning an escape through a castle I didn't know.

The prince's gaze did not flinch. "This whole time you've been here, you have not stated who you are, tried to reach out to your uncle, or made any attempt to flee."

"Your cells are incredibly cushy."

He ignored my flippant reply. "Why?"

I turned away with a lift of my chin, unwilling to tell him, to expose myself any further.

With a sigh, the prince sat down in his chair. He leaned back, placing his hands behind his head. "When my father was alive, he made several attempts toward peace negotiations, but Johan resisted and continued in his campaign against us. Why now do we find our prison cells holding a silent princess? Why now does your king send you as an offering?"

Why indeed. If I had an answer to that question, I wouldn't be sitting across from a scheming magician. He waited, seconds that felt like hours. "In the king's attached letter, it speaks of a woman well versed in literature and who loves to recite poetry. Will you not speak so I can continue hearing your lovely voice?" Humiliation grew to anger. Pride pricked at the back of my eyes. "What answer could I give that you would believe? It's clear you do not trust me, and I have no reason to trust you. I have no answers for your highness."

"Then you agree we are at an impasse?" When I again didn't answer, he gathered my uncle's sketch and tucked it away in his folder. "At one time, we would have no difficulty hanging you for the crimes you've committed against my people—"

"What crimes have I committed? We were at war."

"—but now that Johan declares a desire for this so-called peace, I have no choice but to send word to your king that you are here."

2

LADY ANNA

I SHOT TO MY FEET. THE BLOOD ran from my face. "No!"

Prince Castiel's eyes narrowed at my outburst. "If your uncle chooses to uphold this *peace*, we will permit you to leave with an attendant. Until that time, you will be given room and proper clothes. We can't have your kingdom think you were mistreated within our home."

My head spun. I could feel his walls, my uncle's walls, pressing against me, worse than any cell anyone could lock me in. My breathing deepened as I mentally assessed my situation. I was in no condition to kill the prince, unsure of what additional magic he possessed. Even if I could manage, I didn't need *two* countries vying for my head.

He stretched one long leg out to the side. "For the time being, you are our guest and will be treated with the utmost respect while you remain, Princess. For your safety you will go by Lady Anna—daughter to an unknown country lord, recently deceased. You were attacked by rogue bandits and mistakenly imprisoned with the captives."

My face grew hot beneath his steady gaze. "Why the charade?"

"That's rather obvious, isn't it? No one knows who you are, but I wouldn't put it past anyone to figure it out and take revenge on a sworn enemy. Don't leave your room unattended, and even then... don't leave your room."

My throat tightened in anxiety as my gaze darted about my surroundings, searching for something—*anything*—to sway his decision.

"Please..." It slipped from my lips before I could stop the word.

"What?"

"Release me. Let me leave your country. I won't bother anyone. I'll disappear. You'll never see me again."

His gaze tightened as he regarded me. He sat up sharply. "Why?" His eyes delved into mine, searching my reaction. "Why would a spoiled young woman, a lady of noble birth, not want her only living relation to know where she is?"

My mouth clamped shut.

He rolled his eyes. "Spin your royal woes somewhere else. I don't have time for them, and neither does the king."

Blood boiled at the coldness of his expression—an expression I had seen so many times before on my uncle. This made it easy to shut down. Straight-backed, I stared at the wall, waiting for my sentence.

A knock at the door sounded, then a stout woman entered. Wisps of gray streaked through brown hair. Her brown eyes looked almost bored as she clasped her hands in front of her, calmly waiting instruction. "Your Highness?"

The prince nodded toward the woman. "This is Sameen. She and Lieutenant Mikael are the only two people other than the king and I who know your identity. For your sake, let's hope it stays that way. Sameen will be your lady's maid until your removal." He looked to the woman. "Escort Lady Anna to her room. See to her needs and burn those disgusting rags."

The woman tipped her head. "Yes, Your Highness."

"You will be confined to the east wing with guards posted at your door at all times for your... protection, until you can be claimed. And my lady..." He speared me with his keen eyes. "I wouldn't do anything foolish, or this time you won't be enjoying the hospitality of our prison."

He waved his hand as if shooing a bothersome fly, and with that we were dismissed.

My shoulders dropped. Obediently, I stood before the maid. She watched me oddly before gesturing me to follow. The giant, Mikael, stood just beyond, his arms folded over his barreled chest.

I reached the threshold and stopped. Without turning back, I spoke over my shoulder. "There's a man in your prison that arrived at the same time I did. He's a spy and very dangerous. You might want to keep an eye on him."

There was a pause before Prince Castiel spoke again. "We know."

My bones creaked as I followed behind the maid who jingled when she walked, keenly aware of the heavy steps behind me. My heart sunk, burning in the acid of an empty stomach.

But from that burn, anger rose. My mind snapped to my surroundings, taking in every hallway we traversed, every narrow passageway we passed. Calculating… always calculating my next steps. I was at a disadvantage. I had only seen brief glimpses of Meyrion, Anolyn's castle, between the slits of the prison carriage. The towering edifice was much smaller than my king's, but what it lacked in size, it made up in beauty. It had stood majestic against a darkening evening sky, a great stone giant of pointed arches and flying buttresses, magnificent spires and stained windows. It graced a breathtaking landscape of lush green fields stretching on for miles, a feature afforded by a much warmer climate.

Sameen stopped in front of a doorway, producing a set of keys from her dress pocket. For the briefest of seconds, I contemplated snapping her neck and taking her keys. The maid I could take care of, but the giant was a whole other story. Out on the battle field I might have a fighting chance, if that fighting chance was that he was nearly dead already.

We entered a cavernous room and I almost gasped. A tapestry of bright, cheerful colors hung from the wall, the only decoration in the space. Across from it rested an oversized fourposter bed flowing with a canopy of linens draped from each corner. My body ached as I eyed blush-colored pillows resting upon layers of matching blankets. A single nightstand sat free of clutter on one side of the bed.

Heavy white curtains drawn away from paneled windows revealed the afternoon downpour still ongoing. Two wooden chairs huddled near the roaring fire. In the warmer kingdom of Anolyn, rain fell as easily as the snow in Eira. This was advantageous. In snow, you left a visible trail, but in rain, tracks washed away as quickly as they came if one was careful.

The fireplace beckoned me to its warmth, but despite the tremor that ran up my spine, I waited to be escorted inside. It was too beautiful to be mine.

Sameen cleared her throat, but not for me. She waited for Mikael to make a quick inspection of my temporary apartment. Before he finished, the giant gave me his full attention. With a smirk, he bowed, keeping his pointed glare pinned to mine. His dark grey eyes dared me to do something foolish, then he slinked from the room.

Sameen guided me behind a paneled privacy screen. A large wash tub steamed with hot water, and a new aroma assaulted my sensitive senses.

"What's that smell?" I asked.

She seemed confused. Her hands pushed a rogue strand of gray hair back into place. "Have your never bathed?"

"Of course, but what's in the water?"

"Lavender."

I scrunched up my nose to the strong perfume.

"Give me your robe and underthings," she said, holding out her hands.

My mouth went dry. "Can you afford me some privacy?"

"No."

I closed my eyes and turned my back before stripping off my clothes.

Sameen inhaled sharply, and I knew what she saw to cause her to react as she did. The scarring would be equally bad on my abdomen and chest. When I twisted around her eyes were wide in horror. She swallowed nervously, but schooled her expression, taking the gown from my outstretched hand.

"You'll find soap and a rag somewhere in the water, but soak first," she said, tipping her head toward the bath. Then she hesitated. "The soap will probably sting."

"I'll manage."

She shrugged. Her nose crinkled as she bundled the robe, holding it away from her. She moved beyond the screen, leaving me alone.

I carefully stepped into the tub, shocked with the first touch of the hot water. It took me several seconds to adjust to the heat before I could settle completely. My mind melted as warmth enveloped my skin. For the briefest of moments I allowed myself to sink into its watery depths, wishing I could stay there forever. When the last bubble of air leaked from my mouth, I breached the surface.

Sameen was busily dragging a chair towards the tub. She set it behind me, sitting herself on its cushioned seat. From her deep pockets she pulled a brush and a small vial of some unknown ointment. When she reached for my hair I jerked away, sloshing water over the sides.

Her fingers stilled. "You'll need help with that mess," she said. Her eyes examined my face, waiting for my response.

I touched the matted black tresses. "I'll cut it off."

"No. I can fix it." Although she tried to mask it, concern oozed from her soft brown eyes. "Please."

Slowly I rotated in the bath water, a silent acquiescence. She applied the ointment, massaging it into the knotted strands.

I sat still for several minutes, forcing my nerves to calm through a controlled breath. When I finally rubbed the soap over my skin, I hissed at the sting.

Sameen hummed. "I told you so."

She worked feverishly, but her fingers were gentle as she pried apart the mess of hair. After a second rinse, her tugs became less frequent. The brush felt like heaven against a sore scalp.

A knock on the door caused me to duck into the water.

"It's only the guard," she said as she stood to answer. Whispered voices frayed my already delicate nerves. Sameen returned with a towel and a robe that she placed next to the tub. Heart racing, I reached to scrub the back of my neck, but she took the cloth from me, gently washing away the grime. "You're practically skin and bone, but not as bad as I thought you'd be after months in a cell. Regardless, I've asked for food to be brought."

I wrapped my arms around my knees to subdue my shaking limbs. "Why are you helping me?" I asked, my voice weak.

She didn't answer.

After a minute, she finally spoke. "A missive is being prepared as we speak and will be sent to your uncle. King

Riaan wishes to see you tomorrow… after you see the healer."

I swirled. "I don't need a healer."

She met my gaze. "Yes, you do, and if you don't want me to make known to the king what I recognize your marks to truly be, I suggest you obey his wishes."

Heat enflamed my face. She waited for my answer. I nodded once then sank within the depths of my humiliation.

I sat in the bath until the water lost its warmth and my skin dimpled in cold. Sameen wrapped me in a thick, cream-colored robe that fell to my toes and set me in a comfortable chair in front of the fire. Her fingers pulled through my wet tangles, using the heat from the fire to help it to dry.

"You have a lovely wave to your hair," she said. "And what a wonderful color it has. I thought it was black, but it's really a deep brown, isn't it?"

I closed my eyes, almost enjoying her ministrations.

My lady's maid in Anolyn, Pala, used to do this very thing for me when I was younger and naiver, but the woman was not what she seemed. No one was.

Another rap on the door caused me to jump. Sameen was already across the room. She opened the door a crack to peer out but then skirted back with a bow.

Mikael entered, carrying a silver serving tray. The prince followed his guard but froze two steps within the door when our gazes locked. My breath stilled in my lungs.

"I see now that your uncle's artist is an incompetent fool," he said.

The muscles between my brows tightened. I gripped the handles of the chair, jolting to the edge of the seat. "This is highly inappropriate, don't you think?" His hand flew out to halt me in place. "Please, stay where you are." Piercing blue eyes searched my face and trailed the length of my hair down to the scar on my neck—then to the walls to inspect the tapestry that hung there instead. "You are an enemy and a recently released prisoner. Do you really think we respect your privacy? Besides, we bring you your dinner, Princess."

My ragged nails dug into the soft wood of the arm rest. "I did not know that the prince of Anolyn was such a generous host. I might have left your prison sooner for such comforts."

A smile lit the corners of his mouth. He gave a slight bow. "It's amazing what a warm bath and hot dinner can do for one's outlook on life, is it not?"

"I thought you did not have the time for such bothers."

"I don't."

He tipped his head to Mikael, who handed the tray to Sameen. She set it on my lap—a small bowl of stew and another slice of bread.

My mouth exploded into salivating, but I didn't move to eat.

Mikael began to search the room.

Castiel cleared his throat and peered out the windows to the vast expanse of his royal lawns. Did I sense nervousness in the lines of his face? But whatever I saw in his magnificent profile—for it was magnificent—was gone when he looked at me again.

"It has come to my attention that you have more injuries to you than what was delivered today by Scores." I couldn't control the flush in my cheeks, or the sense of betrayal from Sameen. I should already be accustomed to such treatment.

"Who else hurt you?" he asked, unaware of my mental berating.

I smiled sweetly. "You shock me, Your Highness."

"Was it done by my guards?"

I opened my mouth, but a memory of Scores pinned against a wall by an unseen force caused my throat to swell in anxiety. Despite his sudden concern, I needed to remember and never forget: Castiel was a magician capable of horrors I could only imagine.

I shrugged and stared at the fire. "A warrior cannot flee battle without a few scars. Have no fear, Your Highness. Your guards have been more than gracious."

I lifted the lid to the soup, pretending nonchalance, then almost slammed it shut when my stomach groaned in an impatient declaration. I set the tray on the table next to me, then wiped my suddenly sweaty hands on my robe.

From behind me, a ruffle of blankets drew my attention. I smiled again when Mikael patted down the unused mattress to search for hidden weapons. "Will your guard be turning down my bed?"

Mikael froze in place. His tattoos danced in the fire's light and added to his rather frightening glare. A clawed hand gripped a pillow as if he wanted to tear it in half—

Castiel actually laughed, a soft chuckle that vibrated in the back of my ears. Hands behind him, he paced the length of the room. "Until your removal, your room will be inspected several times a day, so get used to it."

"That sounds more like you. Let's not pretend to be friendly. That would upset my first impression of you."

The prince stilled.

I silently cursed myself. When would I ever learn to shut my mouth as I had been taught?

He waited until his guard had finished with the search. Sameen was hesitant when asked to go with Mikael but did as she was told. I begged her with my eyes not to leave me alone with the magician, but the door shut behind her with a resolute click.

"You don't know anything about me, Princess." Castiel's voice was a ghostly whisper that sent tremors throughout my body. "You want kind, do you? I've known who you are from the moment you entered my kingdom. I've watched you. Waited."

He prowled forward to grasp the handles of my chair. His skin grazed mine. I gasped and jerked from his touch, but he didn't seem to notice. Had I expected a magician's touch to be different from a human's? I cursed my stupidity. Of course they wouldn't feel different. I refrained from shrinking back further despite the flurry of butterflies that sickened the inside of my stomach.

He leaned forward, his face so near that I inhaled the scent of the soap he used to bathe.

It was an impressive show of intimidation—but I'd seen so much worse to be truly scared.

"Do you really think we treat our prisoners so well?" he asked. "Do you think you were properly searched upon arrival? Interrogated?"

My face exploded into uncomfortable blotches of red. My nails itched to scratch out the eyes that delved too deeply in mine, but before I could react he pushed away with added oomph. My chair tipped rearward, but I jerked forward and it slammed back down with a clatter.

Castiel reclaimed his place near the fire.

Hands shaking, I wrapped my robe even tighter around me and forced myself to remain calm. Even then, I heard the nervous lilt to my next words. "If that's true, then—"

"If that's true?" His head snapped my direction, pinning me in place. His eyes saw everything. "Did you never once think it odd at the amount of times you were fed? That you did not waste away to nothing?"

My mouth opened, but nothing came out. I couldn't move, could barely breathe.

He continued, regardless. "I've personally seen to the care of your cell—much to the annoyance of my brother—making sure the least amount of disease crawled through those bars to infect you. You think no one watched you every time you took your weekly walks? Never in the history of warfare has another prisoner been treated as special as you have been, Princess."

"Why?"

"Why punish you for your uncle's mistake? I am more than willing to continue to treat you as a guest and an honorable member of royalty… if you earn it."

A form of hope snaked through me, slow and deadly. "What do I have to do?"

"Tell me what your uncle's plan is. Why this sudden desire for peace? Why send his niece as a marriage offering? And after refusal, why send you to spy?"

A muscled in my neck spasmed. "I was refused?"

One brow raised high. "Does that upset you?"

Embarrassment singed my cheeks. I tsked despite my flurried breath. "Of course not."

"Don't take it too hard. The king isn't easily charmed by a pretty face."

"I couldn't care less what charms him."

But Castiel ignored my indignant response and fixed his stare to the flames within the hearth.

"If friendly is what you seek," he began, his voice a forced calm, "I suggest you be more open with your actions. I'll ask you one more time. Why are you here?"

I swallowed hard. "And I'll give you the same answer I gave before, because it's *true*. I have no desire to be here. I only wanted to pass through."

"Very well." He spun on his heel and quit the room without another word.

I closed my eyes, hating the way my heart settled against my stomach. I heard the door open and shut but didn't look to the source, knowing who entered. I could almost feel her. "You lied to me."

"No, I didn't." Sameen's voice was strong, and nearer than I thought. "I said I wouldn't tell him what I recognize those marks to be, and I didn't. You must be the one to tell him what they truly are."

I set my jaw. And *that* would *never* happen.

I opened my eyes to glare, but her sympathetic expression instantly took the pleasure from the act.

She stood over me with my discarded tray, almost too close for comfort. "Shall I feed you?"

I pished my annoyance. Again, my stomach growled, unaware of anything other than its own discomfort. She placed the tray in my lap and removed the lid to the stew. I sighed and took a bite of potato and steak, barely managing to hold back the groan that bubbled to my lips. Every mouthful was more heavenly than the first. Tears clouded my vision and as I ate, Sameen worked my damp hair into a braid.

By the time she finished, I had scooped my last blissful bite of stew. She watched me closely. Was it pity she felt for me to summon the healer, to bring me the stew, and that now emanated from those soft brown eyes? Her soul radiated goodness—*she* was nothing like Pala.

An easy target. The thought danced wickedly across my thoughts. My face flushed red from the shame, but my mind opened.

I lowered my voice, casting my eyes to the floor. "Thank you. For your kindness."

Her movements slowed as she pulled down the comforter for me. She didn't look me in the eyes when she answered. "I don't need your thanks, but is there anything else I can get you before retiring?"

My spoon scraped against the bottom of the bowl and I stared at it for a moment before meeting Sameen's bemused gaze.

"Can I—can I have a little honey-butter for the bread? It's been so long since I've had anything so good." When she neared, I reached for the hem of her sleeve, gently tugging on it. *Please?*

She blinked. "Of course, dear. I don't know why they didn't bring it in the first place." She spun on her heel, heading toward the door.

"Can you bring a knife to spread it?" I asked in an even softer voice.

She paused, her hand on the grip of the door. She gazed over her shoulder, then smiled at me. "Well, of course I will. How else would you spread honey-butter?"

3
RUNAWAY

NO MATTER HOW HARD I TRIED to suppress it, guilt worked at my gut, twisting a full stomach into painful knots. I tucked the thick butter knife into one pocket of my dress and the small loaf of bread into the other. Sameen had provided me with a nightgown still folded and untouched on a nightstand, as well as a simple gray frock for the next day, no doubt from one of the maids closest to my size. The slippers she gave were too thin to fit properly, but they were better than nothing and would stretch.

She would be punished for aiding my escape, but I didn't have time for guilt. My uncle would soon be on his way.

There were no rules when it came to survival.

But why did I deserve to survive?

I gripped the nightstand when a wave of grief nearly swept my feet from beneath me. My fingers pressed against the wood as I heaved shuddering breaths of too-thick air. My arms and legs shook with emotion I thought to have been destroyed long before. Tears stung my eyes and I groaned, trying to force them away, but still they came. I swallowed against the pain and dropped to my knees.

I tipped my head back to stop the flow of emotion.

Did I deserve to survive? I didn't know, but if there was any type of justice in the world, there were others that needed to die for their deeds before Death claimed me as his. Confusion, fear, and determination warred, but when I had cried every last tear, determination rose triumphant.

My uncle had not won yet.

I dragged the blankets off the bed to the floor and cocooned within their warmth, waiting until the main candlelights were extinguished along my corridor. I counted down the hours.

I had left my kingdom, my home, using methods I said I would never use. It was the only way that had finally worked. Every other attempt had failed. I had discovered the *ability* after I turned fourteen—way past the age it should have manifested.

If gifted, magic bloomed in a child as early as six years old, but never past puberty.

And I was supposed to be gifted. Up until my first day of womanhood, my uncle's behavior changed from patient persistence to manic single-mindedness.

"Your father was a gifted magician. It's your *duty* to defend your country like he once did. Magic flows through the Anouk family veins. It *must* be within you."

"Then why don't you possess it?"

The question was an innocent enough mistake, but one I made sure never to repeat. When my magic finally surfaced, I did my best to tuck it away. I hated it just as much as it must have hated me to let me suffer as it did. Why else would it have stayed away so long? I shook my head to rid my thoughts of such memories. Like it or not, I had no other choice but to use the cursed ability. Still, doing so on Sameen grated. I had used the same trick on Anolyn's prison guards, coaxing more food and water when I could without drawing attention or suspicion. Now, I reached out, utilizing a different but comparable magic, sensing the new guard beyond my door. The connection at first was weak. It was easier when I knew the target, understood the way they ticked.

The new guard's thoughts were simple enough. He loathed the upcoming hours of tedium, guarding a stranger of insignificant value to his career.

Perfect.

I moved to the door and placed my hand to the wooden planks. Holding my breath, I gathered my strength.

Would you help me?

A moment later, the door creaked open an inch and I met the eyes that glared through furrowed, bushy brows. Black skin blended against the darkened hallway.

"I—" I stuttered when the guard pushed it open even more with one gigantic hand, exposing a brute of a man double my size in girth and pure muscle. Candlelight gleamed from a shorn skull. A ragged scar ate through the line of his jaw. His head jerked back upon seeing me. His unreadable gaze swept the length of my gown.

"Did you say something?" Suspicion penetrated his graveled voice.

I bowed my head in mildness, possibly even terror, my heart working wildly. "Forgive me, sir. I cannot sleep. I am so far from my own home and I'm very uneasy." *Might I stretch my legs?*

He blinked once. "You want to go for a walk?"

"Yes, please." But it was more of a question.

He stepped back, giving me space to exit. "Then allow me to escort you."

I swallowed, glancing beyond the door.

"What is your name?" I asked, my voice barely more than a whisper.

"Reese."

He wore the forest-green tunic of an Anolyn foot soldier. "It's so dark, Reese." *Will I be safe?*

One side of his lips quirked up as he regarded me. He offered an arm. "With me? There is nowhere safer."

And for some odd reason, I believed him. *I do not wish to be seen.*

He nodded his understanding and I gently took his arm. Muscle budged beneath my slight fingers and I gulped down a growing swell of anxiety.

He guided me the opposite direction I had originally come, turning down several unlit passage ways. My heart thudded in my chest, my nerves on high-alert. I pulled my knife, fisting it behind my back in case the guard had other plans, but after another minute, a light grew stronger. He brought me to a narrow spiral staircase. He unwrapped my grip, only to transfer it to his hand. He kept me close, down two flights of mind-whirling stairs, tucked behind his larger form. Hushed voices traveled toward us from the first floor and I pulled back, nearly tumbling down on top of him when he whirled. I gripped his shoulder to keep from falling.

I could barely see his eyes or reaction in the cold, hollowed stairwell, but knew he was watching me.

I'm scared.

He let go. "Stay here."

He exited, and I stayed pressed against the wall of the well. I shouldn't have been cowering like some common thief. I was a warrior. The Demon Daughter of Eira.

Stupid, stupid title.

But I was also weak from three months of incarceration, and quite lost. My heart beat erratically, grinding in my ears.

A man called out in greeting and Reese answered. "You're needed at the armory. I'll cover for you until you get back."

A door opened, then closed. Footsteps brought him back to me. "We don't have much time," he said dragging me from the stairwell. "This way."

The guard guided me through a door camouflaged to match its surrounding walls. Twisting and turning we traversed down another flight of stairs. The claustrophobic air in these lower passages robbed me of breath and my head grew light, but then he threw a door wide, and cool air brushed against my face. I instantly inhaled several deep breaths, sighing in relief, but still the guard pulled me into the deep shadows of a nearby building that matched the make of the castle. The smell of flora filled my senses. A hot house, intoxicating and sweet. I could almost be happy.

Farther. I need to stretch my legs.

Following along a towering wall, we moved quickly. A low-hanging fog shrouded us. Although I couldn't make out how far it ran, a river flowed, passing directly along the back side of the castle walls. The smell of mud and moss and mildew thickened inside my lungs. The river could take me to the ocean, but not yet. We kept going. A pathway disappeared into a deep row of trees.

Reese stopped a short distance from that path.

Where does that lead? I asked pointing.

"Into the main city."

And the coast?

"The coast is ten miles more, past the village, and through Forest Hollow."

"Thank you," I said. And I meant it.

"You cannot go now. It's far too late. You'll be killed in that forest." He held my hand tight, refusing to let go. I pressed out with my thoughts.

I would never dream of it. I am just so curious.

"You need to be back inside your room when the other guards return," he said, his black eyes wary. "You are safe in Meyrion."

I nodded. "I understand." *Go back to your post. I will be there shortly.*

He hesitated. "You will not be scared?"

"I know my way back. I am not afraid." It was a lie. I was terrified, but I had to get out of here. *Thank you for everything. Now go, kind sir.*

His lips grazed the back of my knuckles. Moisture stung my eyes as I fought off some unknown emotion. Keeping calm, I pried my fingers from his warm grasp.

I pushed harder. *Go.*

And with that, my guard was gone.

Keeping to the shadows, I raced across the obscured grounds, and sprinted into the foliage that separated the city from Castle Meyrion. My foot hooked upon something sharp and I tripped, barely catching myself on a nearby tree trunk. I swore beneath my breath when the piercing bark scratched into my skin. I wiped the dirt and scrap of blood on my dress. Weakness and fatigue already affected my steps and made me sloppy, but I couldn't slow down.

I cleared the trees and skidded to a stop. Moonlight crept out from behind clouds to cast the town in eerie stillness. A mixture of elation, fear, and hunger clouded my senses. I tore the extra loaf of bread I had tricked from Sameen in half and ate to recover my strength, my mind working overtime to get my bearings. Shops littered the streets, their signs too hard to read. Night pressed against me. The cold air chilled my skin, but I barely noticed the discomfort.

In the distance, a man rounded a corner, his silhouette obscured by the fog. *A city patrolman?* Hands in pockets, he whistled a low tune, his pace slow and relaxed.

I spun and cut between two shops to the back alleys.

I continued through backstreets rank with the smell of sewage and rotten food. At the end of the row, a dim light caught my attention. I picked my way closer. A man exited

through a back door, throwing a pail of an unknown
substance. He wiped his hands on a towel, then tossed it
over his shoulder and went back inside. The smell of urine
and ale assaulted me. I covered my nose as I made my way
toward the front of the building.

Candlelight illuminated the only waking business in
the town of Anolyn. I peered through the windows of a
tavern. Half a dozen patrons sat inside. It must be high-
tide, the main reason a business would be open at such a
weary hour: seamen had come in from port to rest from
their ocean travels.

The magic within me already searched the room for
what I needed—another victim. Two men at the back
played a game of cards. One had tanned, hulking muscles
and a large beard; the other was smaller, younger, with
reddish-brown hair and a cunning glint in his eyes.

Perfect. At least I hoped.

My magic influence didn't work on everyone; I didn't
know why it worked on some and not on others.

Gullibility? Weakness?

I didn't want to hurt anyone like Sameen, or even
Reese. They were good, their souls pure. Like my people
in Eira.

A pang of sadness threatened to distract me, but I
tucked it away. The good and the pure could not help me,
not from the king and his captains. A shiver traveled
down my spine.

I'd only ever used the magic to save my own skin. It
was better when manipulating those with foul
intentions, like the man in the bar. His soul was black as

night. A murderer? I didn't know, but his kind I was used to dealing with. His kind surrounded my uncle and led our army. His kind quailed easily to the fear of a Demon Daughter.

The card game ended. I homed in on the sinister man. *Take your winnings and leave.*

His hands froze upon the money on the table, his eyes narrowed. He spoke to the bearded sailor, who only shook his head and started to deal again.

I lied. *He will try to kill you. Take your winnings and leave.*

The bearded one froze mid-deal; his eyes flashed to mine. Had I connected with the wrong man? But before I could flee, the young man stood, the legs of his chair scraping against the wood floor. He finished collecting his coins and shoved them deep into his pockets despite the other one's objections. He fled.

The man at the table set down his cards and folded his arms across his chest at the same time that the front door to the tavern squealed open. I backed away, oddly revealing myself to the seaman.

He skidded to a halt. His brown eyes rolled over my face and dress as he pulled his fingers through his hair. He was closer to my own age.

"Well, hello, miss," he said, his previous anxiety forgotten. That glint returned, but a handsome smile added something to that cunning face. "Can I help you? Are you lost?"

"I—" I fumbled my words when an unfamiliar emotion wafted from him like bad cologne.

My fingers relaxed from the grip of my knife still concealed within my pocket. I headed toward the alley, but before I could slip into the shadows, I employed a technique I had seen my maids use on the stable boys back at home to lure them into darkened corners. I peered over my shoulder, meeting his eyes, and blinked.

What was I doing?

Flirting? Being coy?

I fled—my steps controlled even though my legs shook. Shock almost floored me when a voice followed.

"Wait!" he called. Hurried footsteps tailed. "Where are you going?" He touched my shoulder.

I suppressed a shudder. Grabbing his hand, I spun, twisting his arm behind his back. He called out, but my knife was under his throat before more than a squeak could release.

I hushed him, bringing my lips to his ear. "Move and you die."

"What do you want, darling?" he asked through clenched teeth.

"I am far from your darling."

"One can hope, can't they? If not my undying love, what is it you want?"

I twisted his wrist higher. He grunted, then laughed through his discomfort. "She likes it rough."

"All I want," I said, "is your clothes."

He laughed again, his voice hoarse. "Lady, you could have had my clothes. You didn't even have to ask."

My brows furrowed at some understanding I knew I was missing. I shoved him away, hard. He faced me. With a wink, he kicked off one boot.

"And I want your wallet," I added.

His face dropped.

Minutes later I plowed through the forest in greater ease than before. Although his boots were slightly larger and his shirt reeked of stale body odor, the pants and cream-colored top comforted me much more than the dress Sameen had brought.

Pala would be disappointed.

I used to hate frocks and evening gowns, and all the layers that came with them. They were ridiculous and confining. It wasn't until my lady's maid and her teachings that I understood the benefits of such frivolous costumes.

No one expects sharpened steel and death beneath delicate folds of silk and lace.

But Pala wasn't here, and something told me deep within that I didn't want her to be, either. She was a traitor. Not to the crown like I was—but to me, her deceit running deeper than I had even imagined.

I pressed forward, quickening my pace toward the harbor located south-southwest of Riaan's castle, according to Reese's directions and my own learned knowledge.

Freights came in and out of Eira's docks as often as Anolyn's, but to sail in our northern seas meant death to an unexperienced sailor. Frigid temperatures and torrential waters killed many of our people in their storms each year. Even if I could survive the journey, there was no way I could escape that direction without being detected. I had committed treason by running away, and King Johan taught that no one was above his throne, not even his niece. I would not risk being recognized by my uncle's men.

Something I thought to be safe from in a foreign kingdom. My battle gear matched that of my fellow warriors, and during combat, I was as fierce as anyone. How had the prince gotten such a canny depiction of me in battle? Although they were only rumors, most that fought against me did die beneath my blade, but not because they had seen my face.

My father, Prince Toma, brother of King Johan of Eira was sacrificed to, and slain in the Demonic Wars—a five-year campaign against the continent by the Wraith Queen herself. It was in this epic conflict that the two countries of Eira and Anolyn buried their differences and fought against an evil menace and her army of lost souls.

Prince Toma and a handful of my uncle's best assassins resolved upon a counter attack. The Wraith Queen never condescended to enter enemy land until the battle was won, and so they would bring the battle to her.

A month after my birth, the enemy suddenly pulled back most of her forces. My father had triumphed, but only one assassin survived the raid to return: Lucan.

The Wraith Queen was dead. When we finally rid our forests from the remainder of her abandoned followers, our people were able to celebrate their freedom from her tyranny and reveled in their saved military. All the while, my uncle stewed over his lost brother and a longing for battle grew within him. He thought Anolyn would be weaker after years of fighting, and when I was ten, he launched his campaign against them…

Two more years of blood loss proved it was *our* country that was weakened. Soon our forces withdrew, but not after severe loss on both sides. The king of Anolyn had been killed in the last battle, but no one knew under whose blade he had fallen. Since then, relationships between our lands had been tense.

Business was still done within the black markets, mostly ignored by my uncle's military captains. Much of Eira's wealth came from illegal trafficking, and only a handful of skirmishes ever broke out at the border anymore.

A sound halted me in place, the snap of a twig. I drew my knife, my breath frozen in my lungs. I turned a careful circle, waiting for something to leap from any of the trunks large enough to hide an attacker—but nothing stirred.

Of course, there was more to fear than being attacked by a man within *this* kingdom.

Forest Hollow. I didn't know much about these woods, but considering the name alone, I guessed it was just as cursed as Varian. The woodland was still but far from asleep.

A chill crept across the back of my neck. Clouds dampened the moon and the canopy of trees that pressed against my paranoid thoughts.

My uncle had taught me about the kingdom of Anolyn since I was a child. Known for its warmer climate and its lush landscapes, the kingdom was rich in bounteous harvests. Its main trading products were its crops, animal hides, and coffee beans… as well as trinkets taken from captured souls and sprites as a method of payment for their deliverance. Shrunken heads, potions and poisons, and evil charms were also a hot commodity among the few magicians that still roamed the land.

My kingdom was nowhere near as beautiful, but when the land finally shed its winter coat and warmth spread its virility, Eira was a glorious sight—for four months, and then it quickly transformed back to its usual snowy landscapes and frigid temperatures.

Whether he did it to keep me safe or to terrify his young niece, my uncle would often tell me stories of tortured souls and demonic spirits that roamed Varian. Even later, our warriors would spin tales of butchered travelers found lifeless along the road and disappearing children that played too close to the borders.

Aside from the halted wars, it was what kept most from traveling through Varian Forest into our neighbor's land. Those that did, stuck to the few well-known and well-marked trails that crossed from one side to the next. It was better to travel in packs. Large convoys of heavily armored warriors went two-by-two, constantly on the lookout. Single travelers purchased the best and fastest horses to make the trek in record time.

I had none of these options when I fled my uncle and had escaped death, but deep-down I wondered what foul creature had whispered my flight in the wilderness that led to…

Light infused my vision as a belated pain exploded in my jaw. I stumbled back, barely keeping my feet before I realized what was happening. A shadowed yet familiar form stalked toward me.

I hissed, wiping the blood from my bottom lip. "Lucan."

"That felt good." My uncle's spy clenched and unclenched his hand. A satisfied smile lit one corner of his mouth. He pushed back his blond locks. "I knew you'd be by here sometime soon. You're so predictable."

"Predictable?" The words hurt my jaw. I crouched low. I had fought him before in training, and had lost. The memory of it quickened my heart to a painful cadence.

A line of three men stretched out to his left and right, blocking my way. Another snap sounded, and three more drew from behind. I twisted, eyeing their enclosing ranks. Their leathers and black hoods masked their faces, but one stood out among the others in a gray dress. The man from the pub smirked.

Trapped.

4

DEMON DAUGHTER

MY HEART PICKED UP SPEED, but I reserved my full attention to the deadliest man of the group.

Lucan shrugged, rolling his shoulders. "I didn't expect you to make me wait three months inside some prison, but oh well." He lunged and swung.

I barely dodged the wild haymaker.

He smirked. "I think it's time for you to come home with me."

"I don't think so." I pulled the dull butter knife from my pocket.

He laughed, as did most of the others, then ignored my weapon completely. "Come, Ilianna. Your uncle misses you."

My brow raised. "You *know* that's not true."

"That's where your wrong, Princess."

He unsheathed his knife. The sound grated against my tightened nerves. I couldn't win against Lucan and six other armed men, not in my current state. My eyes frantically searched for an escape.

One of the cloaked men looked toward Lucan, his black eyes concerned. "I thought you said she was the princess. Why do you draw your knife on her? Why do you strike her?"

"She's not as innocent as she seems, gentlemen." Lucan smiled, his gaze never leaving mine. "My king doesn't hold back from putting his servants in their place, and that is all she is. A servant to the crown that needs to be humbled."

"Whatever you *need* to do, do it quickly. We won't survive this cursed forest for long," one man said, nervously shifting from one foot to the other.

"You paid me to retrieve a runaway princess, but this is wrong," Black Eyes said, stepping away with raised hands.

"It's brilliant." My friend in the dress stepped forward, wiping his mouth with the back of his hand. "I say we have a little fun with her."

I flinched, clutching my knife tighter, unsure of the implied meaning I knew I was missing.

"She is not to be soiled," Lucan growled.

"What better way to humble her? Besides, I've always wanted to sample royalty." He hiked up the hem of his dress to his knees.

Several men sneered, but the one with the black eyes caught him by the sleeve.

"You heard him," Black Eyes said, his voice hard.

The man from the tavern pushed away his roughened grip and stepped toward me. Faster than a whip, Lucan twisted, slamming his blade into his heart. Eyes wide, he gasped and folded to the ground.

Lucan tsked, using the fabric of the man's gray skirt to clean his bloodied blade. "I *said* she is not to be soiled." He kicked the man's body. The others stepped away nervously, no longer concerned about me.

I bolted but didn't get far before my legs were swept from beneath me. I tucked my head and rolled, quickly regaining my feet. Pain took my breath when someone grabbed me by my braid. They yanked me back into the wide expanse of their chest. Their arm snaked around my neck. I cringed when a mouth brushed my ear. "Gotcha."

I rammed my elbow back, earning a feral grunt, then stamped my foot on my captor's toes, loosening his grip. I broke away, but Lucan was there to meet me.

With a downward slash, his blade cut into my arm. A red line instantly drew from the inside of my elbow to my wrist. Unwittingly, I lurched into the hands of another waiting foe.

"That was a warning, Princess," Lucan said, crouching low.

My jailor's touch chafed upon the very fibers of my skin. Instinctively, I threw my head back. A satisfying crack and a cry told me I had hit my mark and the man stumbled. I twisted and sliced my blade across his middle, then plunged my knife into his heart.

The scene slowed to a crawl, forcing me to witness as Black Eyes lurched forward, stabbing into the gut of another that went for me. My mind reeled when he instantly turned, battling another of Lucan's men.

Instincts kicked in and I moved to land a sidekick to Lucan's stomach, but he was prepared. He grabbed my ankle and twisted hard. Pain racked up my leg and I fell, landing face down. I tasted blood from a split lip before hands seized my feet and yanked me back. My body flew over rock and brush that scratched at my face. I flipped over bucking wildly, freeing my legs.

Lucan's boot found my stomach before I could do more. Then again. My breath locked in my chest and my body seized. He wrapped his fingers into my tangled hair, dragging me to my feet. He shook me, jarring my neck. I gasped for air, my breath returning.

Lucan shook me again. "Are you ready to come willingly?"

"Go to hell," I said, my words mumbled through a swollen mouth.

He sneered. With a jerk, he head-butted me between my eyes. A crack sounded in my ears before I felt my body crumple like sand. I blinked against a numbing pain. Lucan drew back his boot to strike again—

His body flew, caught in some invisible snare that catapulted him into an unsuspecting tree. Magic pulsed through the air, standing the hairs at the back of my neck on end.

Lucan slid to his feet just before the newcomer tackled him full-bodied to the ground. Both men rolled and leapt to their feet. Shock infused my already mottled brain when I recognized the newcomer.

Prince Castiel discarded his coat and drew two knives from sheathes strapped to well-built thighs. He glared, crouching low. His jaw muscles rippled. He circled Lucan, his movements smooth yet feral.

Fear infused my thoughts. Why was the prince here? Why did an enemy—two enemies—come to my aid?

Castiel lunged. Moonlight glinted from his blades as they clashed against Lucan's steel.

I crawled the body of the man I had killed, searching for weapons. My fingers wrapped around a knife in his pocket. I scanned the battle, my harried focus caught upon another man—and not one of Lucan's. The bearded man from the tavern leaned against the trunk of a tree, casually observing me fumble. When our eyes met, I pointed the knife his direction, but he stayed where he was, raising his hands in immediate surrender. A bottle of ale tipped from his fingers.

Drunken fool.

A shuffle of feet drew my attention. One of Lucan's men joined the battle against the prince before I could scramble to my feet.

My head swirled, but I braced myself, forcing my body to rise. I panted. My breath ground upon broken ribs as I leaned against a tree.

A cry sounded, splitting my nerves. My original helpmate fell against an enemy sword. His black eyes met mine for a fraction of a second, then he crumpled to the ground, dead.

And oddly, my heart reacted. The remaining blood drained from my face. "No!" The word tore from my lips. Lucan's man spotted me. He ran, aiming his blade at my heart.

Anger rose from deep within, but instead of fighting it, instead of fearing *her*, I smiled, welcoming it, welcoming the pain, welcoming the release. Heat coursed. Black flames devoured bone and flesh. The Demon Daughter rose from her forced slumber, eager to retaliate.

The hired soldier balked, and she relished in the fear in his eyes. His lifeforce pulsed from him like heat from a blazing fire, so strong she could almost touch it. It called to her. Warmed her.

My limbs obeyed her orders and with a scream that rent the air, I flew.

Face to face, I sneered at my enemy, barely registering my blade already thrust into his ribs. I shoved him away and he collided hard to the ground.

I smiled, but suddenly jolted back. My breath hitched in my lungs and pain exploded. Lucan's dagger protruded from my stomach. I screamed. The Demon Daughter receded into her hiding place.

Lucan was a blur as he fled into the black shadows of the forest. Dark liquid pooled from a shoulder wound. With a wave of his hand, trees fell beneath Castiel's power to crush the fleeing spy, but Lucan scampered and weaved through the avalanche like the rodent he was.

I collapsed to my knees, a curse bubbling indistinct from my lips, and the prince halted. Our gazes met and in that instant, I thought I recognized hesitation, perhaps anger, and some other emotion I couldn't identify.

Sparks rained in my vision. I shook my head to rid the reaction, but it was no use. The world spun. Before I fell, Castiel slid to his knees in front of me, his movements slowed by my mental failings. Strong hands caught me. The ground disappeared from beneath my body, swept up into arms I was never supposed to touch.

The prince saved me—a debt that, in Eira, demanded repayment. Confused and appalled, I gazed up to see a neck thick with strained muscles. Of their own accord, my traitorous fingers pressed against a stubble coated face and carved jawline…

He moved them from his skin, holding them in a tight grasp as he scanned the darkened forest.

I opened my mouth to object, but the words left when he pulled me closer. Crushed to him, Castiel's husky voice sent a tremor down my body. "I will not hurt you, Ilianna. I will *never* hurt you."

He ran with me in his arms. The jostled movement kept the pain in my side fresh and prevented me from fully passing into oblivion. I guessed I should be grateful instead of annoyed as I was, but it was all too much. As I fought for consciousness, my mind stewed in a messy mixture of apprehension and annoyance.

Where was he taking me? Would he dump my body somewhere remote? Perhaps then I wouldn't be obliged to him. But that wouldn't make sense, seeing as how we were already in a forest. Would he take me back to his prisons?

Seconds or hours ticked by, keeping a disjointed rhythm with my heart. Soon, the pain from my injuries dulled.

"You should stay awake, Princess." His deep voice stunned me back into a throbbing awareness. I strained to open my eyes, but they did not answer my command. Instead I hummed a response that sounded a lot more like a groan to my ears. It was no use.

Before I slipped into darkness, his voice fought to awaken me again.

"You're going to be alright," he said. "I promise."

But it didn't sound as if he believed his own words.

ঙେ৪

My eyelids were heavy and swollen, my limbs like lead—frozen in a body that buzzed in numbing pain. Whispered voices pulled my attention, and I stopped trying to move at all and focused on their words.

An unfamiliar man spoke low. "Are you sure you heard it right? Her own uncle?"

No response.

"You should have let them kill her."

Castiel let out an annoyed breath. "They weren't there to kill her."

"Then why didn't you let them take her? It could have solved the problem."

"Without knowing the *source* of the problem? Brother, that sounds so unlike you."

Brother?

My heart responded to the connection my mind finally made as both king and prince of Anolyn continued their conversation.

"And *this* is so unlike you."

A pause and then Castiel spoke, his oddly familiar voice sending a strange sensation through my body. "It— it didn't seem right. Six against a single girl?"

A scoff sounded from the king.

Castiel continued. "And we would have learned nothing more than what was already known."

"That Johan is a madman?"

"Not helpful."

"I will send for Melia's mother. Maybe she can solve this riddle."

"And upset the captain of the guard? I wouldn't if I were you. Not until it's absolutely necessary."

"Very well." Soft steps moved to the other side of the room. "If anything happens while she's here, the blame will be on you. I hope I don't have to order you to death."

"Go to hell… and get out of my room."

A laugh sounded, then the door opened and closed.

Silence enveloped the space. Exhaustion pulled at me once again, but curiosity battled the sensation. Concentrating hard, I forced one eye open. Through the watery blur, a face stared back at me, his gaze stoic, his features shadowed by low light.

He reached out, but then drew back his hand.

"Why *didn't* you let them take me?" The words were barely more than a whisper, but I knew he understood.

His eyes bore into mine. "Sleep."

With a sigh, I listened, but sleep did not come easy.

Prince Castiel hadn't saved me from death.

My traitorous thinking delved much deeper into the problem than I wanted. Lucan would have taken me back to Johan—a fate worse than a painful death. Furthermore, Castiel had spared my life in the prison upon first arrival. The brothers were within their rights to kill me. I was their enemy and had trespassed upon their land, yet the prince saw fit to watch over me, giving me more food than a normal prisoner and keeping my conditions more sanitary than that of my inmates—or so he claimed. The combination of all instances and the obligatory life payment was affixed. My existence was forfeit—not that I would tell *him*. If he didn't recognize the significance of what he had done, why should I?

But still the thoughts nagged at my very soul.

Nightmares overwhelmed my mind, never allowing me to rest. Hallucinations from an infectious fever plagued me with a distinct feeling of being crushed. I struggled against an unseen energy I couldn't name as I drowned in a pool of my own sweat. In my visions, a pair of red eyes watched me as I writhed in pain.

Was I dying? Was evil there to claim my tortured soul? I didn't know. But when I woke again, the red eyes and the prince were gone, replaced by a resting Sameen. A mixture of relief and some unknown emotion rushed through me, pumping blood through my weakened limbs. An unstoppable groan bubbled from my lips before I could silence it. Sameen sat up, jarred from her slumber.

She placed the back of her hand to my forehead, then probed the bruises on my face. She stood, moving to the door, and whispered something through the crack. I made to sit up, but pain laced the attempt.

"Hold still," Sameen said as she returned to my bedside. "I've sent for the healer."

I licked dry lips. My voice croaked. "It's not nec—"

"Necessary? You wouldn't say that if you saw your own reflection."

I closed my eyes, almost embarrassed by the pronouncement. I rotated my head side to side to soothe the stiffness in my neck. "I've had worse." I was sure of it.

Sameen's voice was thick with annoyance. "I don't doubt that." Her shrewd eyes watched me.

Lucan hadn't meant to kill me. Compared to others my uncle employed, he could be considered nice. I almost laughed at my ill-humor, but then my breath caught in my throat. Anxiety eddied in my chest.

Lucan.

Had he seen the magic I had used to fight? Would he tell my uncle?

I had always been so careful in the past. My fingers nervously clenched at something other than the clothes I had been wearing.

I peered down to see a fresh nightgown. I had been cleaned, my hair brushed and braided by my temporary lady's maid. Unease ripped through me. How could she take care of me after what I did to her? Did the prince not know about her unwilling assistance? If she had somehow escaped her punishment, my heart was glad for it and I would keep that secret. It was the least I could do after my abuse of her.

Sameen moved about the room, intermittently rearranging a nearly empty space between pacing. It wasn't the room they had taken me to before. This one was plain of any decoration, with only a bed, nightstand, and a rather uncomfortable looking wooden chair. A window gazed out into a new morning, still lowly lit by an unhurried sunrise.

Was she nervous I would tell? Tension was thick upon her delicate brow.

"I won't tell anyone you helped me."

She froze, pinning me with her sharp eyes.

"Excuse me?"

"You have my silence. I won't tell anyone you helped me...to escape," I clarified when she only continued to stare.

"Your silence is unnecessary. I went and told the prince of your tricks the moment I realized what you had done to me. You won't need to confess what I've already declared."

"I'm..." But words left me. Was I sorry? Was that the feeling that settled like a boulder in the pit of my stomach?

Almost on instinct, my eyes searched her for some kind of injury, but whatever she had endured because of my treachery, they were careful not to let it show.

A knock at the door brought me out of my thoughts. An old man with white, balding hair and kind eyes opened without waiting to be permitted.

"Is she awake?" he asked, and Sameen nodded.

She stood back, gesturing with her hand. "Lady Anna, this is Gedeon. He is the kingdom's healer and—"

"I do not desire a healer," I said, pinning him with a direct glare.

His brows lifted as if to say he cared very little for my desires. "I guess that makes sense, now that I've already healed the worst of your injuries."

"I—"

My fingers flew to the stab in my stomach, but there was no pain and no indention. Nothing. My face flushed red.

"You're welcome." He sat in the vacated chair and took my hand. I yanked my fingers from his grasp. His hand froze mid-air as he considered me.

"I was told you'd be difficult. You should know that my king and his brother the prince have requested that I see to your instant care." He waited for me to answer, but when I didn't, he tipped his head to the side. A curious expression wrinkled his already wizened face. "I healed the more serious of your wounds last night while you slept but waited until you were awake for the rest."

My swollen eyes narrowed. "Why?"

He shrugged. "I'm getting on in years, tired from my many travels. A simple healing is harder now than it once was. Some of your scars are too old and too deep for me to completely erase. I have potions and ointments that will heal your lesser injuries, letting me take care of the others without becoming too weak."

"Then save your energy, old man. Leave me."

"I have never disobeyed my king, and I never will. I will see to your injuries with your acceptance, or I will sedate you and see to it while you sleep."

The muscles in my neck twitched, my heart panicked. Slowly, I reached out my hand, allowing him to take it. I looked away and braced against the desire to bolt. Where would I go anyway?

"I had a feeling you were a smart girl. You have the most remarkable eyes I've ever seen."

I swallowed, not knowing what to say.

He chuckled. "Age?"

I jerked back. "What?"

"Maybe not as smart as I thought. How old are you, child?"

Heat infused my checks. "Seventeen."

"So young," he said beneath his breath.

"I come of age in three months."

"You don't say." A smile lifted the corners of his mouth. "In our country, when our children come of age—"

"What makes you think I'm not from here?" I asked, interrupting. According to Castiel, I had been given a false identity for my protection. Had he gone back against his word? I knew better than to trust the word of the prince of Anolyn.

The doctor pushed up my sleeve to expose a blood-stained gauze wrap around my forearm. He pulled a pair of scissors from his bag and removed the old bandage, giving Sameen the scraps and instrument. A cut ran from my shoulder to just above the inside of my elbow. He inspected the wound, not meeting my eyes.

"You're too pale to be from our country, and your accent's not right." He lifted the other sleeve, examining the injuries there. "Besides, I make it a point to introduce myself in each town I visit, seeing to the needs of their people whenever I can. You..." He cupped my chin to examine my eyes. I flinched, just barely managing to keep my seat. "I would have remembered." His gaze traveled to the burn that scarred my neck.

I jerked back. "That one you don't heal."

5

THE KING

"THE BURN?"

I only nodded.

His eyes consumed mine. Even though the color was muted by a milky film that came with living hundreds of years, intelligence and even cunning lurked behind those simple brown eyes. "Why would you want to keep such a horrible mark? The damage you sustained is still relatively new, but it will leave a scar I cannot remove if you do not let me heal it completely."

One side of my mouth tipped up. "Not all scars are bad." Let him think what he wanted. I forced myself to turn away.

He cleared his throat and continued his ministrations. "As I said, when our youth come of age, it's a grand event that includes a week-long celebration and an introduction to the king himself. It signifies their entrance into society, when they must choose what they will become."

My knowledge of Anolyn was very little, but what I did know was far different from what he described. Heat infused my tone. "Your children work as slaves, forced to do jobs given to them based on need."

The doctor smirked. "So you no longer deny you're not from here?" I looked away, refusing the information.

"Well, whoever taught you that lesson was wrong. Members of our kingdom choose their own lifestyle, but it's based on the needs of their community or country. If they cannot choose one, it's chosen for them. They are not slaves, but we do expect our people to work. To contribute."

I tried to roll my eyes, but they were still swollen, which diluted the effect.

He peered at Sameen. "It was late when I attended her. I felt the injury to her stomach and several lesser injuries that I will see to now, but I sense there are others—dated damage sustained prior to arriving here. How far do they extend?"

I heaved a sigh. "My arms and face will be sufficient en—"

"They're everywhere," Sameen said.

I gave her a baleful glare, but she ignored me. She lifted his bag from the ground. "I have a feeling you'll go through all of your product with this one."

"I won't be able to heal all scars and older wounds, but I'll see what I can do for the most recent ones," he said as he rummaged through the contents. "Sameen, help her with her nightdress. Lady Anna, would you please lay on your stomach?"

He stood and moved to the window. Keeping his back turned, he allowed me privacy to undress. Sameen placed the scissors she still carried on the nightstand, then tugged off my nightshirt. While I had grown accustomed to Pala taking care of me, it grated on my nerves being so exposed.

Humiliated, I did as I was told, grateful when Sameen quickly covered my lower half with a thin sheet. "She's ready, Gedeon."

"Wonderful. Lady Anna, I will try to be done…"

His voice trailed off as he neared.

I closed my eyes, ignoring the way my skin flushed in embarrassment. I knew what he saw. What they both saw. But what I didn't know was how I would react when his fingers lightly grazed my skin. Instincts flared. I flew from the bed, at the same time grabbing my cover.

Sameen let out a yelp when I swiped the scissors from the nightstand, knocking it over. My knees gave way and I tumbled to the floor, my legs grudging to respond the commands given them.

I cursed a foul oath, holding the scissors as a weapon.

The doctor's voice was thick in shock. "What on earth—"

"Stay away from me," I said through clenched teeth. I jabbed the scissors his direction, knowing the sheet I held barely covered the front of me.

I inched up the wall.

"Where are my clothes?" I asked through clenched teeth.

"Lady Anna, you are badly injured. Your body needs to rest," he said, unwilling to answer my question.

Sameen's eyes, meanwhile, flashed to a folded pile next to the window.

My legs trembled when I dashed for the bundle, but before I could manage two steps, the door busted open behind me. I inhaled sharply when arms clamped down on mine. Large hands shook the weapon from my fingers and the scissors clattered to the ground.

Red infused my already clouded vision. I bucked and screamed.

Something stung the side of my neck, and I gasped. A second later, the pain released. From the corner of my eye the healer ducked behind the protection of Reese's larger form, a small, dart-like object clutched in his hands.

I twisted hard and fell backward, but Reese caught me and gathered me again to his chest. I beat my fists against his shoulders until my eyes rolled back in my head. A curse fizzled upon my still-swollen lips.

ॐ

When I woke, my eyes opened freely to the sun streaming from a window. I reached to stretch fingers to golden flecks dancing in the light. No pain laced my movements. Birds chirped, their song a soothing balm.

I rubbed that place on my neck where Gedeon had injected whatever it was that knocked me out, but nothing remained except the memory.

I was back in my original room. Sameen sat knitting in a rocking chair that wasn't there the first time, and up against the door stood Reese. His eyes already watched me as I examined my surroundings.

He leaned from the door and commanded the attention of someone just outside. "Warn the prince: she's awake."

Did my face have to keep turning color as it did? I cleared my throat, but nothing came out. What was there to say?

"She will need to be dressed. Immediately," Reese said.

"Very well," said Sameen, smoothing her hair twisted tightly at the back of her neck. "I will as soon as you step out."

He hesitated. A question lingered in his eyes.

I slowly sat up, waiting for the painful rush of blood from my head, but it never came. Twisting, I tried the muscles in my neck. They were sound. "I won't harm Sameen," I said, my voice a croaking embarrassment.

She pished and moved to my bedside. "Of course she won't."

Reese's brows ticked high upon his forehead as if to say otherwise. Heat flooded my cheeks.

"Now shoo," she commanded.

When he had left, she held out a light blue day dress. It draped delicately to the ground in gossamer and lace.

I looked it over. "That color is a little too nice for a dirty prisoner, don't you think?"

"You're not a dirty prisoner any more. I'll expect you to act like a lady, not some wild animal from here on out. Do you understand?"

I hesitated before nodding. Could I do that? I could see myself behaving for Sameen, if *only* for Sameen.

I stood, my mind still reeling over the work of the healer. I felt amazing, the best I had felt in months, perhaps years, even. Sameen tugged and cinched the dress in all the right places, lacing it up the back. "Gedeon is over two-hundred-fifty years old, and I think you nearly gave him a heart attack. Can you tell me why you reacted the way you did?"

I blinked. No one had ever asked me such a thing, but an immediate answer flew to my lips. "I don't like to be touched."

Her fingers stilled. "But I'm touching you now."

I didn't have the heart to tell her that even the feel of her fingers on the buttons of my dress made my skin crawl. She allowed the silence and came around to survey her work. "Will you permit me to do your hair?"

"If you wish."

"If I wish?" Her eyes delved into mine, suddenly thick with an emotion I could not read. "I don't know what life was like for you in Eira, but *here* you're—"

"Safe?" I interrupted. My tone dared her to argue my point.

Her mouth clamped closed. She couldn't promise something she had no control over.

Her next words were slow. "Here, it's different."

I didn't think so. People were all the same. Egotistical. Self-serving. Evil.

Her fingers twirled my long hair into a makeshift style. "Another braid perhaps?"

The prince walked in just as Sameen secured her work. A long, loose braid fell over my shoulder to my elbow.

He crossed his arms over the expanse of his chest. "I see the dress fits," he said, eyeing the handiwork of his servant.

My breath hitched inside my lungs and I looked away to avoid his scrutiny.

"Come with me."

"Where?"

He was already out the door. Sameen prodded me to follow. "The king has requested your presence," he said over his shoulder.

We traveled in a single file. I followed in Castiel's footpath as Reese shadowed mine. I tried to remember the steps I had taken with my guard during the previous night's escape, but we rounded a different corner and went the opposite direction.

My stomach growled loud enough to be heard. The prince's head swiveled to eyeball me.

I only shrugged. "Your generous accommodations did not include breakfast, Your Highness."

He rolled his eyes but refrained from commenting. Was that a glimpse of a smile?

The space opened into a large receiving hall. Carved wooden doors towered at each opposite side, but only one was opened. It poured into a throne room half the size of Eira's, but even then, I turned a circle as I walked, secretly admiring the detailed tapestries and brightly colored flags that hung from walls and draped from ceilings. The ancient stone columns and planked floors echoed our steps. The atmosphere of the space was different. Warm, if possible. Even welcoming.

Confusion tugged at my mind. But where were all the people? The line of peasants seeking their king's aide, and the sniveling upper elite watching with disdain?

Scrawling arches decorated the entries, and wooden beams raised the space high into lofty perfection. They all led to the far end of the hall where a magnificent throne, carved in ancient oak sat empty.

My gaze narrowed. Where was Anolyn's great king? "What's going—"

Footsteps sounded. A man entered wearing nothing but a pair of dirty pants and boots. Perspiration dripped from his lean form. He was only a couple of inches taller than me and skinny, but long muscles corded the length of him. With his skin tanned like a field worker and his black hair a mess, I assumed him to be a servant until he tossed the towel he used to mop his sweat to a nearby attendant.

The attendant bowed deeply, taking his things without complaint, and held out a clean replacement, which was ignored.

The newcomer was followed by a precession of men in military attire, deep in conversation one with another. A woman trailed them, wearing a red gown that plunged in the front. Lustrous black hair flowed to her slender waist. When her black eyes met mine, one corner of her mouth tipped up.

"You're late," Castiel said. His words snapped.

The half-naked man peered over at us. Familiar blue eyes confirmed the shocking revelation. Castiel was the larger brother, but King Riaan Anouk was a force all his own to be reckoned with.

"Ah. Finally." Turning to the line of officers, he waved them away. "Gentlemen, we're done here."

With a bow, they left the room, eyeballing me as they passed. I tried to ignore them the best I could; it wasn't them that set me on edge.

Hard like the stone walls surrounding him, the king's steel gaze watched me—weighed and measured me. Despite my carefully tucked emotions, worry trembled down my rigid spine.

"And what of this lady?" the woman asked, her voice soft. "Are we done?"

The king raised one brow to her question, but he didn't remove his sight from mine. "For now."

She curtsied low then left, smiling at Castiel as she passed.

Was she a mistress? News of any royal nuptials hadn't reached the kingdom of Eira, and since he hadn't introduced her, it was rude to ask.

I stared back at the king of Anolyn, unwilling to appear intimidated.

A faint smile turned his mouth upward, but there was nothing warm about it. "Do you see something you like?" he asked, his voice crackled and deep.

Castiel cleared his throat in annoyance, but the king ignored him.

I looked away, lifting careless brows, and said nothing. His chuckle heated my already enflamed cheeks.

Riaan smirked. "I think I embarrassed her, Brother."

Castiel took the shirt from the servant and shoved it into his hands. "Your *Majesty*, may I present *Lady* Anna."

The king gingerly took the garment but kept his eyes trained on me. "I shock you, don't I, Lady Anna? But this is the first lesson you must learn about Anolyn: we all contribute to the prosperity of this great land. Everyone chips in, even the king."

I didn't care to know anything about his country or his ridiculous lessons. I didn't plan on staying long enough to learn.

He peered over my shoulder to Castiel. "So, this little girl is the reason for all of the commotion within my home?"

"It would appear so."

I cast my eyes to my hands folded neatly in front of me. If he wanted me to respond, he was choosing the wrong tactic.

The king signaled with a nod and the grand double doors slammed shut, leaving the three of us alone. He spun on his heel and crossed the room to his throne.

Castiel sighed and gestured me to follow. I tried to look anywhere but Riaan's glistening back muscles, hating the improprieties of such an introduction. Johan would have never allowed his public to see him so disheveled as this king was. Even though I held no love for my uncle, disgust at such a foreign display tightened my features.

Riaan's voice echoed along with his quick footsteps as he finally tugged his white shirt into place. "Let's not pretend right now. I don't have the patience today... or ever. Princess Ilianna, you've put me into an interesting situation."

An answer slipped past stiff lips without my permission. "I didn't put anyone in *any* situation. I only tried to leave."

He threw himself into his seat and draped a leg over an armrest. He tipped his head to one side and at that moment I realized just how fresh this king must have been. Probably twenty-four, or -five… so young to be king already, but his father had died about five years before. Which meant he took the throne when he was around nineteen. This realization sent my mind spinning.

The king's eyes swept the length of my gown. "As pretty as you are, I don't see how you tricked one of my best soldiers into helping you escape. And Sameen, for that matter." I waited for him to ask the question I could never answer, but he moved on without a breath to spare. "It wasn't what we were expecting, but I guess you can't prepare for everything."

The muscles in my neck twitched. "What?"

His gaze narrowed; a curious expression wrinkled his features. "Her eyes are strangely distracting, aren't they Castiel?"

My gaze snapped to the prince, who nodded. "Indeed."

Riaan shook his head as if to rid an unpleasant thought. "Anyways, do you really think my brother happened to be where he was when he was?" He smiled; his white teeth flashed. "And just in time to save you? I'm so glad to see that my healer was able to work his magic."

I shuddered at the word and cursed beneath my breath. The king and prince were even more stealthy that I gave them credit for. I refused to see the situation for what it was, out of what? Hope? Three months in prison had dulled my wits. "*Idiot.*"

"I take it you're not speaking to *me* that way," Riaan said. One brow tilted up, in amusement or annoyance I couldn't tell. "As of right now, I'm more interested in the man that escaped only an hour after your release. My brother said you warned him beforehand that he was dangerous."

"Yes."

His eyes narrowed. "Why even bother to warn us?"

"I don't know."

"Then what *do* you know?" When I didn't answer he asked, "What's his name?"

I shook my head, irritated at his questions, but more so at myself. Why was I protecting my uncle's man? If I wanted to escape both this kingdom and Johan, I needed Lucan dead.

"His name is Lucan Osrick."

The king's voice remained forcefully calm. "The spy and assassin?"

Of course he would know the name. I bit the inside of my cheek. The metallic taste of my blood combined with my treachery to nauseate me. "Yes."

"And you are not a spy, like him?" Riaan cleaned dirt from beneath his nails.

Dirt beneath a king's nails.

I stared out the window. "No."

"Well, that's nice to hear." Derision dripped from his words.

"Brother." Castiel took a step forward, warning him with a pointed look.

I glared at them both. "I am *not* a spy."

Riaan sat up in one swift motion. "Then why was this Lucan here, if not aiding your efforts?"

I swallowed back the angry bile that rose into my throat. I smiled, my voice sickly sweet. "Worthy King, I will answer your questions, or at least the ones I can, on *two conditions.*"

Riaan gaped at his brother in surprise, then focused again on me. "*Conditions?* And you think you're in a place to demand such things?"

"Do you want to know about this man? I can offer you more than just his name."

His lips twitched. "I will hear your conditions."

I straightened, my fingers clenched at my side. "Swear to get to Lucan before he gets to my uncle."

The king's smile stretched wide. "Done. Why was he here in our lands?"

I shrugged. "I can only assume he followed me when I left."

"You ran away?" Castiel asked.

I only nodded.

"Why?"

I twisted toward the prince. The intensity waring in his stormy blue eyes intrigued me, but why did he look at me in such a way? I raised my chin. "Let's just say that your king was not the only one who rejected my uncle's proposal of a… union."

Was that surprise I saw in his expression?

Another chuckle sounded from the throne.

I turned away and continued. "I would not be offered as a bride to my enemy country."

"I believe you," Riaan said.

Shocked, my attention jerked toward him. The silence dragged to an uncomfortable length as he contemplated me. "Tell me more about this Lucan."

"He's my uncle's best spy and tracker. I can only assume he was trailing me and recognized the ambush by your men. My guess is that he got himself captured on purpose to keep an eye on me."

"You're lucky it was my men that found you and not something else." Castiel crossed his arms over his chest. "It would make more sense that Lucan would go back to Johan and tell him where you are."

I shook my head. "If he was sent to find me, he won't go back to my uncle without me. Johan doesn't tolerate failure."

The prince leaned to whisper in his brother's ear. The blood pumped to my face, but Riaan's reaction was cold, calculating.

"Castiel tells me Lucan is the one who stabbed you."

"Not to kill me. If that was his goal, I wouldn't be standing here now. That wound was to slow me down." And even if I wasn't sure of it, I would be confident enough that they would believe me.

His lips twitched at the corners. "Or to stop my brother from coming after him." Why did I feel there was something behind the statement? Whatever it was, he didn't elaborate. "Thank you, Princess Ilianna, for being so forthcoming. Our messenger to your uncle has been postponed. All efforts have gone to finding this spy. You'll have to make due as our honored guest for a bit longer."

A dismissal was coming, but I wasn't done. Not yet.

I took a step forward and Riaan homed in on the movement. "You'll never find him. Not without my help."

His gaze turned a steely gray, a warning against my proximity. "Oh?"

"Which brings me to my next condition."

A smile tipped the corner of his mouth. "Oh, I almost forgot. Please…" He gestured with a lift of his finger. "Do go on."

I raised my head higher. "If I help you locate Lucan, you'll see that I'm safely escorted to port and placed on the first available ship off this continent."

6

ASSESSMENT

My words echoed off the stone walls, then silence.

The king didn't answer, only studied me for a long while. Just when I opened my mouth to say more, he chortled. The gentle lilt of his laugh sunk the half-risen hope that had grown only moments before.

"This little princess demands a lot in return for her information, doesn't she, Brother?"

"Will you grant it to me?" I asked quickly, not wanting to hear Castiel's response to that question.

"Do you know what waits across the sea in the kingdoms beyond?" the king asked.

I opened my mouth to speak, but nothing came. No, I didn't know, but something told me in that instant that I was foolish to even ask. Pride swelled, cutting through that doubt. "Sometimes one must take the risks, even when the outcome is uncertain."

He set his jaw on tented fingers and peered down his straight nose.

I repressed the desire to squirm beneath his scrutiny.

"The white flag of peace has been raised, but I do not believe for a moment that your uncle intends to uphold such peace. I know his bloodlust."

"That is wise."

"And you. You are his niece—the next in line to inherit the kingdom, a rising star in his militia. Would it be *wise* to trust you or your word?"

I held my head high. "In times of war, I have fought against your people and have taken many lives, but I have no reason to hurt your people now. My uncle's battles are no longer my own. Will you meet my conditions?"

Again, hesitation slowed his response, but finally he slapped the top of his thighs. "Done. Upon your word, you will aid in the discovery of your spy—"

"My uncle's spy."

"Your *uncle's* spy, and upon my word I will personally escort you to Anolyn's port *and* with my most expensive bottle of wine christen your journey."

I nodded, satisfied. "There are three safehouses from here to my uncle's kingdom. If he's hurt, he'll find medical aid and replenish his food supply, but he will not stay long. You'll have to get there quickly. I can show you all areas most frequented by my father's captains as well, but it will be dangerous. The sooner you can capture him, the better."

Riaan stood. "Mikael. Melia."

From behind columns, two guards stepped from their hiding places. Knives lined thick belts on their matching black leather jerkins. Additional weapons tucked in their black boots. Mikael's dark eyes found me, holding me in place as he came forward to answer his king's summons. I stared back, angry.

"So, you have a secret door into your throne room."

"What makes you think they weren't already there?" Castiel asked, but I didn't turn to see his expression.

"They weren't." Detection was key to survival. That I had failed to register the entrance the king's military elite used was worse than a botched-up escape.

"I see you remember one of my men," Riaan said, breaking through my thoughts. My face grew hot. "But it's really the other one you need to worry about."

Mikael grunted in annoyance.

"I think you upset your giant," I said, earning another glare from him.

The second guard, the woman, laughed a low chuckle. Blonde hair—much like so many of Eira's women in fashion—was pulled high into a long, golden ponytail. Pale gray eyes set within an attractive face watched me, more inquisitive than Mikael's deadly glower.

"Bring me paper and a map of both Anolyn and Eira," Riaan said to the first. "Quickly."

Mikael ran from the room in a sprint, much faster than I thought the lug could go.

"And the girls?" The woman's voice was deeper than I imagined. Alto, rich with an accent I didn't recognize.

The king nodded, but it was Castiel that spoke. "Ready my messengers."

Melia smiled, her gaze flitting to mine. "They're already prepared."

She went to the closest window and threw it wide. A second later a piercing, high-pitched shrill fill the air and set my heart racing. A bird call, but unlike anything I had ever heard. She walked smoothly backward, her eyes never leaving the opened window. The king descended, watching with disinterest. Castiel, on the other hand, stood by the woman, his eyes alight.

No one paid me any attention as I instinctively stepped back.

A feral cry filled the air, wilder and more terrifying than Melia's call. A creature of black and white feathers soared into the room. I inhaled sharply, catching more than a glimpse of razor-sharp talons and a deadly beak. It attached itself to the top of the king's throne and screamed. Riaan cursed aloud, more shocked than afraid, but I nearly tripped over my feet in my haste to escape the largest bird I had ever seen. The beast's eyes instantly caught the newcomer and, to my terror, regarded me in distaste.

A second skidded to a deafening halt. A raptor of black and golden plumes, its claws scraped and thudded against the floors.

"Careful, girl," the female guard said, her arms outstretched to guide the bird that stood two heads taller than her. It cast a furtive glance my direction then allowed itself to be shepherded.

Before I could reclaim my breath, another feral squall pierced the air. Castiel opened his arms to a third as it landed directly in front of him. The most beautiful of the trio, its pure black wings flailed wildly as it tried to steady itself. I backed against the wall, aware of their keen senses. I would be their next meal.

"Ilianna, meet my most trusted messengers," Castiel said, his voice strained. "They are—"

"Falcry," I croaked. I knew what they were, but the falcry were supposed be extinct, killed off with the magicians who owned them.

Three monstrous birds of prey perched within the room and flapped impatient wings.

I clenched nervous fingers behind my back and took a step forward, bracing against the fear. "That one's much smaller than the others." But not by much. She still stood taller than the prince, with piercing eyes of liquid gold.

Castiel stroked the feathered neck, and she bent in to him, nuzzling his cheek. "She's the baby." But the bird squawked, indignant at the description.

"They're terrifying, aren't they?" the king said. He moved from his stolen dais of power, but kept his arms safely tucked to his side as he skirted the fowl to stand near his brother. "The largest bird known to our continent. Their feathers are stronger than any shield ever crafted, their talons sharp as knives. She can see miles into the distance. A nearly impenetrable foe and fiercely loyal to their owners, so be careful, Princess. If they don't trust you, they'll rip your arms off and eat them for a snack."

I took a step back. The falcry weren't completely impenetrable. Our history books proved that. Their eyes were targets, as were soft spots just beneath their wings, to the inside, close to their body. But to hit those marks while the creature was in flight you needed an expert bowman, and even then your chances were rare.

Less than five minutes later, I was excused. I huffed an annoyed breath as I followed the female guard to my room. The sun was high, emphasizing the grounds in a beautiful palette of color. My body ached to be outdoors investigating the gardens, river, and beyond. But I would never be able to enjoy them. Not until I was safe, far away from Johan.

Not until Lucan was dead.

I doused the fear that threatened to bring me to my knees.

Castiel and Riaan had scoured maps and took note of all the locations I knew Lucan would hit. Missives were drawn, the information within kept from my traitorous eyes. The prince whispered instructions in an unknown language to his falcry, but I was dismissed after asking what.

"It's not as if I didn't help find the spy or anything," I groused.

Melia huffed a laugh, a deep chuckle that hummed in her throat. Female guards were not unheard of, but rare even in Eira. I had been a warrior since twelve but being in the presence of another felt strange.

"It's still yet to be seen whether your help was actually useful. Don't forget, Princess. You have not earned the king's trust by betraying your country."

I ignored the comment the best I could, and instead allowed the heat of the sting to fuel me. Melia was taller than me, but not by much. Barely an advantage. But she was older than me by at least five years. That could be problematic. Depending on how early she began her instruction and how vigorous the armies of Anolyn trained, she could have the upper hand against me.

I took a deep breath. "I don't need his trust to know what the king will do."

"Oh?"

I paused at a window to admire a garden and allowed my vision to drift to the blue sky beyond. "The youngest falcry will obviously be sent right away." She regarded me with raised brows but said nothing. "The bird is small enough not to gain too much attention, but sufficiently strong to carry missives to waiting men."

"And what makes you think you know this?"

I jerked my chin in the direction of the forest. By now the younger falcry was a dot on the horizon, but still recognizable. Melia hummed a noncommittal sound, but her eyes narrowed.

I continued. "The others will have to wait until nightfall. Think of how your people would react if they were to see such extinct creatures soaring above their cities."

"It's *your* people who think they're extinct, not mine. Mine are still in hopes that there might be a few left—a few your people haven't slaughtered." Anger and possibly hatred tinged her words.

I had found a chink in her armor.

I folded my arms. "The purge wasn't directed toward the falcry, only the magicians that infested our lands."

And it was true. My kingdom was one of the reasons why most magicians were nonexistent. The falcry were casualties of war. Covetous and cowardly, magic users worked their powers to manipulate mortals to their advantage. They could live hundreds of years, inflicting the population with their curse. Tired of their abuse, my great-grandparents battled against those who displayed the ability to wield anything more than a sword. Hundreds had been slaughtered. Those that remained fled into remote parts of the world. My ancestors would have followed them to the end of the earth if karma hadn't sent them reeling.

My father, Prince Toma, was born. A magician.

My father and Johan's parents had tried to keep it hidden and failed. When their son came of age, they set in place a law banning the inhumane killing and torture of magicians.

Which is why the infestation managed to seep back into the continent.

My father was a magician. And my uncle wanted me to be one.

Of course, I didn't find that out until later, when my uncle's desire for me to become what I had grown to fear pushed him to lunacy. I shook my head at the thought and turned to Melia. "Will the little one—"

"Ketrina."

"What?"

"Her name is Ketrina."

It was a strange name for a bird. Too normal. Too human. "After *Ketrina* returns, will she then go with the others when it grows dark?"

"No. She's still too young and impulsive. If there's danger, she won't think rationally. There's too much risk she could be hurt."

I smiled despite the internal warning not to. "Will your king be happy to know you've divulged such information?"

Her gaze morphed to hard steel. "Maybe if you start seeing these creatures as living things with intelligence and feeling, you won't be so quick to hurt them."

I rolled my eyes. "I've never hurt them."

"I'm not really worried you will." She spun, moving in the opposite direction. Hesitantly, I followed. "They know you now. If you betray them, they'll kill you."

"They don't know me."

"Falcry are incredibly intelligent. They need only a second to size you up, darling. I wonder what they saw."

Fear, that's what—although I wouldn't tell her that. "I have no reason to tell anyone about the ugly birds."

She hummed a warning. "And they're very sensitive. You better hope they didn't hear that."

I huffed a laugh, pretending to be unconcerned. At the same time, my eyes scanned the hallways for enormous birds of prey—monsters, straight from texts of ancient folklore, that waited to rip out my bowels.

After another turn we entered another unfamiliar hall and then descended a flight of stairs. "Where are we going?"

"You'll figure it out soon enough."

A minute later, a clatter so familiar tossed me in such sweet nostalgia that I could have cried: the clashing of weapons, and with those weapons, muffled voices. Without a moment's hesitation, Melia threw a door wide. I inhaled deeply the thick aroma of leather, metal, dirt, sweat, and blood. She smiled, walking backward. "This is our training room, Lady Anna, and just beyond that door is our outdoors arena. I thought maybe you'd enjoy getting a closer peek at the king's militia—or what's here, that is."

I swallowed nervously as eyes shifted to her and the stranger she dragged with her. Melia smiled like a cat with a prize, waltzing through the room as if she owned it, and nodded to those that acknowledged her. Curiosity brewed at the surface of every man's face as we traipsed through their ranks.

"Carry on," she said. They did as they were told but continued to steal glances at me through their periphery.

So she was someone high-ranking. Interesting.

She moved to another door and opened it. Sun streamed in on an afternoon current, momentarily blinding me. When my eyes adjusted, I was staring at more than a hundred soldiers, all scantily dressed in what I assumed was their practice gear.

"Why don't they have any clothes on?" I tried to pretend not to be bothered by such a thing as a bare chest, but the heat in my cheeks expanded nonetheless.

Melia smirked, speaking low. "This is Anolyn, Princess. You can't expect them to practice in their full gear amid balmy temperatures all of the time."

I huffed my disagreement. "I see you're not really taking my cover very seriously."

She tsked, but another voice cut into the conversation.

"Lady Anna makes a good point, Captain." Reese had come from behind us. He was similarly dressed as the others in only pants and boots.

My eyes grew large when the sun gleamed from the expanse of a dark chest, hulking muscles, and piercings I had never seen before. I tried to hide my shock at such a barbaric display. "Some of these men might know who she is," Reese said.

She waved a flagrant hand. "These men are too young to know her."

"Still, it's an order."

I lifted the end of my braid, examining the tips of my hair. "Maybe her loyalty only goes so far."

Her hand gripped my wrist. Before I could respond, she pulled me a step closer. Her eyes flashed to mine. "I take loyalty *very* seriously. I'm as loyal as the grave. Never doubt that, *Lady Anna*."

I yanked hard from her grasp. "Call me whatever you like, Captain. I can take care of myself."

Slowly she circled, examining me.

"Melia," Reese's voice warned.

"Resume your post," she said in a snap.

"My post is here."

She tsked. "Poor thing. You've been assigned to watch over this traitor? I almost feel bad for you."

"Traitor?"

"Isn't that what you are?" She leaned forward, whispering close to my ear. "I've heard such fascinating rumors of a child warrior from Eira—that's what I was. But then those rumors changed from child warrior to Demon Daughter. Scourge. Wraith. With each description, the stories became more unbelievable than the next."

"You're right."

"You claim none of those titles?"

"As you said, they're utterly unbelievable." I opened my arms wide. "Clearly."

"I've long waited to meet you in battle, but alas, was unblessed in such a thing."

My mouth clamped shut, my eyes narrowed.

"Well?" she asked, baiting me. "Are you a warrior or not? Or is everything I heard just rumors?"

"I think that's enough, Captain," Reese said, interjecting.

"It's alright." I fixed my gaze to his, but he nearly jumped back, avoiding my eyes. Instead, he seized my wrist and guided me away. I was too shocked to do anything but follow several yards before he stopped.

"Let go," I said, yanking from his grasp.

Melia's laughter followed us. "Come, Lady Anna. Won't you spar with me?" I peered over my shoulder. Someone had given her a wooden knife. She tossed it between her hands.

Reese peered over my shoulder. "She's baiting you."

I narrowed my gaze. "I know what she's doing."

His eyes flashed to mine, then away again. "I'm your guard during the duration of your stay. I will return you to your room."

"Look at me," I said.

His voice was barely more than a whisper. "No. I will not allow you to curse me again." Obviously, he hadn't told Castiel or the king, or he would not be alive to champion me. My heart softened a degree.

"I won't curse you. I didn't curse you in the first place."

Confusion marred his brow, but he finally turned his gaze upon me. "You will not trick me again?"

"No. You will not stop me?"

One brow lifted. "Melia is baiting you, but what you choose to do about it is up to you. I believe you have a right to defend your honor."

I nodded, turning away.

Melia smiled like a feral cat cornering a mouse.

I opened my arms. "I'm at a disadvantage, don't you think?"

"Oh, please." She flipped the knife, catching it by the tip. "Don't tell me a simple dress will stop—"

I whirled, knocking the wooden stick from her grasp. It thumped against the castle's stone wall unceremoniously.

I crouched low. "Now we're even."

She smirked, and I lunged.

7

DUNGEONS

I WIPED THE BLOOD THAT SEEPED from my nose with the back of my hand. It smeared across cut knuckles.

Melia grimaced. "That's disgusting." Her blonde hair, which had started out nice and high in her usual ponytail, was halfway down and matted to the side of her cheek. It looked ridiculous. Not that mine was any better.

I laughed at her purpled eye and split lip. "No more disgusting than your face."

She laughed with me.

It had been almost two weeks since Castiel left with over a dozen soldiers to locate and capture Lucan. During that two weeks there wasn't a day that my stomach didn't twist into knots imagining the worst. I couldn't bear to wait in my room to learn his fate or mine, but Melia had helped ease that anxiety by giving me something to look forward to: a good fight.

Weapons were never allowed, and I was searched every time before we began, but that never bothered me.

An uppercut knocked me and my thoughts off balance. I shook off the hit. She was good. I wouldn't last long against her, but it felt wonderful being in control. A circle of soldiers surrounded us, calling instructions. They blended together, too muddled to be heard. Sweat poured from my body and dripped in all the wrong places. Muscles ached, but the ache made me feel alive. I cleaned my knuckles on the back of the old pair of pants Melia lent me.

Her fist cracked against my mouth, but mine found a mark on her chin.

She worked her jaw, testing it. "Better."

It was the biggest compliment she had given me yet. She leaped forward with a quick jab. I blocked it only to receive a same-handed hook to the ribs. My breath seized before I could cinch up my muscles. I tucked my elbows close for protection and braced for impact to wait out the storm that was Melia.

I had almost memorized her attacks. She was rhythmic, her fighting skills like a dance. I wondered what song she listened to in her head to influence the almost poetic movements. When I found the break in her rhythm, I threw my arms around her neck and slammed my knee into her stomach followed by a double-right-hook, and then left. A satisfying grunt from Melia caused me to smile.

She leaped back and away to distance herself from my blows. "You got out of that a lot quicker than usual," she said.

I pretended not to be excited by the praise, but something akin to warmth pattered from my heart.

Melia crouched low, preparing her next attack. "You should come visit Ketrina with me today."

And that warmth left quicker than it had come.

I mirrored her movements. "So you can feed me to her?"

The smallest of the falcry had been a frequent guest during our training. At first her presence had unsettled me, but the creature never stayed long, becoming quickly bored by our activities.

Melia pished. "Falcry don't generally eat mortals. They prefer sheep or goats. But I think she likes you."

The captain of the guard was trying to distract me, and it was working. I clenched my sore fists. I was better with a knife or a sword—not that she would ever let me near any weapons to prove it—but Melia was better than me in hand-to-hand combat. It was a weakness of mine. Any time I got close to winning against one of my uncle's captains I was always punished for it. She was different.

Taking advantage of my unfocused thoughts, she rushed me, knocking me to the ground. Her forearm pressed like a vice against my throat.

"What have I told you?" she asked, her voice a hiss in my ear. "I can practically read when your thoughts wander. You leave yourself open."

I tapped against her arm to admit defeat, but she didn't release.

"What are you going to do when this is real? When the next one—"

"Melia! Stand down!" At first I almost didn't recognize his voice, but it was Castiel's anger that shot through the space, halting our fight.

She released my neck. Before I could even take a breath, she yanked me from the ground. My world spun on its axis. The group of soldiers that had, only seconds before, stood around us in a tight ring had disappeared without a trace. I forced my vision to focus as the prince stormed toward us, his aura radiating anger.

"What is the meaning of this, Captain?"

Reese trailed him, his face ashen.

Our breathing was ragged. Blood leaked from her mouth, but more dripped from my nose.

She stood erect. "Your Highness..."

But he didn't seem to be interested in her response. His fingers grabbed my chin, forcing it high to better inspect my face. Was that concern in his eyes?

I tried to pull away from him, but his other hand seized my arm. My eyes grew wide; my jaw clamped down. "Let go of me," I said through clenched teeth.

Something clicked inside of him. He dropped his hand to the side. I hadn't seen him in nearly two weeks, but that time had not been friendly to him. A beard thickened his jaw; dirt smudged the exposed skin. My thoughts instantly went to Lucan and anxiety rallied once again.

"What happened?" I asked, but he did not answer.

He whirled on Melia, his voice a forced calm. It sent a tremor down my spine. "Explain yourself, Captain."

"I thought she'd enjoy some time outside of her room," was her simple rejoinder.

"Very refreshing," I agreed, wiping blood from my nose.

His face turned an even brighter shade of red when his eyes focused in on the movement. Castiel produced a

handkerchief from his pocket and went to dab the blood. I
pulled away. He hesitated, then held out the material to
me. Slowly, I took it from his fingers.

Melia watched me, a smirk tilting her lips, but I didn't
know why.

"Did you know about this?" Castiel said to Reese.

Reese lifted his head high. "I did, Your Highness."

"This is treason. What would the king say to hear you
doing this?"

Melia straightened her clothes, unconcerned by
Castiel's temperament. "I think the king would like his
orders followed."

"Excuse me?" I said at the same time Castiel asked,
"What orders?"

She shrugged. "I was ordered to keep a close eye on
Ilianna, but I also have to train. How can I be in two
places at the same time?"

His eyes narrowed. "But if he knew you were—"

"He knows," she said, placing her hands behind her back.

Castiel growled. "Of course he does."

"Really, Brother. Calm down." The king's voice trailed
to us from behind, and we whirled. Riaan sat calmly in a
nearby chair as if he had been there enjoying the spectacle
the entire time. The woman I had seen with him upon our
first meeting was with him. This time she wore a seductive
deep blue gown, her black locks weaved a breathtaking
braid. Upon closer inspection I guessed her to be a few
years older than the king, which I found strange, but her
beauty would make up for any discrepancies in age. Her
fingers slid possessively over Riaan's shoulder.

Next to me, Melia stiffened. Her eyes narrowed at the mistress, her jaw muscles clenched.

The mistress winked at her, and Melia looked away in disgust.

Mikael stood directly behind them. Black combat gear befitted him, a magnificent sword strapped to his side. He tipped his head to me in acknowledgment, and I gave him a bloody grin.

Castiel turned to the king. "Explain yourself."

Calmly, the king gazed at Melia, signaling for her to leave. Her gaze flickered to the mistress, and Riaan, remembering her presence, waved her away as well. Mikael and Reese trailed them both from the room.

"You knew of this?" Castiel asked when the door thumped closed.

"Who do you think ordered Melia to watch over her?"

"You call this watching over her?" he asked, pointing to my face. "You were supposed to keep her safe."

Heat enflamed my cheeks, but I refrained from commenting.

The king lifted his arms towards me with a proud smile. "And here she is. Safe and sound."

And I suddenly understood. He had sent Melia to watch over me—and to assess my abilities. He didn't have to say it, but I knew. It was what I would have done.

Castiel smiled, but there was nothing friendly in the act. His voice was an even, controlled pace. And it frightened me. "Remind me to pay back the favor."

Riaan tsked. "This is so unlike you, Brother. I wonder what spurred such a nurturing side of you." Confusion tinted my understanding, but my heart rate spiked at the hidden meaning. He stood and closed the distance. "But we don't have time for this. The spy is resisting our interrogations."

My heart leapt. "Lucan? You found him?"

"Indeed, Princess. He's secure within our dungeons along with two other men. It seems as if the information you provided was helpful after all."

My chin lifted. Hope sprang within my chest. "Then fulfill your end of the bargain."

The king's blue eyes darkened as he considered me. "Not just yet. It wasn't actually at one of your locations that we found him and his comrades."

"I don't understand."

"Our intel indicates that he had indeed been there, but he evaded our capture. There is only one reason why we were able to apprehend him."

"And how was that?"

"He was betrayed." He removed a knife to scrape beneath his nail. "No one seems loyal to the kingdom of Eira."

"Unfortunately, there are plenty loyal to Johan," I said, spite tinting my words.

"Just not his niece or the men closest to him?" He sheathed his knife.

"His men? Just who betrayed him?"

"You'll learn that for yourself. He's resting now but has asked to speak to his princess. *After* you see Lucan and the others, and after you are healed, of course. We can't have anyone that knows you think we would hurt their princess."

When Castiel opened his mouth to protest, the king interjected. "They were just sparring, Brother. I would think it helped passed the tedium of waiting."

And it was true.

The king's lips twisted into a grin. "My healer awaits you, Princess Ilianna."

Castiel spun. "Come," he said, possessing my hand. He pulled me toward the exist, his grasp tight.

I tried to pry my hand from his, but he held even tighter. My heartbeat increased in speed. His breath huffed. "I was gone for one week—"

"Two."

"What—?"

Frustration nearly closed my airway, but I waited until we cleared the room, waited until we were out of sight from Riaan's all-seeing gaze, before ripping away.

"Stop touching me!" I said, nearly tumbling to the ground from such a violent escape.

He spun. His hands shot out to assist but dropped to his side at my rebuke.

My breath heaved and my heart thundered. "Why does everyone keep *touching* me? And you were gone for nearly *two* weeks, not one." Not that I should care.

"I didn't mean…" His lips parted. Confusion and shock warred in his expression. "My delayed return couldn't be helped, my lady."

"I—" My mouth clamped closed, not knowing how to respond. I was upset, but I didn't know why. I wheeled around. "I can see myself back to my room, thank you."

But still Castiel followed.

I closed my eyes, humiliated by my childish outburst. Castiel had captured Lucan and two others. What was more, there was another traitor in Meyrion to interrogate. None of this would have been possible if it weren't for the prince. I should have felt relieved, but I was far from it.

Castiel was there before me to open my door. He ushered me inside with an outstretched hand, careful not to touch me. He paused beyond the threshold but kept his back to me.

"You should have been better treated during my absence," he said. His low, rich voice trod upon my already fluttered nerves. "For that, I am sorry."

Then he was gone.

I stood there with my jumbled thoughts. Why did he care so much? Wasn't I his enemy? A traitor and a nuisance?

"Just in time." Sameen's voice drifted from behind my privacy screen. The smell of her bath salts floated upon the air, soothing me almost instantly. "The king has asked…" Her words trailed when she took in the sight of me. She stamped her foot. "Not again. I told her to go easier on you."

I almost laughed. Instead I sat on the bed to remove my boots. "I don't need her to go easier on me, and I know what the king wants."

She inhaled a sharp breath. "You are filthy." She yanked me from the bed and proceeded to help me off with my sparring gear, her movements brusque yet soft, as I assumed a mother's rebuke would be.

A knock sounded, and the doctor entered, his reaction nearly the same as my maid's. "It seems I have my work cut out for me again."

"Face only," I said. I didn't have time for anything else. I needed to see Lucan—to see him behind bars which he couldn't escape.

When I finally made my way through to the dungeons of Anolyn, my nerves dangled from a very thin line.

The dungeons were vastly different from its prison. A dank spiral staircase plunged downward, lit by a single torch held by the first man in line. With every cascaded step my throat squeezed harder, constricting airflow. I wanted to scream, claw my way out, but now was not the time for hysterics. Lucan was waiting below, alive and warm and still very much a threat.

The situation should have given me peace. He was captured. But the knowledge did little to soothe. What about the other two captives? And there was another Eirian traitor who waited to speak to me. Who were they? More importantly, were they worse than Lucan?

My heart rate spiked. The prince peered over his shoulder to search my face, but in such dim light I didn't know what he could see. I forced my legs to keep moving and breathed a sigh of relief when the stairwell opened into a cavernous room.

Another torch was lit by the first. Our procession of interrogators spread out, awaiting instruction. Castiel and Reese kept close to me while Riaan and Mikael moved ahead through a tunnelway of cement cells and iron bars. The smell of sewage and mold assaulted me. I covered my nose with a long sleeve to breathe through the fabric.

"This way, Lady Anna." Castiel had returned to using my pretended name in the presence of... what? Prisoners? Murderers? Traitors? Why even bother?

A moment later, a responding terror answered my unspoken question. Something foreign, evil, held me in place.

Cold. I was cold. And alone. And scared. The unseen force slid over my exposed skin and invaded like a disease.

"Lady Anna?"

"There's something down here," I said with a shaky voice I couldn't control. My breath was white from fear. "We need to leave."

His hand was gentle yet firm upon my shoulder. Oddly, I didn't pull away. His contact was so different from the darkness that threatened to undo me.

"What is it?" He stepped forward to separate me from whatever that threatened. Confusion married his brows as he scanned the darkened cells. "Perhaps Reese should take you back to your room."

And then I realized he didn't feel what I felt.

The prince was a magician, but whatever this was, it was only perceptible to me... and he couldn't know about it. None of them could.

"No." I shook my head; the movement made me dizzy. I shrugged his touch, shutting down the fear and the cursed sense. The cold infected the place where his hand had warmed, and I instantly regretted the decision. "I'll be fine. It's nothing," I lied.

His gaze narrowed.

"It's *nothing*," I reiterated and pressed forward.

A moment later, he was at my side again. "Keep away from the cells."

A sharp shriek filled the dank air, rattling me to the core. The leaders of the procession raced ahead, and I followed. Every step hurt the very bones in my body.

The screams got louder the closer we drew. Finally, those that led us stopped. A torch lifted high.

Riaan cursed.

"What's going on?" Castiel pushed forward only to stop dead in his tracks. I tripped upon his heel, but he didn't seem to notice.

"Save me!" Lucan lunged at us, panic in his dark eyes. His arm lashed out between the metal bars, and his head hit the steel hard, as if he had forgotten he was contained in a cell. The impact jarred him, and he dropped to the ground.

Castile spun on the spot to steer me away, but I ducked beneath his arms.

The erratic light from the torch dimmed the effect. It wasn't enough to hide what lay mutilated on the ground. Two bodies oddly kinked, limbs broken at the joints. Scratches and lacerations gouged their exposed skin. Blood leaked from their mouths, noses, eyes, and ears. There was no way I could identify them, even if I tried.

Next to me, Mikael heaved. The vile smell of vomit blended with the dungeon stench, and I gagged despite myself.

"We need to leave," Castiel said, low upon my ears. "Now."

And as much as I thought I wanted to see Lucan dead—as much as I needed to be safe from my uncle—this was so far from what I had desired, from what was right.

I was a fool.

Lucan still breathed, though it was shallow. "We can't leave him here," I said, gesturing to his unconscious body.

A laugh reverberated within the cavernous space. Castiel pushed me behind him. He drew a knife from a sheath strapped to his side. Reese and Mikael did the same.

The blood drained from my face as the dark energy from only minutes before assaulted once again. I searched, but nothing stirred in the abyss.

A voice followed the laughter. "You don't like it? Pity. I thought you'd enjoy my offering."

I pointed to the cell across from Lucan, to whatever hid in the shadows beyond. Additional weapons were drawn. The air felt like needles within my lungs.

"That's the cell of the blacksmith. He's never spoken before," Riaan said, his voice more unsure than I had ever heard.

A soft tsk followed. "I've never had a reason to. Until now."

The king stepped forward, his gaze narrowed and almost curious.

"Stop," I said, pulling on his shirt. He gaped at me. "He's not human."

The thing laughed. A single pale finger wrapped the bar of the cell, but still kept hidden. "You recognize me, don't you, girl?"

I swallowed, my voice hollow in my ears. "It's a wraith." Even though I had never seen one, never felt their presence, I knew he could be nothing else.

"What we brought here was a man. Are you sure?" Castiel asked.

"You can't feel it?" I wrapped my hands around my arms, but it wasn't Castiel that answered.

No, they cannot feel me. Not like you can. The wraith's voice was softer than I had ever heard, and it held a note of approval. Red eyes pinned mine, but the rest of him remained shadowed. Only a faint outline of a muscular face gleamed. "The princess has seen through my mask. I've grown careless in my probation."

I straightened, although I did not feel the forced courage. "How do you know who I am?"

"I know because *they* knew." A finger pointed to the cell beyond and the mangled bodies, but he kept his face hidden. "To enter one's essence is to know them. I know every dark secret they've ever heard. Every sin they've committed."

"What's your name?" The king tipped his head to the side. "And don't lie. You're not the blacksmith we brought here."

A chuckle cracked the wraith's lips. "You can call me Cy."

8

CYRIS

"CY?"

"Cyris, actually, but Cy is just fine."

Castiel took a torch from Reese and stepped forward. "You killed those men?"

Again, he laughed. "From the inside-out. They were hardly men, don't you think? They've preformed evils I haven't even dreamed of. They're more a wraith by nature than I am."

"Why would you care?"

"Can you blame me? The princess herself wanted to see that one dead. Lucan is it?"

"Not like that," I said, interjecting.

"A noose would have been better?"

Castiel hissed. "That coming from someone that mutilated his wife and unborn child? Not unlike what you did to these."

The king interjected, his voice deadly. "It was the *blacksmith's* wife and unborn child the wraith murdered. It's makes sense now. No mortal could have done such a thing."

"Lies." The wraith's hands gripped the bars and the iron groaned beneath his strength. He glared at the king. "There are plenty of mortals willing, for the right price. And I didn't kill the woman and child. *She* did."

"*She*—who?" Castiel asked.

The wraith unflexed his fingers. "Like the princess, I hide from an abusive power."

Silence, and then he asked, "Do you speak of the Wraith Queen?"

I jerked. "The Wraith Queen is dead."

All eyes shot to me, disbelief in their shocked faces.

The wraith hummed. "You've been lied to, little one, and she has not forgotten this island or the people that fought against her."

I shook my head, vehemently. "No."

The shadowed profile stared at me. "Poor princess. He owns you, but already you know that, don't you?"

"What do you mean?" I asked, but my heart dropped into my stomach. Of course there was only one person he could refer to.

"If Johan finds you, there's more coming than the lashes on your back and the burn on your neck."

I covered the mark with my hand.

"Still, it's curious. You've been given every opportunity for influence, and yet... nothing. How many tests did he put you through? How many failed attempts to make you—?"

"Shut up," I hissed. I clenched my hands into fists. "Do all wraiths talk in riddles? What is it you're saying, demon?"

The wraith tsked but said nothing.

Castiel's hand took my elbow to guide me away. "Take Lucan to the prison. Double the guards there. Riaan, you can stay and interrogate this freak of nature, but the princess doesn't have to be here for this."

"You should have let me finish him," the wraith said.

"We're done here." Anger colored Castiel's voice.

"Wait!" A long arm shot through the bars, mere inches from my face.

I wrenched back with a shriek into Castiel. Lightning fast the prince slashed a warning blade across the wraith's outstretched arm, holding me protected to him. Earlier, I had told him not to touch me, but now his strength was the only thing that prevented me from huddling into a cowardly ball on the ground.

The wraith swore, yanking back inside the blackened protection of his shadowy cell. Mikael and Reese moved to guard their king and prince, but Castiel pointed the tip of the blade to the demon within. "Stay away."

A groan morphed into laughter, standing the hairs on the back of my neck. "Do not worry, Prince. Here I am, locked behind your dungeon doors. Besides, it's not through touch alone that I can hurt her." He rested his head against the bars, exposing his face, and I gasped at the beard and tanned skin, recognizing him instantly.

"No," he continued. "Touch alone is not enough. One must be willing to accept a little more than just my touch."

"Wait." I shrugged off Castiel's hold and took a step closer despite the warning from the guards. "I recognize you. You were in the forest…" I shot the king a look. "And the tavern in town."

Cy hummed. Blood dripped down his arms to his fingertips. He smiled, his teeth perfectly white though the rest of him matched the filth that surrounded him.

"Princess Ilianna." He sighed my name, almost a sweet melody.

The king's words held an edge. "How did you get out, creature?"

"I'm a wraith. You have let me in. I have been a guest. I didn't know I couldn't leave as I see fit. And I have done no harm." He smiled wickedly. "Until today."

The king's gaze shifted to the bloodied bodies, twisted into unrecognizable knots.

The wraith smiled. "Would you like to hear the story of the Wraith Queen, great King of Anolyn? It truly is a fabulous tale, and one to learn from."

But the king shook his head. "How do you know the princess?" he asked, his eyes shifting to mine.

Cy pressed farther into the bars, so much that I thought he would break the bones of his face. He lowered his voice, his red eyes wide in intrigue. "I've heard whispers of her name—*she is here, she has come*—but nothing more."

"I do not believe you," Riaan said.

"I care not what you believe." The wraith shrugged then pushed away, rolling his neck as if it pained him. "I heard her when she harnessed the man's thoughts in the bar. I saw her when she conjured the Demon Daughter. It was beautiful."

Castiel stiffened at my side.

Stunned, I froze as the realization of what he was saying hit. Alarm flashed. My heart thundered at a breakneck pace, but I refused to look to the eyes that bore holes in the side of my face.

"Oh." The wraith's voice dripped in derision. "The great king does not know. How embarrassing."

The king spat. "Speak now, demon."

I wanted to run but I wouldn't get far. I clenched my fists and waited for my fate.

"Magic runs in her royal blood."

Silence followed the truth.

℘Ⅽℬ

I pulled at my bindings, but the movement only dug them deeper into my wrists. Ketrina flapped her onyx wings and glared from golden eyes. Her clicking echoed against the walls as she flustered from the ledge of the window. I froze, holding my breath until she relaxed again.

The throne room walls pressed against me like the dungeon had only minutes before. My fists clenched until my nails drew blood. Reese, Mikael, and Melia stood a circle around me, their weapons drawn. Even though her gaze was hard, some unknown emotion darkened the light in Melia's eyes.

Castiel had escorted us from the dungeon, all the while rehearsing everything he had witnessed me do during our fight in the forest. It lay bare my darkest secrets. He had known the whole time—had seen me use the cursed magic—and kept it to himself despite all reason. But why?

Riaan stared at me like I was some wild animal. Frustration and anger seeped from him.

"Again, Princess Ilianna, you are the reason for additional commotion within my quiet home. What do you have to say for yourself?"

I looked away, refusing to speak. Castiel had warned me—told me to do as much before he left for the dungeons to see to the disposal of the wraith. Moments later my hands were bound with rope and I was brought to the throne room to plead my case. But I wouldn't plead.

Ketrina squawked a protest and ruffled her feather, her claws digging into the stone beneath her perch.

"Captain Melia, calm that creature," the king said.

Melia gazed over her shoulder. "She doesn't like what you're doing."

She didn't like what *he* was doing? I glanced at the falcry but couldn't maintain its piercing gaze.

Did the king appear more nervous? He cleared his throat, his face reddening. "I must protect my kingdom, Princess."

"Not from her." Castiel's voice boomed across the expanse. He scanned me as he neared, his eyes growing wide to the bindings at my wrists. "What is this?"

"What does it look like?" Riaan asked.

The prince came to me, concern etched in his brows. Muscles rippled within a tense jaw. He drew a knife, shooting a baleful glare to the throne. "You're upsetting Ketrina."

The king straightened. "Now, Brother—"

Castiel didn't listen. He cut through the rope without any difficulty. "I'll take care of this," he said, turning to the falcry. "Now, go."

With a screech that shook my soul, Ketrina took off into the air, wafting tendrils of my hair.

"It can't be true," I said beneath my breath so that only Castiel could hear.

He searched my eyes for my meaning.

I clarified. "The Wraith Queen?"

He only shook his head.

"But my father. He was sent to assassinate her. He—"

"Prince Toma crossed the seas to stop her. Obviously, something happened to make her pull her forces, but he did not kill her."

My mouth dropped open, but there was no sound. I didn't have the courage to speak. I blinked back tears, watching as Castiel checked the marks on my wrist with a careful touch.

Why would he continue to protect me as he did? To increase a life-debt—one he never mentioned? And why would the falcry protest my treatment? That they cared was too simple of an explanation, one I could not comprehend nor believe.

"The wraith?" the king asked.

One brow rose as Castiel slid his knife back into its holster. "Gone."

"Gone?"

My heart dropped into the pit of my stomach, but I kept my fears to myself.

"He disappeared before I returned. Vanished without a trace."

The king's head tipped to the side as he examined his brother.

Castiel continued. "I've sent Gomez and Verity, as well as a dozen men to search for him, but I doubt the wraith will stay nearby."

"Gomez and Verity?" I asked.

"The older falcry."

"How do we know he's no longer within Meyrion?" the king asked.

"We don't. We keep watch."

"And this Lucan? Have you questioned him?"

Castiel rolled his neck, frustration clear in his expression. "The spy is unconscious still. I am to be notified the moment he wakes."

"You're slipping, Brother. But of all these things, you should have told me about *her*," he said, flicking his fingers my direction.

Heat tingled in my ears, but Castiel stood between the king and my guards, as champion. "I thought you might have her killed."

"And I might still." He slammed his fist on the armrest of his throne, then seemed to check himself. He again leaned back into his chair. "Although, we have other options to us. What do you say, Captain? Should we send for your mother?"

Melia glared at her king.

"Your mother?" I blinked, looking to her.

Melia stood straight, sheathing her sword. "That will be unnecessary. As Ketrina tried to indicate, Princess Ilianna is not a threat."

Riaan watched his guard. "Would you commit treason against your king as well?"

"You know I wouldn't."

He leaned forward in his seat. "I understand my brother's reasons well enough, but you? Explain yourself, Captain."

She dared approach as near as the second step to the dais. "Your Majesty, I have watched over the princess this whole time. During the past two weeks she has not tried to escape, sought for information about our kingdom, or sent or received any type of communication."

Humiliation doused me like a cold wave. She was right. I was truly a traitor. I had left my kingdom without any thought to its survival or success, and did I even care? I closed my eyes, allowing the shame. The people didn't need me. I would only make things worse.

Melia continued. "And she has not once used her magical influence on me."

"That you know of," the king said.

She shot him an annoyed glance. "I would have known."

Riaan tipped his head. He lifted a hand and waved her forward. "Come speak with me privately, Captain."

Melia straightened, then moved to the monarch.

Castiel turned from them to stand with me.

"Why is she doing this?" I asked in a whispered breath. Guilt struck deep within my gut. Would I do the same for her? "She could be hanged for treason. You *both* could." Castiel smirked and I jerked back. "You don't take this seriously."

He leaned to me, whispering low in my ear. "You *really* don't pay attention to anything around you, do you?"

"What do you mean?"

He raised his brows. The corners of his mouth tipped up. "Just watch."

The king took Melia by the arm and pulled her close for a private council. That was all. I almost shrugged at the simple act. I had seen Johan in a similar tête-à-tête with many of his trusted advisors. Was that what she was? Guard *and* advisor?

But then my senses caught upon something else.

Barely perceptible, Riaan's thumb skimmed Melia's arm in a soft circular stroke, familiar, intimate. Despite the hardness of his face, the eyes that usually glared when he looked at me now gazed with appreciation and something else. He whispered a response and when he did, his lips, while only for a fleeting moment, grazed her ear.

Heat invaded my checks when I realized I was eavesdropping upon something a lot more private than a simple council.

But Riaan had a mistress. True, it was not uncommon for royalty to enjoy such company, even when married. My uncle had a collection of favorites, and my father was known to have had a stash of lovers, but I had thought someone of Melia's nature would find such an act abhorrent. And perhaps she did.

Melia stepped back to the middle where Castiel had just defended me.

That flint-like gaze had returned to the king's eyes. "And what of you, Reese? Is her magic what persuaded you? Did she trick you into helping her escape? Perhaps we are all enchanted."

Reese dipped his head. "I told the prince of my interactions. I assumed you were made aware."

The king smirked at the prince. "His promotion?"

The muscles in Reese's face twitched.

Castiel waved an unconcerned hand. "Reese's promotion was due, and with the relocation of Scores, he took the empty seat of Lieutenant."

Reese stepped forward. "Sir, if I didn't earn—"

"Would I have put you as a guard if I didn't completely trust you? The secret of her identity is top priority, but I needed someone who could handle anything she might pull. I didn't know she would use *magic*, but I was even more impressed when you came forward, and how quickly you did so."

"And Sameen?" Riaan asked.

Castiel huffed. "How many years did I torture that good woman with my childish, magical pranks? She might fall for them, but she recognizes them soon enough."

Riaan tipped his head back. "It appears I'm the fool here."

"Far from it, Your Majesty," Melia said. "You asked me to watch her. To keep her close, and I did. She was more than content with the distractions I gave her."

"You mean the thrashings?" Castiel asked, an edge to his voice.

Melia pished. "Those were not thrashings."

The king cleared his throat. "Nevertheless, I was not informed of something vital. So you saw what the wraith saw, Castiel? This conjuring?"

I hardened beneath Riaan's weighty gaze.

"Yes," Castiel said.

His brother rolled his eyes and heaved a heavy sigh.

I looked to Castiel, but he answered the question before I could even ask it. "When you use your magic, you leave a visible mark upon those you use it on."

"I do not—"

"In your case, a faded silvery blue similar to your eye color was present upon their aura, which is why I believed Sameen and Reese that you had influenced them. While it's not a rule, I can see when magic has been used." He turned to the king. "That bit she pulled in the forest is a simple but effective parlor trick used to strike fear into her opponents."

Heat coursed through my body, but I couldn't defend something I had never understood. The Demon Daughter only came when needed. She was my last line of defense, one I didn't control.

He stepped toward the king. "Brother, the only times she has ever used her powers was when it was essential to her survival."

Riaan pursed his lips. "I still think the best option is to send for your mother, Captain."

Melia stiffened, but did not answer.

The king stood and moved slowly toward me. He circled my position. "You are a magician?"

My tongue felt thick inside a dry mouth. "Hardly."

"And yet you possess a magical gift."

"A curse."

He tilted his head to the side. "Wraiths haven't been seen in our parts of the land for over a century, and all of a sudden you show up and we have one within our dungeons."

"If it weren't for Ilianna, his existence might never have been discovered," Castiel said.

"But how *did* she discover him?"

"It was his eyes," I said, but the moment it left my mouth, I regretted it. I glanced between brothers. "They were red."

The king's brows raised. "They were *not* red."

My jaw clamped shut.

"She must be sensitive to his presence," Castiel interjected. "That's not necessarily a bad thing."

Riaan smirked. "Oh?"

I was tired of this game. I cleared my throat. "King Riaan, I have done what I said I would do. I have provided information that led to the capture of the Eirian spy, Lucan. I ask that you honor our bargain and release me. I will sail on your next ship. You will never have to see me again."

Riaan's thumb rubbed beneath his chin. "A tempting offer. However, I can no longer do that."

My heart plummeted with a thud to the pit of my stomach. Again, tears mingled with anger and pricked the rim of my eyes, but I wouldn't cry. Not in front of *him*. "Why not?"

"You're a magician. An unlicensed, rogue magician."

"I'm nothing of the sort."

"You *should* know what that means. After all, your people are the ones that set such a motion forward about untrained magicians."

My mouth snapped shut as the horrible truth sucker-punched me in the stomach.

"I have become aware of your untrained skills, and as such, I am liable for you. I am bound by law to see you trained as a proper magician or killed if unwilling to submit."

"You can't—"

"Or, I can relinquish this knowledge to your uncle and to tell him of what I have learned so that he can see to your proper training."

A vision flashed in my mind: my uncle's face twisted in devilish glee. The image mingled with the wraith's words. *"You've been given every opportunity for influence, and yet... nothing."*

My uncle had done his best to provoke my magic into revealing itself, but I had been able to fight him.

I clenched my teeth. "You would go back on your word? I thought better of the king of Anolyn. What would your people say?"

"That I'm protecting them from harm—the harm that comes from an untrained magician. Have you not told your uncle what you are?"

I clenched my teeth. "No. You wouldn't want me to either."

"Why?"

I smiled, exposing a feral smile. "You know exactly why."

He returned my smile. "As a matter of fact, I do." The king retained his seat. "My conditions stand. I'll give you the night—"

"I accept." The words blurted from my lips before I could stop them.

Castiel's gaze whipped to mine, then away again.

Riaan's head tipped to the side, examining me. "I'm surprised you accept this offer so quickly."

I tipped my head higher. "What choice do I have? If I want my freedom, it's the only *real* option, but if I do this, I reclaim the benefits of our original bargain and the first ship off this island."

Castiel cleared his throat. "Brother, perhaps—"

"Done. But I warn you, Princess. If you fail my trainings, if you try to escape, if you betray our trust again… I won't think twice about killing you myself."

"Brother, I need to speak to you."

Riaan flicked his hand in clear annoyance. "No, you don't."

Castiel's eyes narrowed. "You are not a magician, *great one*. You cannot train her."

"You're right." Riaan stood and swept from his throne. "You'll train her."

9

SCARS

SAMEEN KNOCKED ON THE DOOR twice, as customary, to let me know it was her. It would be unkind not to recognize that the woman catered to my every need, even the emotional ones. I paused when she entered to peek beyond the privacy screen, then continued to undress to bathe. I slipped into the depths of the tub, allowing the heat of the water to infiltrate every aching muscle and drown every disturbing thought. The soap stung the cuts unattended to by the healer.

For a brief moment, I wished I would have let Gedeon work his magic.

"Dinner will be ready in an hour. You will eat with the king and prince," Sameen said as she carried in my robe and towel.

Confusion pulled at my brows as I processed this new piece of information. "Why does the king want to dine with me? I've talked to him *plenty* today." And I was officially annoyed.

"I didn't ask, my lady."

She poured water over my head. I closed my eyes and reveled in the sensation of her fingers in my hair, massaging my scalp. The calming smell of Sameen's oils cheered my senses, but they couldn't fully soothe the frustration at the king going back on his word, or the threat of a demon on the loose.

There had been a wraith in the dungeons of Anolyn. An actual demon. It was rumored that with each conquered kingdom, the Wraith Queen collected these demon warriors herself, outfitting her army with only the wickedest of beings from those continents.

And she was still alive.

I shivered in my water, but not from cold.

Not much was known about wraiths, but they were plagues upon the existence of men. Wraiths, demons, imps—they were known as different things across the earth. Their evil deeds during mortality cursed them to an eternity of torment, denied the very thing they wanted most. Instead they sought for those like them that hadn't crossed beyond life as hosts to do their pleasure.

They were a reminder to mortals of what bad deeds could lead to in the afterlife.

At least they should have been. My uncle had obviously forgotten the priests and shaman that still warned of their presence.

I smiled to myself, hoping that Cy haunted Riaan in his sleep.

I swirled in my bath to Sameen, forcing my thoughts elsewhere. "Your king is something of a prat, isn't he?"

"Compared to your uncle, he's a saint."

And how could I argue with that?

Sameen suppressed a smile and spun me around with strong hands. She doused me with a pitcher of water to rinse the suds from my hair. I coughed through the downpour.

"No," she said. "King Riaan is a really *good* man. Like his father."

I tipped my head, letting the water drain from one ear. Curiosity tugged. "And Castiel?"

It felt like forever before she finally gave me the answer I sought. "Like his mother. Hurry, Lady Anna." She left to prepare my clothes.

But what did *that* mean? I leaned my cheek against the rim of the tub. "Sameen?"

"Yes, my dear?"

"When we're alone, can you call me by my real name?" I didn't know why it was important. Maybe because I had lost my home, my kingdom, and my freedom. While I didn't necessarily regret that decision as of yet, I didn't want to lose my identity too.

She stood next to the screen, a new pair of blue slippers in her hand. "Of course, Prin—"

"Ilianna. Just plain Ilianna."

She hesitated, then nodded.

"Are those for me?" I asked, indicating to the shoes.

She smiled. "New shoes *and* a new dress on the way."

"Really?" Was it excitement that flurried in my chest?

Confusion wrinkled her soft face. "You act so shocked."

Before I could answer, a knock sounded. She jumped with

a clap. "That must be it." She draped a washcloth over the edge of the tub. "I'll return to scrub your back."

I ducked below the waterline to rinse any remaining soap from my hair. When I resurfaced, I wiped the excess from my face. Exhaustion tugged at my mind. I didn't want to go to dinner with the king or the prince. Too many things had happened that day and my nerves were too high-strung. But what choice did I have?

None.

I sighed when Sameen pushed me forward to scrub my back and neck but hissed when she touched upon a sore spot.

"Sorry," she mumbled.

I almost laughed. "It's not your fault."

"Yes it is," the voice said from behind, and I swirled in the tub.

It was not Sameen who washed me, but Melia.

"What are you—"

"I should have known." She nodded, accepting her own statement as fact. Her eyes searched me, her expression hardened. "Had you told me, had Castiel warned me earlier—"

"Stop." Anger grew, and I would no longer cower in my bath. I stood in all my glory, allowing the water to cascade down my exposed body. Melia rose with me.

I had earned ever last stripe received. Every mark. Every bruise. I would not be ashamed. The scars that could not be healed by Gedeon stood as witness to a previous life I would no longer accept as mine. The statement mollified me, consoled me.

My door opened and closed and a moment later. "I'm back. I can't wait—" Sameen gasped when she passed the privacy screen. "Captain Melia, what are you doing here. And Lady Anna, where is your towel?"

"*Ilianna*, remember?" But I kept my focus upon Melia. "And this was not for the prince to tell."

"You were beaten by your uncle," Melia said, but I ignored the accusation. She pointed to my neck. "The wraith said your uncle did that to you. Did he burn you, Ilianna?"

"So this whole time you were reporting on me?" I asked to change the subject.

She crossed her arms over her chest. "Of course. You were a leader in Johan's militia. Would you really expect any different?" Despite my glare, she scoured every inch of my exposed skin before Sameen stepped forward to wrap me in a bathrobe. "*This*"—she flung her hand my direction—"was needed information. I know *all* about my soldiers. There is not a scratch on their body that I don't make my responsibility to know."

I pulled the robe tighter around me and stepped out of the tub. "I am not your soldier."

"Maybe not, but you are my responsibility, and there's a point I'm trying to make that I think you understand."

"No."

"No, what?"

"I don't understand. What does it matter if I have scars? Why do you people believe that scars are so terrible?"

"This is not a secret to keep to yourself, Ilianna. There is no dishonor in the truth. What he did was wrong."

I swallowed hard. No one had ever said that before. Reaffirmed the same truth that screamed from my own soul. *What he did was wrong.* It was *all* wrong.

Melia stood straighter. "Johan is evil."

Tears stung the back of my eyes. "Yes. He is, but I don't need to say it to know it. And over time even your healer can erase what he did to me."

She shook her head, then suddenly seized me in an embrace I did not expect. I froze beneath her touch and she recognized it.

She sighed, her breath against my ear. "Gedeon cannot heal what has been done to you. Only you can." Then she pulled away, releasing me, and took a step back. "I didn't mean to frighten you. I'm sorry."

"You—" I shook my head, confused. "You didn't frighten me."

"And I will never beat you up again."

"You didn't beat me up," I said with a stamp of my foot, but a smile lightened her features. I laughed once. "Melia, this…" And I made a circle with my hand indicating the hidden injuries. "What *you* did, I had control over. I know how I got every mark and for what reason. And what's more important, I was able to fight back. This…" I tipped my neck for her to better see the bubbled scar that lined my skin. "This is a reminder. I will *never* allow anyone to take that right away from me again."

One side of her mouth tipped up as she considered me. "Someday, I'm going to hurt your uncle."

"That makes two of us," Sameen said. Her arms tightened across the large expanse of her chest. Anger burned her cheeks and brightened her eyes. She would be a force all on her own, one Johan had never reckoned with.

A burst of laughter blurted awkwardly past my lips, and then another—a hysterical sound that echoed in my ears.

Melia flinched. A strange expression twisted her beautiful face. And then we were both laughing until tears streamed down our faces. And just like that, I knew we were friends. All of us. It didn't have to be said, it just was.

Sameen tsked. "Well, don't you two make a strange pair."

"Trio," I said, wiping my face with the hem of my sleeve.

She pushed back a rogue strand of gray-lined hair. "Yes, well, I hardly can be compared to the two of you, but regardless..." She held up a dark blue dress of stunning proportions.

I gaped in surprise, but my fingers automatically reached to touch the soft layers.

I had never worn anything so elegant. My uncle had insisted that as his niece, even the dresses I donned needed to be warrior-like. Strong, tear-resistant material, leather-corseted, with straps for a sword and knives—both seen and not.

This gown was different. The material scooped from the neck and flowed to the waist where a satin belt of a deeper shade slung low before draping to the ground. Bell sleeves elegantly fell past the wrists.

Sameen smiled. "You're both going to be late if we don't get you dressed now."

Less than an hour later, Reese escorted me to dinner. Sameen had done wonders with my hair. It hung in a cascade of curls and braids. I hardly felt like me. As we neared the receiving hall, a woman in a purple gown waited just outside the second set of foreign double doors. Her blonde hair flowed to her waist in a similar fashion as mine. I nearly gasped out loud when she turned.

"Melia? What are you doing?"

"Dining with you." She smiled at my shock. "You're not the only one who can turn heads, my lady."

"I—"

She tucked my arm into hers. Again, I stiffened at the familiarity, but she didn't seem to notice or care. Reese led the way. With every step, voices grew. I pulled back, but Melia's step never faltered. I was half-dragged the remaining way.

"You can let go, you know," I said between clenched teeth.

"If I did, you'd turn tail and run."

"You're calling me a coward."

Melia smiled like a cat. "Prove me wrong." She released me, and it took all I had not to do exactly as she thought.

Before Reese could reach the large metal rings to pull them wide, the set of double doors groaned open without being touched. Magic swirled in the air, standing the hairs on the back of my neck on end.

The voices within died.

Despite five rows of tables and matching benches that lined the room, only four people sat within. That could

have settled my nerves if it weren't for the magical
aquamarine eyes set into a sculpted face. The prince's hand
was extended outward but the moment we entered, he
clenched his fist, bringing the doors back to their place.
His gaze traveled the length of my body.

Heat ruptured and flowed down the line of my exposed
neck to the glimpse of cleavage my new dress afforded.

The king peered at his brother with an inquisitive
brow. His expression mirrored my own.

Muscles flexed within Castiel's strong jawline, beneath
a now trimmed beard. He stood, his fingers combing
through this dark hair. He bowed.

I dropped into a curtsey but stood with a jolt when my
delayed attention caught upon a stranger within the room.
Partially blocked by Mikael's larger form, a fourth man
remained seated, unwilling to show his face. Short, sandy
blond hair peeked from a high collared tunic. His pale
hands clenched a goblet of wine.

The king cleared his throat. His chair scraped against
the floor as he stood next to his brother. "Lady Anna,
Melia, come. We have much to discuss."

So his mistress was absent tonight, was she? I almost
tripped over my feet when Melia drew me toward the
table. A curse bubbled from stiff lips and I pulled away
with a sharp tug. I gave her a look, tilting my head toward
the half-concealed stranger. "What's going on?" I asked,
my gaze never leaving the stranger's hands. Despite the
ease that radiated from the king's smile, I was wary of any
new additions to my very small group of acquaintances.
And for good reason.

"Perhaps some of us have forgotten or haven't been taught proper manners, Your Highness," Melia said. Her head tipped high. "When ladies enter the room, the men rise to receive them. Even supposed guests."

The newcomer's fingers released his goblet and cleared his throat. "Yes, of course."

Those three words caused a tremor to jolt through my body.

I knew that voice.

"Forgive me, my lady. I'm out of sorts." As he moved, my heart rate spiked to a painful cadence. "It's been a long time since I've seen the young lady Ilianna."

"You." My breath left me in a whoosh. My fingers dropped to where my knife would have been if I were wearing my normal dresses, but nothing was there. I felt exposed. Foolish. Heat broke out into ugly splotches against my cheeks.

Castiel asked, "Do you know this man?"

I stiffened, my words hollow in my ears. "Captain Weylan Laphel of King Johan's sixth regiment, second son to the Duke of Vaneira, and third cousin to King Johan Drakara." I glared at Riaan. "Why is he here?"

"Princess Ilianna—"

"No." I pointed an accusing finger at the newcomer. "He is one of my uncle's men. A spy."

Riaan's expression was one of disbelief, and I knew why. Weylan was only twenty when he was first promoted to the king's guard. I was thirteen. He was much younger than most captains my uncle surrounded himself with, and had much to prove within the corps. He eagerly set out to do so. His fighting skills were soon unmatched, his cunning in battle feared.

It didn't take long for him to rise in popularity, especially with the added bonus of his rugged beauty. His carved jawline and brilliant smile could melt any debutante. The fashionable women of Eira only added to his status. They were always on the watch for a beautiful face to attach their arm to. A new and upcoming star within Eira's elite, Weylan was eager to prove himself worthy of the king's notice. He was a shining beacon for those of the younger generation.

And an even deadlier foe.

King Riaan threaded his hands in his lap. "He's the one who helped us locate and capture Lucan."

10
UNWANTED GUEST

FEAR LACED MY RESPONSE. I LAUGHED out loud, shocked at the craze in my own voice. "He's fooled you. He's probably working *with* Lucan."

"Never," Weylan said, passion infusing his voice. I wanted to retch against the sound of it.

I turned to the king. "Let me interrogate Lucan. I'll get the truth from him. This man… This—" and I pointed to the newcomer, all words lost to me.

Where was my strength when I needed it? And where was the falcry when I needed them? From outside the darkened window, a shadow swooped by in answer, bolstering me.

The king shook his head. "Now, now—"

Weylan held out a hand. "Forgive me, Your Majesty, but she has every right to be upset. I've done many things for King Johan in the past, things I wasn't proud of."

"Don't make me sick," I said in a growl.

"But it's true, Ilianna."

The blush on his cheeks powered the look of his innocence, but it only fueled my contempt. I would not be taken in again.

A hiss broke through my teeth. "Don't you dare be so informal with me."

"Why? It never bothered you before."

"That's enough." Castiel took a protective stance in front of me.

"Yes," Riaan agreed. "Let's move on to more important matters. Why *are* you here? Why help us?"

Weylan's green eyes flashed from mine to the king. "To ask the kingdom of Anolyn for help."

Memories clamored at the back of my mind, fighting to make their appearance. My fists clenched as I slammed shut that mental barrier before it could burst wide.

Trust me, Weylan had once said. *Trust me.* But then once my uncle called for him to act, he didn't hesitate to do his bidding against me.

I flinched to the sound of his voice. It grated like sandpaper upon every last nerve. While the traitor spoke, Castiel gently guided me to my seat. The king didn't look up when he pulled the chair between him and the prince.

"Johan is manic," Weylan said.

"He is your blood." Riaan placed his chin on steepled fingers, watching him.

Weylan closed his eyes as if the relation pained him. "He was, but no longer. Johan gets worse every day. I couldn't follow his orders anymore, so I left. I now fight with a group of resistance warriors against the crown of Eira."

I laughed. My smile felt stiff upon dry lips. "No one resists my uncle."

One brow pitched high on Weylan's forehead. "*You* did. Do you think you were the only one who suffered? And do you think Eira's princess is so easily forgotten?"

"If what you say is true, why haven't we heard of these resistors before?" Castiel asked.

"We are being snuffed out before we can become too large or get too loud. Several of my men escaped across the border to either find the princess—"

"Why would they want me, if not for my uncle?" I asked.

"To rally your followers."

"I have no followers."

"That you choose to recognize. The others were sent to seek help, but most have died. I managed to make it as far as Leolina and secure a temporary residence when I heard of Lucan's plan to extract the princess from Anolyn's very walls."

A perplexed frown darkened Castiel's brow. "And who gave you this information?"

Weylan shrugged. "Thugs for hire. For months Johan has placed watchmen throughout your kingdom. At the coast. The forests. Near the borders. He searches for his niece. Many are searching still."

I cursed out loud.

Weylan smirked. "You always did have a mouth to you."

"How many know she's here?" the king asked.

"I killed the ones who told me. Most understand the animosity the kingdoms hold toward one another. I, for one, didn't believe she would actually be here. Alive."

I lifted one brow. "And just where did you think I would be?"

"The coast. I had hoped you were long gone by now. I guess I was wrong."

Castiel stiffened next to me.

The king leaned back in his seat. "And what else is it you think I can do for your... resistance?"

"Sanctuary. Food. Anything you can give. There are men, woman, and children trying to get free from a tyrannical leader."

"And that's all?"

"We can't be *any* force to be reckoned with until we are collected. Most die before they can even make it out of the kingdom. Those who have are starving with nowhere to lay their head." Weylan swallowed. "But beyond those basic needs, we will need help to fight against Johan's armies."

The king's answer was immediate. "We cannot aid a rebellion."

I inhaled, unaware I had stopped breathing. Was I relieved that the king would not support my kingdom's outcasts?

Weylan stiffened. "Why?"

Riaan studied him. "Because King Johan has offered us a peace treaty."

"Peace?"

"And for the sake of my kingdom, I must see if peace is achievable."

Weylan smirked. "And you think he's genuine in his peace treaty?"

The king only shrugged. "We cannot afford another war between Eira and Anolyn. Maybe Johan recognizes this as well, seeing as how he's offered his niece as a token of that peace."

Weylan jerked; his eyes flicked to mine. "Ilianna?"

What did he expect me to say? I lifted my head high.

Weylan blanched. "But I thought... Is that why you're here? Did you accept to act as this... this pawn?"

My jaw clenched. "You dare call me a pawn? And what were you for Johan, if not some pathetic marionette? Who pulls your strings now?"

Weylan crossed his arms over his chest. A scowl darkened the lines of his face, making him appear years older than he was. "The king will not honor this peace. Surely you must know this."

I *did* know, but I wouldn't tell him as much.

"While we are grateful for your assistance, Captain, we must allow this peace treaty to move forward."

"I am no longer captain to King Johan." His green eyes searched mine for some understanding I couldn't give. "He has been scouring the countryside for his niece. What will the king do if he finds out that his princess has been here the whole time?"

"The princess is our guest and under our honorable protection," King Riaan said.

"Yes, but—"

Riaan spoke over Weylan's protests. "We do not dabble in family affairs. Princess Ilianna wishes to keep her private relationship with the king of Eira to herself. *We* wish to keep her identity unknown at this time. She may be revered in your kingdom, but in ours she is feared. For her protection, and until this treaty is seen through, she is Lady Anna. I expect you to keep her identity to yourself."

Weylan hesitated, but then nodded.

Riaan gestured to Reese, who opened the door to whisper something to an attendant waiting outside.

"I'm famished," the king said with a smile.

My bones creaked with every step I took to claim my seat between king and prince. Melia took hers across from me and together we sat in awkward silence.

Kitchen attendants brought in steaming plates of food and drink, but with each presented dish, my appetite fled. Weylan's gaze bored holes into me, but I refused to look up, refused to believe he was anything but the con-artist I knew him to be.

"Ilianna." I barely managed to keep my seat when Castiel whispered in my ear. "Will you eat?"

"I'm not hungry," I mumbled.

His fingers touched mine. I whipped my hand away, sending silverware clattering to the ground and stood. Chair legs scraped against the floor and added to the terrible racket.

"She doesn't like to be touched," Weylan said low, making the situation worse.

Resentment and anger caused my limbs to shake.

Castiel clenched the arms of his chair in a white-knuckled grip. "Did *you* have something to do with that?"

Weylan stood. "This is indeed my fault," he said. "My apologizes for causing such an uproar. Please," and he indicated with a wave of his hand to the food in front of him. "As splendid as this offer is, Your Majesty, I am weary from my travels and would like to rest. Would you excuse me?"

"Of course." The king nodded to Reese, who quickly escorted Weylan from the room.

I stared at the closed door, lacking the courage to look the others in the eyes. "I do not trust him."

Castiel said, "We've placed him here tonight, but under heavy guard. He should be gone by the morning."

My place at the table was reset, everything back in order as it should have been. Castiel nodded to my seat and I took it without further encouragement.

Melia reached across to pat my hand. "Maybe I'll take him to the training yard with me tomorrow."

I bristled. "Only if you use him as target practice." The training yard was *mine*.

She smiled. "That can be arranged."

Later that evening, I paced for hours before a dimming fire in a thin nightgown. The silky material felt strange against my skin. A wide-scooped neckline exposed my neck and collar bones. Sameen had warned it was getting closer to the summer months and that Meyrion was well insulated against any remaining chill, but for me it was almost too warm at night.

It was hours past midnight before I slid into bed. Reese was outside my door as usual, my ever-constant guard. Although his presence soothed, I did not feel safe. Weylan was a threat, worse than Lucan because of his craftiness and manipulations. He had fooled me once. Never again.

I pulled the bedsheets to my chin and closed my eyes, but sleep evaded me. I tossed and turned for what felt like hours. My mind fought against a sleep that drained any lucid thought, leaving me with a muddle of complex emotions. They crept through the chinks of my mental barrier I had so carefully formed with Weylan.

Fear, regret, hopelessness… these weaknesses threatened to overwhelm me until something far stronger took their place. My mind seized upon a thought, an entity even more chilling than the treacherous captain.

The wraith Cy.

My heart rate quickened. Dread bloomed and with it, a terrible knowledge. There was something in the room with me.

I tried to wake, to move, but as in the dungeons, an evil presence kept me from stirring.

I focused on the space around me. The threat only watched my struggle—watched and waited. I commanded my fingers to move, then my hand, until the muscles of my body were once again under my control.

I opened my eyes.

Red eyes stared back, so close that I could see the dark rims of the irises. I lurched from the bed in a mad tumble of limbs and sheets. Terror squeezed the air painfully from my lungs and silenced my scream. I fell to the ground and scuttled backward until my spine knocked against the stone fireplace.

The wraith, Cy, watched me, unmoved. I prayed that this was just a dream, that my over-excited mind played yet another trick on me. I couldn't even blink to rid the sleep from my eyes.

A knock sounded.

"Lady Anna? Are you alright?" Reese's voice brought some sense of reality.

There was a wraith in my room. A wraith who hadn't killed me in my sleep when he could have. A wraith who hadn't moved an inch since waking me. A wraith who now held a finger to his lips to plead my silence.

My voice returned with a squeak. "I—" But why would a wraith plead for anything? They were the spawn of hell. They murdered without thought. Destroyed without remorse.

Then why—?

Reese's voice echoed louder inside my addled brain. "Lady Anna?" The knob to my room twisted.

"I'm alright," I said, leaping to my feet. I ran and seized the handle. Light entered through the slit in the door. Heat emanated from the torch Reese held. My eyes braved a glance at my guard. "I'm alright," I repeated weakly. "Forgive me, Lieutenant. Sleep fights me this evening. I may have fallen from my bed as a result of a nightmare."

"A nightmare?"

His eyes dropped to my nightgown that had slipped off one shoulder and then quickly away. I pulled it in place and breathed a nervous laugh. "Foolish, I know. Forgive me for disturbing you."

He nodded, still perplexed, but let the subject drop. I shut the door with a resolute click, sealing the wraith inside with me.

I spun, my hands cold and slick against the wood of the door. Sweat dripped from my forehead. Cy watched me as a carved statue, all expression vacant. And yet he was full to the brim with information. Information I needed. He either had a purpose in being here... or I was a bigger fool than I thought.

Owning my decision, I straightened and forced my legs to move. The fire Sameen had left me with had reduced to a few glowing embers. I squatted low to place a log on the hearth.

"Please, don't." His voice was less than a whisper, yet it rattled me to the bones.

"But I can barely see you."

"Your eyes will adjust. I'd rather not draw any more unneeded attention."

"You mean you'd rather keep me in the dark and afraid."

"I did not mean to frighten you. A compromise, perhaps? One log?"

I set a single log to the dying embers and waited for the fire to bloom and my sight to adjust.

"Why are you here?" I asked, speaking low so as not to be heard. My voice sounded much braver than I felt. "Are you here to kill me?"

Cy chuckled, the sound reverberating from the empty places in my chest. The light from the flames danced shadows on his pale skin. Light brown hair grew ragged to his chin.

"I am a guest in this house, and as such, I cannot kill you. Besides, if I wanted you dead, don't you think I would've taken that opportunity before?"

"Like you did with Lucan's men?"

A smile drew up one side of his mouth. "They killed themselves."

"But their bodies… How is that possible?"

"Do you really want to know?" he asked, his voice an eerie whisper.

A shiver traveled up my spine. "No. Then why didn't you kill me?"

"I thought about it." His brows pinched together as if contemplating the possibility yet again. "You are fascinating to watch. As beautiful as you are awake, you're an unsightly sleeper."

I straightened, lifting my head high. He mirrored me, standing erect. He would have towered over me had we stood any closer.

"What do you want, except to ruin any chance at rest?"

"You put on a good show, but you're just a frightened child. Shall we sit?" He indicated the pair of chairs. His finger trailed the length of my bed as he moved closer.

I jolted to keep the distance between us. "I don't intend to continue this conversation. You should leave. Now."

His gaze traveled the single tapestry that decorated my room, although how he could see any detail I didn't know. "I can choose who I want to see me. I can disappear entirely. But two times you have seen through my guise. Even when you sleep, my presence affects you. How are you so aware of me?"

"This isn't the first time you've been in my room, is it?"

His blood-red eyes rolled to meet mine; a smile stretched across his face. "As a matter of fact, no. I was curious when they brought you back. I had to see you myself."

"See me, for what?"

He sank into the chair but did not answer. One brow raised high as he waited for me to join him. I ignored the warning from within and pulled the second chair several feet away before sitting across from the wraith.

Cy smiled. "Why do you fight against your uncle? Why did you fight what he needed you to become?"

"A magician?"

He cocked his head to the side to examine me. "A magician. An army. And more. He is all you know. The only family to call you their own, and yet you disown him?"

My neck stiffened against the hurt that came. I repeated the very words Melia had spoken that night. "Johan is evil." Saying it aloud solidified that knowledge greater than ever before.

"All men are evil."

I shook my head. "No, they're not."

He shrugged. "Maybe you're right. Anolyn's royal brothers seem to be ridiculously valiant. You're not evil and yet, by every account, you should be."

"Why do you say that?"

He rested his cheek against his hand. "Because it's true. Fear controls the king of Eira. He looks to you as a savior."

11
MORNING VISITOR

SHOCK AND ANGER COLORED MY words. "My uncle looks to me for someone to release his pent-up frustration."

"That's partly true. What do you know about the Wraith Queen?"

I flinched at the jolting shift in conversation. "The Wraith Queen is evil incarnate."

He bowed, his lips a mocking smile. "Besides the incredibly obvious."

"We do not speak of her out of respect for those who lost their lives."

"Keeping you in ignorance. Your uncle *fears* the beast. Do you know why?"

"He would be foolish not to. But what makes you think you know what my uncle fears?"

"I told you before, I know because of what his men knew. What Lucan knew—or as much as I could gather. You didn't let me get too far with him."

My insides shuddered.

"What would you say if I told you Johan had good reason to fear her?" he asked.

"*That* would be obvious."

"Would it? Do you know anything else about the Wraith Queen?"

"Only rumor. Almost two hundred years ago, she came to power. She took an entire kingdom hostage in her greed, then conquered others to satisfy her bloodlust."

He tipped his head back, rolling his neck side to side. "It's amazing what mortals derive. She's taken several kingdoms hostage, and she will never stop until she's destroyed. She's cursed, did you know?"

I didn't, but I remained quiet.

"The Wraith Queen's tale is quite remarkable." His gaze narrowed. "I assume since you're not in prison, the good King Riaan has decided not to kill you?"

My brows creased my forehead at yet another shift in conversation. "No thanks to you."

"You're welcome. Will you be trained or sent back to Johan?"

"How do you know that?"

He smirked. "*Obvious.* You're a rogue magician. It's the only solution to the problem you present."

The truth hit me like a stack of brick. *I was the problem.*

"Stop wallowing," the wraith said, as if he could read my very thoughts. "If I were you, I'd let the prince train me. He's strong. You'll need to be to face the future coming to you."

"And why do you think you know what's coming?"

"The Wraith Queen left something behind that she's not likely to forget. Also, like Anolyn's good king and prince, I pay attention to the signs." His eyes shifted to my door, and a smile lifted one corner of his mouth. "Speak of the devil."

I swiveled that direction, but Cy's voice drew me back. "Like the Wraith Queen herself, you are cursed, Princess Ilianna."

I flinched but suppressed my shock. "Tell me something I don't know."

"You need to find me. We have much to speak about."

And then he was gone. The energy that came with the wraith pulled away, almost painfully. Ice trailed my spine, leaving me more afraid than when Cy was there—a belated reaction from his presence. I ejected from my seat, my breath caught in my throat, and spun in a full circle, searching for any sign of him. Panic welled.

From beyond my room, a recognizable voice commanded entrance, and my heart leaped within my chest. A second later, the door was flung wide and Castiel entered wearing nothing more than his breeches and a thin opened robe that exposed a chest that heaved laden breaths. The light of the fire glinted from two long daggers held in each hand.

I inhaled sharply, stepping toward my fire. "What is the meaning of this?" My voice cracked, thwarting the outrage that should have reigned. Really, I was relieved.

Reese had followed his prince and immediately did a scan of my apartment, even checking beneath the bed.

Castiel's eyes shifted to the darkened corners of my room; however, I knew, could sense, the wraith had disappeared completely. Words almost visible parted the prince's full lips. His gaze fixed on the place where my gown had slipped from my shoulder again, but I did not move to correct it.

"Why are you here?" I asked and was still ignored.

The guard finished his inspection and nodded. Castiel twirled the daggers in his hand, then handed them off to Reese. "Leave us," he said, but I noticed my guard left the door cracked after exiting. His hulking form stood just beyond the threshold.

Castiel watched me. Low firelight glowed warmly from the roughened lines of his rugged face and muscled neck. His opened robe did little to conceal a tanned chest and stomach sculpted from years of arduous training. A scar, a thick line from a stab wound, caught my attention. It marred the left side of his abdomen, just below the ribcage.

My heart accelerated, beating almost painfully. A tremor racked my body and he caught the reaction.

His eyes narrowed. "Please," he said, indicating for me to sit. When I did not move, he grabbed the back of my chair and slid it closer to the fire. Worry set in his expression. "You are shivering. Are you cold?"

"Of course not. I'm only shocked. What is the meaning of this intrusion?"

His grip tightened on the back of the seat. "I told you there would be inspections of your room."

"At this time of night?"

"It's morning, my lady, and it's whenever I please," he snapped, but then he sighed and wiped a tired hand down his face. "Lieutenant Reese worried you were under duress."

I huffed. "I told him it was only a bad dream. I—" I swallowed against the lie that tightened the muscles of my throat. "I'm sorry he woke you for nothing."

"It's not nothing if you are truly distressed." Silence enveloped the space between us.

Heat crawled to my cheeks. I *was* distressed, but it was a combination of so many things that it was hard to choose which was the worst. Was it the shirtless prince standing in my bed chambers? Was it the wraith that had been there only seconds before? Or was it the scheming Weylan?

The last thought squeezed my chest.

It was *definitely* Weylan.

My voice was barely more than a whisper. "Why would it matter to you?"

Weylan would have given me soft-spoken promises of hope through eyes the color of spring, but Castiel only blinked. The muscles in his face tightened as he regarded me curiously. Why did he have to look at me the way he did?

"What is it that distresses you, Princess? Is this because of my brother? That you must be trained by me because—

"It's not going to work," I said in a rush of words. "I told you, I'm not a magician."

A smile touched the corner of his lips. "I hate to be the bearer of bad news, but you are."

"You're not the bearer of bad news." I pointed beyond my room. "That *schemer* is. He's bad altogether."

"My brother?"

"You know very well I'm not talking about your brother. *Weylan*. From the moment he arrived, you should have—

"Sent him to the dungeons to be murdered like Lucan's men?"

I couldn't contain the shudder that climbed my flesh. The image of mangled bodies flashed through my mind. "No. But it's foolish to think that this is not a trap. Weylan is working with Lucan."

"You wouldn't think so if you were there for his capture. But if it pleases you, I'll allow you to ask him yourself."

"You'll allow me to interrogate him?"

One brow raised, giving me a pointed look. "You may *question* him. You won't want to be there for the interrogation." It was a warning.

And he was probably right. I gave in. "Very well. So, what do we do now?"

He shrugged. "While we wait, I assess you."

My face heated and I stepped away to pace. "You assess me?"

"For your magical skills. Which may prove to be difficult."

"It should be quick," I groused.

His eyes narrowed. "Maybe. I'm guessing you just don't know all that's beneath the surface, but this assessment is going to be hard for you in other ways."

I stopped pacing. "Why?"

"Because your magic appears to have a defensive mechanism. Most magical defenses are triggered by your own feelings."

"Meaning?"

"You don't like me."

My heart thundered in my chest as guilt ripped through me. "I never said I don't like you."

"You don't trust me."

"You don't trust *me*," I countered with a snap. Why was I acting like a child?

But the prince surprised me when he said, "Actually, I do." My immediate response caught in my throat. He continued. "You forget, I've watched you over the past three months. I've already made my decision on that subject."

What could I say to that? I clenched my fists. "I trust you," I said, testing the words myself.

Castiel appeared doubtful. "That was a little too easy."

"There's nothing easy about it, but..." I resumed my pacing. My answer poured from my lips without needing any additional thought. "You saved me. You stopped Lucan from taking me. Protected me from the touch of a wraith. Even defended me from your own brother and king. And what have I given you in return?"

Castiel sat in the chair opposite the one I still ignored, a stark contrast to the wraith who had so recently occupied that position. The prince leaned back to stare into the low flames, his arms resting wide, exposing his broad shoulders and chest. "I don't require anything in return, except—"

Almost automatically I moved to stand opposite of where he sat. My heart quickened. "Except?"

"There's a lot that goes into training. It can get…
intimate." His eyes flickered to mine.

Why did I shake the way I did? "I understand."

He turned over his hands to gaze at his palms. "I may
have to touch you. You can't react as you have in the
past, or your magic may shut down. And I'll need to
know the truth."

"About?"

He leaned forward, his gaze penetrating me to the
very core. "Anything I ask you. I won't be able to assess
your magic as I should if you're not completely honest
about things."

"About that…" I swallowed hard against the lump in
my throat. I didn't know how to approach him about the
wraith in my bedroom. Castiel might not suspect foul play,
but Riaan would gain yet another reason to mistrust me.

"What?"

And what could I say except for the truth? I closed my
eyes and took a deep breath. "Reese was right to be
worried. I had a visitor."

"A visitor?"

Finally, I took the chair opposite him. Warmth grew in
the small space that separated us, making me
uncomfortable. "Cy, the wraith. I woke to find him
watching me."

A noise gurgled from Castiel's throat, but he waited
for me to continue. Despite his forced calm, his face turned
an alarming shade of red.

"He—he asked what I knew about the Wraith Queen.
And he said that she left something here—"

"What?"

"I don't know."

He cursed, shooting to his feet. "She's coming."

"Wait. Cy didn't say—"

"He didn't have to. What he said was enough. The Wraith Queen herself warned she would return. We've enjoyed almost eighteen years of peace from her demonic armies. We'd even begun to hope she would never return. But this—I must tell my brother."

I leaped from my seat and grabbed for his arm, but my grasp slipped down to his fingers instead. I clung to them, sliding to a halt. "If you do, he'll suspect me of treachery."

I wasn't strong enough to stop him, and yet he paused to look at our connected hands. His gaze swept the length of me.

"I'll do all I can to prevent that." He pulled from my grasp. "Now get dressed."

"What? But it's—"

"Nearly sunrise. You've attracted this wraith's notice, and that's not a good thing."

"Well, I didn't think it was a *good* thing." I folded my arms tight across my chest.

One brow raised high. "It's worse than you think. Your training starts now."

めⓈℭ

An hour later, I paced the ground nervously and eyed the distance that separated me from the castle. The prince had taken me beyond the wall to a hill that overlooked its grandeur. The morning was warm. Green grass blanketed the ground up until the forest line. The river I had briefly seen on the night of my first escape snaked through the verdant fields, tranquil and unaware of the turmoil rushing inside my soul. This wasn't the farthest I had been since coming to Meyrion, but the distance and the desire to bolt sent my mind reeling.

Reese lounged against a tree with a book, his back to us. I had no idea the guard enjoyed reading, but now I liked him even more.

Castiel stood with his arms crossed and watched as I paced. I ignored the way yet another new dress settled against my skin. I was used to layers of thick cotton, leather, and weapons. Not thin silks and linens designed to accommodate the warm climate. Sameen had commissioned not only one new dress, but several that now lined a cedar boudoir added to the furniture of my room. It was wasteful and far too… nice. She had chosen a light blue fabric for the day, with long sleeves and scooped neck. It fitted snugly down my waist, with a decorative white belt slung low on my hips.

"Shall we begin?"

I ignored his question, giving him one of my own. "He said I was cursed. The wraith did. What do you think he meant?"

He exhaled a long breath. "He's a wraith. It sounds as if he speaks of your uncle, but you already know that." He tried to smile, but it didn't reach his eyes.

I waved away the words. "What did the king say about the incident?" I asked, trying to avoid the training as long as possible.

"He's not happy, but he's processing the information."

I huffed. "Figuring out if I'm to live or to die?"

"No one's going to die unless it's that wraith."

"Then shouldn't we be interrogating Lucan? Maybe he knows where we can find him."

Castiel lifted a brow as if confused.

I connected my fingers in an attempt to better explain. "You know. If Cyris can read Lucan, maybe Lucan can read *him*…"

"I guess it's possible, but I checked this morning. Whatever the wraith did to him, Lucan is still out cold. We don't know what happened to him when the wraith connected to him. Gedeon can't sense anything wrong but doesn't know if he'll ever wake up." He scanned my face, concern etched in his eyes. "We will figure it out, Ilianna, but you are under no circumstances to look for the wraith."

I mentally cursed and kicked at a rock on the ground.

He continued. "There's nothing we can do about it now. Let's move on. When was your magical awakening?"

"Is that what you call it?" I rolled my eyes, walking a slow circle around the nearest tree. "I was fourteen."

"What happened when it did?"

I shook my head.

He blinked. "In the dungeons, the wraith said your uncle tested you. Was this to get to your magic?"

I swallowed. "Yes, but it didn't work."

"Then your magic must have not trusted him and hid from him."

"You speak as if it's a living thing."

"That's because it is. What happened to cause it to finally respond?"

Despite my growing anger, I smiled at the memory. "I was starving. My uncle had sent me to my quarters to be punished without food for a week. Again. But one week became two, then three. The guards didn't care that my body shrank before their very eyes. That I begged. That I cried. I was *fourteen*."

And then I realized what was intended to happen. My uncle was going to let me die.

I turned to Castiel with a look that dared him to show pity, but he only stared back with a face void of all emotion.

After a few seconds I shrugged. "It wasn't anything spectacular. I just… knew. Knew I could change one of the guards' mind. Knew I could convince him to bring me food. Knew I could talk him into letting me go."

I closed my eyes.

"And then I killed him so the king would never know. I waited to be punished for my crime, but my uncle was only impressed by my escape and sent me back to training that day."

Magic had saved my life, and my uncle wanted *it* more than he wanted me, so I did my best to tuck it away. But I didn't know how to bring it back out. And I told Castiel as much.

His voice was a steely calm. "I will help you."

He sounded angry, but of course he would be. I had just confessed to murder. My heart sank. "Look, I didn't know what else to do."

Confusion darkened his eyes until something seemed to click within him. "Oh, Ilianna. I'm not upset with you. How could I be?"

I swallowed against a new lump of unwanted emotion that now swelled within my throat. I peered upward to avoid his gaze. Fat white clouds meandered in a lazy sky. Birds chirped from their branches. Yellow eyes watched me from a perch too high in the trees.

An unladylike yelp escaped my lips.

"What is it?" Castiel was at my side in an instant, daggers drawn.

"One of the falcry is up there," I said, pointing to its hiding place. Her black plumage was stark against the green backdrop. "Ketrina."

He pulled my hand down and just as quickly I yanked it from his grasp. I instantly regretted the reaction. "They don't like to be pointed at," he said in a low voice, sheathing his weapons.

I scanned the boughs for Gomez or Verity, but they were nowhere to be seen. "There seems to be a lot they don't like," I said beneath my breath, and he smiled.

"Indeed, but there are many things that they *do* like. For instance, gossip."

He smiled and reached out a hand. An offering. Slowly, I took it, and he guided me away one cautious step at a time. "If Kitty has chosen to watch us, then that is what she'll do."

"Kitty?"

Castiel only smiled.

I huffed. "I thought Melia liked to have her around as a sort of intimidation tactic."

He chuckled beneath his breath. "Sounds like something she would do, but no. The falcry have their own minds."

"And you don't control them?"

His hand warmed my cold fingers but did little to help my raised pulse. "No. They're too intelligent to be controlled."

"But I read that you can, once they bind themselves to you."

Castiel's head ticked to the side. "Ketrina's not *my* falcry. None of them are."

"But I thought—"

"The falcry are strange creatures," the prince interrupted. "Gomez had a master, but he died in the demonic wars. Verity is Kitty's mother, and neither one has chosen a magician."

"Why?" I asked. Not much was known about the process, but despite popular opinion, it was the *bird* that selected the magician.

He shrugged. "They don't deem it necessary. Falcry are creatures of both light and dark. They can be valiant soldiers and loyal companions, but they can also be lazy and prone to chaos. As of right now, nothing has piqued their interests. That is, until you came along."

He released my hand, taking a seat in the soft green grass.

I remained standing, but my skin tingled from his touch. I changed the subject. "Is intelligence, or lack of intelligence, what controls people?"

Castiel narrowed in on the right focus for my question. "Not necessarily. Sameen and Reese are far from unintelligent."

"Then what is it?"

"I don't really know, but everyone is different. What works for me may not work for you. I understand that you have a reason not to trust people, and I can understand why—"

"Can you?" I asked, my voice raising high. "Can you really understand what I've been through? Do you know what it's like to fear your own blood?'

"No."

My mouth clamped shut. I had said too much. It was too much, all of it. I was a magician. I knew it and had known for several years now, but to say it aloud, to come close to using it of my own free will... it didn't seem right.

"You're right, Princess. I don't understand, but I hope with time you'll come to know that I'm not your uncle."

I shook my head, needing to change the subject and fast. "Of course you're not. Why is it so bad to be a rogue magician?"

"Rogue magicians pull too much energy to them without realizing. You could kill someone that way." He leaned back against his hands." I have a feeling that your magic was late because it was protecting itself, but the power will grow with or without your permission. If you continue to suppress it as you do, the next time you need it, out of desperation or survival, you could harm yourself, or worse, those around you."

"And where exactly do we pull this energy?"

"From everything. Everything has an energy, whether alive or not. We take from that source and shift it to our special gifts."

I splayed my arms, searching for some kind of magical glow I knew was not there. "And of course, we can't see this… energy."

"Some can, but obviously not you. You would've tapped into it a long time ago if you could."

"Of course. So I have to pull energy from somewhere I can't see. Sounds great."

One side of his mouth twisted into a grin. "Luckily, I have the very thing that can help." From his pocket he produced a small vial filled with red liquid.

I instinctively leaned away. "What is that?"

"As I said, something that can help."

I clamped my mouth and glared.

"I thought you said you trusted me."

12
Magical Training

His tone mocked me.

I sighed against the nervousness building within the pit of my stomach and held out my hand. "Fine."

"It's unpleasant, but you'll need to drink it all," he said, placing the vial into my palm. He made sure his fingers didn't touch mine. "And you may feel... strange. Disoriented."

My brows lifted.

"Possibly a little nauseous."

"Is it alcohol?" I asked.

"It's most definitely *not* alcohol, and it will wear off within an hour, give or take. It's a potion made for just this kind of training."

I uncorked the vial and downed the substance in a single gulp.

"That should be enough," he said, reclaiming the bottle.

It was thick, the taste bittersweet with a hint of rosemary. Heat bloomed as it fizzled down the pathway to my stomach. I swallowed hard against the growing nausea.

He continued. "Training can be exhausting. As a new magician, you'll be using *muscles*, if you will, that you've barely ever used. And the potion will make it worse."

I scowled. "Then why am I taking it?"

"Trust me, it's useful."

"Who made it?" I asked, fighting the desire to retch.

"Melia's mother."

"Does Melia's mother have a name?" I shuddered when the potion oozed to the pit of my stomach like a mudslide. "You and the king have mentioned her several times, almost as a threat. Exactly who is she?"

"It's not really who, but *what* she is that matters. She's a seer."

I gasped on instinct, the shock worsening my queasy reaction. Castiel nodded. I braced my hands on my knees. "I'm going to die for sure."

His laugh echoed softly inside my brain. He leaned forward, eye-level. "You're not going to die. Seers are not evil. And it's silly, I know, but we still have a hard time saying her name out loud for fear that she'll hear and come for us in the night."

My face reddened at his closeness. I stood, the blood rushing from my head. "That's the lore of wraiths and demons, not seers."

But I had nearly forgotten that folklore long before. I almost cursed my folly out loud. I had said Cyris's name many times since meeting him. Hopefully it wasn't true.

"Oh, we don't say *their* names aloud either," Castiel said. "Although, I was hoping you saying his name would invite him close enough for me to kill him."

I pished. "Don't tell me the prince of Anolyn believes such silly superstitions."

Because obviously I did, but I needed him to be stronger than I was. Even more terrifying than demons and wraiths, seers were nothing to trifle with. Although they were thought to have been wiped out years ago, rumors of them still spread. They worked within the magical realm, but their powers weren't considered magic. They were supernatural. Some had wisdom gifted from the gods, others had spiritual healing powers to restore the downtrodden. Others even declared to be an actual deity, cast from heaven as punishment for an unknown deed, and only able to return until they served humanity with their life.

Unfortunately, it wasn't that kind of seer one generally heard of. The most terrifying were the ones that claimed the ability to know your future from either dream translation or what they called divine knowledge. These predictions, more often than not, led to tragic accidents or terrible deaths.

No one sought a seer.

Castiel smiled. "It may be superstitious, but there are some magicians that can sense when they're being thought of. They can even locate where an individual is by concentrating on them. I've never asked, but perhaps that's the power that seers rely on. Melia's mother is very powerful, but luckily, she's also a very good woman."

I flinched. "But wait. I thought—"

"That seership is passed on from mother to daughter? Yes. Melia would have taken upon her the title of seer if she hadn't denounced the calling."

"Can she do that?"

Castiel only shrugged.

I braced against a nearby tree and said a silent prayer of thanks as the last of the nausea disappeared. "So what *is* her name?"

He cast a glance over his shoulder to the resting guard several yards away, then came closer to whisper in my ear. "Melora."

"Melora? Melia and Melora Seraphine?"

He flinched, then hushed me with a finger pressed to his mouth. "You better hope she didn't hear you." He backed away, a smile tugging at his lips. "Do you feel better?"

I nodded.

"Good. Now what you should have been taught a long time ago is that we are all connected through this energy I spoke of." He picked a rock from the ground. The sun reflected white from is smooth, gray surface. The prince tossed it high into the air, easily catching it when it fell. His smile radiated across his face and filled me with pleasure.

I inhaled, taking a step back. "Why are you glowing?" The air around him shimmered silver in a gentle breeze, and like him, it was *beautiful.*

He laughed, and the sound traveled across my chest. "It's my aura. The potion you took allows you to see the energy we as magicians' harness. When our mortal senses are weakened due to exhaustion, fasting, sickness, drug, or drink, it exposes us to our *other* senses. The potion is better than those methods, but not as strong as it could be by doing it the right way."

"Which is?"

"Proper meditation and practice."

I groaned, but he ignored it.

"Detached from the real world, you open your senses to the energy around you. Your magic doesn't need sleep or even water to fortify it. In fact, the more you pay attention to it—the more you call upon it—the stronger it will become and the faster it will respond." He reached toward me, holding the glowing rock close to my face. "This is not alive, and yet it has a force that you can now see."

I hesitated before I reached out, my fingers playing in the field surrounding it. The air around the rock felt almost denser.

"When I drop it, it creates a reaction." It fell to the ground with a thump. A visible shockwave rippled across the grass and traveled down the hill. Castiel continued. "We can pull energy from the thing itself, use the energy something holds and releases when acting or being acted upon, and we can access energy created by powerful emotions. Magicians tap into all of that, but in ways that are conducive to the individual."

"How do you use it?"

"Sit down, I'll show you."

I finally did as he asked. In my periphery, Ketrina had abandoned her perch for one much closer.

"Good. As I said, it's different for everyone, but the best way to learn it is to do it." Castiel pointed to the rock again. "Now, watch."

He stared at it, and a second later, it hovered in the air then landed softly upon the grass.

"Now you try."

I took a deep breath, feeling more than a little foolish. I glared at the rock and willed it to raise, but nothing happened. I rolled my eyes and looked away. "I can't do it."

"Don't give up hope so quickly. Let's try something you've already done. What about the Demon Daughter's flames?"

"You mean my 'simple parlor trick'?"

He grimaced. "I'm sure it was more than that, but my brother doesn't need to know everything."

Frustration worked at my nerves. "Only one other man dared to call me the Demon Daughter to my face, and I killed him." I looked to Castiel, but he merely watched me, patiently waiting for me to continue. I took a deep breath and explained. "We got word of a border skirmish that grew violent a few years back. I was sent to regulate. It was meant to be a quick and nonviolent resolution, but a unit of mercenaries from both Eira and Anolyn had taken over the small town."

"I remember that. Two years ago?"

I nodded. "By the time I arrived with a group of soldiers, most of the citizens hung from trees as a threat to those that still survived and now lived as servants. The moment we were seen, they attacked. One man recognized me. He called me that ridiculous name."

"Well, the rumors had to start somewhere. Perhaps I should find the man who drew that sketch of the Demon Daughter. How did you do it?"

"She comes on her own," I said.

"She?"

I nervously wrung my fingers. "It's me. It's rage. It's the magic, I guess."

"Are you saying it activates itself?"

"It only ever happens when I'm in battle and I'm *really* angry."

"And that's it?" Confusion furrowed his brow. "Shouldn't you know more about a power that basically takes over your body?"

I only shrugged.

He sighed. "Very well. What did you do to get Sameen and Reese to help you escape?"

I growled. "Again, I don't know. That magic only ever worked when I really needed something."

"Try it with me." His lips lifted in the corners. His blue eyes captured me.

"What?"

"Try to get me to do something. Here, place your hands in mine."

I tsked. "I don't want to. This is stupid."

I made to stand up, but his hands fastened down on my knees. "Just do it."

His warm energy blended with mine, shooting tendrils of heat through my body. My eyes grew wide. "Get your hands off my legs."

"Make me."

I glared.

His hands flew back. His mouth opened wide, but nothing came out. He clamped it shut. One brow raised.

I mirrored his response, daring him to try again. After a minute of silence, he swallowed hard and cleared his throat. His voice was hoarse when he finally spoke. "Well, that was something, but I didn't sense your magic."

"What do you mean?"

"Like in the forest when you transformed into the Demon—"

"Don't call me that," I snapped.

"When you erupted, then?"

I only nodded, allowing the description.

"I didn't see your mark. I saw you and the flames your power conjured, but not your mark. Maybe it isn't magic."

"Or maybe this blueish hue you think was me really wasn't." I brought my knees to my chest and wrapped them close.

He looked down at his hands to examine them. "Silvery blue—like your eyes. Again, you forget, I watched you for three months. Although infrequent, your magical charm worked on many the guard there."

"My unsettling eyes and my freakish charms," I muttered.

Confusion twisted his features.

"You called my eyes unsettling," I clarified.

A smile tipped the corners of his mouth. "I find them unique. Even beautiful."

I blushed, plucking several blades of grass from their roots. I gasped when their radiance dimmed. "Great. I killed them," I said, throwing them away with a guilty conscience.

Castiel laughed. "You react more to killing that grass then the mer—" He covered his mouth when I pinned him with a glare. A moment later he cleared his throat. "So, you have to be in danger or really annoyed. I can work with that. Touch may also help you."

I flinched. It was true that touch had been effective with Sameen and a few others before her, but not everyone. I told him as much.

"I'm not saying it's a must with your magic, but it probably makes it easier for you to influence your powers. A trigger." He clapped and rubbed his hands together as if to warm them, then reached out to me. "Push me away with your magic."

Hesitantly, I pressed my palms into his. Again, our energies blended. The light from his aura pulsed brighter and I yanked away. It faded. Meanwhile, Castiel didn't flinch, only patiently waited for me to reconnect. I swallowed and clapped my hands against his. My heart soared like a falcry from the warmth of his skin on mine. Power surged. It tingled all senses within.

"Now, push me away," Castiel said.

But did I want to?

The thought whispered in the back of my mind. I shook my head. "I can't." It was a lie. I suddenly knew all I had to do was command, and the magic would obey.

"Come on, Ilianna."

From over his shoulder, movement caught my attention. I pulled from him to stand. "Someone draws near to Meyrion."

Castiel turned. "Riaan is taking an audience today…"

His voice trailed when he saw what drew my attention. The oncoming person dragged something barely recognizable as human on a makeshift gurney behind him.

"Lieutenant!" But Reese had already sprung from his watch, hurrying towards his prince. "Run ahead and warn the king, then fetch the healer."

The guard sprinted from the hilltop at an impressive speed. Castiel lurched two steps forward then stopped short. From over his shoulder he glanced to me. For a split-second a wary expression warred in his eyes. I answered his unspoken question by racing past him after the guard, but he easily caught up. It was hard for him to match my slower pace, but he would not run ahead as I coaxed. The potion—woken by my jostling—roiled like a hostile force in my stomach.

It was only a mile that separated us from the borders of the courtyard, but the distance seemed multiplied by the situation, and by the glow that blurred my vision. With only halfway to go, and without warning, the potion reviled against such ill-treatment and leaped up my esophagus. I skidded to a halt, pitched sideways to my hands and knees, and heaved.

Castiel was at my side in an instant, his voice muffled. "I worried this would happen."

"Go." I waved him on.

"But—"

My voice was strained. "I won't run away. I promise."

"That's not why I worry." His deep concern shocked me, but I would not look at him.

"It doesn't matter. You are needed. Go."

I heaved deep breaths of air, feeling the paleness of my own face. Castiel remained torn, but after a few seconds more, he left me to my own.

Was I upset that he actually listened? I turned from his fading form to collect my wits. I could only imagine what the prince worried about. Did he think I would try to run?

The potion's effect was less, but still everything emitted a soft glow. I resumed my trek to Meyrion, more aware of my surroundings than ever. A shrill cry filled the air. Ketrina circled restlessly about the canopy of trees, but she couldn't risk being seen by more than a dozen spectators. Her golden energy created a halo around her, encasing her.

Fatigue pulled at my body, the effects of Melora's concoction. By the time I made it to the castle gardens, guards, attendants, and courtiers created a wide circle around the gurney and its owner. Fallen to his knees, the shabby man's tears streaked through his dirt-caked face. He forced back everyone who pressed forward to help.

The smell slowed my approach. I paced just outside the circle of gawkers. Most avoided looking at me, but others stared outright, their curiosity bright in their eyes. I could almost hear their thoughts.

Castiel stood next to the man, his hand on one dirtied shoulder. Melia and Mikael approached the nervous din of gawkers. "Step back, all of you. Let the king through."

The crowd shifted, running out of the path of their leader, giving me a direct line-of-sight to Weylan. *Where had he come from?* Hadn't Castiel said he'd be gone by morning? A single guard stood behind him, arms crossed and appearing more interested in the action than with the conspiratorial Eirian.

My insides swam against the tide of the potion. Of course this would pique Weylan's interests. He always did like a good show. Thankfully, he kept his distance. I stepped behind several taller courtiers so as not to be seen.

Riaan was quick to take in the scene. His sharp eyes flashed to mine for a brief moment before observing the main attraction.

Behind him, his mistress watched, her narrowed gaze dashing madly between the hovel of a man and the surrounding crowd, her stance rigid. At first, I thought her thrilled by the excitement until something else caught my attention. Her hand slipped into a secreted pocket in her otherwise fashionable gown—the same kind of pocket that would hide a weapon. The same kind of pocket Pala had sown into every one of my dresses.

The muscles of her neck tensed as she paced to the other side of her king. Perhaps the mistress was more than she seemed.

"What's your name?" the king asked, regaining my attention.

The man shook his head. At first, I thought he would refuse to answer, then, "Oscove. I bring to you the fallen body of my brother, Nolen."

The king placed a kind hand to his shoulder. "Who has done this, Oscove?"

"The Demon Daughter."

Shock and then anger coursed through me. How could anyone think I was capable of such a disgusting thing? Even in my altered state, I would never massacre anyone.

It took effort for Castiel not to look at me, not to gauge my reaction. "Are you sure?"

Oscove nodded. "She's here. She haunts our woods, my prince."

"You've seen her, then?" Riaan asked. *His* eyes did find mine, accusation clearly written within them.

"No, but it's rumored she is here. She arrived on a foul wind and sank her claws into our land. A plague among the living. She'll kill us all."

Castiel called to his guard. "Melia, Mikael, gather your men."

Mikael nodded then sprinted from the scene with Melia flanking him.

"Where is my healer?" Riaan called out.

"He is coming, Your Majesty. He is hurrying," Reese called as he ran from the building, but from the stench and the amount of blood that soiled the gurney, I doubted anything could be done.

"Lady Anna," Castiel said. "Come, please."

All eyes shot to me, including Weylan's.

The king cleared his throat. "If you have no business here, leave." And even though his voice was no more than a whisper, the crowd dispersed.

I jolted to obey, but Castiel's voice stopped me. "Lady Anna."

Weylan, who had retreated to the main castle doors to lean upon the threshold and observe, smirked at my displeasure. His guard stayed several paces away, still overly attentive to the spectacle.

I lifted my head and went to Castiel's side. Oscove's eyes grew large as I drew near.

"What do you see?" the prince asked.

There was no aura that pulsed from him like those that surrounded him. No energy. No light. I turned to Castiel to avoid the gruesome sight. "I'm not a heal—"

"What do you see?"

"Answer him, my lady," Riaan snapped.

I stepped forward to examine the corpse. There was so much blood, but even through the carnage, something caught my attention. "There are no defensive marks on his body," I said, my voice echoing on my ears. "I don't believe he fought back."

Oscove shook his head. "No. Killed in his sleep. He was a good man. A simple farmer. He didn't deserve this."

Nausea threatened my composure. The dead man's arms were broken and lying at this side. One palm rested upward at an odd angle, snapped at the wrist. The way he was attacked was very similar to the fashion Cy had killed Lucan's men.

Something even more peculiar drew my attention. "These are not the hands of a farmer."

Oscove froze. "What did you say?"

"There are old marks on this hand. Slices from swords or knives." I carefully twisted his other wrist to see the inside of his second palm. Matching scores marred his skin.

The brother hissed. "How dare you."

13

THE FARMER

I TURNED TO CASTIEL, ANXIETY in my words. "I do not mean offense. I'm only trying to help."

Oscove's bloodshot eyes narrowed. "Are you accusing—"

"No," I said cutting him off. "But he could have had enemies."

Castiel nodded. "Oscove?"

He scowled at me but answered his prince. "No, he wasn't always a farmer. He was a soldier of your great army, but when his wife died he chose to watch over his little ones. That was five years ago now."

"What was his full name?"

"Nolen Odessa"

The prince flinched. "Odessa?"

"And he had no enemies other than the Demon Daughter. Why am I being questioned by this woman? Who is she?"

"I'm coming!" The healer's voice interrupted. Gedeon's legs struggled with the speed at which he drove them. "Out of the way," he said, pushing past Weylan.

Castiel leaned to whisper in my ear. "Meet the artist of your second depiction."

"What?"

Castiel gestured to the dead man with a tip of his head. His breath was warm on my ears. "Sergeant Nolen Odessa was the one who provided us with the first image of the Demon Daughter in battle."

I flushed. Was he accusing me? Surely, he must know I didn't kill the man. It was suspicious for sure, a revenge enacted against someone who had seen the legend's face and got the ending he should have had in the first place. It was a logical conclusion, except for the simple fact that I was *the legend* and hadn't killed anyone... lately.

"Where are the children now?" Castiel asked.

Oscove jerked back. "What?"

"The children. Where are they."

His mouth opened and closed like a fish. The blood drained from his face. "I—I don't know."

Castiel placed a hand on his shoulder. "We'll send a detail to search for them."

"I am here, Your Majesty." Gedeon almost glared at the young king, more agitated than I had ever seen him, but when he stopped in front of the gurney whatever frustration had been there melted from his wrinkled face. "Heavens alive." He lowered to examine the body, but only managed a stoop. "Poor soul. Who did this to him?"

Oscove and Castiel answered at the same time.

"The Demon Daughter."

"We're looking into it." The prince nodded to Gedeon. "Will you see to the care of his brother?"

"Of course. Of course. Come with me," the healer said slowly, turning to Oscove.

"And what of Nolen?" the king asked, halting his departure.

Gedeon bowed as best he could. "He is dead, Your Majesty. There's nothing I can do."

"But surely your magic can tell us more of how he got hurt."

I flinched. My voice rang in my ears. "*How* he got hurt?" I started then scowled at Castiel. "Why would a Healer know *how* he got hurt?"

Castiel cleared his throat, avoiding my glare.

Gedeon's eyes flitted to me and then away. "As I've told you before, Your Majesty, my gifts only work on those who are alive. I cannot help you." Again, he looked to me, an apology written in his softened face, confirming my suspicions. Then he blinked. Shock, quickly followed by anger, darkened his features. "What's that monster doing here?" The blood drained from my face until I realized it was not me the healer glared at, but someone over my shoulder. I followed his line of sight.

Weylan's brows ticked high on his forehead and he retreated several steps back. His guard also seemed confused. Gedeon grabbed the front of the prince's shirt to whisper several sharp, but lowered words. Riaan quickly leaned in to hear.

Castiel's reaction was even more odd. His spine stiffened. Although his mouth worked, nothing came out.

"Arrest the traitor from Eira," the king said for him. He pinned me with a glare. "Obviously, *we* have more to discuss."

My heart seized, and I fell back a step as several things happened at once.

Reese charged.

Weylan spun on his heel and bolted before his absent-minded guard could even register the command.

Castiel's hand shot out, the aura of his power caused me to blink against the blinding brightness. Through the blaze I saw Weylan fall forward, but the prince was too far away. His quarry escaped from his magical grasp and disappeared into the castle, followed by Anolynian soldiers.

The prince swore beneath his breath and called to the nearest guard. "Escort Lady Anna to her quarters. No one is to enter or leave her room except for me." Without another glance, he pulled his knife and ran toward the castle.

Hands seized me roughly by the arms. Before I could even think, my magic reacted to the mistreatment, and the guard flew several feet away. He drew his knife, but Gedeon tsked, slapping at the man's hand.

"The prince said to escort her, not drag her."

The king raised a brow at me. "I'm glad to see your training has already progressed so far, Lady Anna." Then he smiled and left with his protection surrounding him. His mistress had disappeared in the commotion.

The guard gestured for me to follow, but I had no intention of doing so. Maybe it was foolish, but magic flowed within my veins, bringing with it a new sense of strength I had never felt. Twisted excitement took control over exhaustion. It fueled me, coaxing me forward.

Once inside, I waited until we were alone before I acted. Melora's potion, although not as strong as before, still allowed me to see the guard's aura, a soft shade of lilac. I reached for it with my senses,

We need to search the prison.

The guard flinched, but he did not turn around—did not respond to my magical probe. This time, I stretched, touching his shoulder, and something powerful flowed through me. *Wait.*

And he did. His arm flashed out, as if protecting me. His other hand grabbed the hilt of his sword.

My heart beat erratic and painful. I waited for someone to find us, to capture us, but no one came. Soon I realized that the guard waited for my command. I reached up on my tiptoes to speak low in his ear. "We need to search the prison." Our closeness worked against my nerves. "Please. The traitor could be there." *We need to find him.*

His only response was a nod. He spun around and guided the way.

My heart soared, and my head whirled. I felt giddy. Powerful. Castiel was right. Touch did make my magic stronger. Ironic. He would be mad at me if he found out, but this didn't feel wrong, like when I had tricked Sameen and Reese. Weylan was evil. I had to prove his treachery to the prince and king, and we had to find him before he got to my uncle.

The whole of Anolyn's court detail searched for Weylan, but he was long gone by now. No one paid us any attention as we drew near the prison. The guards that blocked the entrance recognized me, not as the dirty inmate that had only been there two weeks from before, but as a guest to Meyrion: Lady Anna, who daily battled their Captain Melia within their personal training yards.

One held up his hand. "My lady, you should be in your room. The king searches for a convict. It's not safe."

"I know," I said, edified at his description of Weylan. *Convict.* I focused on the new guard's energy. Coming closer. I clasped his arm in urgency. "We believe the man in holding will know more about what's going on. We need to question him."

The guard's eyes grew large as he considered me, but I had already won. "Very well." He stood to the side so we could pass. "But be quick."

"Of course," I said with a serious expression. "Wait here. I will be much more effective alone."

He nodded.

I rushed down the stone steps, assaulted by the smell I never thought I'd forget. I covered my nose with my long sleeve. Low light from the torches hindered my vision, but I didn't need to see to know where to go. After living within this prison for three months, nearly every turn in its mazelike quarters solidified in my memory.

Rounding a corner, I slowed to a stop. Lucan lay on his back on the cold stone floor within the same space he had previously occupied. His hands were bound above his head, secured to the bars of his cell. His bare feet were also tied. A black aura encompassed him.

Had his soul always been like that, so dark?

I cleared my throat, but before I could speak, his eyes flew open.

"I wondered when you'd show your face." His voice was dry and low, scratching at my nerves.

"You expected me?" I asked, feigning confidence. "What would my uncle think of this? Finding you so laid up, unable to do his bidding?" When he didn't speak, I added, "I come alone. I have questions."

He smiled, watching me through steady eyes. "And what can I do for my princess?"

"You can tell me where Weylan will run."

He blinked slowly. "Who?"

I controlled my rising breath. "You know who I speak of. Captain Weylan Laphel, sixth regiment."

"Ah." Lucan chuckled softly. "Young Captain Laphel. He was a promising lad."

"Where can I find him?"

He shrugged. "I haven't a clue."

"You're a liar," I said through a clenched jaw.

"A liar like you?"

Shock colored my response. "I am not—"

"I know what you are, *Princess* Ilianna. I know what you've hidden from your uncle. *You* are a *very* naughty girl."

My mouth opened and closed like a fish.

His gaze searched mine. "What's it like to be trapped as you are? To have nowhere to run? To know there's no escaping him?"

I raised my chin a fraction higher. "I can escape anytime I want."

His laughter shook me to my core. "*Idiot.* He'll find you, and when he does, he'll beat you until you break to his will."

Anger flashed within, but it was nothing to the fear that reigned, the fear that caused me to react in contradiction of better judgment.

Reaching through the bars, I grabbed him by the wrist and wrenched hard, digging my nails into his skin. I tried to tap into that energy Castiel had shown me—tried and failed. There were too many warring emotions to concentrate on the act.

Heat bloomed in my chest, affecting my voice. I glared into his widening eyes. *"Where. Is. Weylan?"*

Lucan twisted, his hands suddenly freed from their bindings. He yanked against my grasp, catapulting me forward. Light flashed when my face plowed into the bars, but fear blocked the pain as gore gushed from my nose.

His hand snaked behind me, securing me in place. He brought his lips to my ear, his voice thick. "Why do you want to know where he is?" Dank breath assaulted.

Where was the Demon Daughter now?

Hiding, like she always did. I was cursed. A weak little girl against the strength of Johan's most valued spy.

"Do you fear he'll run back to his king? Tell him where you are?"

Facial bones grinded against metal. My mouth tasted blood as it ran down my lips to my chin. "Yes," I answered honestly.

"I'm so glad you're awake." Castiel's voice sounded above the echo in my ears.

Lucan's nervous laugh breathed against my cheek. He released his hold on me slowly.

The tip of the prince's blade pressed into the skin at the spy's throat. Castiel's arm slid around my middle, pulling me to him. His warmth soothed my jittered nerves.

Red trickled from the prick of his dagger when he withdrew both it and me from the cell.

I smeared the blood from my face with the back of my sleeve, then pinched the edge of my nose to block the flow.

Lucan watched me, clutching his steel cage. "It's too late, Ilianna." His voice was calm, but a storm brewed in his words. "If your uncle doesn't know now, he will soon."

Melia and Reese and the guards from the prison doors flanked the prince to the left and the right. Melia pinned me with a look I could not read. Shame colored my face and I had to turn away, but Castiel's grip didn't let me get far.

Quicker than I could process, he tossed his knife to his other hand. He caught Lucan by the collar of his tunic then pulled hard. Lucan's face smashed into the bars with a rattled clang. The spy cried out, but a second later, the prince spun me around.

"Secure this spy," he ordered the others. "I want a guard with him at all times. If he escapes again, it's your neck. Melia, Reese, you're with me."

"Yes, sir," all said at once, and they raced to fulfill his command.

Castiel swept me from the narrow prison faster than my brain could keep up with. The world spun, but before I could react to the dizzying effects, the prison doors opened. My lungs filled with a cool, clean breeze, clearing my muddled thoughts. Moisture pricked my eyes, but I blinked back any emotion.

I swallowed hard, my voice still sounded nasally.
"Castiel—"

"No." His words were barely recognizable through the
anger that seethed from him. He gave me a sideways
glance, his eyes hard, then he grunted. Yanking a white
handkerchief from his pocket, he stopped to dab at the
mess of blood at my lips and chin. Steady fingers carefully
tipped my chin to inspect the damage. "Reese, fetch the
healer."

Reese ran ahead.

Again, I tried. "Cas—"

"Not now," he snapped. He closed his eyes as if the
sound of my voice pained him, then quickly stuffed the
handkerchief into my hand. He reclaimed my arm and
resumed his path.

My heart dropped.

I *was* an idiot. Castiel must have thought it too.

What could have been gained from talking to Lucan?
Nothing more than I already knew. He had sent a message
to my uncle of my whereabouts.

I needed to leave. To escape. But I had made a deal.
Was I a woman of my word? I wasn't sure.

Castiel led me back into the castle, his hand tight on
my arm. I could have fought him, but I didn't have the
strength. Not now.

Melia followed, keeping a safe distance until we reached
the receiving hall. Commotion echoed within its normally
calm walls. The captain raced forward to throw the doors
wide into the throne room where King Riaan stood at a
table littered with maps and parchments, along with five

other officers, the same ones I had seen when I first met the king. They bowed to their prince and narrowed their gaze upon me and the mess that was my face.

I glared right back.

"Leave us," Castiel said sharply.

They turned to their king, who signaled his approval, then flowed from the room, shutting the doors behind them. Riaan did not look to us, only studied the maps in front of him.

"A message just arrived," he said, without waiting for his brother to speak. His hand swept across the maps, sending them to the ground. Melia tsked, but stooped to pick them up. "Leave them," he ordered, and she stopped. Then the king blinked, finally seeing me. "What on earth happened to your face? For a falcry's love…"

I shrugged despite my discomfort, and pain laced the movement. "I've had worse." Although it was true, it felt like a lie with both brothers examining me and my every expression.

"How ever did you survive without poor Gedeon to patch you up?"

Castiel cleared his throat, saving me from further embarrassment. "Lucan—"

"The spy is unimportant. As is Captain Weylan."

"How—how can you say that?" I asked, incensed.

He flicked his fingers as if shooing a fly. "Easily."

Castiel flinched, sensing his brother's serious tone. "Who was this message from?"

"From overseas. An ambassador from the kingdom of Ardenya."

"I've never heard of it."

"I don't believe anyone has. You, Princess?"

Slowly, I shook my head. Ardenya had never been revealed in any of my studies. My uncle had never mentioned it either. I glanced between both men, not understanding the direction of the conversation, but Melia guessed it almost immediately.

"The Wraith Queen?" she asked.

"Those are my thoughts." The king gripped the edges of the table. He stared out the grand windows "The Ambassador from Ardenya wishes an audience with the king of Anolyn. The letter does not communicate as to when this ambassador will arrive. It could be next week or a month from now, depending on sea conditions."

I followed his gaze, past the breathtaking view of his gardens and the workers that attended the fields, to the seas beyond. Anxiety screamed within me. I needed to leave. To flee this cursed continent and its problems.

"What is it you see, Princess?"

I snapped out of my thoughts to the sound of the king's voice. He watched me closely, as did Castiel. Both sets of matching eyes observing more than they should.

"I—"

But he didn't wait for my answer. His head tipped to the side, curious. "Do you know why I asked if you knew what was beyond our kingdom? It's because the Wraith Queen has overtaken every last continent that we know of, outside of our own. The countries we once traded with—had any relationship with—we haven't been able to reach with any correspondence in over a decade. Why do you think we harvest so much of our produce here? Because it's no longer safe to send our sailors out. They don't return."

My mouth worked, but I didn't have any response to this new information.

Castiel continued for his brother. "When we do receive communication, it's from another kingdom seeking help from a tyrannical conqueror."

"This message does not convey that." Riaan stabbed a finger at a piece of parchment on the table.

"But if it *is* another kingdom seeking help, can we offer them that assistance?" Melia asked.

"With what? Soldiers? Ships? We barely have enough to defend against Johan."

But we were not at war. "My uncle…" My voice trailed beneath the sharp eyes of the King.

"Just assume everything your darling uncle ever told you was a lie." He returned to his captain's question. "And against the Wraith Queen, our best line of defense is here."

"Agreed," Castiel said.

"If it's the Wraith Queen, this peace with the kingdom of Eira couldn't come sooner. It's imperative we show a united front."

Castiel combed his fingers through thick hair. "Then what's the next step?"

"We message King Johan."

Panic set in, and my voice came out in a gasp. "What?"

Melia stepped forward, standing close to me. "But Riaan, you've seen what he's done to her—"

I held out my hand to stop her. "No, Melia."

Her eyes flashed to mine. "If you won't defend yourself, then I will."

"Except there's nothing that can be done about it," the king said, interrupting. He gave her a look.

Melia's mouth clamped shut and she turned away.

Riaan scanned me. "I'm sorry, Ilianna."

I flinched when actual compassion shone in his eyes. I could handle his abrasive nature, his mistrusting, flippant personality, but this...

He continued. "But for the survival of all, we'll have to come together despite all bad history between our kingdoms. The last time the Wraith Queen battled against us, thousands died upon the swords of her demon army. We are strong, but we will need every trained man and woman available."

I spoke against a suddenly dry throat. "How much time do I have?"

"Before I send word to your uncle?"

I nodded.

He crossed his arms over his chest. "It's already done, and the sooner, the better."

"How?" Castiel asked.

"A missive sent by falcry to our borders. It will then be taken the remaining way by messenger."

My breath whooshed from my lungs. Panic set in and my heart thundered in my chest. The blood drained painfully from my face.

"Why didn't you tell me?" Castiel asked.

Riaan's tipped smile sent a flash of anger through my chest. "You act so surprised. You yourself have kept some important information from me recently. Can you really expect me to share all confidences, considering your new and rather peculiar behavior?"

Guilt did somersaults inside my stomach, adding to the ill effects of the news, and my world began to spin. Sparks grew in my vision. I steadied my breath and forced them back.

Castiel glared at his brother, but Riaan waved him off. "I'm telling you now." The king tipped his head back to the ceiling, rubbing a sore neck. "If there was any other way…"

But there wasn't. My father had died in a valiant effort to stop the Wraith Queen and her assault. If she was yet alive, at least Toma had slowed her for a time. There was no more hiding. No more running, from any of them: Johan, Lucan, Weylan. If this was the ambassador to the Wraith Queen, she would trump them all.

Castiel leaned forward, bringing his face to mine. I instinctively stepped back.

"I will not let him hurt you, Ilianna. He will not hurt you."

"You cannot stop him." His expression pinched. He wanted to argue but I didn't let him. "Besides, our kingdoms come first," I said, despite the pathetic fear that threatened to overcome me. "Our combined forces are the only chance we have of surviving an attack."

"There will be a celebration in two weeks to announce your official arrival to our country. It'll be the first step in securing the peace your uncle so desperately desires." Riaan spoke over his shoulder as he walked away. "In the meantime, let us pray our fears are for nothing." He hesitated at the door. "And will *someone* clean her up, please?"

14

A FALCRY

CASTIEL REJOINED THE SEARCH for Weylan beyond Meyrion's walls. I was dismissed to my room and ordered to stay there until the prince's return. I observed the final attempts by the guards to locate Weylan on the grounds from my window until night impeded my watch. The effects of the potion faded with the sun.

Sameen brought me my meals and kept me company. She helped me ready for sleep, working my hair into a long, intricate braid down my back. She would have stayed with me all night, I was sure, but I sent her to her own bed when her yawning couldn't be contained. I paced the length of my room in my nightgown—a prisoner once again, but this time I didn't mind so much. The stone walls that encased me within also kept Weylan out.

Exhausted, I tucked into a ball in my chair and waited for Castiel, but it wasn't until the outside torches extinguished and the fire in my hearth dimmed that he came.

A soft creak was the only warning that someone had entered. A chill raised the hairs on the back of my neck. He was so close. His presence pressed against me, familiar now, but I didn't turn to acknowledge him. Nervously, I fiddled with the end of my braid.

"Why didn't you tell me?" His voice was barely more than a whisper. It sent a tremor down my spine.

I shrugged, nonchalant. "You should have known I would seek out Lucan. He—"

"This is not about Lucan." Castiel moved around the chairs to stand before me, but still I could not meet his gaze. "You told me Weylan was a spy. A schemer. That he was bad."

"What more did you want me to say?" I asked, my voice monotone.

Castiel crouched in front of me, and I was glad I had not seen his eyes before because they undid me. "You should have told me that he struck you. Repeatedly. That he caused you pain."

Tears nearly blinded me. "Is that what your Healer told you?" I asked, accusingly.

"It's what Gedeon *saw*, Ilianna. His magic allows him to see how an individual received each injury that he heals."

"You should have told me what Gedeon's magic could do. I would never have—"

"Allowed him to heal you?" Castiel interrupted. "To save your life?"

The light from the fire made him glow. His intensity would burn me alive.

Being the coward I was, I glanced away to avoid his eyes. "I wouldn't have died from Lucan's wound."

And why did he appeared to be so upset? Could he really care as much as he seemed? I swallowed against the growing hope and wiped a rogue tear from my cheek. "And what could you have done that would've made any difference?" Nothing ever made a difference. Weylan was too powerful to be stopped.

"What could I—?" His words rose too loud and he made a visible effort to check them. He gripped the arms of my chair and growled. The muscles in his jaw rippled. "When will you realize that what he did—what happened to you—never should have been allowed. He should be punished. Him, and anyone else that touched you. All of them, cast into prison—"

Without realizing what I did, I lurched forward and threw my arms around his shoulders. My face buried into the warmth of his neck. Castiel stiffened beneath my embrace, but seconds later, his tension ebbed. One hand gathered me closer, the other kept us from falling onto the cold stone beneath us.

My mouth pressed into the folds of his shirt at his shoulder, my voice muffled, but comprehensible. "Thank you." And I meant it. Whether his affection—or Melia's, or Reese's, or even Sameen's—was real, I was grateful. It would make leaving this continent a little harder, but not impossible when the time came.

After a few seconds, embarrassment tugged at my senses.

Only yesterday I had commanded him not to touch me. Now, I'd broken my own rule and had flung myself on him. Instead of the anxiety that normally came with such an action, warmth bloomed in my cheeks and flooded my body.

Regaining my composure, I took a deep breath, then pulled away to stand. I smoothed my nightdress with shaking hands. "And since there's no reason to hide it any longer, I promise to let you know in the future."

The low flames from my fire silhouetted him, preventing me from seeing his reaction. "Don't run away." It was spoken in a whisper, but his words shook me to my core.

I swallowed hard to keep the emotions restrained. "And where would I run?" Where *could* I run? I moved to the door and gestured to it with a forced half-smile. "Good night, Prince."

He stood to leave but paused to peer over his shoulder, his eyes meeting mine. His gaze pinned me in place. "Please, do not leave your room until I come get you in the morning."

"I—"

"If you refuse to obey me then I'll sleep outside your chambers."

My mouth snapped closed. Another wave of chills erupted along my spine. I could only nod my acceptance.

"I'll return early in the morning, but until then, I'll send an additional guard to watch over you tonight."

"Reese is out there now. How many more do I need?"

But he didn't answer, only shut the door behind him, leaving me alone to my growing confusion.

Why did he care?

Weylan had pretended to care, and the memory caused my breath to freeze inside my lungs. A numbness trickled into my heart, draining it of any warmth.

Castiel was nothing like Weylan.

Rejecting the possibility, I shook my head and ran a hand down my face. Exhaustion was setting in. I cast myself into bed, saying a silent prayer to the gods that I would be able to sleep despite the tensions of the past several days. It was no use. The room was too hot. The blankets too soft. My nightgown too thick. I slid from my mattress and moved to the window. Three stories up, it was a sheer drop that would break every bone in my body if I fell. No one would be able to scale it.

I was safe.

Unless Cy decided to return.

I growled and unlocked the casing. I threw the window wide. The evening breeze wafted my hair and sent tendrils of cool air through the dense space of my apartment. The smell of a late evening rain soothed my nerves. I took a deep breath, savoring it. Curled into a ball at the foot of my bed to be closer to the cool, I shut my eyes. Still, sleep evaded me.

A rustling noise caused me to fly from my bed with a jolt. A pair of yellow eyes watched me from the window sill and I froze. A heavy breeze rustled through Ketrina's midnight feathers. My heart thundered in my chest, so loud I was sure the mystical bird could hear it.

She leaped from the ledge to my chair in front of the fireplace, ruffling her plumage.

A falcry was in my room. I was going to die.

But all she did was watch me. Moments later, she lowered into the chair, basking in the warmth of the dimming fire.

Frustration made me brave. Almost.

I swallowed against a dry mouth. "Are you here to kill me?"

She tipped her head to one side and then another. Her eyes narrowed.

"Well," I asked, "what do you want?" But she only continued to watch me. I slowly reclaimed my seat on my bed and folded my hands in my lap.

I had a feeling that if the falcry wanted to claim my bedroom as her own, she would do so with little resistance from anyone.

Taking a deep breath, I squared my shoulders. I moved to the window. "Now, that's enough. Shoo."

Ketrina's head twitched. Was that a look of confusion?

"You heard me. Shoo."

She snapped her beak at my hand. Even though she was several paces away, I yanked back to ensure all fingers were firmly in place. I clutched them to my chest, my words sounding braver than I actually was.

"Fine. You want to sit in my chair, it's yours. But only for tonight."

I sat back down on my bed, folding my legs beneath me. "I don't know what gossip you expect me to share. I'm really a dull person, so..." I huffed, rolling my eyes at my own idiocy.

Did I really think she was going to answer?

But the falcry were mystical birds. Tales about them had seemed so farfetched to me at the time, but now that I had an actual, physical manifestation of one resting in the very chair I had just vacated, I could believe them all. Ketrina's yellow eyes watched me as if I were the one on display, but I refused to squirm beneath her gaze. I stared even harder.

After a while her eyes drooped, mirroring mine. A melody danced at the edges of my subconscious, its notes a soothing balm. My eyes rolled back into my head and I jerked awake, and yet Ketrina continued to mesmerize.

I didn't remember falling asleep

ഇരുന്ന

Ketrina was gone the next day. In fact, I wondered if her presence had been real at all, or whether it was just a dream. Had the prince been a dream as well? But when I rose from bed, a large black feather decorated the floor, the only proof that the night had indeed happened.

For a week straight, I had dreams of bloodied farmers, evil blacksmiths, and the falcry. Of the Wraith Queen.

Training was put on hold. The prince claimed he couldn't get away from his duties, but I knew what he was doing. I watched him leave every morning to continue his search for Weylan. Part of me was annoyed with him. My training had once been so important, but now so easily overlooked. But the more feeling, emotional side of me, appreciated that he seemed to care.

Melia no longer collected me for sparring. I was less than pleased with her new gentle method of friendship and decided to force her hand. I had almost gotten ready in my sparring gear when Sameen arrived with breakfast and clothes—although not the clothes I had grown accustomed to.

I held up a pair of brown pants and a cream-colored shirt. "What is this?"

Her answer only confused instead of enlightened. "Or you can wear this one." She displayed a mud-colored day dress with long sleeve and attached hood.

"How about neither? I'm going to spar with Melia today."

"Not going to happen. She's taking over the prince's duties today and *he* has requested you join him."

I grimaced, flicking the drab material. "And I've been reduced to peasant status?"

She rolled her eyes. "There are no peasants in Anolyn, Princess."

My brows pinched together. "Truly?" But even as I asked, I had never seen a beggar to soil the front steps of Meyrion or plead the king for amends. "How do the boys manage that?"

"The boys? You mean the king and prince?" she asked.

I gave her a cheeky smile.

She responded with an indulgent sigh, ignoring my impertinence. "I'm sure poverty still exists. You can't control everything, but as Gedeon told you, each citizen is required to work."

"And what about Weylan's escape? He's out there. I shouldn't be working. I should be looking for him."

"The prince is seeing to his capture, and you know he wouldn't take you anywhere if he wasn't sure of your safety. Today is the first day of harvest. He would like you to join him."

Again, I stared at her, not fully comprehending her meaning until she held up both the shirt and the dress for me to choose between. It was her turn to smile, and the smugness of it caused any remaining hopes to crumble.

"What am I supposed to do?" I asked.

"I'm guessing the prince will find something." She tipped her head to the side, a curious expression pinching her features. "Castiel is more content than I've seen him in a long time."

My heart squeezed oddly. "What's that supposed to mean?"

"Maybe you have something to do with it."

I flinched, mentally shaking my head. "I truly doubt that."

She shrugged then dangled the clothes in front of me, impatient for me to make my selection.

"Does it matter what I wear? You choose."

Speechless, I climbed into the clothes—the pants and shirt ensemble. It was a drab thing with long sleeves and a neckline that scooped. It had only one thin layer of protection above my undergarments. I tugged on my boots while she carefully picked apart my braids then piled the wavy mess high into a loose bun.

Would I be forced to muck out animal stalls or sow the field? How did one even sow a field?

"This feels strange," I said, tugging at the shirt.

"From what I hear, you wear men's armor into battle. Why is this so strange to that? Besides, you'll be grateful when the afternoon gets warm." Then she laughed at my somber expression. "Cheer up, *Ilianna*. It's not such a terrible thing."

But still anxiety draped upon me like a sickness. When Castiel came to release me from my cell, as it were, he almost laughed at my expression.

"You look miserable."

I opened my arms to display the obvious reason, then noticed what he wore.

In a matching ensemble of brown slacks and cream top, we were ridiculous, a pair of royal yokels. Although *he* made the outfit look almost good.

A smile lifted the corners of his mouth. "Are you ready for some fun?"

"You're teasing, right?"

"Not at all. Today, I travel to Rhyolyn, a little town not too far from here."

I laced my fingers in front of me in an effort to remain calm. "Weylan? Lucan? The Wraith Queen?"

He ticked off his fingers. "My brother leans to the extreme; this messenger might have nothing to do with the Wraith Queen. Lucan is unwilling to discuss anything further, I have scouts searching for Weylan, and you'll be with me."

Anxiety gnawed at my nerves. "I'd rather stay here." But why? It would be better to go with the prince instead of waiting like a sitting duck where Weylan knew I'd be. Grumbling, I followed him.

Outside stood two magnificent horses: one a blue roan with tall, white stockings, the other a buckskin beast with golden tones. He tossed his black mane and stomped his dark legs, impatient for his rider.

Castiel called to him. "Calm, boy." His hands rubbed down the horse's sides. "This is Dhema." He glanced over his shoulder. "Do you ride?"

"Of course I do." But it had been a very long time and I wasn't that great at it. In fact, when I was younger, I was deathly afraid of horses until my uncle discovered the fear and punished me with extra lessons. Now I could appear as confident on one of them as anyone else. My insides were a whole other problem. "Which one's for me?"

He indicated the blue roan with the nod. I steadied my nerves and went to the waiting attendant. I allowed him to give me a hand up, wondering if he felt the tremor in my bones. If he did, he didn't say. I swung my leg over, thankful when it cleared the saddle. My hands shook, my white-knuckled grasp tense around the reins.

Castiel was already in his seat, his horse steady beneath his sure grip. He studied me. Did he see the coward, the fake that I was?

"Her name is Amaya. She's very calm."

"I'm sure she's wonderful," I said without feeling. I quickly smoothed my hand down her neck, mumbling beneath my breath as I patted her. "Please don't throw me. Just, please don't throw me."

We set out at a comfortable pace. Amaya was easy enough and seemed content to follow the leader. Then Castiel slowed, a constant vigil at my side. He kept conversation to a minimum, no doubt in effort to calm my nerves. And it worked. A warm sun peeked from behind thin clouds. The fields we traveled were a lush green, plump from a good rain. Wildflowers speckled the landscape. The sound of the horses' hooves against the dense earth soothed. Even the forests appeared less ominous than before. How could anyone think evil lurked within them?

Except that it did—evil that fought for someone as terrible as a Wraith Queen.

I shuddered. "What's the first harvest?" I asked, breaking through my moroseness.

He turned from me, no doubt to hide a mischievous smile that still shone at the corner of his mouth. "You'll see."

When Castiel increased the stride, it almost felt nice. We traveled northeast for an hour before coming upon Rhyolyn; the small town bustled with movement.

My anxiety returned.

Homes of brick and mortar lined the single street, pressed up against each other without much space between, but the farther we rode, the scenery changed. The homes grew farther apart. Now of wood or even straw, they spotted the land without much rhyme or reason. Beyond them stretched an orchard. In a large field, citizens readied tables decorated with flowers, streamers, and painted signs. The scent of breads, pies, and flora infused the air. My mouth watered. Children played games of chase, barefoot along dirt roads.

The Wraith Queen and her demon hordes destroyed small towns like these, reducing them to stubble. With barely any protection at all, they were as good as dead against her force.

Unaware of my grim thoughts, the children stopped to wave to their prince then resumed their games, their laughter echoing through the streets. Others recognized Castiel and came offering drink, which he took with warm smiles of thanks. I, too, was offered refreshment, which I refused as kindly as I could.

They surrounded him, inquiring after the honorable king, of the rising Captain Melia, and other kingdom gossip.

Tiny fingers pulled at my clothes, asking questions I could not hear over the ruckus. They received me, a stranger, as warmly as they did the prince without a second thought.

Well, most of them did. The younger ladies watched me with pointed looks, jealousy brimming from beneath fake welcomes. I smiled at them all, enjoying their discomfort.

Since when was I so petty?

The prince descended his horse. He held out his hand to help me but did not touch me yet. I took his offering, his fingers warm against my cold skin, and slid from my horse. When he caught me, his thumbs dug into my rib cage as he transferred me from Amaya to the ground with ease. He released me and instantly, we were swarmed by men and women offering drinks, baskets full of baked treasures, and sweet candies.

"You've made it!" A man entered the circle of admirers and clapped the prince on the back. The newcomer's clothes were ragged and dirty. Blondish-red hair fell to his shoulders. Freckles spotted a handsome face. He appeared to be Castiel's senior by roughly a decade, but the sun-worn wrinkles on his skin could have added several unfair years, impairing a proper guess.

The men hugged, and my mouth fell open.

What prince hugged a commoner? I shook my head, not sure why I was so surprised by what he did. Besides, was there anything truly wrong with such a display?

Again, the man beat a friendly hand on the prince's back. "Just in time, my boy. Just in time. We were waiting for you." Soft brown eyes found me over Castiel's shoulder. "And what beautiful creature have you brought to our town?"

My face heated crimson at the compliment. In Eira no one had ever dared to compliment me. My uncle taught that such attentions were considered ill-bred and they were not allowed. Despite my raising, I found myself almost enjoying the attention.

Castiel turned. "This is Lady Anna. I hope you will welcome her as you do me. Lady Anna, may I introduce the leader of this town, Mayor Ashley Belau."

I curtsied the best I could in the ensemble given but felt foolish for doing so.

Ashley smiled and wiped the dirt from his hands on his pants. "I hope you wouldn't even question that, my prince." In a grand sweep he bowed like I was royalty, although I was sure he didn't suspect the truth.

In Eira, when presenting themselves to myself or the king, mayors and alders put on the façade of pomp and wealth. They simpered and preened, they bowed, and they kneeled, prostrating themselves to the almighty king and his lineage. It was disgusting.

"Welcome, Lady Anna," Ashely said, then suddenly, he clasped my hand in his and kissed one of my knuckles.

"And might I add that I could get lost within your mesmerizing eyes forever."

I gasped. "Oh!" I barely restrained myself from pulling away.

"Alright, alright," Castiel said, nudging Ashley away with a peevish smile, but the twinkle in Ashley's eyes made me laugh despite my previous discomfort.

I clenched my hands together, fighting the desire to wipe away the remnants his kiss may have left on my skin. I swallowed. "It's a pleasure to meet you, Mayor—"

"Ashley. Just Ashley, my lady," he said with a wink.

"Very well. Ashley. Can you tell me why I'm here today? The prince has been quite hush-hush about it."

He turned to Castiel in dramatic awe. "You haven't told her?" But without waiting for a response, the town leader looped his arm through mine and swept me away. I was too busy concentrating on not falling to bother about the contact.

Laughter sounded behind me. Castiel trailed at a leisurely pace, conversing at ease with several townspeople. More stopped what they were doing and followed us with their baskets and drink. Children ran ahead, racing to beat us to our destination.

"Lady Anna, today is the first harvest. A grand day of celebration."

Ashley pointed to an orchard. The trees were towering giants with big, dark leaves, their limbs thick and strong, and heavy leaden with plump foreign fruit I had never seen before. Workers busily laid blankets beneath the larger ones. The townsfolk waved as we drew near. These

were Castiel's people. This was his life. This was *real.*
Castiel was real.

The mayor continued. "It's the best day of the year, when we reap what we sow. We work hard, but we also eat, drink, dance, and if we're lucky, regret our decisions the next day!"

15
FIRST HARVEST

A NERVOUS BREATH BUBBLED TO my lips, but I managed to contain the near-outburst. Ashley's affable humor was catching.

"It sounds as if you've already starting the drinking, my friend. Perhaps a tad too early," Castiel said from behind. Several people laughed at the comment.

"Not a drop, my boy." He lowered his voice conspiratorially and leaned toward me. "But that will come soon enough, my lady. And as I said, you're just in time." He stopped, releasing my arm with a smile and another deep bow.

Castiel reclaimed his position next to me. His eyes searched mine, and although his smile was genuine and warm, apprehension shone through.

I nodded to ease it, a smile tugging at my own lips. I could almost see the energy the people emitted, feel the glow of their auras without the need of Melora's potion to aid me. Their enthusiasm intoxicated, overwhelming my anxiety, and I found myself more curious to see what would happen next.

"Attention!" Ashely's voice rang over the rest, silencing the crowd. "Attention my people! Once again, the good prince has graced us with his presence and his assistance. The time has come!"

With growing excitement, men, woman, and children ran to the orchards and picked up the blankets beneath them at the corners, spreading the material wide like a net.

They looked to Castiel, barely containing their glee. I didn't understand why until the prince lifted both hands high into the air. He paused and gazed over his shoulder to me, a mischievous twinkle in his blue eyes, increasing the dramatic intensity.

I shook my head at his childishness but smiled nonetheless.

Closing his eyes, he twisted his fingers as though wrapping around an invisible object, then pulled down. Trees shook, almost violently, and fruit fell from the branches in a downpour.

Shrieks of joy filled the air.

Seven trees had been affected by Castiel's powers, and now seven groups competed at a frantic speed to collect their spoils into a makeshift net. The spectators clapped and called out wild instructions to the participants, watching their women giggle and fall. With the fruit gathered, the fastest of them raced to the waiting town leader and the prince, but such a task did not appear easy.

I clasped my hands to fight the desire to join in the fun, my competitive nature boiling to the surface.

Four men in the lead dragged the overladen sack of produce, along with a mother and child that had collapsed on top in fits of glee. They tugged and grunted while all else cheered for their chosen team.

Ashely howled at the sight. When the competitors arrived, he took one of the leader's hands and held it up. "The winners! Go collect your spoils!"

The men fell upon the sack with the woman and child, heaving great breaths of air.

Ashley playfully pushed one man to the side to open the net and grabbed a deep-red fruit the size of a fist. He lifted it high. "To the first harvest of the season!" Then he tossed the offering to the prince.

Castiel caught it and sank his teeth into its flesh, biting off a chunk. Mouth partially full, he too raised it to the sky. "To the first harvest!"

The crowd cheered, and I couldn't help but join in the celebration.

I glanced to the prince. "That was—that was *amazing*," I said, wonder in my voice.

Castiel chuckled. "*That* impresses you?" he asked, speaking around his mouthful.

I rolled my eyes to hide my smile and turned to the mayor.

"What is it?" I asked, gesturing to the celebrated fruit.

Ashley's head twitched. Confusion marred his expression. "It's—it's a ruby-sweet. Named for its dark red color. You've never—"

"Of course," I said, grasping my mistake. "I didn't recognize it. I've never been to a harvest."

He gave Castiel a strange look but shook it off. "Well done, my prince. As always, well done." He handed him a goblet of amber liquid. "And here's to another prosperous year!"

The prince drank deeply, then offered some to me. And how could I refuse?

I downed the remaining liquid. All the while, Castiel watched me, a curious expression on his face.

"Some of the best mead in the kingdom, my lady," Ashely said, with another wink. He claimed my cup just as a woman passed with a basket of baked goodies. He traded the goblet for a slice of bread and shoved a bite in his mouth. "I remember a day when we couldn't keep both princes away from a harvest."

I could understand why. All around us the townsfolk ate, drank, and picked the remaining fruit the prince's power had been unable to harvest. I had never witnessed something so amazing as this small town's festivities.

"Where did you say you come from, my lady?" The question shocked me from my good mood.

Before I could even think of a lie, Castiel answered for me. "Lady Anna hails from near the north border, which is why her skin is so frightfully pale."

Ashley laughed at the comment and at my offended gasp.

"And it's *also* why we must get some more sun on that skin. Come, my lady." The prince held out his arm, another offering. "Our time grows short before we must go."

I threaded my arm through his.

"Very well, Castiel, but one minute—" Ashley skipped to a table where yet more drink lay waiting. "For the journey," he said, handing me another wooden goblet of mead. "And to your good health, my lady."

I looked to Castiel, wondering if such a genial toast bothered him, that Ashley paid such attention to me. He only smiled... and the whole world slowed. His warmth matched that of the sun, and he cast that light upon everyone who surrounded him. His people.

Had I done that for my own people? Did I deserve equal praise from Eira, a kingdom I had never served, never loved, never saw past my own afflictions?

Castiel leaned forward to whisper in my ear, effectively jolting me from my sullen thoughts. "He'll only ply you with more if you don't drink now."

Ashley shrugged. "Tis true."

I chuckled and took a long draught. We left the mayor to his mead and meandered farther into the orchard. The prince plucked an empty basket that lay against an abandoned tree. As we walked, I handed him my remaining drink. He took it without question. Though the effects of the mead numbed my anxieties, worry still managed to seep through.

"Will you tell Ashley of the king's suspicions. Of the Wraith Queen?" I asked.

The lines between his brows deepened. The desire to smooth the worry from his face nearly overtook me, so that I had to look away.

Finally, he answered. "No. Until our suspicions are confirmed it wouldn't do any good to worry them."

I nodded, watching children weave in and out of the orchard in a game of cat and mouse. Castiel worked his magic on several more trees as we went. Ruby-sweets littered the ground, waiting their turn to be collected in baskets—not that the individuals *within* the orchard cared much. Most of the families stayed to the outskirts closest to the town, near the activities, while couples meandered the fields. They held hands and sometimes snuck additional privacy behind the trunks of the trees that towered above them. They didn't worry over the improprieties of being caught wrapped in each other's embrace, but why should they?

I blushed at the intimacy of it, my heart racing. Should I go back? And what did the prince think? Did he worry about the rumors that would start if we were seen alone, unescorted, in a secluded part of the orchard?

But Castiel didn't seem to notice.

"Here we are," he said, interrupting my thoughts.

"What?"

He released my arm. "This should do nicely."

My face heated. "For what?" I asked again, my voice harsher than I intended.

He placed the basket beneath the tree then glanced to me. "For practicing, of course." He shifted to pull something from his pocket and held it out to me. Melora's potion. "Willing to give it another go?"

A breath whooshed from my lungs. "Oh."

"What did you think I brought you out here for?"

"I—" Was that laughter in his eyes? "Never mind."

One side of his lips quirked up. "Indeed."

I shuddered at the thought of another drink of Melora's brew. "I thought we were supposed to be helping the town."

"I can't do *every* tree. That would sap my strength. Besides, this has been done for hundreds of years without my help. They can handle it on their own." He wiggled the vial between his fingers. "It won't be as bad this time. Just a sip. Only enough for an hour or so."

"Fine." I snatched the bottle from his grasp and uncorked it. The mead had made me brave. I plugged my nose to the taste and sipped, then stole the remaining mead as a follower.

Castiel jolted a step. "Wait—"

But he was too late.

I swallowed hard against the combined taste then tossed the empty cup back to the prince, followed by the potion. He easily caught both, pocketing the vial.

"You might regret that."

The mead dulled the burning effects of the potion and quickened its decent. "That poison needs a chaser. It's terrible. You'd think the all-powerful Melora would make it taste better." I rolled my neck, concentrating on the movement instead of my stomach.

Castiel grimaced, putting a finger to his lips. "You probably should be careful of—"

"Getting drunk?" I asked with a smile.

"No, saying her name. But yes, that too."

"She's not a wraith, remember?"

He rolled his eyes but smiled.

"Besides, I was reared in my uncle's militia from the age of twelve. I can hold my own. Just don't let me fall asleep in the saddle on the way home."

His brows raised high as he considered me, but I only wiped any remnants off with the back of my hand.

"The amount you drank is too small to truly affect you." He jumped to grab a high, thick limb then heaved himself to it. The leaves rattled when he tossed a leg over to straddle the branch. His strength was impressive.

Who was I fooling? Everything about him was impressive.

His legs swung playfully. "You did well today."

I hummed, leaning against the tree for support. The world was tipping. "I didn't have much of a choice, did I."

"Yes, you did. You *almost* seemed at home."

I didn't answer. A deep longing nearly overwhelmed me, and I suddenly regretted my earlier statement. More than ever, I wanted to find *home.* I wanted to leave, start over in some new place where no one had ever heard of Eira, of Princess Ilianna or the Demon Daughter. I could serve the people and work as the king and prince did. But Anolyn was *not* that place.

He gazed into the canopy of leaves. A snap sounded just before a ruby-sweet fell into his waiting hand. "Hungry?" he asked.

I shook my head.

"Very well." He tossed the uneaten fruit into the empty basket and gave me one of his most rewarding smiles. "Now you try."

"We've been over this."

He cocked his head to the side. His blue eyes captured mine and I had to look away.

"Fine." I scanned for the nearest ruby. Melora's potion was working. A hazy cloud emitted from the tree, and I focused on it. The afternoon heat beaded on my forehead as I squinted and glared at the object until my teeth ground against each other. I released the effort with a sigh and shrugged.

"Come, my lady," he said, reaching to me from the branch.

I slapped away his hand. "I don't think so."

He appeared offended. "That's not a request. It's a direct order."

"You don't say." I scanned for a better branch to climb, preferably one a little closer to the ground.

His voice whispered close to my ear. "Ilianna, come join me."

I inhaled and jerked away, shocked by his sudden closeness. Except that he wasn't close at all. He was in the same place he had been before. "How—how did you do that?"

"Parlor trick." A devilish smile lit his eyes.

I narrowed my gaze. "If I fall and break my neck, I'm returning as a wraith to haunt you in your sleep."

"Who says you don't already?"

My breath caught in my lungs, but I pretended not to hear his comment. What did it mean anyways? Did he worry I would escape? Did I give him nightmares? And why did I blush the way I did when he watched me like this?

His aura shone like the moon from his skin. It was beautiful. He was beautiful.

Castiel laughed, then reached for me. "Do you know how to climb a tree?"

I shook off the effects and snorted. "Of course."

"Well, this will be the easiest tree-climbing you'll ever do. Take my hand."

And I did. He pulled, but it was more than his strength that lifted me from the ground. His magic cocooned me in a soft glow, allaying the strain of my body against gravity. I felt light, like the clouds hovering in the distance.

He guided me to a place next to him and I settled the best I could on top, grateful for the first time today for Sameen and her choice of breeches instead of a dress. My nerves balanced like I did on that branch, and carefully I moved a few inches from him, my fingers clutching to the limb.

"I wish I could do that," I said, shocked by the admittance. I once mistrusted anything magical, but Castiel didn't use his magic the way I knew Johan would wield it.

Castiel leaned against the trunk of the tree, stretching one long leg out along the branch. "The moving of objects is not every magician's gift. That doesn't mean we don't try to see if you can. And I have other tests I want to perform today."

Regret bubbled within. I never did well with tests. My uncle enjoyed giving them, and I enjoyed failing them all. But with Johan, I couldn't show what I was capable of. With Castiel it was different. I didn't want to fail with him.

The haze from the potion blurred my vision. Despite knowing what it was, I still blinked to clear my sight, without success. I splayed my fingers against the bark of the tree, then froze against its rough skin.

Warmth spread from my hands up my arms and coursed through my chest. Peace washed over me, and with it a sense of happiness I had never felt. The tree's lifeforce pressed back. Alive and inviting, it supported our weight with its strength. I closed my eyes to the sensation and allowed it to draw me in.

"I can feel it," I whispered, afraid I would scare it if I was any louder.

"Feel what?" Castiel asked.

"The tree."

"Are—are you being serious?"

I could hear the disbelief in his words but couldn't understand why. How could he miss it? She was strong and fertile. She stretched toward the sun in her desire to continue her progression, anxious to shed her remaining harvest to make room for new growth. Her fruit, a gift to those that maintained her, needed to be removed.

And I could help.

Reaching out through our connection, I felt every leaf, every twig, every stem of the ruby-sweets. It would be nothing at all to snap those remaining stems—

A roar swelled past me as a flood of ruby-sweets rushed to the ground unaware of anything or anyone in their path. Castiel swore as he reached for me, but I was knocked from my meditative state before he could grab hold. I cried out, tumbling backward, only managing to keep my grip and my legs wrapped around the branch. A second later Castiel toppled past me.

When the final fruit fell with a thump, I called to him from my perch, my voice a strange octave I had never heard.

"Castiel!"

He groaned.

I peered about for a way down, but the haze from the potion disoriented me. "Are you injured? Prince?"

"What in Anolyn's green pastures—? What did you do?"

"I—" But I had no answer to give. "Is there a reason I'm still hanging here? Are you dead?"

He sat up. "Of course not."

"Then get me down."

My mind whirled with the dizzying mixture of mead and potion. I eyeballed the distance, not trusting that I could make the stretch without falling on my face or breaking a bone. Gedeon would be disappointed if I got hurt yet again.

Castiel grunted and got to his feet.

My face grew hot as blood continued its path to my head.

He moved below me. Our eyes were level, his expression thoughtful; then he twisted, dipping his head to the side. His brows cinched together, wrinkling his handsome features as he scanned mine. He looked to the mess of ruby-sweets on the ground.

My hands sung in pain and I adjusted my grip, aware now of the scrapes from the sharp bark.

"That was—*amazing*," he said. And he smiled again in that way that made everything except for him disappear. Firm hands took hold of my waist. "Let go. I've got you."

I squeezed my eyes tight and obeyed. He flipped me over, guiding me carefully to the ground. When I opened them, I was tucked safe to his chest.

My blood rushed from my face, making me light-headed. I allowed him to keep me close until my world stopped spinning, then gently pushed from him.

"What did you do?" he asked.

I displayed my hands as if in explanation. "I told you."

Castiel tsked, seeing only the scrapes on my palms. He pulled a handkerchief from his pocket and wiped at the scratches.

"No, no." I batted him away. "Castiel, I could *feel* the tree. With my hands. Couldn't you feel it too? She wanted to be harvested, and my magic—my *magic!*" I inhaled a sharp breath and clapped my hands together. Something I could only describe as joy coursed through me. Despite everything I had ever been taught, every lesson my uncle beat into me, every ingrained warning, I jumped up and down like a silly schoolgirl. "Castiel! My magic! It worked!"

16

MELORA

I SHRIEKED AND GATHERED HIS FACE into my hands. "I have magic I can use!"

Castiel huffed a laugh. Capturing my wrists, he held them in his grasp. "I never doubted it."

"Touch really does help."

"It makes sense."

"It does?" But I shook my head to whatever meaning he was trying to get through and whirled in a circle. Melora's potion intensified the sensation. I wanted to soar with the falcry. The prince only watched me, a growing smile upon his handsome face.

I knew I was acting ridiculous. I had used my abilities before—but not in *this* way. This felt different. This felt good. I stopped twirling, my breath heavy and uneven. "Can you see it? My magic?"

"Indeed."

"Is it blue?" I ran to the tree but all I saw was her greenish hue. I touched her trunk. Relief coursed through her branches.

Castiel's voice came to me from over my shoulder, close enough to make me whirl to the sound. "Silvery-blue."

For the next hour we practiced. I harvested a half-dozen more trees for the town, but also tested my touch on other objects. While I couldn't elevate a stone the way Castiel could, I was able to focus my powers on the aura of the stone and send it away from me—not far, but it was impressive enough to the prince.

Castiel stood in front of me, his hands outstretched. "I want you to try your powers on me."

"What?"

"While the type of power you're wielding can be used for good, it can also be for nefarious reasons. I want to see what you're capable of."

"Is that smart?" I crossed my arms over my chest as a sudden wave of guilt swept over me. "What if—what if I asked you to take me to port?"

He was quick to respond. "You wouldn't do that."

"Are you sure?"

He took my hands in his. "Yes."

I flinched at the intense expression in his eyes. He trusted me. But had I done anything to earn that trust? Did I want to?

I gripped his fingers and focused on his aura, that connection to his soul—his soul that was good despite everything I had come to believe about men. I closed my eyes and pushed my desire upon him.

He jolted back, removing his hands from mine. A smile built in the corners of his mouth.

"Very well. I'll go get you more mead, and even some lunch, but not because your magic is forcing me to do it."

I gathered the full basket from the tree. "But how can you tell you're doing it of your own free will?"

He smirked then confiscated the basket, offering his arm instead.

Without thinking I took it and together we walked back into town.

After lunch, we did more work, but directly with the townspeople and using our hands instead of magic. We climbed ladders into the foliage and plucked ruby-sweets until our fingers smelled of fruit. Soon, like so many of the other men, Castiel discarded his shirt to the dirt beneath him. I, on the other hand, sweltered beneath my clothes as well as an apron now wrapped tightly around my waist.

I tried to not stare, tried to not appreciate the lines of his muscles as he worked. Tried not to notice the way sweat glistened from his shoulders and chest. Unlike Mikael, not a single tattoo marred his marvelous sculpture of a body—because that was exactly what it was. A pristine sculpture worthy of notice. He turned to me, and I spun, almost plunging to my death from the branches.

"You should pay attention to what you're doing, my lady."

I cut back my colorful response and tried not to look at him at all. Feeling warmer than I ought to, I climbed down from my branches picked clean to empty my heavy-laden apron into the basket of a passing woman.

I rolled my neck, stretching sore muscles, then meandered away toward the table of breads. Something I could only describe as peace filled my lungs, nearly stopping my breath.

It felt wonderful.

"Here you are, my lady," said a young girl who watched over the baked goods, and she handed me another cinnamon cake, one of many slices I had gotten that day.

I curtsied in my garb and strolled the town at leisure.

Contentment washed over me like a soothing balm. It was like all my cares from the previous day had melted beneath a warm sun and hard work. For one of the first times in my life it felt good to be alive. I wiped the crumbs of cake off on my apron, wishing I had thought to take another cup of mead. I barely noticed when I reached the outskirts of town. It was a small town, after all.

A woman waited just beyond the worn road. Braided light-blonde hair fell over her shoulder to her waist. Pale eyes watched me from within a striking face. She wore an attractive deep-blue dress that flowed to the ground. Jeweled bracelets decorated her wrists. When our eyes met, she raised a hand in salute and beckoned me further.

And why not speak with her? She was lovely.

I jolted, surprised by my altered mind. The woman froze, attuned to the change in my state. Still, a voice I had not recognized until now coaxed me forward.

Come speak to me.

I shook my head. "Who are you?"

"Hello, Ilianna." Her accent was as beautiful as she was, and there was something so familiar about her face.

I took a step forward but kept my distance despite her lure.

"Who are you, and how do you know my name?" I asked again, my words stronger than what I felt.

"I know your name as you know mine." The way she smiled prompted knowledge… and then fear.

"I don't know—" My breath seized in my lungs. Shock and instinctive panic warred within my mind. Their likeness was uncanny. It was Melia, but it wasn't. Melia was *her* daughter. And Melia's mother was…

My voice trembled. "Melora."

Melora Seraphine. The seer.

But it was impossible. This woman appeared to be no more than a few years older than Melia. I stepped away.

Her eyes caught the movement and intent, then flashed again to mine. She took a willowy step forward, holding out her hand. "There's so much mistrust in you. Hurt. Fear. You think you are alone, but you are far from it, Ilianna."

I swallowed, my tongue too thick. "I would never dare assume such a ridiculous thing."

She tsked. "It's like an infection, but it spreads more like a plague. You must heal it before it feeds on your soul, leaving you exposed. She'll find a way in."

"Lady Anna!" Castiel's voice carried to me from over my shoulder, but I ignored him.

"She, who?" I asked. When she didn't answer, anger grew, supplanting fear. "Do you mean the Wraith Queen?" But who else could she mean? Seers were known for their tricks with words and double meanings. How could one believe anything they said?

"Lady Anna." Castiel's massive form was in front of me then, blocking my view to the seer. His eyes scanned my face, worry embedded deep within them.

The seer's voice cooed. "My prince."

He closed his eyes and took a deep breath but kept himself between us. "Mother Seer. What a lovely surprise. I see you've met my friend."

But now she had eyes only for the prince, leaving me forgotten. "It's always such a delight to see you." She closed the gap, her long, lean form graceful, her dress wafting in a sudden breeze. Could a seer control the elements?

She reached slender fingers to Castiel, who took them to place a gentle kiss on her knuckles.

Those slender fingers clutched him closer. He lurched forward. "I always said Melia should choose you. Whoever takes upon them *your* yoke will reap the benefits of a fine… bloodline."

My eyes grew large at the double-meaning.

Did the prince blush? "My brother is the better choice."

She sighed. "But is he?"

Castiel cleared his throat. "Come, Ilianna. It's time to go home."

"Wonderful." Melora thread her arm through his. "You can escort me to your brother."

The trip home was even more uncomfortable than the ride to Rhyolyn. Melora traveled on the back of Castiel's horse, her arms securely tightened around his middle. As if in recognition of her presence, the horses doubled their speed. As much as I wanted to, it was almost impossible for me to ponder this woman—the seer—while clutching the reins for life and limb.

It took everything in me not to retch. My world was
still spinning when we made it within the castle walls.
Melora hung on to Castiel as we entered, ignoring me
completely. Mikael and Reese met us outside the throne
room.

Mikael held out his hand, halting us. "The king is in
council," he said, his voice distant and formal, but his eyes
grew wide upon seeing who decorated the prince's arm.

Alarm shot through to my innards and I clutched at
my stomach. "Is it my uncle?" The nonsensical question
flew, unchecked from numb lips as the blood drained from
them. Even though I did not look, I could feel the seer
watching my reaction. Could she read my thoughts?

Mikael's face betrayed nothing. "I am unable to answer
any and all inquiries."

Castiel balked. "Excuse me? Step out of the way,
Captain."

Reese's jaw flexed, and Mikael stood taller. "I would,
Your Highness, but the king has given direct orders
that you are not to interrupt his meeting. He wishes you
and my lady," he said with a glance toward me, "to join
him for dinner." He looked to Melora, his smile tight.
"And I'm sure the king would want you to join as well,
Madam Seer."

One brow pitched high. Alarm flashed in Reese's eyes as
the seer considered both men. "If I wanted to see him now,
young ones, I would. But it's just as well. I need to rest.
Maybe a warm bath and a change of clothes." And even
though she returned his smile, it seemed more like a threat.

"Of course, ma'am," Mikael said.

She twirled and laced her arm through the prince's.
"And I'm sure the prince would escort me. I take it you've
kept my room ready?"

Castiel's gaze flashed to mine, an apology. "Of course.
Reese, please take Lady Anna to her room."

I wanted to refuse his request. To demand that he stay
with me—although why, I didn't know—but the prince
was already being dragged away by the impatient seer.

Emotion rooted me in place. Anger, disbelief, fear—
they warred within, eager for victory over the other. I
reached inward, sensing my magic for the first time
without the need of the seer's potion. I cast it from me but
it was too late. Castiel was gone and I was alone.

I closed my eyes to the unwanted sting.

"My lady?" Reese's soft and impossibly deep voice
almost soothed. When I opened my eyes again, he stood,
waiting, concern within his expression. "Will you allow
me to escort you?" It was a request not an order, and I was
grateful for the distinction. I took his arm.

In a trance I moved, my brain fighting against use
until we reached my door. I released Reese's arm, but
before I could step away, he seized me by the wrist.

I inhaled, shocked, and spun to glare at him, but
Reese's appearance disarmed me immediately. Concern
swam in his big eyes.

He leaned forward, speaking low. "Johan is not here.
Don't worry, Princess."

Relief broke my defenses as emotion sprang to my eyes.
Without thinking, I wrapped my arms around his
incredibly large neck. Reese froze beneath my embrace. I

wondered if he was afraid of me, or worried I would trick him again, but a second later a firm hand pressed between my shoulders. He patted my back then peeled me from him. I did not bother to check the tears that flowed down my face. His warm fingers gently wiped one from my cheek.

"If your uncle comes, it won't be any time soon. The falcry would have the missive to the border by the first night, but while they are fast, our carriers are not. It's at least a three-day ride from the border. Even if your uncle were to stop what he's doing—"

I almost laughed at my stupidity. "He wouldn't." It would take six days by carriage after receiving the missive—that trek was doubled in the winter. No matter the season, I wasn't that important for him to rush from his throne. I had several days—weeks, most likely.

"Go. Get ready for dinner."

"Thank you, my friend," I said, and I wasn't shocked to realize I meant it.

Time crawled at a snail's pace. I had been bathed by Sameen and dressed in a soft lilac gown long before dinner's arrival. A book I had taken from Meyrion's library did little to catch my attention. I just held it, flipping through pages I did not read. Something had happened, something important, but what, I could hardly guess.

If it wasn't my uncle, then who else claimed the attention of the king? Could it be the Wraith Queen herself? I doubted it. There would be triple the guard if *that* were the case. Could it be Weylan, or even Cy the demon? But even that didn't make sense. Why keep his brother from entering the throne room? I felt the snub acutely on Castiel's behalf and stewed over the meaning.

A knock at the door sounded and I raced toward it. Melia and Reese waited in full combat gear to escort me. "So, can we discuss yet what this is about?" I asked as we ushered down the hallways. "And why do I feel like I'm being led to the gallows?"

"Always so dramatic," Melia said behind me, but while her words were meant to tease, there was an edge to them.

"Not yet, my lady," Reese added, and I gave him a small smile.

As hard as it was, I remained quiet. There was a strange feeling about the castle. Several armed guards I had never seen paced the hallways, sliding sideways glances at me, their hands on the hilt of their weapons. Unfamiliar voices floated toward us from the reception hall. Additional guards stood sentinel at the entryway, barring our entrance.

"Melia, Captain of the Guard, and Lieutenant Reese, escorting Lady Anna. Our presence is requested."

The guard dipped his head and stepped aside. The sun had not yet disappeared, but already candles dotted the dining hall and hung from candelabras. Mikael paced the room as four men and the king's woman conversed in hushed tones near the table already set with dinnerware and full goblets of wine. I had seen the men before, but only in passing, when they were trailing behind the king. They were obviously advisors or councilors.

The mistress was, as ever, beautiful. Elegant. Her gown was a solid black masterpiece that barely covered her ample chest. The light from the surrounding candles shone in her sleek black tresses, tucked into a neat ball at the back of her neck.

The men wore brown leather jerkins and matching breeches that didn't fit with the military garb of Anolyn's militia, but neither were they of the appropriate age for battle. Retired, perhaps?

Castiel, the king, and Melora were nowhere to be seen. Melia and Reese left me to take their assigned positions about the room, their rigid nature so against everything I had grown to know about them. Tension rippled in the cavernous space. I shrank into myself, hoping no one would notice me.

But it wasn't to be.

One man stepped away from the group of five. He was the oldest one, maybe early sixties. Gray streaked the sides of his impeccably combed hair. Confidence—no, arrogance—wafted from him like a bad cologne. I lifted my chin a little higher as he neared.

He stopped, bowing low. "Welcome, Lady Anna."

I tipped my head in acknowledgment then looked away. "You know who I am?"

He cleared his throat. "I make it my personal duty to know anyone who ventures near my king and prince. Now, may I ask just what it is you're doing here?"

My spine snapped erect, my cheeks reddened.

"She's here on my orders, Vega." The king entered dressed in a black tunic, leather breeches, and matching boots. The belt that slung low on his hips displayed more weapons than I had seen him wear since my arrival. He didn't address anyone else but sat at the head of the table without another word.

Vega pinned me with chocolate-colored eyes before moving to the table. Castiel had yet to come, but Reese tipped his head toward my spot and pulled out a chair to the left of the king. That earned me a few pointed looks from the others, especially Vega. He took the seat next to where I could only assume Castiel would claim, and the mistress chose to sit next to him.

A man with several gruesome scars on his face, jawline, and neck took the place next to me, settling in without so much as a word. He didn't even try to make eye contact, for which I was grateful.

"I assume you took the time to get to know each other?" Riaan asked.

They glanced to each other. "Not formally, Your Majesty," his mistress answered, returning her pointed attention to me.

"Then allow me," the king said. Pointing to the one nearest to him. "Lady Anna, this is General Vega, my father's most trusted advisor." Vega's eyes bore holes through mine, but I ignored his pointed stare. Riaan nodded to the man with the scars. "General Dag." Then to another man that barely managed to remain buttoned beneath his girth. His bald head gleamed from the exertion of breathing. "General Beau." Next in line was a man who appeared as frail and thin as a woman. His delicate facial features appeared far too pale to be from Anolyn. "General Amara." Finally, the king's fingers gestured to the woman. "And this is Madam Siana." The woman inclined her head, her onyx eyes cold, calculating. The king continued. "All trusted advisors of my father, the once great King Cassius Anouk."

"You do not claim the title of General?" I said, immediately turning my attention back to the woman. Now that we were properly introduced, my curiosity got the better of me.

She didn't flinch, only sipped from a goblet of wine. "My kind are rarely part of the king generals."

My brows raised as I measured that little bit of information against my own experience in the courts of Eira. "Very curious. A woman, not of the same ranking of the audience she is routinely seen with, and yet privileged to circulate with them. That makes you one of two things."

Her eyes narrowed in warning. "And what would those be?"

"Because of your beauty, my original, *incorrect* guess was mistress—"

I paused, partly wondering at the glimmer of mirth in Siana's onyx eyes. She sighed dramatically. "It's not for the lack of trying."

Riaan choked back what sounded like a laugh, and I could feel Melia's gaze boring upon me.

"My lady—" Melia began, but I cut her off.

"However," I said, "knowing the king as I do now, I doubt he would participate in such salaciousness. Then your beauty is only of consequence and my concluding conjecture would be special forces. A select guard for the crown of Anolyn."

One corner of the woman's mouth tipped up and she inclined her head. "And the king's personal assassin."

I nodded, cataloging that piece of information. "Indeed?"

The king laughed out loud and clapped his hands as if he enjoyed my little show.

General Vega cleared his throat. "Your Majesty, why—"

"No questions until *after* dinner," the king interrupted. "Believe me, we will not be eating much once we begin, and we'll need our strength."

Vega's eyes grew large.

"Where's my brother?" Riaan asked.

"Forgive me, Your Majesty." The voice was sweet, childlike. I turned to see Castiel leading a girl to our table. She clung to his arm as if unstable on her own legs—a young miss with long, light-blonde hair that fell in curls over one shoulder to her waist. Pale eyes found mine, and she smiled.

I inhaled a gasp and pitched my gaze toward Melia. The question in my eyes was clear. She answered with only a single nod.

The seer was now a youth of no more than thirteen. Thin and gangly, with scrawny arms, she looked tiny in a dress that barely fit. I was not the only one to recognize her.

Chair legs scraped against the floor, one tipping over, clattering to the ground as the men and woman scrambled to their feet.

17
SETBACK

MELORA HALTED HER STEPS AND Castiel too. He pulled the child-seer behind him as if protecting her, but it was not she who needed protection. The seer smiled up at him adoringly, and I clutched the arms of my chair.

Vega covered his heart. "What is the meaning of this?"

"Why is she here?" Madam Siana stepped smoothly away from the table, her hand shifting to the knife that would be strapped beneath the folds of her dress.

Fear and anger infused the room. It was gratifying that I was not the only one taken back by the seer's very presence. Melia's cheeks blushed pink, not from the shared emotions of the others.

"Sit down," the king ordered.

Mikael at the doors shut everyone within.

Riaan straightened. "Melora!" He opened his arms wide, smiling as I'd never seen him do before. "What a pleasant surprise." But behind his smile was something else— something foreign to his usually calm demeanor. Discomfort.

The seer watched the others reclaim their chairs before turning her full attention to the king. "Your Majesty." She gave a petite bow. "But where is my daughter?"

"I'm here, *Mother*." The captain stepped from behind a pillar.

The seer swept forward to awkwardly embrace her child who towered over her by at least a foot, then she tugged Melia's hair pulled high on her head. "You look so... severe."

"And you look young," Melia said.

She waved a hand down the line of her thin body. "You too could have all this."

Siana huffed her annoyance, gazing to the ceiling.

Castiel took Melora by the hand and carefully guided her to the table, but the seer shook her head at the offered seat and moved closer to the king.

"I believe you're in my place," she said, eyeing General Vega.

He sputtered, his face turning an even deeper shade of fury, but quickly moved to the end of the table.

Castiel took his seat next to his brother and across from me, and finally his blue eyes flickered to mine, stealing my breath. Concern and something else I couldn't understand mingled in his penetrating gaze. My heart thudded almost painfully inside my chest. It was only a moment before he looked away, but it was enough.

I dropped my gaze to my hands to hide the warmth in my face. Why was I acting like this? Was I still under the effects of the mead? But it wasn't the mead or even Melora's potion that was to blame.

Dinner was served. Steaming plates of roast and potatoes, vegetables and breads were brought to the table. All ate in silence. It appeared even the Generals and Madam Siana were unaware of the king's reasons to gather us. With Melora there, I was all but forgotten, except by Vega who took turns glaring at both myself and the unwelcome seer.

Melora pushed her food around the plate more than eating it. Did seers even need to eat? Not much was known about them. She was the first I had heard of to change ages. In fact, their ages were unknown. Not many were ever documented, and those who were lived well past three or four hundred years before dying gruesome deaths by those who hunted them down. I had never heard of one dying by natural causes.

What was the reason for her sudden appearance? Had Riaan called for her? I refused to believe it was because I had spoken her name aloud.

When everything was cleared away, the king threw his napkin to the table and leaned back in his chair. "There's been another murder."

I flinched.

Castiel slid a glance my direction, then asked, "Who? And why wasn't I told sooner?"

Riaan cleaned his nails, feigning nonchalance. "Oh, did I say murder? I meant *murders*. Seven more people have been found dead, their bodies broken and dumped in the forest. They were brought to the throne room to be inspected by our healer."

Castiel's jaw worked. "And the culprit?"

The king smiled. "The Demon Daughter."

My breath caught in my lungs. I tried to not squirm, to not give away anything to cast blame upon me, as I was sure the king had already done.

Castiel's eyes pinned me in place, but it was to the king he spoke. "And the reason you didn't allow me entrance?"

"Your whereabouts had to be verified."

And if *his* whereabouts had to be verified, then mine did too.

"That goes for all of you," the king added. "Those who brought the bodies say there are witnesses."

The others murmured to their neighbors, aghast—all but the seer, who peered about the room as if bored.

General Dag crossed his arms over his chest. "But if there are witnesses to seeing the demon herself, why do we need to be interrogated as such?"

"The face was not seen, just a so-called specter. But the town is spooked. They are sure that it was her."

"You know our loyalties. Why question them?" Siana asked, her voice a measured calm.

Vega slammed his fist upon the table. "Of course, we're loyal. There must be something that can be done. Surely this is an attack straight from Eira."

"I agree," Madame Siana said. "Johan is sending his attack dog, and the bitch needs to be put down. I'd be happy to perform such a task. In fact, I'll put them both down. All you have to say is when."

My nails dug into the napkin at my lap.

"Ladies and gentlemen, calm down. There was a day that I might have agreed with you, but that day is not today."

"Is this girl the witness?" Vega asked, staring at me from the end of the table, his voice accusing.

"No." Riaan smiled again, a wicked glint to his eyes— and suddenly, I knew what was coming. He nodded toward me. "*This* is the Demon Daughter."

I schooled my expression even as shock ripped through my body. An equally stunned prince flinched, meeting my steady gaze. There was a moment of silence before all hell broke loose.

General Vega jumped to his feet at the same time as Castiel. Both men drew their knives. Next to me, Dag attempted to seize my arm and I reacted on instinct. I twisted fast, clamping one hand down on his wrist. I jerked up hard at the same time as I pushed against the back of his elbow. His face slammed into the table with a crunch.

The assassin moved. Faster than a snake's strike, her knife flew. I hauled to the side, knowing I wouldn't be able to dodge it completely and waited for it to strike my shoulder, but it careened off at an angle, impaling itself into the seat next to me.

Magic infused the air.

Faster than I thought possible, the prince soared over the table to protect me as General Beau reached to grab me. Castiel's powers threw him to the ground.

I shoved Dag away, releasing him as the prince backed me toward the wall where Melia stood, waiting to receive me.

"Put away your weapons," Riaan said, but his voice was barely heard over the shouting.

Vega lowered into a crouch. "This is the one that killed your father, Riaan. That killed *my* king."

I stammered, clutching to Castiel's back. "Wait, what?"

A wave of anxiety coursed through me. No one, not even Johan, knew who had killed the previous king of Anolyn. It was said he was betrayed by his own.

Castiel held out a hand, as if to calm a panicked horde. "That is rumor only."

"But rumors start from somewhere, my prince," Siana said darkly, shifting to protect the king. She turned to him, a promise in her eyes. "Say the word and she's dead."

"Stand down," the king ordered, but her stance remained rigid.

General Beau gripped the top of his chair, already out of breath and looking like he would faint, but Amara remained in his seat, watching the scene play out.

The assassin, on the other hand, circled us, her gaze set on me.

"Stay back," Melia warned her.

The woman smiled widely. "And what are you going to do about it, sweetling?"

Melia's eye narrowed.

The king tsked. "Look at her, Siana, Vega. She's a child."

I flinched, my face on fire. "I'm *not* a child."

The king gave me an exasperated glare. "Maybe not anymore, but Vega, look at her. She's only seventeen. My father died five years ago. Would a twelve-year-old girl have been able to best such a seasoned warrior and magician?"

My breath stopped in my lungs. The king had been a magician?

Vega glared. "Perhaps a demon—"

"Take your seats, you fools, or I'll have you thrown in the dungeons. Do you honestly believe I'd dine with my father's murderer? Stop upsetting your prince. Brother, sit down now."

"Why didn't you tell me?" I asked, refusing to move from the protection of Castiel. "Why didn't you tell me that the kingdom of Anolyn thinks I killed your father?"

"You did!" Vega bellowed.

"Enough!" The king's voice echoed from the walls.

Slowly Vega lowered to his chair, his eyes moving from one guard to the other. Finally, he spoke. "Forgive me, Your Majesty."

The room was silent. My heart squeezed painfully within my chest. "I—I didn't kill your father."

The king turned to me, his face red. "I know. The moment I saw you, I knew it had all been fabrication. We didn't have much information about the warrior girl from Anolyn. We weren't even sure it was you when you arrived—the princess with such a terrifying name. Not until Castiel finally coaxed it out of you did we learn your hesitancy to even claim such a ridiculous title. While I'm sure your skills are quite the thing, I knew you hadn't done it."

"We both knew," Castiel said.

Emotion welled inside my throat and stung my eyes.

The king stood, his arm lifted my direction. "Ladies and gentlemen, may I introduce Princess Ilianna of

Eira. She has been a guest in our home for over three months now."

"Three months?" General Amara asked. His soft voice held disbelief and awe.

"And you didn't tell us her real identity?" Siana asked. She glided to her seat but never took her gaze from mine.

"She wished for her presence to stay unknown, and for good reason."

The assassin huffed. "Then she's smarter than I first gave her credit for. But do you think it's wise to unveil her? Many will want retribution for their fallen king."

"They'll be informed of their incorrect beliefs and the importance of this union between kingdoms. Many have already seen her and worked with her, thanks to Captain Melia. They will come to the same conclusion as we have."

"And what is that?" I asked.

His chin lifted a fraction. "That you are not the murderer of my father or an immediate threat to Anolyn." He turned back to his council. "I believe someone is trying to sabotage this peace King Johan is seeking by creating a fake Demon Daughter."

"How do we know it wasn't her?" Vega asked.

"Vega." Castiel's voice warned, but it didn't stop the general.

"The king and prince may have accepted this girl is not the killer of their father, but that does not mean she's not the killer now."

"The princess has only ever killed in battle," Riaan said.

But that wasn't true. Castiel knew of the others now, too.

The king continued. "And she has been watched closely."

"You don't think she could have snuck out to do it on her own?" Siana asked. If there was someone in the room that would understand that, it was an assassin.

"Or maybe she has someone doing the work for her," Dag said.

"I guess that's a possibility, but why?" the king asked.

Vega crossed his arms over his chest. "To incite a war she never wanted to be over. If her uncle wants peace, *she* must not want it. Princess Ilianna is as bloodthirsty as her uncle once was. She should be hung as an enemy to Anolyn."

"Princess Ilianna is a guest in my home, as are you all. She has been under direct supervision by my captain of the guard and the prince himself. She has been guarded day and night. She has not been allowed to leave this castle unescorted. Demon Daughter or not, the princess cannot walk through walls. Whoever is killing these men is not doing it under her orders. She has agreed to our reasons to keep her identity unknown and she has been a good guest. If her uncle wants peace, then he will get it, and I will not allow revolutionists or evil to stand in the way of that."

It was a good speech, *if* that was what my uncle wanted, but something deep within told me it wasn't.

"I do not think the princess holds your sentiments. Do you, Ilianna?" the seer said, finally speaking. She had been all but forgotten.

"What do you mean?" Castiel asked.

Everyone watched me. I stepped out from the protection of the prince. "Your Majesty, you know that I've never been sure about my uncle's intention for peace."

"And you still think that way?"

"I don't know. For our sakes, the sake of your kingdom as well as my own, I hope he intends to keep it, but I would be watchful of his arrival. Be careful of what information you share with him."

"Your caution is noted. That still doesn't help us with what to do about this murderer who kills in the name of the Demon Daughter."

"I will go myself and capture this deceiver," Castiel said, reclaiming his protective stance in front of me.

"No." It slipped out, sharp and almost crazed. I clutched at his arm, but he ignored me.

"I'll go as well," the seer said, her voice light and almost playful. "Something tells me I'll be able to stir up the true identity of this murderer."

"Very well," Riaan said. "You will leave with a party of soldiers at dawn. No later."

Castiel nodded.

"And my daughter?" Melora asked, pinning the king with her interesting eyes.

He froze. "What of her?"

The blood drained from Melia's face.

The seer smiled. "I would like her to be my escort."

"You'll have the prince."

"But I feel my daughter is necessary in this journey. Are you going to deny the blessing of my own blood, Your Majesty?" She lowered her head, her hands clasped together as if in prayer. "That would be very unwise."

Riaan made a visual effort to remain calm. "Very well, Melora Seraphine. You may take your daughter, but you have *one* week—until the celebration to announce the arrival of the princess. You will all return before that evening." He rose from his seat, his hands clenched in tight fists. He glared at the council members. "The princess is not to be harmed. She is a guest and is under my protection. If she is harmed, those involved will be put to death. You're dismissed."

The members of the council stood and bowed to their king. They were the first to leave, but before I could follow, the seer halted me with a hand at my chest. Her delicate fingertips were ice cold. I barely managed to stay beneath her touch.

She spoke low, shooting tremors up my spine. "I hope, for *your* sake, you will never disappoint me again, Your Majesty."

The king spoke. "Excuse me?"

"We are not done here. Not yet." The seer faced him. "Why did you not call for me the moment *she* arrived?"

All eyes turned to me. My cheeks grew hot.

"Don't push it, old lady." The warning in the king's voice was clear, but the seer overlooked it easily.

"You apparently underestimate her significance in the events of the future."

"Significance?" I asked, annoyed. Since when did I ever hold such a calling? I was a nobody, lower than my uncle's boot.

"What significance would a runaway princess be to you?" Melia asked, but Melora ignored her daughter.

"And stop dressing her as if she is some soft, pampered princess. She is anything but, and she needs to play the part."

"And what part is that?" I asked.

She surveyed the length of my lilac gown in disgust. "She's a princess from Eira. A snow-driven, war-loving country. She is the daughter of Prince Toma and niece to King Johan, both powerful enemies. You make her appear positively normal."

A stab of reality jolted through me. She was right. I wasn't normal. I didn't belong, now or ever.

"But do we want our people to fear her?" Castiel asked. He too examined me as if I was on display—which I was.

"Your people are not stupid. If you try to make her look like everyone else, you will incite controversy. Show her for what they know her to be. Acceptance will come sooner than not."

"*Your* people?" I asked.

One brow ticked high upon her porcelain forehead. "Eirian blood runs in my veins, girl, and that of my daughter."

Of course it did. I practically rolled my eyes as the likeness to my country's people dawned.

She continued. "But I belong to no king or country." She smiled, glancing from her daughter to Riaan. "There must be a union between our two kingdoms if we are to survive."

While she didn't come out and say it, I internally cringed at the underlying meaning to her statement.

Castiel avoided my gaze and red flushed in the king's cheek, but he dodged the statement smoothly. "There's an ambassador coming from overseas. Will he bring news of the Wraith Queen?"

The seer closed her eyes. "Yes. You must build a strong alliance now."

"Peace with Anolyn is being negotiated. Even now—"

"A union is not negotiable." Her eyes flashed open and she looked to me. "You must come to accept this."

I ground my teeth to keep from replying and glanced to Castiel.

"If you choose to ignore my words, you'll pay the price. We all will."

"You've seen this?" Castiel asked. "And what is the price if we do not succeed?"

She shrugged. "I do not see everything. As you witnessed by the few who attended this evening, the arrival of this little princess will upset many."

The king looked at only the seer, avoiding all other gazes. "Precautions are being set in place as we speak.

"I will personally see to her protection," Castiel added.

"How?" I asked, shooting him a glare. Despite my efforts, hurt infused my words. "You'll be gone searching for a murderer."

"And will it be enough?" Melora asked. She traced one finger up her delicate arms, enjoying the touch of her younger skin. "It's interesting you didn't think it wise to council with me on the union of two great kingdoms. Have I grown so old and useless as to not merit consideration?"

Tension rang through the colossal room.

"Beware, young king. Don't let your pride, your fear, be your downfall."

Riaan raked his fingers through his hair, then plastered a smile to his face. The effort seemed almost painful.

"Will you council with me now?" He moved toward her to offer his arm. The seer took it with a dark twinkle in her young eyes.

18
REPLACEMENTS

THE MORNING WAS A BEAUTIFUL palette of dusty rose, gold, and lilac splashed against a cloud-speckled sky. Already fifty soldiers in full armor lined up on their horses behind Castiel, Captain Melia, Lieutenant Reese, and the seer.

There must be a union between our two kingdoms if we are to survive.

I tried to ignore the warning from the seer time and time again but failed miserably. While she didn't come out and say it, the implication was there.

This was why I had run away from my uncle in the first place, what I tried to escape: marriage to someone I did not nor could not love. I prayed Melia didn't read into her mother's words.

I rested my head gently against the cool glass of the window. Now that I had met the king of Anolyn, the thought was not so abhorrent as it had been only months ago, but it was not the king that drew my attention.

Castiel was an impressive sight atop his spirited steed. He was flanked by Melora, who now appeared to be about thirty and could pass as her daughter's sister instead of mother. How strange that must have been for a child to grow up with a being that could change her age to whatever she wanted. It was unnatural. Even creepy.

Melora matched Melia's severe mohawk braid and black officer's dress of leather and breeches, but while Melia was draped with all manner of weaponry, the seer sported only a single knife. Did she even need it? But the two looked terrifying seated next to each other.

And my heart longed to go with them instead of being trapped in the confines of my room. I imagined how I would look in my full combat gear, riding the front lines with Castiel at my side. Anyone who beheld us would quake and tremble in fear.

I smiled at the thought, but my mind quickly slipped back into reality and my shoulders sank.

After dinner we had been sent back to our rooms. Castiel left to see to Melora's needs. He didn't return to speak to me, and he didn't say goodbye. The neglect stung, but I knew it was foolish to be upset by such a small thing. I gripped the skirt of my morning gown, wrinkling the once smooth fabric.

I couldn't hide from my uncle, I couldn't outrun the brothers of Anolyn, and no one could escape the Wraith Queen. I pushed away from the windows to pace my room. *She* was the ultimate problem that had to be obliterated before I could be free.

But could I do what needed to be done? If I married the king, I would be forever away from my uncle. Riaan, while arrogant and scheming, was a good leader and good to his people. Could I unite with him to save my kingdom? To save his? Could I live as his wife, and sister-in-law to Castiel? Could I see the prince married to someone else in the near future?

Even as I thought it, my heart protested.

I spun on my heel and raced from my room. On the other side of the door, Mikael stepped in front of me. I barely managed not to collide into him. A second guard flanked him "Where do you think—?"

My words came almost too fast. "Either take me yourself or let me go on my own, but please, allow me see them off. I will return. You know I will."

He gave me a strange look, then motioned to the other guard. "Go with her."

I didn't wait to see if the guard followed but half-ran through the hallways of the castle. By the time I made it outside, Castiel had done his final inspection of his troops. I sprinted out into the open, not caring what spectacle I would create. The prince was not looking my direction, but Melia was. She cocked her head and nodded, saying something I couldn't hear over the rush of wind in my ears. Castiel twisted in his seat, surprise on his face. He guided his horse around, then leapt from his saddle.

Melora watched me from afar, her expression unreadable, but I didn't care. She could watch me all she wanted.

I slowed, suddenly self-conscious, my breathing heavy.

Castiel met me halfway. "What's the matter?" he asked, concern etched upon his handsome face. "What's wr—"

"Are we such enemies that you would leave without saying goodbye?" I asked, shocked by my own breathless words.

He flinched, then ran his fingers through his dark mane. "Of course we're not enemies."

"Then why not say goodbye?" I asked again.

The corner of his mouth flickered. He spoke low so as not to be overheard. "Ilianna, in my kingdom, if you plan on seeing the person again, if you *want* to see them again, you do not say goodbye. It's bad luck."

And for some odd reason, my heart felt as if it would break in two. "I didn't think you believed in bad luck."

One brow tipped high. "There are many things I believe now that I never did before."

My body froze as his thumb gently grazed the line of my jaw. I braced for my usual reaction, but his touch soothed instead of disturbed. "Practice your magic while I'm gone. There's a vial of Melora's potion on my desk in my room."

He glanced over my shoulder to the guard I had all but forgotten about. "Make sure she gets it."

"Yes, sir."

"I'll be back soon. Less than a week."

"You have three days," I said, my words clipped.

"Oh?"

"That should be more than enough for the renowned Prince of Anolyn."

He nodded. "Alright. Three days."

He dropped his hand and backed toward his horse. In one fluid movement he had regained his seat to turn his steed back toward his troops. He didn't say goodbye and he didn't look back. I watched as the band of soldiers rode through the courtyard gates until they disappeared into the surrounding countryside.

Someday, I would disappear too. As I thought it, a plan solidified in my mind, deadly but firm. I mechanically retraced my steps to my room, unseeing, uncaring.

Johan didn't want peace. That truth screamed from my soul. There was something else he wanted, but what that was, I didn't know. No matter the cost, I had to stop him.

I would not marry Riaan, and I would never go back to my uncle. I would kill Johan before ever returning to Eira.

I was unprepared the last time I had tried. The burn on my neck was proof. But I had acted rashly at the time. Now, I would train. I would train like I had never done before, and with the enemy of my uncle. With Riaan's men. Melia had already taught me so much. Castiel could teach me even more.

I would kill the king of Eira, and when the kingdom fell to me, I would hand it over to the king of Anolyn and his brother, Prince Castiel. They were good men, capable of uniting and leading two kingdoms into battle against an evil Queen and her demon horde. Perhaps I would stay to ensure victory, but when it was all over and the blood of battle leeched from the fields, I would finally flee this plagued continent.

This righteous awareness took hold upon me and solidified in my mind.

I barely heard the commotion until I was nearly at my door. Several guards moved about my room. My escort ran ahead and was immediately redirected by Mikael, who stood with three other guards I had never seen at the entrance. My steps faltered. "What's this?"

Mikael ignored me, scanning a parchment he held. "The furniture will obviously stay, but take whatever personal items our gracious king has gifted and bring it."

Sameen was at my armoire, helping guards to gather its contents.

"Wait." I hesitantly stepped inside. Fear laced my heart. "What's going on?" I asked. My uncle's face flashed into my mind. Had he arrived? Where was Reese and his comfort now?

"Forgive the intrusion," Mikael said with a partial bow, finally looking to me, "but there was a mistake with your room. Would you come with me, Princess Ilianna?"

I flinched upon him using my real name. Despite the king's earlier assertion, Princess Ilianna was an enemy in this kingdom. A suitable room would be in a cell with Cy the wraith. "But—" My voice scratched against a suddenly dry throat and I swallowed, trying to relocate my composure. "But I like it here. I'm fine with staying—"

"Your highness is very kind with pardoning such a horrific mistake, but I assure you, the king will not rest until you are comfortably situated in our guest quarters, nearer to him."

With a dramatic wave, he gestured for me to leave. The other guards were busy gathering my small collection of things, but they were paying close attention to everything I said. What other choice did I have?

I followed him as he guided me down the hallways to a part of the castle I had never been. "The celebration came early, I see. Is that why we're using my name so freely?"

"The king will announce you to the kingdom, but the guards and those that work closely with us have all been notified of the situation."

Again, *I* was a situation. "I see."

Two guards stood at attention outside a large door, watching as we neared. Their gaze slid to me. Coldness seeped from their expressions and I tipped my chin even higher. Mikael ignored them completely and produced a small keychain from his pocket. He unlatched the door and I followed him in.

Flowing, lilac-colored drapes had been pushed away from two large, open windows at the opposite side of the space. Dust masked as silver flecks of fairy light danced on a cool morning breeze. It smelled of freshly cut roses and soap, the evidence of such on a table in the corner of the room. A four-poster bed of ornately carved wood and wrought-iron dwarfed the rest of the space. Yards of cream-colored linens hung from the centermost part of the mast and swathed over each pedestal all the way to the ground. Blankets of white and creams, lace and silks, folded over the mattress with more pillows than one could ever need.

A decorative vanity table waited between the two grand windows, the top coated with an oversupply of feminine paraphernalia. A bathtub twice the size of the one

I had previously been using sat behind a tufted, cream and yellow privacy screen, with even more roses on a private table with soaps, lotions, and brushes.

It was one of the biggest, most beautiful rooms I had ever been in… and yet it only filled me with a sense of loneliness.

Mikael cleared his throat. "Sameen has been relieved of all other duties and will be your round-the-clock lady's maid until further notice. There will be a guard at your door at all times of the day." He smiled, though it was not friendly. "I have been given the honor of seeing over your security detail until the prince returns."

"That should be fun for you," I said, although I assumed he felt the sting of the task even more than I did.

"You will find every comfort you could possibly desire in this room. It's yours, but as of right now, the king requests your presence."

"Now?"

"As soon as you can be ready. Today, you will meet his guard." He moved to the armoire and opened it. On the inside panel waited a leather ensemble of black boots, breeches, and jerkin. It matched the uniforms worn by Castiel and Melia, but no weapons.

My shoulders drooped as again the desire to join them hit me. "But I've already met so many of them."

"As Lady Anna."

I sighed. "There's no difference."

"But there is. You're Princess Ilianna. *The Scourge of Men*. The dreaded daughter to the feared Prince Toma and the niece to the powerful King Johan. They must be allowed to see you as you truly are." He folded the parchment and left without further instructions.

I had no desire to inspect the room, or to see the other material delights encased within the boudoir. I was Princess Ilianna. I was cursed to be feared. To be hated. Which is why Riaan and his brother would be better suited to run my kingdom.

When Sameen arrived, she pulled my hair high and braided it down the center of my skull until it stopped at my waist. Mikael remained just outside the room, and together we left for the training yards. It was a familiar walk, and for a time, a comforting one. But it wasn't Melia that waited with a smile and a fight at the other end of the walk. It would be the king and a long line of men that probably hated me—me, my king, and my country. Not that I could blame them, especially with the rumor that I had killed Riaan and Castiel's father.

Everything had changed. The walls of the castle pushed against me, more heavily than any cell my uncle could put me in. With Castiel and Melia gone, I was nothing more than a murderer. The training room was eerily empty, the weapons put neatly away in their appropriate places. Our steps echoed against bare floors as we crossed the room to the exit. Mikael threw the doors wide.

The familiar smell of fresh hay, grass, and leather filled my senses but did little to soothe my nerves when faced with the sight of an army. My legs stopped on their own accord. Mikael moved into the line of warriors to stand at attention with his comrades.

"Just in time." I inhaled a sharp breath as King Riaan's voice came directly behind me. How had I not heard his approach? He circled to stand in front of me and bowed low, but his blue eyes never left mine. He wore black leather breeches, a white tunic, and a leather belt decorated with two ornately carved knives "You do us a great honor, Your Highness."

"What is this about?" I asked, scanning the full yard.

He peered over his shoulder to the line of soldiers and smiled. "The seer was adamant about this particular course of action, as well as many others." He cleared his throat. "And I, a humble servant, obeyed." He reached out with one arm and waited for me to take it, which I did. It was the first time I had ever touched the king of Anolyn. His muscles were hard beneath his tunic, and standing so close, he was even taller than I thought. A fine specimen for sure, but he paled in comparison to his brother.

My face blushed at the thought, and the king noticed.

His brows pinched together in artificial concern. "You seem flushed, Princess Ilianna. Are you well?"

"I am perfectly well, thank you, good king." I lowered my voice. "I assume they believe I killed your father?"

He leaned down to bring his mouth closer to my ear. I braced against the desire to bolt and froze when his breath caressed my cheek. "They have been properly enlightened. Don't worry."

I looked to the ground. "You're too kind, Your Majesty."

He guided me toward his audience but stopped several yards away. "Princess Ilianna of Eira, may I introduce you to the pride of the kingdom, the great men and women of Anolyn's army."

As if on cue, the squad of soldiers called in one great shout. The sound echoed on the expansive yard and rang through my ears. My heart rattled within my chest.

I scanned the line, my sight catching upon the king's assassin. She stood away from the rest in soldiers' garb, curves vanished beneath heavy leathers and exposed weapons. Her flexed arms crossed tightly, and her dark hair pulled back in an unflattering twist at the base of her neck. I ignored her and continued my inspection. In the sea of men, I only counted seven women. Whether there were more in the deployed troops I didn't know, but it seemed far fewer than Eira's. Something to improve upon, for sure.

I took a deep breath. This is what I was used to. My uncle had done this before every battle ever fought. I was a talisman, my uncle had said. Despite the anxiety that drew upon my breath, I fought my instinct to shut down.

"King Johan of Eira desires that we set down our weapons of war and has offered up his only niece in good faith as mediator to start negotiations. By my order, she is not to be harmed. You will treat her with respect and honor this peace."

He nodded to me and I responded.

"I am grateful for this opportunity," I said, my voice more timid than I wanted. I cleared my throat and spoke louder. "The uniting of our kingdoms is far overdue." And improbable, if my uncle had anything to do with it.

The king nodded. "As many of you already know, there are whispers of the dark power from overseas—that the time for the Wraith Queen's return is upon us. Now more than ever, we must set aside all differences as we once did and combine forces to combat this terror."

Response rippled through the ranks, though good or bad, I couldn't tell. Guilt rang within my chest. For the sake of these people, I hoped I was wrong and that my uncle truly did want peace. But it didn't matter. I would kill Johan, and the brothers would bring that peace no matter what.

"Princess Ilianna, do you think the Wraith Queen will tremble beneath the force of my army?"

I tipped my head higher and peered down the lines, knowing my answer. "They are impressive, indeed. But do they fight as good as they look? Will they be able to defend against the Wraith's demonic horde?"

The king smiled. "Only one way to find out."

With a signal, the warriors spanned open to create a great semi-circle. The shuffling of boots and crunch of dirt beneath a swell of militia increased my anticipation. Stage complete, two men stepped into the center. Both carried wooden training swords and a practice shield. They bowed to one-another, then they charged. A fantastic battle ensued. I was drawn in, mesmerized by the clash of their weapons and brute strength. The cheers of the surrounding soldiers sent a wave of nostalgia coursing through me. There was so much that separated our two countries, but this... this we had in common. The call of battle, the smell of blood, sweat, and dirt, the duty to king and country... they were the same in every land, and it was wonderful.

The battle came to an end. I matched the king's enthusiasm and cheered for the victor. Several battles followed, each more intense than the one before. It was a brilliant display, and I was eager for more. An easy hour passed before a break in the exercise.

"What do you think, Princess Ilianna?" the king asked with a wave of his hand.

I nodded with a lift of my brows. "These men are expertly trained. A remarkable show of talent and skill. Did you train them yourself, Your Majesty?"

He walked the semi-circle of soldiers. "There was a time when I did, when I shared the barracks with my fellow soldiers, drank and ate from their tables, fought side by side... but my time is now spent elsewhere."

I nodded, turning a circle. "It's to be expected. A king cannot always remain on top, and the older you get, the more your champions will lead your great army."

A hint of a smile tugged at the corner of his lips. "Are you challenging the king, Princess?" Riaan asked. Whispers between soldiers grew as they sized me up against their leader.

I covered my heart with a hand. "I? I am only a girl, far from your equal in battle, but rumors of *your* greatness spread even through Eira. But perhaps others would be afraid to win against their king out of fear of punishment."

That got a few whispers and more laughs as I played to the crowd.

Even Riaan chuckled. "But how can I back down to such a challenge?" He turned to his warriors, his arms uplifted. "One hundred gold pieces and an upgrade in rank to the individual cunning enough to defeat me." Another murmur rippled through the crowd, but still no one stepped forward. He spoke louder. "Do not be afraid, my brothers and sisters. I have always cheered your progress."

Finally, a soldier moved into the ring. The size of Reese, the volunteer stretched his large arms. His eyes held a cunning to them that worried me for the sake of Riaan. "I accept your challenge."

19
A King's Challenge

Again, the king smiled. Suddenly, he whipped off his shirt and snatched a weapon from the nearest rack.

I tried to avoid admiring at the way his muscles rippled with every smooth move the king deployed, but I failed. The heavy clunk of the practice swords beat along with my heart, faster and faster with every strike. I watched in awe Riaan's precision and grace in motion. He saw every move and found every open weakness. Before the battle could really begin, it was over.

Another opponent leaped into the ring, and then another. Five challengers in all—including one woman. Each wielded a different weapon. A sword, a knife, a staff, an ax. He dispatched them all. The fifth and final match was arm-to-arm combat.

The new soldier was several inches shorter than Riaan, and even more skinny, but something told me not to underestimate him. Faster than the lash of a whip, the competitor lunged, landing a punch to the king's jaw.

Riaan barely moved in time to block a second hit, but then he had the man's arm in a lock, twisting it up and behind his back. The man countered with a solid elbow. Riaan stumbled toward the line of soldiers, freezing everyone in their place. Blood leaked from a split in the king's lip. And he grinned.

Riaan tore forward.

The man leaped back, but he wasn't quick enough. The king landed a solid uppercut that sent him flying. He rolled, barely making his feet in time for Riaan's next attack. The battle lasted twice the length of the others, but still ended the same. The soldier fell to the hard ground on his back, his wrist still in the king's masterful grip. The man tapped the dirt to show his defeat.

The crowd roared their approval of their king. Riaan raised his hands high above his head, the sweat of battle glistening from every pore. Blood had dried on his lip and chin, but the king didn't seem to notice—or maybe it was his trophy. I almost laughed at his proud display.

Riaan turned, his hands upon his hips to watch my response to his victory. One brow raised.

I laughed and then clapped my approval. "Truly, you are amazing."

"And what about you, Princess Ilianna?" Mikael's voice rang out above the rest, effectively silencing everyone. He walked through the crowd of men, his sight trained on me. "Maybe you cannot stand against the king of Anolyn, but what about a lowly soldier?"

I lifted my hand to the others. "I see nothing lowly about these warriors. I'm honored to witness such a display."

"Pretty words, pretty words, Princess. But come now..." Mikael stepped into the ring. "Friends, we have the *Scourge of Men* here, right in our very own training yard. Surely, she has some techniques she could show us. Some new moves known only to Eira."

Both cheers and scoffs erupted, and my heart nearly exploded. The sneer on Mikael's lips spoke volumes. This would be no friendly competition, but I had no choice. The king now lounged on the ground, leaning languidly upon his hands, completely unconcerned by the hostility oozing from his personal guard. He tipped his head to nod his acceptance.

Adrenaline raced through my veins. "Very well."

Mikael pulled off his shirt, stretching a barrel-chest and arms bigger than my waist.

First the king, and now his guard. Was it an intimidation tactic to take off one's clothes before a fight? Whether to intimidate me or annoy, it worked both ways.

His tattoos danced to his movements. I couldn't help but stare at the artwork, which looked almost alive. A sea of black ink moved to his muscular rhythm. Dark ocean waves beat upon two magnificent and detailed ships, both with swarthy captains at their helms. An angry falcry decorated one corner of his shoulder and chest; its feathers stretched down his arm, coming just past his wrist. A mermaid adorned the other. Beneath the ships, just at the navel, the artist of this oceanic scene had inked a whale that disappeared beyond the line of his breeches.

Was he once part of the king's navy?

"There's a lot more to me than what you see, Princess." Mikael's voice cut in to my thoughts, and I flinched.

One corner of his mouth tipped high as he regarded me. I wasn't sure what he meant, but I was sure I didn't want to know.

My legs shook as I walked, but I refused to allow anyone to see the anxiety dripping from my very soul. Even though out of practice, I had done this hundreds of times before. Melia had allowed me to train, but never with weapons—wooden or otherwise. I focused on the rack of practice swords and chose one good for my smaller frame.

The stick was light, the grip a nice fit. The weight was easy enough for me to manage in one hand. I twirled it once, and again, maneuvering it to get the feel. I stroked its dulled blade; its sanded edge soothed. I breathed in the scent of it, of the yard, and closed my eyes.

Someone cleared his throat behind me, impatient for battle, but I ignored him. The sword felt alive in my grasp—

Suddenly, I recognized something else, something I had never felt before because I didn't know how until Castiel and Melora's potion. Although the awareness was not as strong without the elixir, I could sense the connection to my sword. I spun it around, again swinging it in my grip. I tested its balance. Through my touch the weapon's energy coursed within me, strange and invigorating. A tingling sensation traveled down the length of my arm.

Had I always been able to do it before, or had Melora's potion woken the power inside me? Confidence pulsed. "Shall we wager on this fight?" I asked, my back to him.

Mikael grunted. "Gambling is for the weak who trust luck instead of skill."

I rolled my eyes and faced him. "Are you always such a bore?"

He spun, yielding a powerful strike with his weapon. It clanked against mine, reverberating painfully up my arm. And I smiled. My answering parry had him stumbling back.

Noise erupted as soldiers called out to their leader. Energy vibrated through the room, alive, warm, and familiar. I twirled my wrist, spinning my sword in a fluid circle. My joints were stiff, but this was my calling. This was what I was good at. The crowd pulsed with both excitement and trepidation. Mikael walked the circle, working his muscles. He rotated his sword deftly in a figure-eight, then attacked again.

His strength was impressive, but he was not fast. His muscles impeded agility. I deflected his next heavy blow in time and kicked away, planting my foot in his gut but its effect worked against me and I stumbled backward. Already, weakness threatened the joints in my knees. I barely managed to keep my feet before he attacked again. An upward block deflected his next strike—but I would not be able to match him for long. I had to work fast.

I leaped back, distancing myself from his offensive reach. Blood and energy surged into the palms of my hands, warming stiff arms. Shifting back, I drew my sword in tight and stacked one fist atop the next.

On his next attempt I lunged forward and dropped to my knee, ducking beneath his heavy swing. I spun, lifting my sword, and the blade sliced behind his knee.

He roared at the point loss and paced away to glare at me.

I was in trouble. This was more than a simple competition. It was there in his eyes, but there was nothing to do about it. Siana had moved to her king's side to whisper something in his ear. They watched unaware of the threat in Mikael's gaze.

Mikael ran at me and dropped a downward blow so powerful it worked against him. Energy coursed through me, connecting me to my weapon. I twisted my wrist, rotating the blade around his to glide up his sword. I sliced beneath his armpit, then whirled fast, swiping at his middle.

I had won.

Riaan stood and clapped his congratulations, but there was no approval in his eyes. From my periphery, I spied Generals Vega and Dag as they crossed the yard, their expressions blank.

The soldiers groaned, but others laughed and even cheered for my victory.

Mikael tossed his wood sword to the front-line soldiers and pulled a knife from the sheath at his side. Sunlight reflected upon the sharpened metal. I backed away and glanced at Riaan. General Vega was at his side to whisper something in his ear, momentarily distracting him.

And Mikael took that advantage. With a covert jerk of his head, the soldiers finished the circle, effectively blocking the view. I doubted the king would notice. In fact, I was sure the generals were in on this little scheme.

My pulse quickened as my heart raced near out of control. I eyed the steel in his hand. "What are you doing?"

His face was hard as stone. "Showing everyone just exactly who you are."

OF BLOOD AND DECEIT 263

"And what's that?" I asked.

"An enemy."

The muscles beneath my eye twitched. "And if I refuse?"

He huffed a laugh. "I'm not giving you that choice."

"You're a fool." I spat, then held my arms out wide. "Would you attack someone unarmed?"

He blindly reached with one hand and a soldier slapped a dagger into his waiting palm. With the flick of Mikael's wrist, the blade impaled the dirt in front of me.

I lowered to pick it up but kept him in my sight. "Very well. Best hurry it up before the king realizes what's going on."

We circled each other. Every step deliberate. Steady. Contempt painted Mikael's face a violent shade of red. This was personal to him. He needed to prove a point. What that was I didn't know, but *that* would be his number one weakness.

The soldiers crowded closer together, sending a wave of claustrophobia over me, nearly dousing my courage, but I shifted my step and crouched low.

No one cheered as Mikael lunged.

I stepped sideways to deflect his attack with a downward swipe. He jumped back as I advanced, then spun into me, his fist colliding with the side of my head.

I fell to the dirt, hard. My mind whirled with the impact, but I quickly rolled from the ground and sprang to my feet.

He was too strong.

I changed my focus. On his next attack, I ducked in close, blocking his wrist with my guard arm and hit his hand with the butt off my blade. The knife knocked from his grasp and thudded to the earth. With all my leftover strength, I shot upward with a hard uppercut to his chin. A satisfying crack sounded, but that satisfaction didn't last long before I was blasted away by a heavy frontal kick.

Sparks invaded my vision as I flew to the ground. My breath whooshed from my lungs.

The assassin was suddenly there in front of me, crouching low to better see me. "Get up," she said, as if I had forgotten what I needed to do.

I gave her a look. Pain racked my body, but I managed to twist away to avoid getting stomped by his massive boot. I shot up, dizzy and weak and empty-handed. I scanned the ground to find my weapon yards from me. When had I dropped it?

The giant charged.

"Excellent match." Riaan appeared in front of me, a smile on his face.

A scuffle of dirt sounded beyond him as Mikael desperately shuffled to avoid plowing into the king. Siana stepped in front of him, glaring the captain down—and the giant visibly shrank.

The knives miraculously disappeared from the ground, and the crowd disappeared even faster. I looked to the king, but his expression betrayed nothing. How much had he witnessed?

I wiped blood that flowed from a split on the side of my cheek and nodded to Mikael. "A worthy opponent, for sure." The words worked upon a tense jaw. I reached out a hand to him. He considered it a moment before he seized it, pulling a little harder than needed, then walked away with his comrades.

Riaan took me by the elbow to guide me away and into the castle. "Well done, Princess. A fantastic display of fierce technique."

My answer was flat, emotionless. "It's been an honor, Your Majesty. Now if you wouldn't mind—"

"—you wish to rest before dinner. Of course. Come with me." His steps were quick as we moved inside to the training room, then beyond. I blindly allowed him to lead, not caring that Siana probably followed behind as security. My mind was abuzz with thoughts too muddled to make sense of them. I barely registered the king's next words. "I will not be able to join you this evening. I hope you don't mind."

"Oh." I clasped my hands together. "Of course not. And in that case, I'll eat in my room."

He nodded. "Perfect. I'll tell Mikael."

My breath hitched, but not out of fear. "Your Majesty—"

"You may call me Riaan."

My head jerked back. "Oh? Alright. Riaan, I don't think Captain Mikael is quite with you and this plan of yours."

His response was automatic. "Mikael is loyal to me. I'm sure he had his reasons for this display, and I'll trust them."

I nodded. So he *did* see the scuffle.

"You did very well, going along with his little scheme. If anything, he helped prove you are *not* our enemy."

Anger caused the cut on my cheek to throb, but I clamped my mouth shut. I very much doubted that was

Mikael's reason for doing what he did, but the king wouldn't believe me over his personal guard. I would need to steer clear of the captain as much as I could.

Riaan cleared his throat. "Tomorrow, I ride with my men to the eastern borders toward Varian. Will you join me?"

I answered automatically. "Is that an order?"

"Of course not, Ilianna. You're welcome to stay here with Mikael as your—"

"I'll join you," I said, then seethed when Riaan smiled.

Only a single security guard stood outside my door. I could hear Sameen working inside, no doubt moving things around to better suit her duties.

The king stopped short. His mouth opened as if to say something. He reached his index finger to gently graze the skin beneath the cut on my cheek.

Reflexively, I brushed aside his touch.

He dropped his hand. "You should have Gedeon take care of that." Before I could respond, he moved away. Siana watched me, a curious glint to her onyx eyes, but then she spun around to follow her king.

My breath left in a whoosh. A mixture of confusion and worry battled within.

He did not love me. He did not trust me. But Melora had found a way to coax him into pursuing me, that much was clear, and I needed to put a stop to it.

I nodded, agreeing to my own conclusion. On our ride the next morning, I would tell him.

My room now smelled of new perfumes overlaid upon the scents of soap and roses. Sameen peeked beyond the privacy screen, instantaneously eyeing my injury, but I put up my hand to stop the scold I knew was coming.

"You don't need to call for Gedeon. Leave the poor man alone."

She folded her arms. "And what would Castiel say?"

"Castiel's not here." As if she had to remind me. "But the king is, and when I go for a ride with him tomorrow, I want those that watch me to see it."

"But why?"

I needed Mikael and anyone else that shared his same feelings to know I could stand up to a bully. But I didn't answer her.

Sameen sighed and opened the armoire. She drew out a deep burgundy riding dress.

"No," I said. "I'll need something more suitable for riding. I'll wear this again." I sat down on my cream bed. The mattress sunk low and inviting.

"But the king—"

"The king will be traveling near the forest. If it's as haunted as rumors speculate, I doubt he would want me defenseless. I am the Princess of Eira, an enemy to many of your countrymen until now. I would be foolish to go unprotected." I crossed my leg over my knee and tried to untie my boots, but my fingers shook, my body still coming down from the high of battle. I clenched my hand.

My lady's maid gathered a brush from the new vanity table. Next to the mirror sat the vial of Melora's potion the guard had retrieved for me. I eyed it warily, but Sameen didn't seem to notice.

"They won't always see you as such, Ilianna. It only took me a moment to realize you were not who the stories claimed."

"I was, though." Giving up on the strings, I grunted as I endeavored to pull them off using sheer force. "Maybe I've changed, but we can't expect everyone to be as clear-minded—or insane—as you." Still the shoes wouldn't budge.

She laughed, then knocked my hands away. "Who took care of you before I came along? You act as if you've never had a lady's maid."

I leaned back as she made quick work of the laces. "I did. Sort of. Her name was Pala."

Sameen glanced up. "Did she not take care of you?"

I shrugged. "My uncle never allowed me to believe I was anything but a bastard."

"But you are a prince's daughter. You are *royalty*."

I fingered the burn at my neck. Only the memory stung now. *"Barely."*

Her eyes flashed to mine. "You *are* royalty, and to treat—"

"It is what it is," I interrupted. "I cannot begin to understand the things that flow through my uncle's brain. If I tried to wade through that abyss, I would never resurface."

She nodded solemnly, as if she understood my convoluted statement. "Then, what was Pala like?"

"Scheming."

"What?" Disbelief crossed over her features before she schooled the emotion.

"She didn't so much take care of me; rather, she reported on me."

Sameen stood to help me remove my jerkin. "Reported what?"

I stretched my sore feet. "Who I spoke to. Who spoke to me. What I studied. What I read. What I did that day. Who I trained with. What I ate. When I bled."

"Excuse me?"

I nodded. "Everything."

She visibly trembled. "What on earth would your uncle want with all of that?"

"Information is control. The more you know, the more power you have over them, or so he says."

Sameen watched me as she processed my statement. "I guess he isn't wrong, but—"

"I know." I closed my eyes, letting my worries melt from me like snow on a hot summer's day. I was no longer under his so-called protection. No longer a slave to his whims. I was safe for the time being.

After my bath, Sameen kept me company for the remainder of the day. She grimaced when I took Melora's potion. I needed enough to last the rest of the day, but it wasn't as if there were instructions on the bottle. After two small swallows, I sat on the floor and waited.

The reaction didn't take long.

Sameen's aura was a shimmery lilac. She watched me work my magic—or lack thereof—and cheered my pathetic progress. In truth, I didn't feel much like training, but I had told Castiel I would. At first it was slow going, but then I was a child learning to play with a new toy. It was fun in its own way. I practiced picking up small things about the room and sending them cascading to the opposite wall. Sameen would gather them and bring them back for me to do it again.

I should have tried to do more but going out to the forest with my lady's maid to strip trees bare of leaves was probably not an option right now, and without further guidance, I really couldn't do much.

After several hours, the sun was behind the horizon. Dinner had come and gone. Sameen dressed me in my nightgown, almost as exhausted as I was. She wilted in the chair before the fire, her eyes scarcely open. Mine blurred to the dim light of the room. The flames in the hearth were nearly out. Not wanting to disturb her, I crawled on hands and knees to retrieve a thrown brush, but as I did, my slippery awareness connected to its energy and pulled it toward me. It slid across the floor, scraping over the stone.

I flinched to the feel of the handle in my grasp, then stood to replace it on the vanity table.

The potion's effects swept a sweet sense of delirium over me, lulling me to sleep. I creeped beneath my sheets to sprawl in the center of my bed.

An image of Castiel's face met me in my instant dreams, and I smiled. I would have to show the prince my new parlor trick when he returned.

20

TAKEN

A SHARP PAIN STABBED MY NECK.

The jolt woke me from sleep, but blackness coated my vision. Alarm shot through me as I kicked and flailed against restraints I couldn't identify.

Something clamped down on my mouth, nearly suffocating me. An acrid scent invaded my nostrils. I shut down my breath and grabbed at my restraints—ice-cold and hard as steel, but nevertheless, a hand. I wrenched back on a thumb and my captor grunted.

My fingers pulled at the material covering my eyes, but it didn't help.

A shadowed figure stood above me, more wraith-like than flesh and blood. My head spun, reacting to the injection. I had seconds.

The thing shoved the pillow into my face again, but I grasped at their arms and clawed through their black shrouds until I found skin.

Not a wraith.

Nails dug into flesh. Power and fear infused me, and I sent the intruder flying back. He smacked into the wall with a thud then slid to the ground.

Not knowing what I was doing, I clapped my hand to my neck and willed my powers to pull the poison from my bloodstream. The skin beneath my touch grew hot and wet.

A muffled curse caught my attention, but before I could roll from my bed, a gloved hand seized me by the wrists. He slid a dagger to my neck, and I froze. From beneath his black cloak, a tattoo peeked from the cuff of his sleeve.

Feathers of a falcry.

In my fading lucidity, an idea formed. Before I slipped into oblivion, I grabbed the knife by the blade. It sliced into my skin. I smiled at the pain as the darkness overtook me.

ᴈᴑᴆ

This time it was different. Had my powers drawn the potion from my bloodstream, or was it just my anger that kept me from passing into pure oblivion?

Either way, I was grateful. And annoyed.

I passed in and out of consciousness for hours, days, weeks. I wasn't sure. My body rattled along with my bones until I felt reduced to powder, before finally succumbing to the numbness.

A groan escaped my lips, unbidden. Then another prick in the neck…

❧❦

My body crumpled, boneless, to the ground. The smell of earth and pine entered my lungs as dirt and brush scratched against my face. A cold breeze tickled the back of my exposed neck. I still wore a nightgown. In a deep fog, I waded with my thoughts, my mind working faster than my body. Voices whispered from all around. I searched for their source without success, but my eyes wouldn't open.

I didn't want to be here. I wasn't *supposed* to be here. Someone had taken me from Meyrion, from the only place I'd ever felt at home. Moisture stung my eyes. I shoved my emotions back to the pit they came from and forced myself to remain calm.

I breathed through the frustration. I didn't want to draw attention, and I most definitely didn't want another dose of whatever medication they gave me. The drug had to be from the healer—a heavier concentration and longer lasting than before—but whether Gedeon was a willing participant in my capture I wasn't sure. My soul rebelled against the idea. What reason could he have for wanting me gone?

But what reason did Mikael have for wanting me gone? His involvement was very easy to believe. He had never liked me. I was an enemy. But to go contrary to the orders of his king? That was tad too treasonous for the trustworthy captain. His motives had to be good enough for the guard to go against crown and country.

Or had Riaan lied?

The last time Castiel turned his back, his royal brother bound my wrists for an informal interrogation. Now he sent the prince away to search for a murderer killing in my name.

Could that be a coincidence?

A fly buzzed in my ear, and I barely managed to not flinch. I dared to crack my eyes, but my blurred vision stopped me from seeing where I was. The voices grew louder, then a nearby door squeaked. Footsteps crunched against a rock-strewn forest floor. Warm fingers probed the temperature of my forehead.

"Are you sure that stuff will wear off soon?" Lucan's voice, deep and harsh, came from a distance. Despite my pretending, my body stiffened.

Boots ground against the dirt. "The guard said no more than a day."

If my body was able, I would have rolled from Weylan's touch. Two of the three men I most hated stood over my should-be-unconscious form. Blood pounded in my veins fiery hot, burning the residual side effects of the healer's potion.

"We're running out of time," Lucan said, "and this place gives me the creeps. We need to leave, soon."

"It's getting late. We shouldn't be traveling in the forest at night."

A scoff cut through the air. "Don't tell me you're scared, Weylan. You know those tales are meant to frighten little children, don't you?"

Weylan's response was clipped. "I'm not afraid, but I'm also not a fool. And what about the farmer? Oscove helped us get her here. Without him—"

"Well, the freakshow's disappeared, hasn't he?"

"*Well,* she'll be easier to transport if she can ride. You can't just keep drugging her."

My uncle's spy laughed. "You expect her to come willingly?"

"Once she hears the alternative, she won't fight. It won't be long before she's awake. I'll get her some water."

Lucan was the one that grunted now. "Fine. I'll go look for the lunatic. But with or without him, we leave in one hour. They'll be coming for her."

His footsteps trailed away, leaving me alone with Weylan. I listened to his movements, trying to formulate some kind of plan. The further away I got from Anolyn, the harder it would be to get back. But is that what I really wanted? I had no idea how far we'd come and how deep we were into the forest.

"You can stop pretending you sleep, Ilianna," Weylan said, his voice close to my ears. "And don't worry. Lucan's gone."

My eyes cracked open. They burned from dryness, but they cleared quickly as I blinked away the haze.

"Though I can understand why you'd pretend to be dead in front of that maniac." Weylan grabbed me by the shoulders and lifted me to lean me against a tree. At his touch, anxiety hit with alarming force. He squatted in front of me, jaw clenched as he peered through familiar green eyes.

He lifted his hand to brush aside a rogue strand of hair, but I jerked away from his touch.

"I don't fear Lucan as much as I fear you." The words barely sounded human, but they were true, nonetheless. I coughed against the dryness of my throat.

"How can you say that?" Hurt infused his voice, but it did nothing to affect me.

"Easily. His motives are open for me to see and know. You lie. You deceive, and you're very good at it." How had I ever found him attractive?

"You don't understand." He closed his eyes and took a deep breath.

But I didn't care to understand. "Sameen?"

His eyes flashed open, confused by my sudden change of topic. "Who?"

"My lady's maid. She was in the room with me. Did you hurt her?"

He made a face. "Of course not. She was tranquilized as well. She won't remember a thing."

"And are you going to hurt me again?" I asked.

"Are you going to come with me willingly?"

"Go to hell." I tried to spit, but I had no saliva.

He lifted a brow but worry wore in his expression. "I'd go there and back again if it meant you'd hear me out."

I scanned my surroundings. A few yards away there was a dilapidated shack. I nodded to it. "Oscove's?"

He only hummed in the affirmative.

My gaze narrowed, and I tried to roll my neck to the side. The memory blurred in my mind. "That was the man who brought his dead brother to the castle, wasn't it?"

"The very one."

The farmer's home was small with stone and mud walls and a thatched roof in need of repair. The fences that separated field from farm tipped haphazardly to one side or the other. There were no animals in the stalls, and whatever crops were long since dead.

I lifted my hands to find them tied together with a crude rope, one palm wrapped with gauze. Exposing my binds, I glared at him. "What do you want, Weylan?"

It could have been a trick of the healer's concoction, but concern brimmed in the surface of his eyes. "I've made a bargain with Lucan to help get you out of Anolyn."

"And what makes you think I wanted to leave? I've made bargains too, you know."

"The people of Anolyn are not your people. Anolyn is not your kingdom. Castiel is not your prince."

At the mention of his name, my face heated.

Weylan glanced away. "And I don't like the way he looks at you."

I shifted. "What are you talking about?"

"He watches you too closely."

A scoff cut through my forced calm. "I am an enemy and a traitor. Of course he watches me closely. And I know these aren't my people. I'm not an idiot."

He smiled as if I were. "These people would hang you the instant they learn who you are."

A weight sat in the pit of my stomach. He was right.

"Listen, Ilianna. Lucan wants to take you back to your uncle."

I smiled, exposing my teeth. "I'd sooner die—"

"I know. I have no intention of taking you to him. You'd never be safe from him." His eyes trailed to the burn on my neck.

I covered it with my hair. "Then where? Your resistance?"

He stood to pace the forest floor. He glided his hand over his tightly trimmed hair.

I blinked, trying to force my vision. "How did you get me out?"

"We have our ways."

My palm tingled at the memory of Mikael's blade against my skin, and I almost smiled. "Mikael was more than happy to help you, I gather."

A smirk twisted his features. "You're very clever. I've always thought that. Well, we couldn't have done it without insider help, and then there was Oscove. Did you know he was once a soldier?"

"Of course." I remembered the markings on the farmer's hands. He may have changed occupations, but there were some things a person couldn't erase.

"He knew Meyrion's layout." He shifted closer. "Can you move?"

"Help me stand," I said.

He did as I asked, steadying me when I swayed. I looked down to see someone had put my boots on for me. Lucan wouldn't have cared if I froze. I ignored the bothersome thought of Weylan touching my bare feet and legs.

"If you have no intention of letting me go with Lucan, just what do you expect to happen when he returns?"

Weylan grinned. "I don't expect him to return."

Boots rustled in the distance. A dozen men rushed into the vicinity. I stepped wide and crouched low, readying for an attack, but the men merely stopped in front of Weylan and saluted. They wore the clothes of commoners from Anolyn, but their paler skin screamed Eira.

"Report," Weylan commanded.

One man glanced to me, then answered. "They are circling him as we speak."

"And their orders?"

"Kill on sight."

Weylan clapped his hands. "Excellent. Gather any supplies you find here. We'll assemble with the others at the next checkpoint."

My heart raced. I needed to think fast. To get away. "You're very sure of yourself," I said, turning to face him. "Do they know who they're up against?"

Weylan pished. "Of course."

"Do you?"

The wrinkles between his brows made him appear older than he was. "Even the feared assassin Lucan Osrick can't defeat against twelve of my best soldiers."

He moved to the side of the shack where a horse was tied to a fence post, and I followed. "The way you spoke to the king of Anolyn made it sound as if these resistors of yours couldn't lift a sword."

He shook his head, giving me a look that warned me to hold my tongue. He didn't know me well enough if he thought that would work.

"Lucan is Johan's assassin," I reminded him.

"He's just a man," Weylan said in a whisper. He stepped in closer. "And I may have made our plight a little needier than the truth, but if I had been able to convince the king to help, it would've made a takeover all that easier. No thanks to you."

"Do you expect me to feel bad? To help?"

"You should want to help. Your uncle did everything in his power to keep you under his thumb, and yet you fight against the ones that could free you?"

"You free me by taking me captive?" Again, I held up my tied wrists and the fresh wound for him to see.

He lifted his hand as if to take mine, but I pulled away before he could touch me. He hesitated. "Listen, Ilianna. There's—" He pulled his fingers through his hair. "There's more to it than what I'm saying, but I can't tell you more until we're safe." He cut a line to the farmer's hut. As he got to the door, a man on a horse galloped into the clearing.

His face red, the soldier leaped from the animal. "He's gone, General."

Weylan balked. "What do you mean?"

"The assassin. He's—"

But his voice broke, then gargled to a stop. The point of an arrow protruded from his neck, cutting off his remaining words.

I jerked back, nearly falling over in my retreat.

The man fell to his knees, grasping for the arrow. Weylan moved. He seized my arm and twisted, catapulting me through the door of the shack. I painfully rolled over the dirt floor and knocked over a small wooden table that collapsed on me. I groaned, turning over on my back. Papers fell to the ground in a flurry, but the room was covered with them. Drawings. Dozens of them, pinned to the walls and fallen to the ground.

"Stay down," Weylan ordered from outside. Did he forget I was still tied?

"I'm a sitting duck in here," I said through clenched teeth, but he was already gone. I scrambled to my knees, searching for a better place to hide, barely registering the sad state of the cottage, and spied a darkened corner. A tub, small but cast-iron, hid there.

I crammed myself behind it and fingered the edges until I found what I was looking for. A rusted shard of metal protruded from the edge. I moved my bound hands to saw though the bands. A paper floated down from the wall to land inside the tub, and I froze.

The picture was a charcoal sketch, so familiar to me… Because it *was* me.

And I had seen one like it before. The sketch the prince showed me on the day of my release from prison. Castiel had said it was sketched by someone that had seen my face and lived to tell the tale. A soldier named Nolen Odessa. Nolen's body had been brought to the castle by the farmer, Oscove.

My gaze traveled the walls. They were covered with sketches. Some charcoal, other's blood. Some crude and angry, but others beautiful portraits, so like my own face without the flare and prompt of the Demon Daughter. How could this man have known me so well?

They were all the same… except for one.

I crawled to the space on the wall where a drawing stood in stark contrast to the others, and I plucked it from its place.

A picture of me, holding a ruby-sweet. No flames. No Demon Daughter.

I dropped the picture.

The body of Nolen had been brought to the king *before* we went to the first harvest. The artist—Nolen, wasn't dead. Oscove *was* Nolen.

Lucan's voice rang over the din of battle outside. He had brought with him his own army.

I cursed, but the words froze on stiff lips when someone appeared in the small room next to me. I stumbled back into the stick wall of the shack.

Cyris the wraith watched me, a curious glint in his eyes. "Why does the Demon Daughter cower?"

"The Demon Daughter sleeps, and I'm not cowering. I was thrown in here." I displayed my bound hands.

One brow quirked up. "And those stop you from fighting? Curious. No wonder he worries for you. Help is on the way." Then he disappeared.

"Cy—"

But at that moment Lucan and three other men blasted into the room, blades drawn. Red covered Lucan's hands and shirt, but the blood wasn't his.

He smiled. "Hello, Princess."

I shot to my feet but crouched low, readying for attack.

Lucan nodded to the others. They spanned out, blocking all escapes. "Why don't you come with me?"

I glared. "I'd rather not."

He twirled his knife and sheathed it. "I'd hoped you wouldn't be willing." Dropping low, he moved forward with lethal grace.

I had no weapon. No way to escape. The wraith's words grated on me.

And those stop you from fighting?

Fists clenched, I shifted into a defensive stance Melia had taught me and waited for their attack.

A sound pierced the air and traveled painfully along my spine. A second later, the roof was ripped away by talons that raked across a soldier, instantly killing him. The other men dropped to the ground shielding their faces. I scuttled to the wall as Ketrina soared away with a bone-chilling cry. The shack never stood a chance against the strength of the falcry. The roof tumbled to the ground in a dusty heap.

Without looking back, I leaped over their prone forms and tumbled out the door. The soldiers had stopped fighting, shock etched upon their faces. They seemed frozen in place by the witness of the mythological bird and the collapsed building, but my sudden appearance snapped them back into focus. The battle recommenced. I scanned the darkening sky for Ketrina, but she was gone. The sun hung low, dulling the effect of carnage that surrounded me.

A soldier ran at me, and I twisted, landing a solid kick to his stomach. When he doubled over, I came down on the back of his neck with my bound fists. He crumpled to the ground.

An arm seized me around the shoulders. Another snaked and tightened against my neck, cutting off my airway. Weylan dragged me toward his horse as I kicked and flailed beneath his strength.

Could I use my magic? I grabbed for him, but my bound hands couldn't make a solid grasp. He twisted me hard and picked me up, flinging me over his shoulder, which slammed into my solar plexus. My breath knocked from my lungs and sparks of light sliced through my vision. In a last-ditch effort, I flung my body hard. It was enough to loosen his grasp. I fell to the ground on my side, slicing my arm on a jagged rock. I reeled for air.

Weylan was on me a second later. My head pulled back as he yanked me by my hair. He slid his blade beneath my neck. his voice rough against my ear. "You'll come with me, Ilianna, or I swear I'll kill the prince and your friend... what's her name? Melia? I'll slaughter them both."

And there he was, the Weylan I knew so well. I closed my eyes and stopped struggling, recognizing the promise in his words.

"That's my girl. Now—"

"You weren't going to leave without me, were you?" Lucan's voice cut through the tension like a knife.

Weylan glared at me, a warning in his eyes, and stood. He faced Lucan. "Was thinking about it." His lips twitched at the corners. "You know Johan's rule is coming to an end. It's only a matter of time before he's overthrown."

Lucan laughed, slowly moving through the trees, inching closer. Blood leaked from a split on his forehead. "And who's going to replace him? His bastard of a niece?"

My jaw set and I rolled to my knees. "I don't want anyone's throne. I don't want any of it. I'm not a pawn."

My uncle's assassin scowled at me. "Haven't you figured it out yet, fool? That's all that you are. To anyone. No one cares about Ilianna Drakara. No one ever has."

I tried not to let his words affect me, tried not to hear the truth in them, but failed.

My voice came as a whisper. "Just go. Both of you. Leave me alone."

Someone called out to Lucan. The handful of soldiers remaining had finished off the rest of Weylan's men. They crept forward to close the trap.

Lucan smiled. "As you can see, that's not going to happen, Princess. You're coming with me."

"I don't think so," Weylan contradicted. He crouched low, his knife at the ready.

"No one is going to take her," another voice said, but not one I had expected. Oscove—or rather, Nolen—came out from behind a tree, a crossbow in his hands. He aimed it at Lucan, then Weylan, but seemed to think twice and aimed it at Lucan again. Lucan's men stopped their advance.

He beckoned me to him with frantic gestures, but I stayed in place.

"What are you doing?" Weylan asked, raising his hands high.

"I didn't help get her out of the castle so she could be your slave." Nolen adjusted his target. "I did it to set the Demon Daughter free. That's her destiny. To be free."

"Is it really?" Now Cyris joined the group, his hand shoved deep into his pockets. "What an interesting situation you've gotten yourself into, Ilianna."

Nolen eyed the stranger tentatively; the others didn't seem to recognize his presence at all.

My brows pinched together, but I ignored the demon. "Nolen, you need to leave," I said, even though my heart twisted in disagreement. I rose from my knees. "Go."

"It's been so long since I've seen you. I—I've searched for you for so long." He spoke to me, but his eyes scanned the line of men, his movements erratic. "When I found you at the castle, I thought you would recognize me. I hoped—but how could you?" He laughed, a tear falling from one eye. "I'm not the same anymore. I tried to get your attention so you would come for me."

"My attention? How—" My heart dropped into the pit of my stomach. "You—you killed those men, didn't you?"

His glance shifted to mine. "They were all bad. You would've killed them if you knew what they were."

From the corner of my eyes, Lucan shifted.

"Don't," I said, pointing to him. Nolen refocused his attention back to the real danger.

Stealthily the wraith inched toward Lucan.

"Set her free, now," Nolen said with the jerk of his head to Weylan. "And if you do anything to hurt her, the first arrow goes through your eye."

Weylan took a slow step toward me, his arms still raised. "Ilianna belongs to Eira, Nolen. The Demon Daughter can help her people."

"You're a liar!" he said with a strange laugh. "If you truly believed that, then you would know her true identity—the identity your people have given her. To many of the Eirians, she is an angel. To *me* she is an angel. Set her free. Now!"

Weylan reached out with his knife to saw through my binds. They dropped to the ground.

Nolen motioned him back, and Weylan complied.

I gently placed a hand to his arm and guided him away from danger. Weylan's horse was saddled and ready. If I could just get him on it with me—

Nolen looked to me and smiled. It was only a fraction of a moment, but it was all Lucan needed. A breath of air and a gasp was my only warning. A knife protruded from Nolen's chest. He reached for me and I grasped his cold hands.

A shockwave of grief shuddered through me as I gathered him close. A scream ripped from my lungs. I tried to keep him up, but it was no use. He folded to the ground. Even in his last breaths he watched me, expectant. Pain and anger erupted in one deadly explosion.

Nolen had wanted to see the Demon Daughter freed, and in his last breaths, he would. I opened my arms as she tore from the depths of her prison and my body became hers. Flames of black and gold engulfed me.

21

RESCUED

WEYLAN'S HORSE REARED WITH A frightened scream. It bolted, taking with it several others that had recently lost their owners.

The Demon Daughter smiled at Lucan, reveling as the blood drained from his face. Fear transformed him to a coward in what would be his final moments.

She couldn't blame him. His dread called to her— wanted her to draw from its force.

"Kill her!" he screamed.

The group of soldiers shrank back, but only a moment before their courage pushed them forward. They charged, and the Demon Daughter sensed her new targets.

Their essence wrapped around her like a warm blanket. She pulled them to her, eager to greet, and cut through them like wheat. One, two, three, and four fell before they could even lift their weapons to strike. The others ran.

Cyris raced toward Lucan, wrapping him in his arms. My uncle's assassin convulsed, then dropped to his knees beneath the weight of the wraith.

A laugh bubbled to her lips. In the distance, the Demon Daughter recognized Weylan on his horse. The coward was escaping, but she would get him soon enough.

The mortal Lucan, however...

She moved to reclaim her initial target, but the assassin was no longer there. Only the shell of a wasted mortal.

Red eyes glared from beneath a wash of blond hair, his arms raised in surrender. The wraith had taken away her fun.

"Kill Lucan and we lose our advantage against your uncle," Cyris said.

The Demon Daughter opened her arms and smiled. "What more advantage do I need, wraith? Perhaps I'll kill you instead." Even though they stood far apart, the wraith's dark energy was stronger than the average mortal's. She reached out to touch the strands of his very soul. Power raced through her as she connected to him.

Cyris shuddered, drawing back a step. "Kill *me* and you lose everything you need to know about your past. I can tell you who you are, Ilianna."

She stalked forward. "What does Ilianna care for an identity? I have given her enough to know who she is."

"Ilianna, snap out of it," he yelled, and for a moment, I recognized who he talked to, but I wasn't ready to come back. The Demon Daughter was powerful. When she was in charge, things didn't hurt so much. Ilianna didn't hurt so much.

She flew across the expanse that separated her from her prey and snatched Cyris by the throat. She lifted him high, taking the knife from his own sheath.

Ketrina screamed from somewhere above, and my attention snapped to the sound. Hoof beats thundered through the forest.

"Ilianna, stop!" Castiel's deep voice boomed, strong and familiar.

Quicker than she had come, the Demon Daughter receded. Lucan's body dropped to the floor.

I gasped, turning to see the prince barreling toward me on his magnificent blue roan, Dhema. A line of soldiers followed close behind, including Melia and her mother. My head spun. My legs felt like lead. Emotion sprang to my eyes, but I forced myself to be composed. To not break at the very sight of him.

He leaped from Dhema, then froze. His arms opened wide. His troop slowed to a halt, swords drawn, arrows aimed.

"Put your weapons down, you idiots," Melia hissed, and hesitantly they obeyed.

Reese pushed his horse forward, standing sentinel between me and more than a dozen armed soldiers. He glared them down.

Cyris's ragged breath caught my attention. I peered at him as he struggled.

"Stop, Ilianna. You don't need to kill him. Just come away." Castiel took one cautious step forward. "It's alright."

"I wasn't going to kill him," I mumbled, the words barely intelligible.

"Then come away from him. Everything's going to be alright."

I swallowed against the tightness in my throat. "Why do you keep saying that?"

His head tipped to the side.

"Ilianna?" Melia slid from her saddle to stand next to her prince. Concern twisted her features.

"And what—what are you doing here?" I asked.

No one cares about Ilianna Drakara. No one ever has. Lucan's words echoed over and over again.

Castiel gestured with his hand, and the other soldiers, led by Melia and Reese, directed their horses toward the ruined cottage. They checked the dead bodies and surveyed the total damage. Only Melora, now in her mid-twenties, stayed on her horse, watching me with expectant eyes. Her blonde mohawk braid flowed down and over her shoulder. She looked like her daughter in every way.

Why were they here? Why had *he* come?

I tipped my head back and scanned through the canopy of leaves to find the moon beyond. Suddenly I shivered, my breath white against the chilled night. Without more than a muffled groan from the branch she chose, Ketrina landed in the boughs above.

"You told me I had three days, remember?" Castiel asked.

I nodded.

The prince watched me, concern etched in every line of his handsome face. "I was done in two."

I choked against the emotion that tumbled from me. In the next second, I was in his arms not knowing how I had gotten there. My heart shattered, leaving me exposed. Raw. I was on display for everyone to see.

He wrapped me even closer. He smelled of leather and spring, his body warm and comforting. The strength of his arms as he trailed gentle strokes up and down my back was a soothing balm amid the torrential storms of my soul.

I didn't have the strength to look too closely at the meaning behind Castiel's revelation, or even my own behavior. Whatever his reasons for being there, it didn't matter. Castiel was with *me*. And he acted like he cared. Maybe not in the way I cared for him, but he cared whether I lived or died, and that meant something.

"This is very moving, and all, but…" Cyris's slow drawl pulled me out of my meditation. Despite the warmth of Castiel's body, my skin chilled. "Might we move to other more pressing matters?" He sat up slowly and rolled his neck side to side, then stretched his long arms, as if testing them. It was strange that this was his new form, but red eyes glowed from the depths of Lucan's face.

Castiel stiffened beneath my touch. "Melora, remind me why we're not killing the wraith?"

The seer dropped from her saddle and strolled to the wraith. "He's invaluable," she said, but she kicked the wraith's boot lightly with the tip of hers.

Castiel grunted before turning his attention to me, his expression grave. He searched my face, but what he sought I didn't know. "You're pale," he said. "You must be starving."

I blinked. "I—" I had no idea how long it had been since I'd eaten, but food was the last thing on my mind. "I'm fine, for now."

I twisted in his arms. He still hadn't released me, for which I was grateful, but I peeked beyond his shoulder to the wraith only a few yards away. Melora squatted in front of Cyris. From a leather bag slung around her shoulders she pulled a curious device—cylindrical, with an odd-looking scope attached. She thumbed his eyelids open to scan his pupils.

He growled and pushed away her ministrations. "Enough, old crone. I don't need your strange medicine."

My brows raised, but Melora only laughed. She tapped the device on his bent knee. "This is not medicine, and you're older than I am, you geezer." She straightened and held a hand out for the wraith to take. "Tell me what went on here and what the mortal knew."

"Wait." I shifted in Castiel's embrace and gently pressed against his chest. He understood my meaning and released me. Cold invaded the moment we separated. "Is—is Lucan dead?"

"The assassin is no longer." Cyris's brows lifted as he scanned me. "There's a bit of soul that remains, but not much, and what's left begs for death." It was still Lucan's voice, and yet not. The slow way Cyris spoke and his languid, calm air were different from the once precise, surgical movements of the assassin.

"That doesn't sound like Lucan to give up so easily," I said.

"And why did you kill him instead of taking him captive?" Castiel asked.

"I'm only as physically strong as the body I take. I wouldn't have been able to overcome him in my old form. He would've kept coming for Ilianna, and he would have killed her in the end."

"If that's the truth—"

"It's the truth," the wraith interrupted, shifting to his knees. "I have no reason to lie to you."

A cold wind whipped through the trees and set my teeth to chattering. Castiel moved to the saddle bags on his horse and withdrew a small wool blanket. He placed it over my shoulders. I shivered, pulling it tighter around me.

"Cyris works with me," Melora said. "We're not killing him because he's the only one who can shed light on what's coming."

I shuddered. "The Wraith Queen?"

She nodded. Cyris accepted her help and pulled himself up. He slapped the dirt from his hands. "This Lucan knew nothing more than his men, although his memories of going to Ardenya confirmed what we suspected."

"Ardenya?" I looked to Castiel. "Isn't that—"

"The kingdom the ambassador is coming from. Yes," he answered.

Melora grunted and shoved the instrument back into her leather bag. "We'll go over that later. We must face the battle in front of us."

"And this wraith is necessary?" Castiel asked.

She nodded. "Cyris has been my informant for almost thirty years."

The prince eyed him warily. "Did you know he was a prisoner in our dungeon?"

"Of course. I put him there."

"Why didn't you tell us?"

"I'm telling you now. Don't let the others know what he is. As far as they're concerned, he's yet another traitor from the home of Eira." Her eyes shifted to mine. "That shouldn't be too hard for them to believe."

Even though I had disassociated from my kingdom—rejected it as my own—her sting hit home. Shame colored my cheeks and sank like mud into the pit of my stomach. Had the kingdom of Eira fallen so low? But it had not always been so. Not according to our history books.

The seer took the reins to her horse and clicked her tongue. The animal followed her instantly. Cyris trailed behind, heading towards the shack. Already, Castiel's men had constructed a fire that blazed bright beneath the shadows of the dark forest.

"We should get you warm," Castiel said. He gently placed a hand at my arm to guide me, but I shifted away. His gaze narrowed. "What's the matter?"

"How did you find me?" I asked, my voice no louder than a whisper.

He took a deep breath. "We got word of your abduction earlier today, and I came."

"And that's it? You knew where I was?"

He shrugged. "I went off a hunch."

I twisted to better see him, but still he kept me close.

"A little more than a hunch." He tapped his boot against the trunk of a tree. "Before I knew you were missing, we of course were working on finding those who murdered in your name. I started the mission by separating the unit to speak with each of the deceased family members. Strangely, when we found them, they were more relieved to hear their kinsmen were dead, and they had no additional information to give."

"What?"

He nodded. "Every single one. In fact, the only relative to mourn over the loss of these victims was Oscove, and he disappeared before being questioned. So I searched for him."

"Did you find him?"

He tipped his head to the side. "The only Oscove we found was an eleven-year-old boy."

My brows cinched together.

"But people *did* remember his brother. Nolen Odessa: an eccentric hermit that went crazy after the demonic wars. The townspeople said his wife ran away with her children to her sister's house in the next town over. We rode there, and I was able to speak with her. She carried a locket with a picture of her husband, and shockingly—"

"Nolen was Oscove," I finished for him.

Castiel flinched. "Yes. How did you know?"

"You'll see." My eyes drifted to the shack where scores of sketches peppered the damaged walls and floors. "Oscove said my people knew me as something else—not the Demon Daughter."

He shook his head. "That I don't know, but when we get back, I can look into it as well. We'll figure it out, Ilianna. It will take time, but we'll figure it out. Together. Can you trust me?"

My mind ached along with my body. "Can I trust you? You're here. And you did all of this—"

"You gave me a direct order, Your Highness," he said, interrupting. A smile lifted the corners of his mouth. "I didn't have much of a choice."

I almost smiled back. "So I've been gone for two days?"

"This is the third day." His expression grew wary. "My brother soon expects our return. We need to leave if we're going to get back in time for your celebration, but will you tell me what happened and how you were abducted?"

I rehearsed to him everything that I had remembered the night of my capture, although I left out seeing my attacker's tattoo. Mikael would pay for his actions, but in my own way and time. For now, the prince would know that Weylan and Lucan acted alone.

Castiel touched the binding that protected the slash wound on my hand, his jaw muscles tense. Soft finger turned my hands to expose the rope marks on my wrists. "Why did you let them bind you?" he asked.

I almost laughed. "What choice did I have?"

"Don't you remember the first harvest in Rhyolyn and what you did to that tree? Your touch alone worked better than even my magic."

I opened my mouth to object, but then I recalled the night of my abduction and the brush I was able to draw to me through some connection.

When I told him of my practice, a smile touched his eyes. "When you realize your true magical potential, you'll be *truly* terrifying."

It was meant as a compliment, but it hit sorely upon my gut.

"Your abductors would never have stood a chance," he continued, but I had to change the subject.

"I believe they used Gedeon's sleeping potion," I said.

His face dropped. He cursed beneath his breath, dragging his fingers through his hair, "I know what you're thinking—"

"I *don't* think Gedeon helped. I think Lucan and Weylan stole it from him."

Castiel let out a breath, nodding. "I am so sorry, Ilianna. I should have been there."

"Nonsense."

His eyes flashed to mine.

"You discovered who was killing in my name—"

"*You* discovered that," he interrupted. "*Without* me."

"But I wouldn't have if Weylan and Lucan hadn't acted in your absence. They probably knew it was their only chance."

Again he swore, using a much more colorful dialog, his face turning a dark shade of red.

Hesitantly, I touched his cheek. "Thank you."

He pulled my fingers from his face and kissed their tips. "Nonsense." His voice was amazingly gentle. "When I finally found you, you had almost everything under control. Your parlor trick did most of the work."

I knew he wanted to ask how I had done it, but what could I say? The Demon Daughter was not under my control. Far from being angelic, she was chaos. She was power, and not the kind Castiel taught from.

But I couldn't give her all the credit. "That wasn't done by my parlor trick," I said, pointing toward Nolen's home, or what was left of it. "Ketrina."

His eyes grew large upon the wreckage. He hummed. "I wondered where she had disappeared to, but that makes sense."

"Gomez and Verity?"

He shook his head. "They're back with my brother. Ketrina has a mind of her own. After delivering the king's message about your abduction, she took off. You know I don't exactly control her. Obviously, she went to find you herself. See? You didn't even need me."

But I did. More so now than ever. The acknowledgment never made it past my stiff lips. "She probably saved my life. You both did." A shudder rippled the skin on my back.

Concern broke through his calm demeanor. "Let's get you warm."

I allowed him to guide me to the waiting fire, but it wasn't the cold that affected me. My parlor trick had saved me from a bad situation, but I had no idea how I had incited the reaction. There was no incantation, no summoning. She had just come.

Castiel stood me near the fire. However, before I could even enjoy its heat Melia drew me away, a change of clothes slung over her arms. She led me toward Nolen's shack. I stopped.

"No. Not in there." I had seen enough of Nolen's artistry to last a lifetime. I didn't need the Demon Daughter's eyes watching me as I stripped nearly bare to change. Melia watched me, waiting for a reason, but all I could manage was, "You'll see."

She shrugged, shifting directions. I followed her behind the shack to change with her as guard. "They're not clean," she said, "but I assume they're better than what you're wearing now."

Gratitude filled my heart as the cold night seeped through the thin nightgown. "Thank you." Her travel-worn leathers fit better than expected. When I finished dressing, Melia nodded her approval.

Castiel surveyed the inside of Nolen's home with Melora and Reese. Melia went to join. I warmed myself at the fire instead.

Soldiers carried Nolen's body from the forest and buried him with the other dead, and my heart chilled. He had tried to save me. The Demon Daughter, at least. To set her free. I wasn't sure what that meant, or why it was important to him, but I was oddly grateful.

Reese's warm presence pressed against me. He gently bumped my arm, nearly knocking me over, and held out a chunk of bread to me. A tiny yellow wildflower draped across the top of it. I peered into his dark eyes, so surprisingly kind...

I shook my head.

Confusion crossed his features. "What's the matter? Are you not hungry?"

I took the bread from him, careful not to let the flower fall. "Why are you so kind to me, Reese? You always have been."

He huffed, again nudging me with his elbow. "I don't think I have much of a choice, do I?"

My shoulders dropped. "My magic is not controlling you."

"No, but my conscience is." He faced me, lifting my chin with one finger. "My mother always told me I could read people better than anyone. Said I had a nose for sniffing out the good from the bad. Do you know what my nose tells me about you?"

"What?" I asked.

His brows creased together as he scanned my face. "Despite what I'm sure you've been told in the past, you're a good person, Ilianna. Better than most." He gently picked up the wildflower, so small in his hands, and tucked it into my hair just above my ear.

I frowned, trying to touch where he placed the flower. "I'm not so sure about that."

He tsked, pulling my hand away, then he tapped his nose and winked. "Always trust the nose. Now eat."

"Thank you, Reese," Castiel said, coming from the shack with Melia.

Reese nodded.

"We cannot stay here," Melora said from behind.

I whirled. How had she gotten so close without me knowing?

Her face glowed eerily, highlighted by the flames of the fire. "We must get back to Meyrion."

"You sense this?" Melia asked, one hand on her mother's arm.

"I do."

"Very well," Castiel said, and he glanced at the nearest soldier. "You. Put out the fire. We leave now."

The soldier flinched. Casting his voice low he said, "But sir, what of the spirits?"

Another soldier afraid of the spooks that haunted the forests.

The seer answered. "The spirits will avoid us tonight."

The soldier nodded and left to follow Castiel's orders.

Melora's eyes grew distant as she stared up at the stars. "We have one in our midst more cursed than they."

It was spoken so the others didn't hear, but my gaze shifted toward Cyris as he stared into the dying flames.

The others quickly set to work, dousing the fire with dirt and stamping out the embers. Castiel and Melia collected as many drawings as they could from Nolen's home. Melora whispered something in the wraith's ear. Curious, I neared with silent steps.

Using some sense special only to her seer ears, Melora raised her head and nodded. "Princess."

I froze. My gaze narrowed. "Why do you change your appearance so much? Do you like to frighten everyone?"

She flashed a set of brilliant white teeth. "Do I frighten you?"

I lied. "No."

Cyris snickered.

The seer cut him a sharp glance before answering. "Unfortunately, Princess, that is a misconception. I do not enjoy spooking the common folk." She cast her eyes round about, then nodded me to approach.

Tucking my fear, I edged nearer.

She whispered. "The truth is, I don't control my age."

"What do you mean?

"Just what I said, girl. You're a magician. Your lifespan is much greater than a normal mortal. You'll live two hundred or more years. You will age slowly. I did as well, but as for a seer's lifespan, it's yet unknown. I may be an immortal. I have no clue. My body rejuvenates daily, but lately it's been… malfunctioning."

"How?"

"The moment I fall asleep, it begins a metamorphosis. My guess is that I'm so old, it can't remember what age it's supposed to be."

"Are you serious?"

"Why would I lie?"

I didn't know, but the truth was so farfetched. "How long has it been malfunctioning?" I asked instead.

"Oh, for fifty years now."

"So, you're saying Melia had to grow up with—"

"A mother that was sometimes a child, like she was? Yes. Although my age never drops lower than puberty."

I grunted. "That would be interesting. For Melia."

"I assume it was, although she's never talked to me about it. It was even stranger for people to see me pregnant as an eighty-year-old woman or even worse, a thirteen-year-old girl."

"Actually, the thought makes me laugh," Melia said, interjecting. She led her mother's horse to her, a curious expression upon her beautiful features. She shifted her attention to me. "And you were right about the shack. Someone should set it on fire."

Melora smiled and then allowed her daughter to assist her in mounting.

Castiel's spoke from over my shoulder. "We're just about ready. You'll ride with me, Princess."

His voice tantalized. I released my breath slowly. "Perhaps I should walk, since I was the one to scare away the other horses." In truth, I wasn't sure sitting with him would be wise. Already, I had made a scene, throwing myself into his arms. Stories would spread abundantly when we returned, and with them a possible backlash.

But it was more than that. Now I was acutely aware of just how much I liked being in his arms.

"I could sit with Melia," I added.

"My saddle's too small," she said, not meeting my gaze. My face heated.

Castiel guided me to Dhema. The blue roan lightly stamped his foot and shook his mane for attention.

"Come, Princess Ilianna," the prince said, gliding his hand down his horse's flank. "I'm sure the great warrior is used to having her own horse, but that's not an option. We've got a lot to discuss and a long way to go."

"Alright," I said, scratching at the space between the horse's ears.

"Is there something wrong with sitting with me?" A wicked glint sparkled in his eyes.

"Nothing at all. It's just that you are a prince. You deserve your own horse. But if you don't mind, I'd love to ride with you."

The rest of the unit had already mounted. Melia and Melora led them away. Only Reese stayed, pretending not to watch our exchange. Castiel cupped his hand to give me a lift-up. To avoid any more of a spectacle, I pushed my boot into his make-shift stirrup and swung my leg over the saddle. Dhema held steady when the prince mounted next.

"Excuse me," he said, before he placed his hands on my hips. I inhaled as he shifted closer, settling me more comfortably in front of him.

He took the reins, his arms around me, and at his touch a jolt of adrenaline pumped through my blood. I sat rigid, but as he urged his horse forward the constant motion of the ride made noncontact impossible.

My mind trailed back to Weylan and the shack. To Nolen and his countless pictures. I shuddered despite the warmth of Castiel's body.

"What is it?" he asked, concern etched in his words.

"Is—is that what I look like?" I asked, my voice low.

"Pardon?"

"In Nolen's shack. Is that what I really look like when the Demon Daughter takes over?"

He hesitated a moment before answering. "Yes."

I shook my head. "When you showed me that sketch in your office, that was the first time I realized she was... real."

"When did she first come?"

Within the pit of my stomach, nausea churned. I shrugged, and my shoulders tingled as they brushed against his chest. "I don't remember."

It was a partial truth, but what I *did* recall didn't make sense. Something warned that I might not want to know.

Castiel's reluctance played in the space between us. "Sometimes a magical awakening can be traumatic for a young magician. The power can wipe clean its wielders temporary memory, sapping their physical and mental strength. Perhaps it was the same for you when the Demon Daughter first entered."

"Maybe."

And with that, the conversation dropped. Soon we caught up with the others, who moved out of the way as Castiel pressed forward to take the lead with Melia and Melora.

"So, what must we discuss?" I asked when they were in earshot, partly to get my mind off of Castiel's nearness.

But Melora put a finger to her lips. "Not here. We're being watched."

"What?" I tensed and Castiel's arms tightened around mine. My gaze darted from tree to tree. "I thought you said it would be safer in the forest."

"No," Melora answered. "I said the demons in the forest would leave us alone, but that doesn't mean they won't watch."

My eyes scanned the trees, its features now too dark to see anything clearly.

Castiel leaned down and spoke into my ear, his breath warm on my neck. "Don't worry, Ilianna. You're safe."

I gazed back to meet his blue eyes, and that was a mistake. His mouth hovered so close, his beautiful lips parted as if to say something more, but he froze. I twisted back around, flushed.

We rode through the forest two by two. Castiel led the unit with Reese at his side. After a few hours, my muscles unclenched, and I found myself leaning into him. His arms tightened around me and my heart swelled. His scent comforted, and the constant, rhythmic walk of the horse soon lulled me into sleep. I dropped my head against his chest and allowed the warmth of his body to infiltrate every cold space in my heart.

22

Wraith Tales

"Ilianna." Castiel woke me from a deep sleep. His hands gently rubbed mine; heat from his breath tickled my neck. I smiled and peeled myself from him. His leathers had worn marks into the side of my face, my mouth dry from being open while I slept.

Lovely.

I quickly wiped the sleep from my eyes. Dhema shifted beneath my jerky movements. I patted his neck to calm him. It was still dark, but we had stopped in front of a large stable and barn attached to an inn. An old woman holding a candle stood beneath the entrance while Melia spoke to a thin, white-bearded man.

"What's going on?" I asked.

Castiel shifted behind me. "We're changing horses and hopefully getting something to eat."

The old man looked to the prince and nodded, signaling we could enter.

"Wonderful," he said.

I moved forward as he slid from the horse. He lifted me from the saddle with ease. I didn't need his help. I shouldn't have *accepted* his help either, but I wanted it. I wanted more of it. More of his touch. More of his nearness. More.

Something warned from within that it wasn't mine to have, but I ignored it and followed close to him. Melora stepped in front to block our entry. Castiel reached back to take my hand, halting me.

The seer's blonde braids were darker from days of not being washed. Dirt smudged her cheeks. "Conduct your business with the innkeeper, Prince," she said, her eyes never leaving mine, "but the princess I must take. She needs instruction."

Castiel pulled me behind him further.

Melora smiled at his reaction. "Don't worry. We will not stray far. You may have our food brought to us." She pointed to a nearby soldier as he passed. "Young man, build a fire. There." And she gestured to a place near the forest line.

The soldier paled then hustled to obey without waiting for the prince's consent.

Castiel watched Melora pointedly. "You shouldn't go near the edge of the forest."

Melora removed dirt beneath her nails. "I'll have the wraith with me. He'd be better to guard against what lurks in the trees."

"In that case, I would prefer to join you."

Her gaze slid to his face. A slow smile spread her lips. "You can trust Cyris."

"I'd rather not."

Her chin raised as she tried to stare him down even though she was a whole head shorter. "You dare go against my wishes?"

"My lady, you cannot ask me to have faith in what I should naturally mistrust. Besides, Ilianna's is a magician in training and I'm her teacher. Whatever you're introducing her to, I need to be made aware." His grip tightened on my hand.

She glared, one brow raised. "I could curse you, you know."

His head dropped to the side. "But you've known me since I was a child." He reached to tug on a stray wisp of her hair. "Would you really do that to me?"

Was he flirting with her? My face flushed.

"Bah." She batted away his hand with a roll of her eyes. "You're lucky I like you, but mark my words, Prince." She poked his chest hard with a thin finger. "You're not going to like what you hear." She stomped away to where the guard was busily constructing her fire. He gazed up from his work, double-timing his efforts when the seer drew near.

Dread kneaded my stomach into painful knots. What would the seer say that would affect the prince? I extracted myself from his grasp. "Perhaps it would be better—"

"Go to the fire with Melora," he said, cutting me off. "I'll be there with food and drink as soon as I finish with the innkeeper. His finger softly traced a line down the side of my cheek, then he vanished inside the darkened inn.

By the time I sat on the cold ground, the fire was well on its way to a nice blaze. Melora rested across from me, her gaze transfixed on the brilliant flames.

A few moments later, the hairs on the back of my neck stood on end, indicating the nearness of the wraith, Cy. He claimed the spot at Melora's side and examined me unabashed as I examined him. It was Lucan's body, but everything else had changed. His expressions, the way he spoke, the calm air surrounding him.

He winked, and I looked away.

Castiel arrived with the innkeeper's wife and daughter in tow. The women carried bowls of stew with a side of bread and butter.

Before she left, the wife promised to have everyone fed within the hour. Her husband would have a change of horses finished in no longer than two.

The prince gave her his thanks, and the women left us to eat in silence. Castiel sat between me and Melora and ate his dinner quietly. My eyes traveled the length of his face, but whatever emotions he had, he tucked them close.

I ladled hurried bites of stew, barely tasting them as they burned my tongue and slid to my empty stomach. When we were finished, a soldier carried off our dinnerware.

"So, what's this about?" Castiel started, an annoyed tint to his words. "And why are you here, Cyris? Who are you?"

Cyris wiped his mouth with the back of his sleeve but didn't meet the prince's gaze. "The answer to those questions is one and the same. I am the reason the Wraith Queen exists. I'm her creator."

Silence enveloped the space between us. Finally, Castiel spoke, his voice deep. Deadly. "If that's true, why shouldn't I kill you now?"

The threat had no effect on the creature. "Because no one knows more about her than I do. More importantly, I'm the only one who knows how to kill her."

Melora cleared her throat, setting a hand to Castiel's crossed legs, then releasing it. "The Wraith Queen has a name. It's Theia."

I gasped, leaning away. "Don't say her name."

Castiel's brow tipped up. "I thought you said you didn't believe such superstitions."

I glared. "I was only surprised *you* believed them. I never said I didn't."

He hummed, accusingly.

"She's right, of course," Cyris said. "But even if she did hear us, there's nothing the Wraith Queen could do about it."

"What do you mean?" I asked.

"Well, the distance is one problem. A wraith must be relatively close for that to work, but even if the need was strong enough, or the wraith was powerful enough, they couldn't come just by command. I'll get to that later, but as of right now, we're safe. But—"

I interrupted again. "So, it's true then. If I called your name…?"

One side of his lips tipped up. "Maybe I'd come, maybe I wouldn't."

My eyes narrowed, but he only smiled.

"As I was trying to explain," Melora said, annoyed. "Theia once belonged to one of the most powerful families within the kingdom of Ardenya."

"Ardenya?" I asked, glancing over to Castiel. Our eyes met, and the same recognition lit his features. *The ambassador.*

"My home," Cy said. "It was a kingdom of magicians and seers. *Dark* magicians and seers. Home to some of the most powerful families and ancestral magic ever known. Seekers from all over the world would face the seas to travel to our country in search of the darker arts."

"Then why isn't your kingdom more common knowledge?" I asked. If my uncle had heard of it, I would know. He might have even tried to send me there.

"We worked hard to keep our home hidden through powerful enchantments. Only rumors of it existed, but those brave enough to venture were tested before entrance was permitted. We knew our gifts were special, valuable, so we stocked this knowledge in our secret vaults, only ever revealing our powers for the right price. Our kingdom grew in wealth, but it was a deadly trade. If our visitors survived, they would leave with information too evil for anyone's good."

I sat transfixed as Cyris's story played out in the flames. The brilliant glow of the fire threw shadows on the surrounding woods, making the trees dance. My heart beat an irregular cadence to his words.

He continued. "The larger, more celebrated clans in Ardenya feuded among themselves, not satisfied with their lot. They wanted more—more power, more wealth, more prestige. Whole families were slaughtered without any repercussions to the murderers. They had to be stopped. They needed to die. So, I cursed them."

"Why you?" Castiel said abruptly. "What made you take it upon yourself to stop them?"

He swallowed. Raw emotion blazed in his eyes. "My family name was well-known, and one of the worst. Our biggest rival was the family of Meurig. Theia Meurig—now the Wraith Queen, killed my wife and children. My parents. Everyone I loved." The wraith waited for Castiel to respond, but that seemed to be a good enough explanation for the prince.

"I wanted them punished. All of them. They didn't deserve to live. *I* didn't deserve to live. I shut myself away in my parents' library and devoted my remaining life to creating something powerful enough to affect the entire kingdom. After months of study, I concocted a magnificent curse, both dark and pure. A righteous ending to a truly wicked people.

"I went to the center of the kingdom and released my creation. Something that potent should have killed me, but instead of dying, I was flung from my body and land, doomed to never return."

My words nearly stuck in my throat. "And your kingdom?"

Cyris's brows pinched together as his voice faltered. "My magic was *supposed* to bind every dark magician to the continent, so they could never pass on their wicked traditions. This worked for the most part, and it's the reason Theia won't come to you when she hears her name. I hoped that when they continued to kill each other off, or when their lifespans were over, their souls would be bound to the land as wraiths to haunt it forever. In the end, it would be an entire kingdom of wraiths—not quite dead, but not alive either. Centuries of investigation, of searching for those who survived the trip to Ardenya, confirmed my curse had worked. But then Theia—the very one responsible for the slaughter of my family—stumbled upon a loophole.

"Our enchantments didn't work against those ignorant to our location. Occasionally, a storm would maroon a ship on our land. A sailor named Isaac wrecked his ship upon the island. Normally the wraiths would kill any trespassers instantly, but Theia was at the shore that day and this particular sailor was handsome—the first human she had seen in years. She was not yet a wraith. She took compassion on him and protected him, kept him. They had a child. A girl. I assume by then the sailor realized what was happening. He killed Theia as she slept and escaped with the babe."

My heart picked up speed as Cyris continued his narrative.

"Now a wraith herself, Theia was enraged, but after a time she sensed a bond forming between her and her child. It grew stronger day by day and when the child became of age, the connection solidified. The link to the girl allowed Theia to leave her home. She crossed the seas. The bond was so strong that the daughter, too, waited for her mother to come. When Theia found her, she immediately took over, inhabiting her body... and thus she discovered a magic more powerful than even the dark magic she and her family had wielded before. Ancestral magic."

I shivered despite the heat from the fire. "That's disgusting."

Cyris viewed me curiously. "Wraiths are pulled to occupy that which is stronger than themselves, but there has to be a certain level of... damage to that soul. However, because the girl was her offspring, no matter the level of corruption, Theia could infect her without too much effort. She took over the girl. The girl's kingdom was now connected to the Wraith Queen, and because of her presence, Theia was able to bring over any wraith in Ardenya that would follow. And with every generational member, Theia's power increases."

"Wait." Castiel held up a hand, his eyes narrowed. "She becomes more powerful in her offspring?"

"Generational magic. Magicians naturally grow more powerful with each generation. This is the same concept. Theia's power grows with each host. She has repeated this pattern time and time again to kingdoms all over our world. As a result, demons not of her kingdom are drawn to her rising strength. It's those demonic creatures that she sends against the nations she cannot yet take over."

Cyris paused in his tale, allowing us to finally speak, but no one did. What could we say?

Melora finally interjected. "The curse has become warped. It has shifted from what Cyris created it for into an entity all its own. Now it protects itself. It wants to survive."

"Any land Theia possesses, the curse recognizes as her ancestral land," Cyris said. "And I'm flung from it, which is why we have to act now."

"Why are you telling us this?" I asked. It aligned with what we knew, but if it was true, what could be done?

Cyris was thoughtful. "The first Demonic Wars were a cover for what the Wraith Queen truly desired. Her offspring."

I balked. "You're saying there was a child of hers here?"

He nodded. "A boy, but Theia won't take over boys. She kills them and restarts the process."

Castiel shook his head. "Why not just take over the body of another child?"

Melora answered. "She could, but her powers only increase if she takes on as host of her offspring, *and* it can only be the oldest living of the current host."

"First-born rights." Cyris's lips twisted. "She'll change out bodies after twenty years or so. When she abandons them, they live as her servants—a shell of what they once were. We call them pryors."

I glanced over to Castiel next to me. His face was pinched in what I could only guess was the same frustration that coursed through me. "And what happened to the boy?" I asked, not sure I wanted to know.

Melora's response was devoid of any expression. "Cyris helped me hide the father and the son, but we failed in saving him. The Wraith Queen found and killed them both.

I swallowed. "How does Theia keep getting these men to… to…"

"Copulate with her?" Cyris smiled, the fire glowing in his eyes. "In every kingdom she takes over, she keeps human volunteers."

"She tortures them?" the prince asked.

"No. She makes them wealthy beyond their dreams, treats them like royalty. They become her spies and deliver the victims she needs."

Castiel's eyes narrowed. "This ambassador from Ardenya? Are you saying the ambassador is a spy coming for her next... donor?"

Cyris hummed. "No."

"Then what?" he snapped.

The wraith stared into the flames. "The child is already here."

I pulled my hands down my face. If the child was already here, then they must have an idea of where. We would find her, bring her to the safety of Meyrion, guard her night and day until the Wraith Queen came to claim her, and then we would kill the menace. "Where is she?"

From the line of trees, a snap caught my attention, like a twig breaking. Adrenaline pumped through my veins as I scanned the forest. A pair of glowing embers burned from the shadows, and my breath nearly stopped. I reached out, grasping Castiel's leg.

"What is it?" His hand closed over mine. Concern swam in his eyes.

My voice came out half-strangled. "Something watches us. In the forest. Red eyes."

The prince jolted from his seat and pulled a knife from his boot.

Melora tsked. "Stay where you are, Prince. You can't see them. Not like Ilianna can."

A second pair of eyes lit the space next to the first. "There are two now."

The seer smirked, picking up a long stick from the ground. She examined the tip of it. "There are many more than that; those are just the ones brave enough to come closer."

Frustration seared when Castiel looked again. "I don't see anything."

I turned to Melora. "Why can I see them, and why am I just seeing them now? Why not every time I entered the forest with my men, or when I came from Eira to Anolyn?"

She threw her stick into the fire. "Two likely reasons. I'm guessing you've always been able to see them but didn't search very hard. They would have stayed away, like they do now. And also, my potion has permanent effects. If it opened your eyes, like it opened Castiel to auras, you will always be able to see them now."

I glared at the prince, but he threw up his hands in defeat. "I didn't know."

"You were young when you first took the potion, my prince. I don't normally tell my students such details. As for the demons, there is nothing to do. Best ignore them, Princess."

"But what if they attack?" I asked.

She sighed. "I told you they won't."

"Why?"

"Because they fear someone more cursed than they," Cyris interjected, frostily. "They fear the offspring of the Wraith Queen."

I flinched when his gaze and then Melora's fell to me. Castiel glanced between the two conspirators before gaping at me in both disbelief and shock. The space went silent.

Heat flared to my neck and face. The muscles in my jaw tensed. I leaned in, glaring at the wraith. "Liar."

"What reasons would I have to lie?"

"You're a wraith. Lying is second nature to you."

He flicked his fingers as if shooing away a pest. "You speak of demons. I'm not a demon. I'm probably not even a wraith."

My jaw clenched. "Go to hell."

He opened his arms wide. "Already there, darling."

"I—" The words caught in my throat.

My world slowed. I turned to Castiel, but he only stared, the blood drained from his handsome face. Did he believe the accusation? Truly, it was some kind of sick joke What was the wraith's object in casting such blame upon me?

My attention snapped to Cyris. "I'm not this—spawn of the Wraith Queen. I'm the child of a mistress. A commoner."

He shook his head sadly. "You're the daughter of a powerful magician and an evil sorcerer—one more powerful than the world has ever seen."

My chest tightened, my heart racing erratically. I searched the wraith's eyes, but there was no deceit in them, only determination to force his truth upon me. Anger flared. My voice shook when I spoke.

"Then why am I still alive?" I lunged toward the prince and yanked his knife from his boot, but Castiel's hand caught my wrist before I could plunge the blade into my heart. I slapped my free hand on his restraining arm. Power flew through our touch, sending him cascading from me. The knife fell to the ground several paces away and I scrabbled to take it up, but the moment it was in my hands again, arms wrapped around me, securing me to them.

The wraith's frantic pleas raked through me. "No, Princess." Cyris's skin was ice cold, a deadly warning that he was far from human. I shuddered in his iron grasp. "Please, return the knife to your prince."

Melora watched me from across the flames. She hadn't so much as flinched. Castiel was back on his feet, unharmed. Deftly, he removed the weapon from my grasp.

My skin crawled to the wraith's touch as a guttural moan bubbled from my lips. "I refuse to be the host of that... that creature," I hissed through my teeth.

His breath rasped against my ears. "Then keep living—or she'll spawn again. She'll find another victim, take one from another long list of volunteers and create another child. I'll have to begin the hunt all over again. By the time I find them, it could be too late."

"Let go of me," I raged, but Cyris's hold only tightened.

"Release her, or I'll kill you myself," Castiel said, his voice close.

With a jerk, the wraith let go, suddenly yards away. I fell forward, barely catching myself from landing face-first into the dirt. I pushed upward, then leapt to my feet. The others were already there to meet me. They surrounded me. I spun a circle as anxiety welled within.

Melora raised her hands as if in defeat. "Princess, you need to calm down. To listen. We don't know how she tricked your father, but when she killed her son, she was forced from this continent. Toma followed her."

"To assassinate her." But even as I said it, I heard the lie in my words. The lie my uncle had told me.

"No," Melora said. "He thought himself in love. They had a child. You. Lucan's memory confirms our suspicions. It was the assassin and a woman servant of the queen who brought you back. I don't know what became of your father, but I know you are the only one who can defeat the Wraith Queen."

I laughed. It was a pathetic, hysterical sound that grated on my nerves. "How can anyone fight her? You said so yourself: she's powerful. *Too* powerful."

"*Except* when she creates a child." Cyris watched me, reading my every thought and expression. His eyes delved into mine. "Theia willingly weakens herself every time she procreates. Her magic splits. The curse splits. Both go to her child. It went to you."

I shook my head and swallowed hard, trying to ignore Castiel's eyes that watched me so closely. I couldn't look at him. How could I ever face him again? Movement caught my attention. Melia stood outside the inn door, gripping the frame, her expression unreadable.

"You see," Melora said, taking a step closer. "You are Theia's only weakness. If you live, she is weakened. If you live, we can defeat her."

"The others couldn't defend against her infiltration," I said, my mouth dry.

Cyris nodded, his voice *almost* tender. "But you… *you* have been groomed for this, and yet you are unaware of her effects. Your uncle has prepared you for this very thing, and you fight. This is unheard of. As young as puberty, the Wraith Queen begins infiltration, preparing her host children. By the time she comes, they long for her to take over."

"How do you know—"

"Because I've *seen* it," he yelled.

Melora placed a calming hand on Cyris's arm. "Part of the reason we failed to protect the boy was because he fought our help. He wanted her to find him. We only prolonged their reunion. But you're different."

I glanced between them. "How?"

"Does she speak to you?" Melora asked.

The muscles between my brows creased. "No."

"Has she come to you in your dreams?"

"Of course not," I snapped.

"Then you're not under her influence. And you're a magician. The very first magician she's ever spawned."

"Your uncle—" the wraith began, but I cut him off, shocked by my own hostility.

"Don't speak to me of my uncle," I hissed. "Why would you want to help me?"

Cyris hesitated before answering. "This Wraith Queen killed my wife and children, but it took their loss for me to see what my kingdom had become. She won't stop taking life. Enslaving it. She'll destroy our very world. You're Theia's lineage, and the curse will continue through you if you don't stop it. We must align."

I raised my hand, waving away his words. My legs shook, but I pushed forward, not seeing as I hobbled to the trees.

"Let her go," Melora said behind me to Castiel.

Castiel.

A sob leapt to my throat. It took all I had to suppress releasing the dam that nearly drowned me. I shook my head and the action made my head spin. I couldn't be the Wraith Queen's daughter, and yet I couldn't sense the lie of Cyris's words. How did I not know? All these years? My mother was supposed to be a nobody. A peasant woman. A whore.

No, she was worse than that. A soul-sucking, child-infesting… there were no words to describe the thing that bore me. My life, every aspect of it from conception to near adulthood, had been a fabrication. A hoax. How had my father come to be part of it all? And why him?

"We don't know if it's true," Castiel said behind me, but his voice held no conviction.

I almost laughed. No. The prince knew it was true just as I did. I searched for the red eyes within the trees that so intently watched us before. They had disappeared. Chased away by my closeness. I tipped my head to the stars, but they were covered by thick, dark clouds.

I turned to the group, not meeting their gaze. They had kept close behind me, most likely afraid I would try to harm myself, again. "The ambassador?"

Melora answered. "A spy, of course. Probably the one that delivered you to Eira. When do you come of age?"

I stared at her blankly, but Castiel answered for me. "In two months."

The seer nodded. "More than likely, Theia is worried about her investment and is sending someone to check in."

"How much does my uncle know?" I asked, my voice strange and foreign to my ears.

"I don't know. It's interesting how he's... raised you. He knows something, but whatever it is, he's keeping it close to his chest."

Of course he was. "Then, what do we do?"

A smile lit the corners of her mouth. "We fight."

23

ARRIVING HOME

THE REMAINING JOURNEY WAS long and dreadfully uncomfortable. The innkeeper found me my own horse. The wraith became my riding companion. Suddenly, the prince trusted him enough with my safety, stating he wanted Cyris to be available to answer any questions I may have, and to protect me. Not that I needed protection. Apparently, I was terrifying enough on my own to keep any fabled spirits at bay.

My heart twisted painfully, my emotions too close to the surface. Since when did I become such a delicate female? But I wished Castiel hadn't heard the conversation with Melora and Cyris. He had avoided me since, barely meeting my gaze each time he walked the line of soldiers. If I were being honest with myself, I would admit that he needed to know. My immediate response to Cyris's news had been rash, but I still hadn't ruled out death. I couldn't possibly affect the Wraith Queen—my mother—as much as they hoped.

My mother.

A sigh blew through my stiff lips as I closed my eyes to the panic rising in my chest. How could I be the daughter to that… thing? The very person responsible for the most violent and fearsome war Eira had ever faced. My mother.

I cringed. I was happier thinking the woman that bore me was a lowly commoner, a mistress to the inconstant prince.

It was late morning when our company came in view of Anolyn's castle. The unhindered sun beat a beautiful glow on the glorious, grayed fortress. A sense of peace folded over me as my gaze longingly traced its arches and spires.

That peace quickly faded. Countless soldiers and staff dotted the landscape, erecting great canvas tents and building fire pits. Streamers and flowers hung from poles and wrapped tables. A distant sound of music floated to us, but was soon drowned out by the thundering of hooves as a unit of armed soldiers stormed across the green fields straight toward us. Castiel signaled for all to stop, and the company obeyed.

I peered behind and nearly laughed. We were a bedraggled sight.

Mikael led the coming squad, his gaze lethal as he scanned our group. My hand tingled where his knife had cut into flesh. He didn't know I had recognized him that night, but he would find out soon enough.

"Seize the assassin from Eira," Mikael said.

Immediately, a ring of soldiers converged, their weapons circling the spy as he sat upon his horse, but Cyris didn't flinch.

"He's not a traitor," I said, kicking away the sword of one. The soldier glared.

Castiel's voice shouted over the sudden commotion. "Stand down."

"Take him," Mikael commanded, ignoring the prince, "and search the others, beginning with her." He pointed to me.

I gave a cheerful grin. I'd let the traitor have his fun, for now.

Castiel's face grew a violent shade of red. "No one will touch her, Captain, if you value your life. What's the meaning of this?"

Mikael's head lifted a fraction. "A mandatory search, sir. Orders of the king. All personnel entering must show identity and be examined. Soldiers belonging to our majesty's army must promptly report to their commanding officers. All others will be relieved of their weapons. *You* are the only exception."

"I will see him at once. Princess Ilianna—" Without looking back, he motioned for me to accompany him.

Mikael held out a hand. "His Majesty is not expecting the princess and she must therefore await his—"

"Enough," Castiel barked.

"Sir, the—"

"Captain!" Hoof beats drew our attention. The king in all his regal glory, raced toward our company, his assassin and four guards in tow. Riaan wore all black leathers, a magnificent sword strapped to his side. He raised a hand to silence his ambitious guard. "That'll be enough." He circled Melia, examining her quickly. The nod she gave him was barely perceptible, but it was enough to extinguish some of the angst in the king's expression.

Siana neared, again wearing the clothes of a soldier.

"What happened to your fancy gowns?" I asked in a low voice.

One corner of her lips quirked upward, but she didn't answer. She moved toward her leader.

Riaan's horse circled his brother. Castiel's borrowed steed danced uncomfortably, but he skillfully controlled the beast. "I'm getting a bit tired of this, Brother."

"The captain's only doing his duty. I was beginning to think you wouldn't make it in time and I'd have to hang you for failure to follow orders."

The prince rolled his eyes. Castiel's larger frame shadowed the king's, but that didn't make Riaan any less threatening.

The king peered over Castiel's shoulder to me, the sun absorbed by his dark, freshly cut hair. The muscles between his brows raised as he regarded me. "Princess Ilianna, what a relief to see you alive and uninjured." He registered the cut on my hand. "Relatively uninjured. You must be exhausted and famished."

His gaze traveled to Cyris, although it was Lucan he saw. "I suspect there must be a reason why this snake is not in shackles, Brother?"

Castiel huffed. "There is, but it cannot be discussed here."

"Then, come" He directed his horse toward Meyrion. "Captain Melia, bring your mother," he called over his shoulder.

I spurred my horse, falling into place, the others not far behind. Two fresh soldiers broke from the group and flanked the wraith to the left and right, both with weapons trained on him, but Cyris didn't seem worried.

As we neared the commotion that built in the courtyard, attendants stopped in their work to bow.

Riaan smiled to each one. "Unfortunately, I can only offer you food, Princess. As you can see, rest is only for the dead." He examined me from the side. "Ketrina arrived this morning, after disappearing a few days back. Do you know anything of this?"

"Yes," I answered. "She—she found me and helped me out of a rather difficult situation."

"I see." His focus returned to my bandaged hand.

"It's only a scratch, Your Majesty," I said, tucking it from his view. "Please do not bother Gedeon with it."

"Gedeon's not here. He's playing midwife for a difficult pregnancy." The king grimaced. "I'm not sure when he'll be back, but Sameen will be relieved to see you. She's been worried sick. I'll send her to you right after our debriefing. You can fill her in on everything, and she can fuss over you and get you ready for your celebration."

It was my turn to cringe. "Surely, that could be cancelled?"

"Absolutely not. Now is not the time to stick our heads in Anolyn's deep soil. We must move on. Besides, your dresses are ready for the grand ball."

"Ball?" Dread did a number on my nerves.

A smile tipped one side of his mouth. "Why, of course. If things progress as I fear they will, this might be the last celebration for many. And in any celebration, there must always be dancing."

I lifted my chin, staring straight forward, hoping he didn't see the fear drain the blood from my face. "Warriors don't dance."

"Speak for yourself," Melia said. I speared her with a sharp look. She only smiled.

Siana chuckled darkly.

"Whoever heard of a princess not dancing at her own celebration?" A wicked glint entered Riaan's eyes. "But perhaps you are worried for your safety. Brother, do we need to relocate Princess Ilianna?"

Heat crawled my face. "Again? But they've already relocated me."

Riaan stared straight forward, the muscles within his jaw tense. "And within the first night you were abducted."

"You cannot protect me from everything."

"I already have plans to ensure her safety," Castiel said, and I flinched at his voice. He still avoided my gaze; I was surprised he even cared. "These plans will be put into place this very evening."

Riaan gave me a patronizing glance. "It's for the best, considering the new circumstances, Princess. If I could relocate, I might feel safer doing so, as well." He shuddered dramatically.

"What is going on, Brother?" Castiel asked.

The king's brow quirked, his voice low. "The esteemed Ambassador from Ardenya has graced us with her presence."

My pulse thundered painfully. My gaze fell to the prince, but he didn't look at me. What would he tell his brother? So much had changed from the time I was taken by Lucan and Weylan. Would I even be welcome anymore?

"Then it has begun," Castiel said in a quiet voice.

The king nodded. "Time for debate is over. We must act now and see where it leads. The night of the ball I will announce the arrival of our beautiful Princess of Eira and the peace Johan desires. We will announce it in front of the ambassador to show her our commitment to fighting any enemy that challenges us."

"And then?"

"We wait for her response."

"Why not counsel with her now? Why wait?"

Riaan's head ticked to the side. "I've tried to speak with her, but she is the most peculiar thing. My gut tells me she's from the Wraith Queen, although she does not say it. She won't even give her name. She only says she must wait for word from her master. She is… odd."

"Odd?" Melia asked.

Riaan shrugged. "That she watches us to report back to her mistress is no surprise, but she also does not eat. She barely says a word, only wanders the corridors at all hours of the day."

Castiel flinched. "Unaccompanied?"

"Of course not, and we demand that she remain in her room during the night hours."

"She's a shell," Melora said in a hushed voice.

"A pryor," the wraith corrected.

"You don't know that," I said, quickly.

"Whatever she is, she's unnatural," the king said.

I scoffed. "Why let her roam at all? Why is she not in a cell already?"

Riaan tsked. "Ilianna, you of all people should know that we don't go throwing visiting dignitaries into prison. And what good would that do to lock up a mere ambassador?"

"I agree with the king. We must wait for her to deliver her message, but if she is a pryor she cannot see me, or Cyris for that matter."

"Cyris? Did we find the him?" the king asked.

"I am here, Your Majesty."

The king's head whipped around to glare at the wraith. His horse jutted to a halt. "You—Castiel what is the meaning of this?"

"You'll have to trust me, brother—"

"Now is not the time for this," Melora said. "We might be recognized, and the wraith's deception in my plan is a must."

The seer reached into her saddlebags as her gaze traveled the great castle walls. She withdrew a black cloak and wrapped it around herself. She pulled the hood down low, almost over her eyes.

Cyris nodded, shielding himself as well.

Melora continued. "As soon as our business is concluded, my king, I will excuse myself. I must prepare for what she might bring."

Riaan spurred his horse forward. His gaze was lethal as he stared Cyris down, but he waited until we had dismounted and were securely within his throne room before asking more.

Reese and Mikael remained outside the doors with two other guards, shutting us within. Siana stood apart from the group, silently watching her king.

Riaan circled the wraith. "Alright, fill me in on all the particulars. Did we find the murderers? Who took Ilianna? And why is this man not three feet underground?"

I steeled myself to hear it all over again. As Castiel took turns with Melora and Cyris explaining the details the king wanted, Melia listened with her arms crossed over her chest.

I remained silent. Anything I said would be immediately rejected anyway. I was tainted. A risk. I had been from the moment I had arrived at Castiel's home. But now it was worse.

Riaan's face solidified as the story progressed, hardening into a mask of steel. Only when he heard of my attempt to end my own life did he cast a glance my direction, but his expression remained unreadable. I paced away, not wanting to hear my fate replayed yet again. Melia broke from the company to take a stand at my side.

After a silent moment, I swallowed against a dry mouth. "Don't want to hear the rest?" I asked. "To hear how far I've fallen?"

She snorted. "Always so dramatic."

I glared.

"I already knew, Ilianna."

"What do you mean?"

"Melora is my mother. You don't think she told me of her suspicions long before? Alright, maybe not too long ago, but she told me everything the night before we left."

"But, then—"

"What does it change? Did I think you had deceived us all? Tricked us into believing you were some innocent chit, all the while plotting your treachery upon my kingdom?" She crossed her arms, staring toward the others hovering around the king and prince. "Surely you know I'm much smarter than that."

"You didn't tell the king, then?"

"It wasn't my story to tell," she said simply.

"I need an interview with Princess Ilianna," Riaan said, interrupting our conversation. "Alone."

I flinched when all looked to me. Even Castiel watched me, but distantly.

Riaan walked away from everyone. "The wraith is under the care of the seer. See that he behaves himself, or he'll be thrown from my home." He climbed his dais of power and cast himself onto his throne. The others, even his assassin, left without a backward glance, abandoning me to the stoic king. Castiel disappeared last through the double doors, and Mikael resealed them shut.

"So, this little girl is the reason for all of the commotion within my home?" Riaan asked. It was the question he had offered to Castiel the very first time we met.

I didn't answer.

He tipped his head to the side, considering me. "The daughter of the Wraith Queen herself. Ilianna Drakara, heir to the powerful Prince Toma and the infamous Theia. The untapped power that must flow through your veins…"

I closed my eyes, sick to my stomach.

"I bet that's what your uncle wanted to ignite in you."

I gritted my teeth. "Then he went about it the wrong way."

Riaan chuckled softly. "No doubt. Well, what do you suggest we do?"

Apprehension plagued me. "What do you mean?"

"It's your life, Ilianna. I won't pretend to understand what must be going through your mind, or how you must feel." He leaned forward, his hands clasped. "But suicide? Really?"

"You have a better solution?" Although I sounded strong, sickness nearly stole my nerve.

He drew a knife from his boot, examining the blade. "I believe you should do as the seer suggests. If what the wraith says is true, then this is our opportunity to destroy the beast once and for all. You are a gift to this nation."

A laugh burst from my lips. "I'm a curse."

"You are a blessing, Ilianna. Not a curse."

"Blessing?" I nearly choked on the word. "What chance do I have against this lunatic? Someone that infests the souls of her own children to become stronger through some black magic? *And* I'm a magician—doubly cursed. How much more powerful will she be when she takes me?"

Slowly, he stood. "You believe she will take you?"

I didn't answer.

Carefully, he extended his knife to me, delicately balanced on his two palms. It was a beautiful instrument sharpened to a deadly point—an offering. "Then what would you do if the choice was yours?"

I hesitated, then grabbed the knife by the hilt. One hand clamped down on my wrist, so fast I had no time to react. An iron grip chafed against my skin. I jerked back, but his hold kept me in place.

His eyes stared into mine, holding me fast. "You'd leave us to face her alone?"

My mouth opened to respond, but nothing came. Shame colored my cheeks.

"Dammit, Riaan." Castiel's voice was like ice. From the corner of my eye, the prince darted toward me. "Ilianna, stop—"

Power surged into my fingertips and I yanked free of the king's grip, deftly moving away from both royal brothers. I lowered into a crouch and Castiel halted, his hands raised. I had all but forgotten about the secret entrance into the room. Had he heard the entire conversation?

"So now you care? Is that all I am to you? A means to an end to the Wraith Queen?"

Slowly, he straightened. "Of course not."

"At least your brother was willing to give me the choice."

"Is that what you want? Truly?"

I growled. With the flick of my wrist, the king's blade flew from my fingers, hitting the oak throne dead center. Without waiting for their response, I turned on my heel and pounded on the double doors for release.

Mikael opened them. Reese waited beyond.

"I wish to go to my room."

Mikael peered beyond my shoulder to the king, but I couldn't. I didn't have the courage to see Castiel's disappointment.

"Where is the ambassador, Captain?" the king asked.

"She wanders the garden with three of your soldiers, Your Majesty," Mikael said.

"Good. Quickly take the princess to her room. Lieutenant Reese, find Sameen."

I stormed by the guard without waiting to see if Mikael followed, earning several strange glances from an unusual amount of security. As I climbed the stairs, I was slowed by half a dozen soldiers in the stairwell. They pressed themselves against the stone walls for me to pass. Some whom I recognized from the training yard murmured their apologies then went their way. I hesitated, watching their descent as I finally registered the changed atmosphere of the castle. An eerie sensation pricked the back of my neck and traveled the length of my spine.

"Princess?" Mikael waited on the steps below me, annoyance clear in his voice.

I slowly restarted my ascent. "Was anyone hurt the day of my kidnapping?"

The hesitation in his voice was barely detectable. "The soldier that stood guard at your door was found unconscious, but alive."

I hummed. "Probably given the same injection I was."

Mikael grunted. "The knot on his head would suggest otherwise."

Had he been the one to deliver that blow? "I see. Well, I'm glad to hear he was at least left alive." I released a heavy sigh, my nerves on a tight string. If I was going to do this, there would be no better time. "Now that we're alone, I feel this is the best time for you to kill me, so no one else is injured during the attempt."

Mikael's steps halted. "Excuse me?"

I laughed, and the Demon Daughter within stirred to the crazed sound. "Believe me, it's for the best if you do." I faced him, a whole head higher on the stairs. Lifting my chin even higher, I glared. "Shall we begin?"

"What do you—"

I took a step down, excitement rising. "Nolen was murdered. Your guard was injured. All because of *you*."

His jaw clenched. "I didn't injure any guard or kill this—this Nolen."

"No, but you might as well have." I tipped my head to the side, examining the red splotches erupting on his cheeks. He wasn't a very good liar, which meant he didn't do it very often. That at least was encouraging. "Do you know why I have this?" I held up my hand to expose my injury.

One side of his lips quirked up, mocking, "How should I?"

"Because it was done by your blade, and when Gedeon heals it, he'll see what I saw. The arm of my captor, and the feathers of a falcry on the exposed skin of his wrist."

24

CONFRONTATION

THE SMUG SMILE SLID FROM HIS lips as the blood drained from his face.

I took a step down, closing the distance. "If it's all the same to you, I'd rather you be a man and kill me yourself. If you can."

His teeth set, his jaw clenched. "No."

"Are you afraid that if you do it in the light of day, with extra security roaming the corridors, you won't be able to cover up the murder?"

"No."

"Because no one will be able to take the fall for you, right?" When he didn't answer, I took another step down, bringing us eye to eye. Anger electrified the space between us. The demon inside growled. "Coward."

His gaze narrowed. The muscles in his jaw worked. "I'm not a coward."

"Then prove me wrong."

"How?"

I shrugged, nonchalant, but that wasn't the answer my demon wanted. She paced within, still hoping. "I don't know. Personally, I'd take me up on the offer."

"I didn't want you dead. You weren't even supposed to be hurt."

"Then what, Captain?" My voice echoed from the concrete walls. "Why help Lucan and Weylan? Why go against Riaan?"

He grimaced at the mention of his king.

I smirked. "I honestly didn't think you capable of treason."

Anger flared in his eyes. "I'm not a traitor. I just wanted you gone. Riaan himself wanted it at first."

"Are you saying he doesn't want that now?"

His smirk mirrored mine from just a moment before. "You think my king had something to do with your abduction?" He laughed. "He's young, but he's a good man. He would never go against his word."

"But you would."

"For the safety and benefit of my kingdom, yes. You're a threat to Anolyn."

I tsked. "I don't want to hurt your precious Anolyn."

"Maybe now you don't, but you are a Drakara. You'll be as bloodthirsty as your father and uncle."

Bloodthirsty.

The word hit me, strangely. I blinked as shock and shame battled for ownership. If he only knew what my family line was capable of. The Demon Daughter rolled her eyes, relinquishing any control.

Mikael smiled. "You know I'm right, don't you?"

"You're a fool," I said, rallying. "The Wraith Queen practically beats upon our doors. You'd risk the peace Riaan seeks?"

"Lucan said your uncle wanted you home and that he'd keep any peace needed to fight any upcoming battle. Both he and Weylan promised to take you to Eira. *That's* where you belong. Not here. You'll lead my kingdom into ruins."

I snapped. "I don't want to lead any kingdom anywhere. I never wanted to be here in the first place. I wanted to get away from my uncle. To start over somewhere new and live my life as I choose!"

"And yet I'm the coward?"

I glared at him. "Perhaps *you* are the one who needs to leave."

"No."

"Where will they send you when they hear of your treason?"

"My place is here, protecting my king."

I ripped off the bandage, exposing the torn flesh, still red from the cut of his blade. "Then from here on, you'll do what I say no matter the cost."

He grimaced. "You'd blackmail me?"

"Absolutely. But like you, Mikael, I have a soft spot for both of the brothers of Anolyn, and heaven help me, I'll protect them, even above my own king and kingdom."

"Truly?"

Shocked by my own words, I laughed. "Is it such a surprise I have no love for my uncle?"

His eyes narrowed, then slid to the burn mark on my neck. "Is that from *him*?"

I lifted my head, angling it so he could see it better. "It was given as a reminder of his power over me."

He shook his head, his expression darkening. "I can understand why you'd hate the lunatic."

"I don't need your sympathy," I said, my face flushed. "But I believe you genuinely care for *your* king. I also believe you to be a good man, Mikael, but I can't keep looking over my shoulder for the next time you'll betray me."

His chin raised a fraction. "I'll never betray you again."

"We'll see." I turned from him, almost daring him to stab me in the back. Pricks of imaginary pain assaulted my spine, but Mikael made no attempt on my life.

I stepped from the stairwell to the hallway that took me to my room. A woman came from the opposite direction. When she saw me, she gasped, dropping the basket of linens. Sameen ran for me. I was tackled in an embrace too strong to pull away from. Her warmth soothed.

She held me from her, searching my face. Tears streaked her cheeks. She clutched my arms, then pulled me inside the room, but before she shut the door she shouted an order to the stunned captain. "Call for a bath to be drawn. Immediately."

Mikael nodded, a strange expression on his face.

I lazed in bliss as Sameen brushed my hair, drying it before a warm fire. I had bathed for more than an hour, washing the grime of the past few days from my body and soul. Sameen had washed my hair twice, massaging my scalp until the headache I'd been ignoring reduced to a dull throb. Then, she dressed me in a beautiful new nightgown fit for a queen. The white material draped so soft against my skin I barely stopped myself from cocooning within the folds of fabric. Scooped wide on my shoulders, it kissed the skin at my collarbone then fell to my toes. Lulled into a deep sense of relaxation, I sank in my comfortable chair, basking in the care of my maid's attentions.

Even after I told her the horrible truth of my lineage, Sameen still fussed over me as a true mother would. Why didn't she care? Only Castiel had reacted rationally, but he was right to shun me as he did.

I sat up, feeling the sting of his rejection acutely. He would never look at me the same again, but why did it bother me so much? Caught up in my thoughts, I didn't hear Sameen's question.

"What?" I asked.

She gave me an exasperated look and placed her hands on her hips. "I really think I should sleep in here with you. Should I have a guard bring in a cot?" She placed the brush on my vanity table.

I waved off the suggestion. "Of course not. I'm not going to subject you to such uncomfortable sleeping arrangements."

"But—"

"Thank you for your care." I stood, stretching sore muscles.

"I really think—"

I wrapped her in my arms, embracing her. She froze.

"Thank you," I said into the material at her shoulder. "For always taking such good care of me."

She patted my back soothingly, then gathered my dirty linens and left me alone. For a long while I stared from my window, watching the sun set past the horizon. I pulled my chair closer to the glass and tucked my chilled feet beneath the folds of my nightgown. My mind raced yet could not complete a full thought.

I was the Demon Daughter to the Wraith Queen. That title had to have spawned from somewhere. Had my uncle created it? Who else of my kingdom knew of my lineage?

Guards walked the grounds in pairs, their torches dotting the gardens and fields. Did the pryor walk the grounds with them, escorted by the king's soldiers? If she were the descendant of the Wraith Queen, that meant she was my grandmother, or even great-grandmother. I shook my head at the absurdity.

Should I look for her? But even as I thought it, the answer twisted in my stomach. No.

The creak of my bedroom door drew my attention. I tipped my head to the side, waiting. "If that's someone here to kidnap me again, at least let me change into something else."

The door pushed open and Castiel entered. He wore tan breeches and an unbuttoned white top that exposed his muscled chest. He was barefoot. "Do you find that amusing, Princess?"

My chin rose at his formal tone. "And what if I was serious?"

Castiel spoke to someone behind him, their voices too low for me to understand. I rose from my chair. Reese's familiar shadow stood just beyond the threshold. The prince closed the door.

"What is going on?" I asked. "Another search?"

"Your new sleeping arrangements. Reese is the only one who knows about it. The only one I trust with that secret, outside of my own brother."

"And just what are these new arrangements?"

Castiel peered about the darkened room but he did not answer.

I crossed my arms protectively over my heart. "I see you're still not wanting to talk to me."

He walked to the fire to lean upon the mantle. The dying flames claimed his attention. "It wasn't that I didn't want to talk to you."

"Then what?"

His fingers threaded through his thick, dark tresses. Finally, he looked to me. "What Melora said… what Cyris said—it was a lot to work through. I needed time to think."

"Oh, it was a lot for you to work through?" Although I tried to hide it, pain laced my words. "Well, I'm sorry it was so difficult. I know I'm a burden. I always have been."

He tsked. "You're not a burden. I just had to figure things out."

"Whether or not to kill me?"

He spun, shock twisting his features. "Of course not! For the love of Anolyn's… I just can't think clearly around you, Ilianna!"

My heart broke at the sound of my name on his lips. "What is that supposed to mean?"

Again, he said nothing. Frustration seared through me, deeply, painfully. Why did my eyes sting? Why did he affect me so much? My words tumbled out on a whispered sigh. "Just leave, Prince."

I moved toward my bed, wanting nothing more than to cast myself into its embrace, never to emerge.

Suddenly, Castiel's hand seized my wrist. He pulled me to him as his other arm snaked around my stomach and tucked me closer. I gaped and tried to wrench away, but his strength held me in place. His voice was rough at my ear, the sound vibrating deep into my chest. "Ilianna, I didn't come here to argue."

"Then what?" I angled my head to glare, but my scowl fell flat against his weary expression. Like the other day when we had traveled together, he was so close, his mouth only a breath away. But this time I didn't pull back. My gaze fell to his lips, so perfectly sculpted like the rest of him. His crystal blue eyes traveled my face. Heat sparked like flint between the small space that separated us and suddenly I couldn't breathe. I couldn't move.

Slow and warm, his hand glided up my side to my arm. Fire bloomed where his touch grazed. He lifted my wrists open to the side. "Were you at least taught how to dance?" he asked low in my ears.

I swallowed. "Yes."

"Do you remember the steps?"

I lied. "I don't know." It wasn't that I hadn't been taught. I wasn't *allowed* to dance. Ilianna Drakara was a warrior, not a fool, and King Johan didn't believe in letting his niece participate in such frivolities.

He leaned down. His deep voice caressed my neck as he spoke. "Step forward with your left." Without waiting for my response, he guided me, and I could do nothing but comply. "Step back. Now, forward with your right. And back." One hand slid to my waist, gently twirling me around. "Turn in a circle to the left. And curtsy. Circle to the right. Curtsy."

What was I doing?

Before, I had shunned the touch of others, terrified of ulterior motives. Of being hurt or betrayed. But this was different. With Castiel, there was no anxiety or fear, only intense… there was no word to describe how I felt.

I closed my eyes and allowed him to steer me through several more actions, his touch electrifying my every sense. Every time I moved, he pulled me back to him, securing me in place. The steps he taught were almost the same from what I had learned as a girl, with only slight modifications, but no one had ever shown me like this.

"I remember," I rasped and drew away from his touch, but the prince spun me around on the next turn and I over rotated, stopping face to face with him. I froze in his arms. Only inches apart, his crystal eyes overtook me and darkened to reveal something I had never seen before. Something I didn't understand but was powerless to stop.

With a gentleness that nearly undid me, his fingers traced the length of my hair down my back, eliciting a shudder that traveled throughout my body. I inhaled his scent and reveled in the soft touch of his calloused hands. Slowly, almost painfully, he leaned in. My breath caught, then gasped when his lips brushed against mine. Then again, and again.

And my heart shattered into a million pieces.

I loved him.

He pulled away, and his hands cupped my cheeks, gently wiping the tear that trailed the length of it. His fingers traced the burned scar on my neck.

He rested his forehead to mine. "I'm sorry. I shouldn't have—"

"Why?" I broke away.

His head twitched. His eyes narrowed, confused.

"Why shouldn't you have?" Braver than I felt, my fingers pressed against his bare chest. Reaching up on tip toes and staring directly into those eyes, I kissed his lips. Then again. All thoughts fled when Castiel's fingers threaded through my hair to secure me to him. His other arm pulled me even closer.

A mixture of elation and fear did a number on my senses. On a falcry's wings, my heart soared, but I worried at how hard I would crash to the earth when Castiel decided he was done with me. Then I realized—it didn't matter. I desired this. *Needed* this as much as I needed him, and I would take what he would give.

Two knocks at the door forced us apart much too soon. Castiel pulled back to look at me.

Passion. It was passion that darkened his eyes and emanated from him. It matched the heat amplified by my every nerve.

His finger trailed the line of my jaw, then he went to the door and opened it. Reese entered carrying a cot and several blankets. I stepped back in strange awe as Castiel directed him near the dying fire.

He took my hands in his when Reese clicked the door closed. The intensity of the moment had faded by the interruption, but not enough. I waited with bated breath, my lips tingling with a desire for more.

Castiel cleared his throat. "I shouldn't have kissed you, because I will be the one ensuring your safety during the nights until the ambassador leaves, and now I will struggle to keep from compromising you."

He must have read my reaction as trepidation, but that wasn't what caused me to burn.

Lifting my hand, he pressed his soft, marvelous lips to the back of my knuckles. "Don't worry. I'll be a perfect gentleman… from now on." A smile lifted the corner of his mouth. "Reese is the only one that knows, and besides myself, he, Melia, and Sameen are the only ones I trust right now with your safety."

I considered my words before I spoke. "Not Mikael or your precious generals?"

Castiel stilled, then released my hands to spread out the blanket over the cot. "Mikael was the one in charge of your safety before. While I don't know if he had anything to do with your abduction, I will not risk having him watch over you. Not for a while. And the generals—well, they're still not exactly on the same page yet." He turned to me, then groaned. "I'm starting to regret my decision."

"I'm sure your assassin would be more than happy to watch over me," I said, enjoying the moroseness of my humor. Castiel scowled in the familiar way that I loved.

A knock at the door interrupted, and Sameen entered wearing a white cap and nightgown. When her eyes fell to the prince, her expression pinched as her arms wrapped around her chest. "I already told the princess I would stay with her tonight. Surely, you can and *should* sleep in your own room, my prince."

Something that sounded an awful lot like a laugh huffed from Reese before he shut the door behind her.

Castiel gestured to the cot. "It should be comfortable enough, my dear."

"And where will you sleep?" she asked, her eyes shifting uneasily to the bed.

He almost smiled. "On the ground in front of the door, of course."

"Nonsense," I said, interrupting their conversation. They seemed to forget I was in the room. "Sameen, you will sleep with me."

She flinched. "I should think—"

I waved off her words. "My bed's big enough for five grown men. It's silly to have it all to myself. Castiel, you take the cot but sleep near the fire. I'm sure you'll wake if you hear any commotion." I refused any further argument by crawling to the opposite side of my mattress to make enough room for my prudish lady's maid. I pulled my blankets to my chin and gazed at the ceiling, listening as my orders were obeyed. Silence settled upon my room. I curled to my side, barely making out Castiel's shadowed profile against the dim light of the fire.

I loved him. The shock of that realization spun my thoughts and made me dizzy. I had once thought myself in love, but this was so different from what I had felt for Weylan. No more than a child when I fell for my uncle's young star, I didn't know what atrocities he could be capable of. His flirtations and motivations were manipulative, and like my uncle, he played a game I could never win. Castiel had no ulterior motive.

There must be a union between our two kingdoms if we are to survive.

Melora's words raked through my mind. I squashed the memory with the twitch of my neck. I could never marry the king of Anolyn. While strong and good like his brother, Riaan wasn't what I wanted. Besides, as much as they tried to hide the truth, it was obvious he loved Melia, and Melia loved him.

I closed my eyes, sinking into the depths of my soft bed. Sameen's delicate snore calmed.

My uncle had to die. The Wraith Queen had to die. I would hand my kingdom to Anolyn, our two countries to be ruled by a hand that could lead my people towards peace and resourceful living. And I would—what would I do?

The question plagued me as I fought for rest. Finally, I drifted off to sleep and dreamed of sailing away from this plagued continent.

But this time, I wasn't alone.

25

PREPARATIONS

MEYRION BUZZED WITH MORE activity than I had ever
seen within its walls. Much to my dismay, I wasn't
allowed to explore. I had to watch the preparations from
my lonely window as every able hand hustled to clean,
cook, and decorate for the two-day festivities. Castiel kept
to his word and left me alone the entire night, much to my
chagrin. Not that he had any choice with my lady's maid in
the room, and not that I had wanted him to… to do
anything to compromise me.

Or did I? Warmth flooded through every pore of my
body. I touch my lips, remembering the way his had felt
on mine.

I should have been with him.

He had breakfast brought to me and Sameen at a most
terrible hour and left before the light of dawn, giving me
some terrible excuse as to why I was not permitted to join
him or to participate in the arrangements. I was the guest
of honor—although I felt that most of that honor was

shifted to the new and more fascinating visitant, the reserved ambassador from Ardenya. I had yet to witness her for myself.

Sameen left after eating to take care of my washing. Locked away in my room, I paced, my stomach twisting as the kingdom of Anolyn arrived in hordes for the grand feast. They pitched tents along the outskirts of the king's land. Sameen had said this was customary, especially for those civilians traveling from a greater distance. It all seemed crazy to me. I observed from my window as great pits of fire dotted the courtyard, smoking pork, chicken, and beef. The smell traveled along the soft spring air, filling my lungs and causing my stomach to growl a pitiful noise. Musicians played their instruments and sang, their voices blending together in an odd collaboration.

It was all a show put on by the cunning King of Anolyn. But would it be enough?

No one knew that a snake lay hidden within their den, waiting for the perfect moment to strike. Why was the ambassador here? And why hadn't she delivered whatever message she was sent to give? Would the Anouk brothers let her live once she delivered the message?

A pang of guilt ripped through me. The answer *should* be no, but did Riaan and Castiel have it in them to do something so hard? The Drakara family would have no qualm in killing the messenger of an enemy.

Eira had always been considered harsh, and not only for its weather. Only during the Demon Wars had the two opposing countries come together for any resemblance of a union, but now we would try to do so once more. An announcement would be made that very evening, an accord between Anolyn and Eira, and then I would be introduced.

How many countrymen would line up to take my head?

Although I thought it better to cancel the cursed festivities altogether, I knew the king was right. It was important for Riaan to demonstrate to the ambassador that united we would fight against her master and any army she could bring. She would then take the message to her queen.

Sameen entered with attendants trailing her—two young girls, barely of age. Their fresh faces observed me with wide eyes and barely suppressed curiosity. One carried flowers, ribbons, shoes, and other paraphernalia I was sure a sensible woman had no need of. The other, a silver tray laden with lunch, the smell of which caused my mouth to salivate.

Sameen brought gowns, several of them, all different colors stacked high on her strong arms. She gently hung them within my armoire, then directed the girls where to place each item they carried.

I absentmindedly played with the ends of my long hair until the young ladies were shooed from my room. "Am I allowed out of my confinement?"

She picked through the things the girls had brought, not looking at me. "You will eat first, but then we must get you ready." She turned to me and her expression pinched. "Why are you still in your nightgown?"

I shrugged. "Why bother getting dressed if I'm to stay up here? Besides, it's very comfortable."

Sameen snorted in artificial annoyance. "Well, the prince will gather you as soon as we're done, so we must hurry. The festivities will start soon."

But still I lingered by the window. "Why don't I eat with the townsfolk? The food smells delicious."

"The prince demands that all food you eat is prepared by our kitchen and is checked for poison by the cook himself."

"Do you jest?"

"Princess Ilianna—"

I held up my hand. "Never mind, I get it." I was the enemy.

I was dressed in record time in a simple, cream-colored day dress embroidered with gold-colored stitching. A gold belt was the only decoration. Sameen sat me down at the vanity and arranged my hair into a long, loose braid, interweaving ribbons throughout.

From the pile of female fripperies, she drew a crown of pale pink, blue, and green wildflowers, but before she could set it on my head, I jerked away.

"Flowers? No."

"Ilianna, you are Princess of—"

"I am the Demon Daughter of the Wraith Queen, and niece to Johan Drakara. I have never worn a crown of flowers, and I'm not going to start now."

She placed one hand on her hips. "And you're proud of that ancestral line? Why don't you show these people that you're not some bloodthirsty, untrusting foreigner?"

My mouth clamped shut.

She continued. "Crowns like these are worn by *all* eligible maidens during the daylight activities. It's an Anolyn tradition, and in Anolyn, we take those seriously."

An eligible maiden? Is that what I was? In the mirror I watched as my cheeks turned a shade of pink. It that what Castiel thought of me as?

"Fine," I puffed. "But only because it's a tradition, and I will respect the people of Anolyn." If my uncle ever saw me like this, he'd have me stripped bare and beaten for shame and insolence.

Sameen smiled. "That's a girl."

Castiel collected me after I ate. Worry wore the lines of his face, but when he saw me, that worry slipped. His gaze traveled the length of my dress, admiration clear in his eyes. He lifted my hand to his lips, and I blushed. "You're beautiful."

"That she is," Reese said from behind, and I smiled at him.

I took Castiel's extended arm. Reese followed close behind. "Until the ball tonight, I will continue to introduce you as Lady Anna. While all our staff and army know who you really are, they've been instructed not to reveal it to anyone."

"Which means a lot of people already know," our guard said. "So, the fact there's no one waiting outside with pitchforks is a good sign." Reese smiled, in obvious good humor, but nothing of what he said cheered me as it did him.

"Your men would go against your king that way?"

Castiel examined me, his expression soft. "You're fresh gossip, Ilianna. We expected it."

Outside hundreds ate, danced, and played games I had never seen. They stopped and bowed to the prince, showering him with affection and speaking to him as they would their friend. The king was also among his people, talking and laughing as if he were just another citizen. Captain Melia was with him, stunning in a similar cream-colored dress. Purple flowers crowned her flowing blonde hair that fell to her hips in waves and braids. Her mother was nowhere to be seen.

There was too much detail to take in. Too many conversations I couldn't hear. My vision narrowed, unable to see past the citizens clogging the once opened landscape, hindering me from locating the true danger that lurked. I squeezed Castiel's arm and he looked down. I tipped up to my toes to whisper in his ear. "The ambassador?"

"She will join us this evening," he said through stiff lips.

I nodded as a little anxiety slipped from my chest. Attached to the prince's arm, I could *almost* feel happy, but something warned me against it. Although the day was warm, chills rippled across my skin. Something was coming, I could feel it. The Demon Daughter paced within her cage, sensing my ill-at-ease nerves.

Is that what brought her on? My fear? I swallowed, forcing the sensation back, and tried to pay attention to my surroundings.

Rather than have someone test my food for me, I refused any offerings in the kindest way possible. It wasn't easy. Treats, meats, baked goods, and delicious-looking candies were shoved at us. The smell was enough to weaken my knees, but I wouldn't subject a food tester to such fears as poison.

Time slipped by quickly, and soon people left to get ready for the ball. Those that camped on the grounds had it easy enough. Others headed into the nearby town.

The prince escorted me inside as soon as we could slip away, and I released a nervous breath. The afternoon had gone off without a hitch, but there was more to come. The dance would be open to everyone no matter their station—yet another difference between kingdoms. It made sense. If the people of the kingdom were happy and felt a connection to their king, they would be more willing to work and be productive. And when required, they would fight and protect their homes.

The king of Eira, didn't deserve the loyalty of his people. After I killed my uncle, it would be wise of me to give Riaan and Castiel the crown.

I nodded, confirming my own judgment.

Castiel's brows lifted. "What was that?"

I glanced away. "Just thinking to myself."

The closer we came to my room, the more distressed I felt. Castiel opened my door and let me pass through.

And I froze.

A woman clad in a lavender dress stood next to my bed. Heavily gray-streaked brown hair tumbled past her waist, unbound and almost wild. Her porcelain profile appeared more doll-like than real as she stared at the empty blankets, one hand extended above the covers. Upon our entrance, she turned. Red eyes fixed on mine.

My heart stammered to a halt, then picked up speed.

Castiel quickly blocked me from view. I half-stepped from behind him, peering over his shoulder on tiptoes.

"Ambassador, why are you here?" he asked.

She didn't seem to notice him. Her head tipped oddly to the side to better see me. Chapped lips lifted into a broken, peculiar smile, set into a face that was my own. My feet moved on their own accord, stepping around my protector to get a better look. Her eyes rolled to the back of her head and she swayed on the spot. I bolted to catch her, but Castiel's reaction was faster. He grabbed me to hold me in place.

"Castiel—"

"No," he said low in my ears, but any assistance was unnecessary. The woman steadied herself on the corner post of my bed.

She blinked, then bloodshot, silver-blue eyes stared up at me. I inhaled, gripping Castiel's hand wrapped protectively around my waist.

"Excuse me," she said, her voice an octave too high. She peered around the room. "I must be lost. Can you direct me to my room?"

With raised brows, Castiel called for Reese but didn't let down his defenses. Our guard entered, his eyes widening in response to our uninvited guest.

"Wonderful." She smiled at Reese in a daydreamer's haze. She moved toward the door but paused as she passed me. "Aren't you lovely, dear." She reached to touch my braid pulled over my shoulder but stopped when I flinched away. Blood encrusted her torn nails.

"What happened to your hands?" I asked in a gasp.

She clenched her fists as if embarrassed. The gown she wore was pressed with clean lines, but red smudges smeared where her touch had rested against the fabric. "I fell while in the garden. I should get cleaned up. Excuse me," she said, then left with Reese.

My breath whooshed from my lungs, my pulse beating at an irregular rhythm. "It was her." I clasped Castiel's hand to my chest, desiring the warmth of his fingers. "For a moment, her eyes were red like the wraith's. It was the Wraith Queen."

"Are you sure?"

"Yes." But then a groan escaped my lips. "No. Not for certain. But for one moment there was an entirely different being staring from her eyes. She has—she has *my* eyes." A silvery-blue. Pain erupted in my chest and my throat tightened. Castiel gathered me in his arms, protecting me from my own torturous thoughts.

"Ilianna." An urgent voice whispered at my door before Melora pushed it open. Now well past one hundred, her gray hair fell from a messy bun at the top of her head. Black smudged the loose skin of her wrinkled cheeks, and she didn't even register Castiel's presence as she shuffled barefoot into the room. She held out a small bowl filled with a muddy substance. "Quick, take this and follow the pryor, but don't let her see you. When she enters her room, coat the entire door frame with this."

"What is it?" I asked, examining the bowl.

"Just do it!"

When I reached to take it, suddenly Melora grabbed my hand and a sharp prick stabbed into my finger.

I cried out. "Hey!"

Castiel lunged forward, holding my arm. "Melora, what—?"

She waved him off, seized my finger, already coated in red, and pinched. Her papery thin skin felt strange against mine.

"A final ingredient," she said as a single drop of blood fell into the mixture.

Anger pulsed like my throbbing thumb. "You could have asked."

"No time." She dropped my hand and mixed in my offering, grunting as she worked.

I sucked at my abused thumb. "Will it kill her?" I asked.

"Fool, we don't want to kill her. Why do the Drakaras instantly jump to killing?"

Heat drew to my cheeks, but I kept from commenting.

Again, she held out the bowl. "Follow her, but don't let her see you. Coat the entire door frame."

"Why don't you—"

She tsked, interrupting. Her voice scratched in her throat. "Because I must rest, and the spell will be more effective if it's done by a descendant. *Now*." She pushed the bowl against my chest with a grunt and shoved me out the door, much stronger than any old lady should be.

I ran. Castiel's footsteps followed behind.

"I don't know where I'm going," I said over my shoulder, and the prince sprinted ahead.

We climbed the spiral staircase one flight up and raced down another hallway. Before we rounded a corner, Castiel stopped, holding out an arm for me to wait.

Reese walked quickly away from the ambassador's room. I could almost feel his unease as he made his escape. Two guards stood just outside, appearing as apprehensive as him. A chill crawled my body, but I shook it off. This was not the time for fear.

Castiel followed as I neared the closed door. He put a finger to his lips to silence the guards, and they instantly moved to block any view of our actions. Anxiety took my breath. My heartbeat pounded loudly, painfully within my head. Holding my hand as steady as I could, I coated the paintbrush with more paint than was necessary and slathered on the primal sludge.

༄ళ

Castiel led me through the hallways and I followed blindly, caught up in my thoughts and an extreme amount of adrenaline. I didn't know what the potion would do to the pryor, and I worried over whether it would hurt her or not. But why did I worry?

"At ease," Castiel said.

Shocked, I stuttered to a stop between two guards. Mikael's lips twitched in the corners when he nodded to me. The other I recognized from the training yard only.

"Tell Sameen she is to bring Princess Ilianna's things here," Castiel said. "And if anyone hears of this, you'll both be put to death."

The other's guards face paled, but Mikael appeared unconcerned.

"Yes, sir," they said in unison.

Castiel pulled me past the soldiers and into the very same room he had brought me my first day of meeting him. I don't know why that knowledge caused me to blush like an idiot, but I turned from the prince to avoid notice.

Nothing had changed. Books still littered the floor, and more paperwork coated his desk. A fire blazed within the hearth, making me sweat.

What was wrong with me?

"This way," he said, and he opened another door. "You'll stay here until we can figure out something else."

I froze at the threshold. More neatly stacked books ascended one wall all the way to the ceiling. Steam rose from an already filled bathtub that sat next to a stone fireplace with no privacy screen. Above the mantle, a menacing beast of fur and claws hung with another one mirroring it upon the floor. But what caught my attention more was the gigantic mahogany bed draped with deep red blankets and plush pillows.

I flushed again, pointing to the tub. "I had a bath last night," I said stupidly.

Castiel cleared his throat. "The water was drawn for me."

Heat crawled my neck and burst into ugly patches on my cheeks. I moved to the fireplace, stepping over the head of the beast. "And what did these poor bears do to deserve such treatment?"

"Those aren't bears," he said, but didn't answer anything further because a flustered Sameen entered, unhappy and out of breath.

She gasped, dropping the two bags she carried and quickly ushered the prince from the room. Despite my objections, my lady's maid still forced me to wash in the prince's tub after seeing residue from Melora's potion on my hands and arms. I shivered in the warm water, covering my nakedness with my hands. It wasn't because of Sameen. She'd seen me more times than I could count, but I couldn't shake the feeling of being watched, and the thought chilled me to the core.

The ambassador had somehow found my room and gotten inside. Where had the guards been? Was that to be my fate? My grandmother's red eyes flashed into my memory.

And where was the other red-eyed freak, Cyris? Had the seer tucked him away somewhere?

So many questions and more flooded my brain while Sameen proceeded to dress me in the most beautiful gown I had ever seen: a silvery-blue dress with silver piping and belt.

"To match your eyes," she said. The sleeves covered to my wrist, then draped open and flowed nearly to the ground.

She let most of my hair fall in waves to my hips, adding an elaborate braid that drew from my temples to the back of my head.

When she spun me around to look into the mirror, the fabric shimmered against my pale skin and contrasted wonderfully with my dark hair. The woman reflected in the mirror was not the same as the girl that had first arrived in Anolyn. Although still pale, color bloomed upon her cheeks. And she was not as reed-thin as I once was. A healthy, regular diet had added to my curves and softened the sharpness of my face.

"Beautiful," Sameen said from behind me. "But we're not finished yet."

From within one of the bags she drew a blue velvet case, and within it was a delicate circlet of silver vines and flower. She skillfully pinned it in place.

Mikael waited for me when I was finished. His shocked expression was enough to cause me to blush, but he wasn't the one I wanted to impress tonight. Two new guards stood outside the doorway, refusing to even look at me. Music floated to us as we drew closer to the reception hall. Reese spied our arrival and rushed to collect me from my guard. Mikael preceded us into the throne room.

My head spun to the noise of hundreds of voices talking, laughing. It was a hive of commotion, more than I had ever seen or heard. I clung tighter to Reese as he led me through the throng of packed bodies that pressed against me and jostled my steps. Once again, there was no pomp or ceremony. Castiel laughed with his people and the lively king danced with commoners. Melia danced with Mayor Belau. Gedeon had returned, paler than usual but still smiling as he conversed with several citizens.

Upon the dais, several additional chairs aligned to the left and right of the king's empty throne.

The music stopped.

26

AN ARRANGEMENT

"MY GOOD PEOPLE!" RIAAN'S VOICE rang above the din, and we halted near the front of the space. "Welcome, my friends! I hope you have enjoyed your time here and know you are always welcome!"

Cheers erupted at his words.

"I have several announcements to make before we continue with our evening of celebration. First, I'd like to welcome a guest from overseas."

My breath hitched in my lungs. Riaan's arm spread to the side, and the Wraith Queen's pryor appeared with two of the king's guards.

Silence enveloped the crowd.

The pryor's nervous gaze shifted about the room. Again, the silvery-blue shade shocked me, but it wasn't the color of her eyes that caught my attention. Before, the woman seemed barely lucid, as if in a trance. Now, her smooth demeanor had disappeared. She shook with anxiety. Her forehead shimmered with sweat.

Could this be the effects of Melora's potion? Had I made her sick?

The ambassador stopped next to the king.

"We welcome the ambassador of Ardenya to Anolyn, and hope she finds her stay among our people enlightening."

The ambassador bowed, then quickly stepped away without a word to stand at the side of the room. Several people cleared a place for her, their eyes nervously shifting away from her panicked expression.

Castiel's familiar presence pressed against me when he took Reese's place. I sighed in relief as his hand clasped my elbow. I looked up to him, but his gaze was transfixed upon his brother, his jaw tense. The prince was a specimen of elegance. A white top and dark breeches did little to hide his masculine beauty and muscles. Sweat gleamed from his handsome brow.

The king continued. "But this evening was originally planned to celebrate an even more important announcement. Almost four months ago, we welcomed within our community a guest that you know by the name of Lady Anna. But my good people, that was an invention to hide this individual's identity until we could guarantee the success of a future arrangement."

Arrangement.

The word cut through my gut like a knife. Surely, he didn't intend to go forward with *that.*

"Brother, bring our guest forward."

The request rang in my ears. Panic nearly caused me to bolt. Castiel's touch alone allowed me the confidence to move, but every step was painful. What could I do? How could I refuse the king in front of this crowd? Maybe Castiel would intervene—unless he'd already agreed to this *arrangement.*

I wanted to scream.

A murmur erupted over the audience.

Castiel brought me to stand next to the king. My head spun as the blood drained from my face, but I managed to gaze out among the sea of faces.

"I was young when my father died," Riaan said. "And yet you put your trust in me. Because of your unshaking faith, I have devoted my life to serving you and you have become my friends. My brothers and my sisters, I ask that you once again put your trust in me. An evil threatens to return. Because of this threat, we must once again align with our neighbor."

More murmurs erupted. The king paused until the rush calmed. "As a show of peace, the king of Eira has sent us a gift. His niece, Princess Ilianna Drakara." A roar of voices followed. I swallowed against the tightness in my throat, but the king pretended not the notice the chaos. "He does this in hopes that we can put behind us our past and unite against a common enemy."

"And who is that?" a voice shouted from among the throng.

The king paused to eye the questioner. "The Wraith Queen."

Gasps and screams sounded throughout the room. Questions flung within the space. Castiel placed a steadying hand at my back.

Riaan called for silence and his audience obeyed. "Calm down, my friends. She is not here yet, and we don't know when she will arrive, but I would be a foolish king indeed if I were not to prepare my people for her coming. As you know, Princess Ilianna is a warrior."

"Who has killed many of our friends. Our family," someone shouted—someone who sounded an awful lot like General Vega.

Castiel stepped forward, tucking me behind him. "In battle only."

My eyes scanned the crowd and found him along with the other generals, but it wasn't the men I was worried about. It wasn't until I located the assassin that I could breathe again. Siana watched me, a smile on her face and a gleam in her eyes. Her hands were free of any weapons, but I knew there were many hiding beneath the folds of her gown.

"She's a murderer!" another voice cried.

Riaan interjected with a powerful voice. "But how many of her kinsfolk in Eira could say the same of me? Of my brother? Of you?"

Silence enveloped. I observed the room, my face blazing from the heat of my shame and embarrassment. Some glared at me as if they could kill me with their very eyes, but not all looked upon me with hate. Others appeared merely curious.

"But she's still murdering in our country," a man said, yet the voices of the crowd simmered instead of boiled.

Riaan shook his head. "An investigation was made and the culprit was found. An impersonator only. Princess

Ilianna has been here for nearly four months among you. During the times of those murders she was with us, under the watch of both myself and my brother."

"I can testify to the character of the princess." Mayor Belau pushed his way forward with Melia. He faced the others, both arms raised. "Princess Ilianna spent an entire day in the service of my town, on the day of the First Harvest. I'm as shocked as you to hear of her true identity, but I know she's not what you think."

No, I wasn't. I was much worse. Not only had I killed many of their people, I was the daughter of their cruelest nightmare. This was the retribution I was due.

"But I am," I said. The words croaked within my throat. I stepped around Castiel, my face exploding into embarrassing shades of red. "I *am* what they think." I gave the mayor an apologetic look, then turned to the people.

I took a deep breath and raised my voice to the room. "I *am* the feared warrior you've heard of in your stories. The Demon Daughter. And you're right, and have every reason to hate me. But know this: what I did, I did because I was commanded to do so. I pray that perhaps this is a good enough reason for you. Or perhaps it's not." I shrugged a faux nonchalance and paced the dais in front of the king. Castiel tensed as if he wanted to shield me, but he held his ground.

And I knew what I had to do.

Silence entombed the space. I moved forward, raising my voice. "What you don't know is that the prince saved my life, a debt that in my kingdom I am obliged to repay. My life is forfeit. *His* life is forfeit to *you*, and because of that, the warrior you hate and fear is now yours, and now I will fight." A chill traveled my spine as I spoke the words, realizing they were true. Despite my previous hopes of sailing from the continent on the next available ship, I couldn't leave. Not yet. "I will fight until my dying breath to protect your kingdom and those you hold most dear."

Several cries of approval rang, lifting my confidence. Mikael pressed forward, stopping at the side of Siana. I glared at them all: Mikael, the assassin, and the generals.

"I will fight side by side with your honorable warriors, even the feared assassins, and with their help, I will destroy those that lift a hand to molest this people. I will abolish those that seek to bring you into their bondage." I pointed to where a wide-eyed ambassador pressed herself against the wall and glared. "Send this promise to your master. *This* is one country she cannot take, for we will defend it against her evil, or if we fail, we will burn it to the ground before she can infest our mother earth."

The ambassador paled beneath my wrath before I addressed my true audience. "But if we survive—if the battle ends and we are finally rid of the Wraith Queen once and for all, I will swear an oath that the kingdom of Eira will never again lift up arms against her neighbor, or if it does, I will abandon my rights to that kingdom and become an Anolynian forever and be adopted as her faithful daughter. This I swear!" A roar of approval nearly deafened as the people of Anolyn cheered. Suddenly at my side, Riaan clasped my hand and raised it high above our heads, joining in the cheer of his people.

In my periphery, I registered the ambassador being escorted away by several armed guards. Lucky to be in Anolyn, my grandmother would keep her life to pass the message to her daughter, my mother.

It was a while before the cheers calmed, but the king allowed the swell. He smiled with them. Castiel stood by my side, his face devoid of all emotion. What brewed within? Surely, he wouldn't be upset that I had won the approval of his people. He should be pleased.

Riaan signaled for silence and the crowd obeyed. "We have a lot of work to do, my people, but our labors can wait until we have once again united as friends and countrymen. Tonight, we celebrate!"

With a wave of his hand, the music resumed, even more boisterous than before. Laughter rang and my head spun.

"Good job, Your Highness," Riaan said with a wink. He bowed, pressing my knuckles with his lips. I nodded uncomfortably, then slid my fingers from his grasp. A chuckle reverberated deep within his chest. He took Melia from the Mayor and led her to the center of the room to join the dance. He paused at Mikael's side. "Double the security around the ambassador and tell me if there is any change."

Several countrymen nodded to me, taking a moment to size me up before continuing by. A woman even stepped forward to embrace me quickly before racing back toward the dance. Sameen had arrived to enjoy the festivities and a drink with a gaggle of older women at the far side of the room. When she saw me, she beamed, lifting her glass high.

"May I?" Castiel's voice caused me to whirl. He bowed low but kept his eyes on mine.

My heart nearly stopped. "I don't think this is the time," I said, wringing my fingers. I should have been watching the ambassador. We should have been preparing.

He placed his hand to my shoulder and my skin blazed at his touch. "My brother's right. There's nothing that can be done now. Come; the evening's almost over." His touch trailed a line down my arm, eliciting a shudder, then his fingers hooked mine to gently tug me in the direction of the others. Hypnotically, I followed to join a circlet of dancers with the prince. My joints creaked as I worked through the movements, my face ablaze.

What if I made a fool of myself? What if I forgot the steps? But when Castiel gathered me close for a reel around the ring, I all but forgot any concern. Melia met me in the center for a lively dance with the woman. Who cared whether I made a fool of myself, for she did as well.

Then the music slowed, its tune almost heart-wearingly painful. Castiel reclaimed me. His crystal blue eyes entranced. I loved him. It was so clear to me now. I didn't even care if he didn't love me back. I would be his whether he wanted me or not. I would stay with him, be his warrior, protect him and his people, and find happiness in the service he desired.

Too soon, the song ended, followed by a slow clap that reverberated against the stone walls. Those around me scanned for the source of the acclamation.

"Wonderful! Wonderful!" A loud and bone-chilling voice cried over the commotion of the crowd. "Lovely, just lovely." King Johan of Eira stepped from behind King Riaan's empty throne, wine goblet in hand.

A muffled cry tumbled from my clamped lips. Shock pulsed through my chest, and my vision blurred, but every other sense heightened.

The crowd near Johan shrank, externally reacting as my body would have liked. Perhaps they recognized him, or perhaps they sensed evil. Either way, tension grew thick, quickly dousing the once gay atmosphere. My heart seized in my chest. Lucan, or rather, Cyris followed closely to him, the hard line of his face so familiar that only the red eyes of the wraith gave away his true identity—red eyes only I could see.

With the jerk of his head, Castiel signaled to Reese, who was already on his way to us.

Gray heavily streaked the sides of Johan's curly, dark-brown hair. Exposed tufts of chest hair twined in and around a thick gold chain and royal medallion. He wore his leathers and furs—hunting trophies that he believed proved his prowess and cunning—and his black leather breeches that bulged around the width of his muscular legs. He seemed even larger than I remembered.

His black eyes found mine among the sea of Anolynians. "Amazing!" He raised his goblet high. "Good people of Anolyn, I commend you. How you ever got my niece to dance is a mystery. But watch her twirl."

By others, it might be understood as a compliment, but I heard the true derision beneath. I would be punished for my insolence later.

I cursed beneath my breath and forced my thoughts to clear. I was not in Eira. To keep up pretenses, Johan would be on his best behavior.

He would also not be alone. What army had he brought with him? I scanned the packed room but caught upon Riaan pushing through the crowd instead. On his way there, he snatched a cup from someone's hands. They did not complain or even seem to notice.

Reese arrived at my side and stepped partially in front of me. Before Castiel could move, I clasped tightly to his hand to stop him from leaving me. Riaan had already arrived to intercept my uncle anyway.

"Your Majesty. What an honor." The king of Anolyn smiled a lopsided grin, swaying slightly, but he was far from drunk. It was an act.

Johan's brow ticked high. "Ah. The eldest son of Cassius Anouk." He pitched a glance to Cyris's host, and the wraith nodded. Was this another play by the seer? Had she sent Cy to intercept my uncle? "It's an honor to meet you." Johan extended his hand and Riaan jovially clasped it, laughing.

Then the king of Anolyn turned to his audience. "My friends, the great leader of Eira, King Johan Drakara!" He raised his glass and his people followed suit, slowly, toasting our new guest. Before another word could be spoken, Riaan signaled for the music to resume.

Johan narrowed his gaze at the start of a new set. A muscle in one eye twitched as he tried to hide his disgust for what he witnessed. "And where has my niece disappeared to? Didn't I just see her dancing?"

My voice stuck in my throat, but I relinquished hold on Castiel and neared daringly close to my uncle. I could feel the prince shadow me.

"Ah. There she is." Johan's gaze traveled my face, then the length of my gown. In his mind, I would be indecent without my warrior's leathers, even at a celebration, but he refrained from commenting on my clothing. "Amazing," he said again in artificial awe. "Four months has only increased your beauty, my niece." He reached to me and I stiffened, becoming marble and ice. His thick finger trailed a clammy path down my cheek.

His touch was a promise of punishment to come. I barely suppressed a shudder. "Thank you, Uncle," I finally managed, my voice strange in my ears. His appearance always reminded me of a bear—frightening, with a mass larger than most. He used his size as his one and only strength, thinking all else was unnecessary, and who would dare test that truth? Unlike the brothers of Anolyn, the king of Eira never actually fought for his kingdom, but to challenge the supreme ruler brought death.

Reese, Mikael, and Melia circled near. Even the generals kept a close distance, but the assassin had disappeared. I prayed a silent prayer that her knife would find its way to Johan's back; however, I doubted my luck.

Johan tipped his head my direction but kept his attention fixed on whatever liquor he held. "What an amazing speech you just made, Ilianna. I wasn't in time to hear it all, but I don't doubt it was riveting. You were always good at riling up our companies for battle, weren't you?"

I didn't know what to say. "Uncle, may I introduce you to Prince Castiel Anouk, second son to Cassius the Great."

Castiel inclined his head. Even though he rose to the same height as Johan, my uncle tipped his chin up to peer at the boy in front of him—because that was all the prince was in his eyes.

"Why are you here, Uncle?" I dared asked, then braced for the back of his hand.

Johan pretended not to hear me, only turned to Riaan. "I must demand an immediate audience with you. I'm afraid this merriment is as premature as your governance."

My hackles rose on the back of my neck, but Riaan handled the insult well. "Oh?"

"And I demand the presence of my niece as well."

Riaan tipped his head. "I may have an empty room we can retire to. I assume you have guards you wish to attend you?"

"Of course." At his signal, six men detached from the crowd, gathering behind the body of Lucan. Their clothes matched that of the local commoners.

Riaan's gaze narrowed. "I see you all made it through my security without any problems."

Johan shrugged. He paced to the throne to eye it with more interest than anyone should have shown. "Not without *any* problems. I'd say I left well over a hundred men outside the borders of your country, and a dozen in that little town just past your hills. Oh!" He turned a mocking smile to me. "And I brought Pala with me."

My heart sank into the pit of my stomach.

He continued. "Actually, I couldn't keep her away. She missed you so."

A figure detached herself from the crowd. Oil shimmered from her black hair, highlighted by the flames of the overhead candelabras. Pala folded her hands neatly in front of her slight figure. Her brown eyes warned there was much more brewing within than the calm picture she displayed.

Riaan smile kindly at Pala, then looked to Johan. "I'll have the guest quarters made up for you and your men. Your lady's maid can stay—"

"With Ilianna, of course," Pala said. She took a step forward. She barely came to my chin, yet the arrogance that emanated from her overcame any problem with her height. "I will return immediately to the princess. By the state of her appearance, it's obvious she's been without proper care."

Riaan's brows tipped up. "I'm sorry, dear lady, but that is out of the question. You are our guest and will be treated as such."

"Truly?" Her fingers flicked my direction. "I'd be frightened by such treatment. Tell me, is it common in your kingdom to neglect royal guests?"

Johan let out a hearty laugh, not allowing the king to respond. "Throughout the years the woman has never held her tongue, but still she shocks me."

A guard rushed to King Riaan and whispered in his ear. The king nodded, then re-acknowledged Eira's king. "If you'll come with me."

Johan gestured to Lucan-Cyris and together they and their company followed behind Riaan, along with Reese, Mikael, Melia, the four generals, and two additional guards. Pala waited for me to join her, but Castiel wound my hand through his arm, claiming me, then gestured to the woman. "After you."

She glared with pursed lips, but left without a word.

My fear set in. I looked up to Castiel, seeking comfort from his kind, familiar eyes. He reached to cup his hand on my cheek. "It's going to be alright," he mouthed.

I kept my voice lowered. "Lucan? Did you know?"

He nodded once. "We told Cyris to be on the watch for Lucan's master. We didn't think…" His whispered voice trailed.

That he'd be here so soon? That he'd ever come?

After two flights of stairs and several heavily guarded hallways, we came to a room adjoined to multiple suites I had never been permitted to enter.

"This is my private study," Riaan said, turning a circle. "A library of books added upon with each generation of Anouks. We will be uninterrupted here."

"Marvelous. Just marvelous," my uncle said, but the library could hold no interest for him. I'd never seen the man pick up a book. I wasn't sure he even knew how to read. Lucan-Cyris smirked next to his leader, giving me a red-eyed wink. I flinched.

General Vega walked the outline of the room, eyeing me as he moved, but Dag, Beau, and Amara kept close together, arms crossed. Reese and Mikael stood as guards just inside the door by Johan's men. Lucan-Cyris watched me closely, transfiguring his mannerisms to match the former tenant so perfectly that I shuddered inside my skin. Melia took her position by the king of Anolyn. The energy around me shifted when Pala slid close behind, causing the back of my spine to prick painfully.

Johan continued. "I didn't know there were so many books in all the world. It almost makes my heart ache. Speaking of which..." He pick one from a shelf and thumbed through the contents. "When you left, Ilianna, you made my heart ache. Almost broke it altogether."

I swallowed, realizing I had to answer. "I'm sorry, Uncle. But isn't this what you wanted?"

He hummed. "You came straight here?"

I eyed Riaan and he nodded, barely perceptible. "Of course," I said. "Where else would I have gone? You made your request clear of me, my uncle."

"And so, you left your home, without saying goodbye, to fulfill my commands on your own?"

"Of course," I lied again.

"Heartwarming," he said, turning away to fake interest in a tapestry that hung over the low burning fire. "Truly heartwarming. Just like it was to hear that your people, King Riaan, are so eager to accept a union between our kingdoms." He spun, eyeing Riaan with a baleful look. "But that was not what I agreed upon."

27

PROPOSAL

RIAAN'S BROW TICKED UPWARD. "Didn't you send your niece as an offering of peace?"

"I sent my niece as an offering of marriage as the *price* for peace. Surely, good king, you must know that nothing of value is given for free."

"The Wraith Queen beats at our door and you worry over price?" Vega asked.

The king eyed the general. "What door does she beat at? Not mine." A smirk twisted Johan's features. "Where are you getting your false information?"

Riaan's lips thinned. "The ambassador from Ardenya, the Wraith Queen's homeland, is here at this very moment, awaiting a message from her master."

Johan's head jerked back. "Is this a farce?"

"Not at all, Your Majesty. That is the very reason for our announcement this evening, to display our willingness to combine powers against her."

He appeared impressed. "No doubt that will send a

message, but I'm not swayed. My niece was an offering for marriage."

"That is not something I can accept."

Johan tipped his head to the side. "I'm confused. Why? Surely she would make a most pleasing wife in many ways."

An appalling noise projected from my mouth. My face exploded into awful shades of red. "Uncle, please."

But Riaan was quick to answer the king of Eira. "I am betrothed to another." He took Melia by the hand. Despite the situation, I beamed at her. Awkwardly, she smiled back until my uncle drew our attention.

"You choose marriage to a commoner over someone of royal blood?"

Riaan smiled but there was nothing friendly in the gesture.

"She's far from common, I assure you," I said, my voice raised above the others. "And she is my friend."

Johan tsked. "But—"

"I have asked for Ilianna's hand, instead," Castiel interjected into the already heated conversation, shocking me into silence.

My uncle's voice pitched low. "Excuse me?"

Heat enflamed my entire body. I gawked, but Castiel ignored me. He stepped forward. "With your permission, King Johan, I request the honor of marrying your niece."

Johan's gaze narrowed at Castiel. I could see his devious brain working, planning his next steps.

Riaan cleared his throat. "Might I speak to you? Alone, Johan?"

My uncle's gaze flashed to the king of Anolyn as if he'd forgotten he was even there. "Of course." He dropped the volume he held into Melia's hands as he passed, then exited with Riaan through a side door along with a single guard from each kingdom. Silence enveloped the dense space.

"Your uncle's a charmer," Melia said, replacing the discarded book.

"That's him on his best behavior," I snapped, then grabbed Castiel's hand to drag him away for a more private conversation. I headed toward the first set of double doors.

"That's my brother's bedroom," the prince said, and my face heated. The generals quickly moved out of the way as I adjusted my direction to another set.

"Any objection to this one?" I asked, not missing a step.

"I didn't have any objection to the first one."

I rolled my eyes at his attempt to flirt.

"And where do you think you're going?" Pala asked, blocking our way.

My breathing spiked and I barely held back several feral words. "To speak to my *betrothed*."

"You will not leave the room with that man." As she spoke, her dark eyes glared over my shoulder at Castiel. "It's highly inappropriate."

"Indeed," Lucan-Cyris said, speaking for the first time since arriving.

I speared him a glance but directed my hostility to the lady's maid. "So is your firing your opinions at the leaders of a hosting kingdom, and yet you still do. Stand down."

I pushed past her, but she clamped her fingernails into my arm.

Pent up anger and frustration pressed against the edges of my tolerance, ready to break free. "You will remember your place, dear lady, or I will remind you of it."

"Your uncle will hear of this."

"Then it will be no different than it was. You do not change."

Cyris laughed, low and menacing. The sound traveled uneasily across my chest. How far would the wraith take this deception?

I glanced over to Melia, who watched the dramatic scene with barely suppressed curiosity. "Please have Miss Pala escorted from the room. Make sure she is seen to her quarters. And if she objects, ask if she would find the prisons to her liking." I wiped away Pala's grip. "We all know I did."

I pushed past my stunned lady's maid into a room of simple decorations. Several chairs circled a desk in the center. A map of the continents spread out on the top thereof.

I released Castiel to turn a circle, wringing my shaking fingers. "What have you done?"

He almost smiled. "I solved a problem."

"Solved a problem?" I threw my hands in the air, then checked my voice, lowering it to a whisper. "I'm a problem now?"

"You know that's not what I meant."

My shoulders lifted. "Then what did you mean? You don't even love me."

Light flashed in his eyes. His head tipped to the side, searching my face. "Is that what you want? Love?"

I looked away. "Love is for fairy tales and children." It didn't matter that I loved him more than I had ever loved before. It wasn't possible for it to be reciprocated. I didn't deserve it.

"Surely you don't believe that," he said, his voice a caress. My skin zinged at the touch of his finger beneath my chin as he pulled my attention back to him. He leaned in, bringing his face eye-level. "Is it my love you require for us to be betrothed?"

My heart sank. Once upon a time I would have said yes, that it was both a necessity and an honor to claim. But that was a long time ago, before life taught me a lesson so very different than the fairy tales I snuck into bed. Before Weylan and his fabrications.

"No," I lied. "All that I require is—"

"What, Ilianna?" His hand gently traced the line of my jaw and I closed my eyes as a heaviness tugged at my heart. If I were brave, I'd tell him. *He* would be enough to make me happy. His love was unnecessary. Warmth played within the small space between our bodies, and I closed my eyes, relishing in the sensation. A chill coursed through me when his words blew against my skin. "What if I told you that I *did* love you?"

Pain seized all breath.

"What if I told you I have from the day I carried you home from the forest. That—"

I drew up on my tiptoes and kissed him to silence the words I couldn't believe to be true. It wasn't real. His warm hands held my face as he returned the kiss, dragging me closer, closing any space between us. And my mind reeled in the sensation that was all Castiel.

How could I not want this? I trusted and needed him. He was everything. Did I care that he probably only wanted to marry me for the safety of his kingdom? No. It was what I would have done if I were as brave and good as he was.

Someone cleared their throat and I jumped from Castiel's arms. Riaan watched us with mild interest. "It may be too soon to celebrate. King Johan wishes to speak to his niece. Alone."

My stomach twisted. "No." I stepped back, into the safety of Castiel's arms.

His warmth gave temporary relief. "Surely, he would not mind if I were there."

Riaan shook his head. "He specifically asked for privacy."

The prince stiffened. "All those wounds on her back." He gestured to the scar on my neck, a mark I had all but forgotten. "That burn mark. That's all because of him. You know that, right?"

"If he tries anything, of course we'll intervene. I will not allow him to harm Ilianna in my home, but we cannot stop him from having a private conversation with his niece."

Like the Eirian lakes in winter, ice immobilized the chambers of my heart, painfully chilling me to the core. I breathed through the frost-bitten panic. How did I intend to kill Johan if I was too afraid to face him alone now?

I took the prince's hand to gain courage from the warmth of his touch and gazed into his beautiful eyes. "It's alright," I said, hating the lie. "He just wants to talk." But Johan could never allow me to be happy—which was another reason he had to die.

The muscles of Castiel's jaw worked as he searched my expression. "I—I'll be right outside the door." I knew he wanted to say more—to do something—but there was nothing.

"Alright." My fingers slid from his tensed grip. Steeling my resolve, I headed for the door and entered another of the king's suites. This one was also simple in design: a receiving room with fireplace, couches, and a table with chairs off to the side for private meals. Paintings and tapestries decorated the walls, the largest of them catching my gaze. It was a marvelous depiction of a woman with midnight hair in a burgundy gown. I could only assume this was the wife of Cassius Anouk. She gazed down at me with the same blue eyes as her sons.

Johan waited with his back to me. A warm fire burned in the grate. He leaned upon the mantle, a fresh drink in his hand. I stopped across from him.

"The king is very affable," he said gazing into the amber liquid, swirling the contents in his glass. "I could *almost* like him." Which meant he hated him.

Anger grew within my chest. "Perhaps you should get to know him better."

"*Perhaps* I should *congratulate* you, Niece. Even if you didn't snag the largest fish of the lake, the one you caught is too big to go unappreciated."

"I don't know what you mean."

A deep chuckle rumbled. "Don't you?" He threw back the remainder of his drink and dropped the empty glass on the mantle with a thump. "If it makes you feel any better, I believe the prince loves you. The king told me himself that his brother has been enamored of you since your first arrival."

His eyes dropped to the peek of cleavage my gown afforded, and I wanted to do nothing more than run from the room.

"And look at you. How could he not? You've grown into quite the woman, with curves and all."

I tried to hide the hurt in my words. "That's what regular meals will do to a person, I guess."

"You've quite the cushy life here, haven't you? Grown soft. Perhaps if you would've put more effort into seducing the king—"

"I didn't *seduce* anyone. I didn't even want to be noticed." I clamped my mouth shut. It was too close to the truth and my uncle sensed it.

He smiled. "So this *is* a farce."

My eyes dropped to the mess of chest hair that twisted and tangled around his golden medallion like weeds. "This is no farce, Uncle. I will marry Castiel."

"Come, come, Lilipad."

Blood froze within my heart. "Don't call me that. I never liked that name."

He pretended not to hear me. "Regardless of your failure, this sacrifice is no longer necessary. Your kingdom desires your presence. *I* desire your presence."

Emotion nearly overpowered me, and I turned away from him. A tear streaked down my cheek, unchecked but thankfully unseen. "Even if it's not what I want?"

He spun, pitching his voice low. "How dare you. Return to your festivities with your pathetic prince. Twirl and dance like the fool you are with those simpletons the king surrounds himself with. Drink yourself into a stupor for all I care, but you are leaving with me. Tonight." He pushed from the fireplace and strode toward me. Before I could bring myself to move, his hand caught hold upon my hair at the nape of my neck, his nails scratching into my skin as he did. He yanked me to him, my vision coating with sparks of light. "Be outside the gates at the third watch. Do you understand?"

I clung to his wrist to keep from falling, speaking through clenched teeth as pain racked my scalp and neck. "And how do you expect me to leave without alarming Riaan's security?"

He shook me, rattling the insides of my brain. "Be creative, Lilipad. But refuse my wishes, little girl, and I'll slaughter every man, woman, and child in the surrounding town. All in the name of the Demon Daughter." A smile darkened his features. The stench of alcohol on his breath burned my nostril and tainted my breath. "It shouldn't be too hard to convince the kingdom of Anolyn to hang you after that."

My heart stopped. He meant every word.

He released me with a push that sailed me into the back of a thick, wooden chair. I toppled to the ground with it, a sharp pang traveling up my arm upon impact.

I heard the door open, and Castiel exclaimed a string of curses before he was at my side, pulling me up from the wreckage.

"What is the meaning of this?" Riaan demanded.

"The clumsy chit fell. If you'll excuse me," Johan said, mumbling as he left the room.

I didn't hear the rest of his murmurings. It didn't matter. Whatever he did say was nothing I needed to know. My mind whirled in a mass of pain, confusion, and hurt.

What I *did* need to know was where my uncle would sleep tonight. Johan would stay to validate what the king told him. His men would search for the ambassador— maybe even try to kill her—but my uncle wouldn't do it himself. No, he would lounge in his room and direct his guards to carry out his orders. And drink made him tired. He would rest before traveling.

A thought entered my brain. Perhaps it was cowardly, but if I could kill him as he slept...

Castiel said something to me, cupping my cheek as he spoke. How disappointed would the prince be when he found I had murdered my uncle? Would Riaan cast me out? Of course, there would be no punishment if I were dead, which would be the more likely outcome.

"Ilianna." Castiel's voice pulled me from my thoughts. Shocked, I realized my face was wet. Had I been crying? "Are you hurt?" he asked. "What happened?"

Could I tell him what I planned? No, he would try to stop me, or find another way around it. But there was no other alternative. No one knew the king of Eira better than myself. He would never allow me to marry the prince or to stay in Anolyn.

My heart broke when I realized I *wanted* to stay. These were more my people than Eira's citizens had ever been. Even when they had been told who I was, they hadn't tried to kill me as I thought they would.

"I'm going to kill that bastard!" Again, Castiel's voice shocked me into reality. "Ilianna! Are you hurt?"

Riaan stood next to his brother, eyeing me in a mixture of concern and curiosity. I straightened the circlet that had fallen haphazardly to the side of my head. I was probably a mess. "I'm fine."

Castiel growled, but he gently took my hand and returned me to the king's library, where the others, minus my uncle's men, waited with stunned expressions. Reese's jaw worked as he examined me from head to toe. Melia's expression was careful, as was Mikael's. The room's silence was almost more painful than my uncle's touch.

I released the prince's hand. Raising my chin, I glanced to each one of Riaan's men. "King Johan of Eira says he'll consider the prince's offer. He keeps early hours and will retire now but should have his answer by tomorrow."

It felt awful lying to them. With the way they all watched me, I wondered if they sensed the falseness of my words, but I couldn't focus on that now. I looked to Castiel and my energy left me in a single exhale. "It might be best to know where he'll be staying tonight so I can avoid being in the vicinity."

The prince searched my eyes for one long moment, then nodded and signaled for Reese to take his place. "I must talk to my men," he said.

I was too overwhelmed. I stayed behind as he and Riaan joined their generals and Melia to converse in hushed tones over the king's desk, but I had no desire to hear their conversation.

I sighed and placed a hand on Reese's massive forearm.

"Are you alright?" he asked, his voice low.

Grateful for the concern etched into his words, I nodded. "I need you to find and warn Sameen about my old lady's maid. Pala won't like that she's been replaced. She might not respond well to the imagined spurn. Please tell Sameen to go to my new quarters and not to leave. I'll come to her as soon as we're done here."

Reese bowed then went to Castiel to whisper my instructions in his ear. Castiel looked to me with raised brows, then nodded to my guard. Reese raced to fulfil my command, sliding past Mikael at the door.

My eyes met Mikael's. With a covert nod, I signaled for him to come.

He obeyed, taking a stance at my side. He watched the conversation of his leaders. "You trust me to guard you?"

I cast my voice low. "I'll do a lot more than that."

28
PRACTICE

A SMILE TIPPED THE CORNER OF Mikael's mouth. "Oh?"

"I need you to send a private message to Siana for me," I said.

"The assassin?"

"Tell her to meet me in my room before the end of the festivities. No one else can know."

"And just where is your room now? Even I don't know where the prince has put you."

I tsked. "If she's as good as I hope she is, she'll find me."

Mikael huffed a laugh, but the all emotion slid from his face quicker than it had come. He studied me, his brows pinched low over his eyes. "For what it's worth, I hope you succeed," he said, then left the room without another word.

Melia strode over to me. "And why did you just send away two of your guards? What are you up to?"

I shrugged. "I'm worried over Sameen."

"And you want to know where your uncle has gone to?"

Perhaps Melia wouldn't mind so much when I killed him. "Of course."

"The king has offered Johan the very chambers you recently vacated. Pala is in the room of your first arrival." Her head ticked to the side, watching me with probing eyes. "I'm sure wherever the prince has tucked you, you'll be safe."

"I'm not worried."

"But are you happy?"

"What?"

She smiled. "His announcement tonight. I'm assuming it came as a shock to you?"

"He's only doing it to appease my uncle."

"You're a terrible liar. I've known Castiel since we were children, and I've never seen him respond to anyone the way he does you. He loves you."

I swallowed against the rising lump in my throat.

"And you love him," she finished with a nod. "The once terrifying Demon Daughter of Eira has grown softer than an Anolynian lamb."

I jabbed my elbow into her side, but she didn't so much as flinch to the assault. I scanned her profile, admiring the strength in every line of her features. "I'm happy for you. And the king."

Her gaze caught mine. "I told him he should choose you."

"That's ridiculous."

She shrugged. "Before I left to search for your killer, I impressed upon him the importance of such an alignment and told him he should pursue you."

Annoyance flushed through me. I crossed my arms over my chest. "Well, he didn't."

One brow shot up as she regarded me.

I rolled my eyes. "It worried me that he suddenly became more familiar and cordial, but nothing more."

She huffed a laugh, her attention returning to her betrothed.

"What made you decide to accept him?" I asked.

"I didn't accept him. *He* accepted *me*." She spared me a rueful smile, a laugh in her eyes. "The whole time I was gone, I cursed my foolishness. When we heard you'd been captured, I was worried, but once we found you and you were relatively sound—" She snorted, scanning me from head to toe. "—I decided to put the screw to my mother's words. When we returned, I asked him to marry *me*."

Just then Riaan glanced over to his fiancée with a look so smoldering that I blushed for her.

I coughed, glancing away. "I'm happy for you. But what of your mother? And why haven't I seen her?"

Melia's expression was vacant. "I haven't discussed my attachment to the king yet. And since she's left, I won't be able to discuss it with her anytime soon."

"She left?" Why did a sense of panic suddenly fill my chest? "When will she be back?"

Her shoulders lifted. "Next week. Next year. I never know. She said something vague about preparing for the imminent battle she feels is coming."

"That's helpful."

Melia hummed her agreement.

A rush of voices caught my attention as the meeting around the king's desk broke apart. Castiel and Riaan moved to our sides, followed by the generals, their expressions grim.

Riaan spoke first. "Princess Ilianna, we'll triple the guard around your uncle. In the morning we'll see what his answer is and when he intends to return home. Melia, we need you to send the falcry—"

"Not Ketrina," Melia interrupted. "She's still too young."

Riaan nodded. "Send Gomez and Verity then, with a message to the borders to discover if what Johan is saying is true and if his men are really outside the boundaries. We'll also send spies to the town to locate these men Johan says are there."

"Will the people travel back to their homes tonight?" I asked as Johan's threat repeated within my mind.

General Amara answered. "The closest towns may, although most will stay in tents on our grounds."

"Perhaps when they leave it would be best to have them escorted back with guards."

Riaan nodded. "Do you think Johan's men would attack the town?"

My eyes narrowed. Could the king know of Johan's plans? I didn't dare ask. "If what Johan says is true and he does have men here, and he feels provoked to do so… yes. He will."

Riaan gave Castiel a meaningful glance. "Then we'll have no choice but to find these men and silence them."

"And you don't think killing them will set off Johan?" I asked as alarm coursed through me.

He smiled. "Who said anything about killing them? That won't happen unless they make the first move. We'll just send two ready men for every one of Johan's and be prepared for the worst. Right, Generals?"

Dag, Beau, and Amara all gave their verbal consent, but Vega only nodded, watching me with an unreadable expression. I met his glare with my own until he left with the others to carry out his kings' orders.

I waited for them to shut the door, then turned to those who remained. "Cyris?"

"He'll watch your uncle and report when he can," Riaan said.

Castiel touched my shoulder. "We need to return to the festivities. We don't want the townsfolk to think there is anything wrong." His hand swept a strand of wild hair from my shoulder. Then he cursed again.

I jumped. "What—"

"He *did* hurt you." His fingers reached to touch my neck, but I covered the damage with my hand and winced at the pain. Johan had drawn blood.

"It's only a scratch."

Castiel's eyes grew large. "It's only a—Ilianna—"

"If you please, gentlemen, I've had an incredibly long night, and with the recent..." My voice trailed off; I was more tired than I had ever been. "I wish to retire to my bed. Please."

Concern and some other emotion I couldn't put a name to deepened the wrinkles of Castiel's handsome face.

I intertwined my fingers with his. "Please."

I could sense Riaan watching us—feel his eyes upon our connected hands. How strange it was for him to see me allow any affection—to allow any type of contact at all.

But Castiel's touch was different. "Brother," the king said, "Ilianna may retire, but I need you to return with me."

Castiel nodded, his thumb rubbing circles upon my skin. "Very well. I'll escort Ilianna to her room and meet you after."

That satisfied Riaan, who offered his arm to Melia and left.

As we walked, music floated to us from the festivities below. An eerie chill crept through my body. The good people of Anolyn had no idea that at this precise time, a madman held the closest town hostage, plotting to kill each and every one of them when they returned if I didn't obey his wishes.

"Why didn't you use your magic on your uncle?" Castiel asked, breaking through my morose thoughts.

"I—" I clamped my mouth shut.

"You are powerful, Ilianna. More so than you know."

I huffed out a breath. "But all my life, I've hated magicians. And when I realized what I was becoming, I kept it hidden to stop my uncle from gaining the satisfaction that I was the magician he always wanted. I can't give him that satisfaction now."

"That doesn't matter anymore. You're not the same little girl. What you did at the First Harvest—no one so inexperienced as you are has ever been able to do so much. You either learn to use your magic to defend yourself or get comfortable with me never leaving your side."

As we moved down the hallway leading to the prince's private suites, he halted me by the wrist and pulled me close. One hand wrapped behind my back, possessively, the other lifted my face, bringing our lips nearly touching.

My breath hitched in my lungs and fire exploded to his touch.

"And I mean *never*, Ilianna. You'll be so sick of me, but I won't care. I'll protect you from even yourself if you won't see it my way."

"That won't be necessary," I said, leaning away from him.

"Then stop hesitating. Stop holding back. If you keep practicing and using this magic as a day-to-day thing, you'll become even more powerful than that parlor trick you rely on. The Demon Daughter will have nothing on Ilianna Drakara."

A pang of jealousy hit, strange and intense, but it didn't come from me. Nervously, I tucked away the bizarre sensation. "Very well," I said, stepping from his grasp. The heat from his body fled. I wished I could stay in his arms forever, but I couldn't. Castiel couldn't be with me for what I had to do. "I'll practice with Sameen before I retire. Thank you for seeing me to my room—to your room."

He gently placed his fingers along the length of my jaw. "I will be back as soon as I can. There'll be extra guards at both yours and your uncle's doors. He will not bother you again tonight."

No, he wouldn't. He had already given me the message he wanted to give, and now he would expect nothing but complete obedience.

"Nothing's going to be the same after tonight, is it?" I asked, knowing the truth whether he chose to answer or not.

Castiel's touch stilled. "No. But do we want it to stay the same?" He pressed his lips to the inside of my palm in a pleasingly intimate gesture, then spun on his heel and left me at his door.

I froze, in awe of the man who had offered for me. He was heart-shattering and remarkable in every way, but could he ever be mine? Cold seeped into my pores.

Sameen arrived, exhausted and a little befuddled from too much drink. When I made to apologize for interrupting her fun, she waved it off. "Nonsense. After your uncle arrived, I sobered right up." She shivered, giving me a knowing glance, then proceeded to change me from my evening dress into my nightgown. "I knew you'd be needing me, and rightly so. Besides, it's better to leave the merriment to the youth, whose bodies will not suffer much for their revelries."

A low fire crackled in the prince's spacious bedroom suite. While my lady's maid prepared our bed, I perused Castiel's room, even glancing within his armoire when Sameen wasn't watching. Not that I found anything worth sneaking a peek at. Castiel was apparently a minimalist, his possessions relatively few compared to what... well, what I expected of other royalty.

It was hard to pull my thoughts away from the nauseating fact that my uncle festered within what had become my home, infecting its walls with his sickness. Regardless, I directed Sameen to sit across from me on the floor. I hadn't practiced my magic in days. Melora's potion stayed tucked away; I didn't dare use it. I couldn't afford to be weary. Sameen, on the other hand, I needed to tire out, and I had only a few hours in which to do so.

Then I would finally face my uncle.

And die.

I shook away the thought and gathered different objects of all shapes and sizes. First I focused on casting things away from me as the prince had taught me to do, but when I tried to bring them back, nothing worked. Castiel was able to lift Lieutenant Scores off the ground several inches. I either didn't have that power or didn't know how to hone it. But then I remembered something else.

On the day of the First Harvest as well as the night of my abduction, I had been able to work through touch. And not even direct touch.

I took a deep breath and placed my hands flat to the cold stone floor. It was harder without the seer's potion, but not impossible. I closed my eyes, envisioning the objects Sameen placed on the ground in front of her. After a few minutes of concentration, I moved the book a fraction. Then a few minutes later, I drew it halfway to me. Then all the way. Sameen, who watched in awe, clapped her approval.

"I've never seen Castiel use his magic that way. It's—"

"Absurd," I finished for her, but it was what I could do.

"It's not absurd," she said. "Think about it, Ilianna. It's different. That means it'll be unexpected. That is always a good thing."

And she was right. Tucking my frustration, I splayed my fingers upon the cold floor. I closed my eyes and concentrated on the feel of every divot and groove of the stone. I breathed and pressed firmly against it.

Warmth pulsed in my fingers and traveled up my arms. A delicious excitement lifted the corners of my mouth as I sensed several lifeforces pressing back. Each had a different flavor and temperature. A book, a plant, and Sameen, who prayed to the gods to give me strength. Drawing upon our connection, I tugged, and Sameen gasped. "What in Anolyn's blue sky—" A rush of shocking curses flooded the room as she flew across the floor on her bottom. She slid to a stop in front of me, her skirts scrunched in an unladylike heap above her knees.

Despite the foreboding gloom that had settled upon me, a laugh bubbled past my lips. Two guards ran into the room, armed and ready. Sameen jumped to her feet faster than I'd ever seen her move and shoved them back out the doors.

She turned to me, hands on her hips. "Next time, young lady, move the plant!"

ॐ

Sameen snored soundly. Exhaustion had claimed her quickly, rendering it unnecessary for me to fake my own sleep. Curled up on my side and beneath the comfort of several layers of blankets, I watched the door to Castiel's room in the low light of a dying fire until the hair on the back of my neck stood on end. A cold draft was the only sign of intrusion.

Siana.

An involuntary chill crawled my skin as the slippery devil, cloaked in black, slid through the prince's window without a whisper. I sat up, and she froze, waiting for my reaction. I held her gaze. Then, not really knowing what I did, I carefully pressed my fingers to Sameen's cheek. Concentrating on my powers, I willed her to stay asleep before I slipped from bed.

The assassin's invisible blade pressed against my back as I crept to the far end of the room, but if Siana wanted to kill me, I doubted there was much I could do to stop her.

Her voice came to me from over my shoulder, too close for comfort. "You wanted to talk to me?" Amusement shone in her eyes, but her face was a stone mask. Beneath her cloak, she wore leathers of black that hugged her uniquely curved body.

Forcibly, I reminded myself to breathe, more anxious than I cared to display. "I was beginning to think you wouldn't come."

"I was intrigued. But I'm even more shocked that the prince has you in his quarters. Castiel has never had a woman in his chambers before. Ever."

I cataloged that piece of information. "I need to get out of my room. Tonight. Without the prince knowing."

She lowered the hood of her cloak. One brow raised. "To escape?"

Spine rigid, I forced myself to say the words out loud. "To kill my uncle."

Silence settled within the room. I fought the desire to squirm beneath her narrowed gaze. Finally, she spoke. "And why would you want to do that?"

"For the very reason *you* would want to… and more. Johan is forcing me to leave. He doesn't want a union between kingdoms. It's all been a lie."

"What *does* he want?" she asked carefully.

If I only knew. "Whatever it is, it won't be good."

Suddenly, I doubted my haphazard plan, but it was the only one I had. Death mocked me, ready to claim me one way or the other. Either I would die facing my uncle, or the reaper would accept my soul when I lost it to the Wraith Queen herself.

"The king and his brother will be busy with their men tonight, ensuring the safety of their people against your crackpot uncle. *I* must protect the crown. What made you think I'd help you?"

I paced to the low fire in the grate. The last time I'd faced my uncle, I had lost, but I was unarmed and unprepared. The memory of it burned beneath my ear. It had been right after my most recent punishment, carried out by Weylan himself. Beaten to the brink of bitterness, I didn't think my uncle could subject me to anything crueler than he'd already done. But then he announced his plan to give me to the king of Anolyn.

It was the last straw.

I had grabbed the closest weapon to me, a letter opener, and advanced on him, but he was quicker. His weapon? An iron poker pulled from the red-hot flames of his hearth. My punishment remained for everyone to see, a reminder of what Johan was capable of.

Practically the only father I had ever known, he never loved me, and he never would. I was nothing to him other than a way to gain influence over his people and power over his enemies.

I rolled my neck to alleviate the imaginary pain. "All I need is for you to make my guards disappear."

"When?"

I glanced at the sleeping form of my lady's maid. "Soon. Within the hour."

Siana huffed, her voice low. "You ask a lot, don't you?"

My gaze returned to the assassin. "And I'll need a weapon."

She froze. Then a hint of a smile tugged at her mouth. Wordlessly, she unbuckled her belt strapped with not one, but two long daggers. Keeping her eyes on me, she dropped them into my outstretched hands.

29

DEATH OF A MAID

SILENCE BLANKETED THE CASTLE. An eerie moon shone brightly upon the grounds, highlighting a sea of tents filled with slumbering countrymen.

Sameen rested in a deep sleep and hopefully would stay that way until it was all over. The assassin had left the same way she had entered, and I waited impatiently for her signal.

I didn't have to wait long. A rap at the door sounded. I scuttled to the bed where Sameen still slept and again pressed my fingers to her skin. A pulse of magic vibrated through my touch.

"Sleep sound," I said, then exited the room.

The assassin waited for me beyond the threshold. Two guards stood several paces away, their back toward us. I raised my brows, gesturing to them.

She shrugged. "The best I could do in such short time was to replace your current guards with my own men. They are loyal to the crown, and to me."

I nodded, slipping down the hallway the opposite direction, but the assassin's continued presence pushed against me. I whirled. "What do you think you're doing?"

"Protecting my investment. If you're unsuccessful, I'll be there to clean up the mess. Can't have this come back on me."

I hummed. "So you'll kill me if I fail?" An old fear threatened, nearly changing my mind altogether, but I couldn't run anymore. Not from my uncle, not from the Wraith Queen, and not from Anolyn's assassin. I added Siana to the growing list of people that wanted me dead.

She smiled. "I'll kill your uncle, too, if that makes you feel better."

I huffed a laugh. "Actually, it does."

Taking a deep breath, I headed toward my old room. Down a flight of stairs, I paused to peek around the corner to ensure the hallway was clear. I slowed to a crawl, then around another corner.

Two shadowed mounds littered the ground in front of what should have been my uncle's room. A hitch in my throat stopped any warning as the assassin rushed past me. She dropped to her knees to inspect the bodies. "Your uncle's men," she said, telling me what I already knew. "Dead."

Blood pooled upon the ground from stab wounds to their chests. Both had been killed recently.

Without knocking, Siana entered Johan's room, then froze. Fear momentarily held me in place before I clamped down the emotion and followed her in. The room was empty. The lilac drapes had been crudely slashed, and upon the window sill was a single candle with a glowing flame. Apprehension thickened within my stomach and my breath squeezed within my lungs. I whirled, jolting from the room, but Siana seized my wrist before I could get far.

"Let go," I growled.

She pulled even harder. "Obviously, you aren't the only one who wanted your uncle dead. Who else?"

I glared at her. "I don't know." But then the memory of Castiel's words rang through my mind. *I'm going to kill that bastard!* A moan escaped my lips, but I covered it with a grasping answer. "Perhaps the wraith might want him dead."

"As well as the prince," Siana said.

I rallied. "The prince would n—"

"Castiel would never stoop so low as to murder the king of Eira in his sleep, as deserving of it as he is," she said, pinning me with a condescending glare. Her voice softened a fraction. "He would, however, offer a challenge to the one who harmed the woman he loves."

I cursed beneath my breath.

She lifted her head. "And rightly so."

I nodded, gesturing to the window. "That's Johan's signal for aid. He's gathering his men to him."

The assassin raced to the window and pinched out the light, but it was too late. They were already on their way. I hurried back to the stairwell, where Siana caught up to me. "Where are you going?" she asked, following close behind.

My heart ached to find Castiel, but my mind told me I had to finish my business with Johan. The king of Eira signaled for his troops because he felt threatened, and that meant more would die tonight. "I need to find my uncle." I had to stop him—to get him to call back his men. If all else failed, I would vow to return home with him to get him to leave. I would protect the people of Anolyn.

"How many will come?" Siana asked.

I shook my head. "I have no idea how many have followed him here." A sinking in my gut warned that this whole affair was nothing but a military campaign against Anolyn. Perhaps someone found out and attacked first. "He wouldn't have killed his personal guards."

Even in the darkened hallways, the assassin held my gaze. "You must find him. Whoever killed his guards was probably coming after him and he knew it."

And whoever it was, they had ruined *everything*.

"I must go to the crown," she finished.

We reached the stairwell and Siana split off from me, heading up. I preceded down to the throne room.

Suddenly alone, panic twisted my gut into knots. Cold seeped through my clothes, chilling me to the bone. At the bottom floor, the hallway opened into the reception hall. The moon cast its glow through the grand windows, highlighting a hunched form across the expanse of the room. I skidded to a stop as the mass moved. Light reflected off a blade it held just before it plunged it downward. A sickening sound of steel gouging flesh resonated within my ears. Despite the alarm pealing inside my brain, I ran forward.

It wasn't one large figure, but two smaller ones. As the ambassador yanked her bloodied blade to strike again, I slid to my knees, grasped her wrist, and twisted. The knife fell from her fingers, and I deftly picked it up with my free hand. Holding the stolen blade to her neck, I peered down to the victim: Pala, her dark hair pulled high in a severe bun, her gray dress made darker by the blood pouring from her heart.

Keeping the blade on the ambassador, I checked Pala for signs of life, but there were none in her. A chill ran up my arm to the touch of her cold skin. Multiple stab wounds peppered her body. Sickness threatened to weaken me, but I pushed it back.

I gritted my teeth, lifting the blade closer to the ambassador's skin. "Why?" It was the only thing I could think to say. I held no genuine love for my former lady's maid, but she was someone who had taken care of me since I was a child. While she had never shown me an ounce of concern past the duties she was given, that didn't mean I wanted her dead.

The ambassador's breathing came out in gasps. The moon cast an eerie glow, reflecting on her strange eyes. My eyes.

I removed the knife from her throat and she scuttled back until she hit the stone wall behind her. She shook her head. For a moment I thought she wouldn't answer. Then, "She was a spy. She was *her* spy."

"Who?" But my brain connected with what she was saying. "No. She was no spy to the Wraith Queen. She was a spy for my uncle." That was what she did—spied on me for my uncle.

"Johan is a puppet. Pala was a spy. Evil."

"She was only a lady's maid."

The ambassador gripped both sides of her head, lacing her fingers into her wild hair. "Evil." She tucked her knees close to her chest and tapped her forehead hard against the bones.

I scowled at the pathetic creature shaking in her own skin. "Who are you?"

Her familiar silver-blue eyes pinned me in place, dread embedded deep within them. She displayed her long, slender hands. "What did you do to me?"

A strange mixture of compassion and guilt tugged at my heart and I answered honestly. "I was given a potion to paint around your door. I assume that when you passed beneath it, whatever spell it held stopped your master from being able to follow."

A tear slipped down her cheek as the blood drained from her face. "No, no, no. You can't do that."

I lowered my voice. "But don't you see? It worked. You are free of her."

"No, no, no."

"What is your name?" I asked again, reaching to place my hand on her. "Tell me your name."

She jerked away from my touch. Wariness pulled at her face, but finally, she answered. "Deylah."

I nodded. "I can help you. We can protect you from Theia."

At the mention of the Wraith Queen's name, Deylah's eyes grew wide. She doubled over, pulling at her hair. "No. No one can help. She'll kill me. She'll kill us all."

A scream rang through the night and suddenly the pryor was on her feet. She drew back several paces from the sound. We both looked to the large double doors as beyond, another bone-shattering cry muffled from the outside.

The ambassador bolted.

Drawn between several choices, I hesitated. Johan should have been my priority, but I had no idea where he was or what the commotion was outdoors. It was obvious that Deylah had killed the men outside his room. The stab wounds inflicted to Pala were the same given. If I didn't stop the pryor, would she continue to kill?

I growled and leapt to follow her.

My breath caught in my lungs and pain erupted at my skull. I grabbed at the hand that held me by a fist-full of hair. Another hand clamped over my mouth before I could scream. Pinned to my uncle's massive chest, I fought as he half dragged me, kicking and flailing, through the grand double doors of the throne room.

"Bar the doors," Johan said. His breath smelled of rank liquor and rotten cheese.

Lucan-Cyris shut them behind him, pressing his back to the thick wood.

Fear coated my throat, making breathing near impossible. I gripped the hands that covered my face and held them as I bit into the flesh of his palm. Johan cursed, flinging me to the ground. I rolled and shot quickly to my feet.

"You rabid, feral beast!" My uncle shook his hand to rid the pain, disgust on his face. "Feral! You were always too much trouble for what you're worth."

My eyes adjusted to the darkened throne room. Moonlight glowed through the windows and onto the stone floor, but it wasn't enough to cast the lurking shadows away. Cold infiltrated my muscles and penetrated my bones.

A gasp drew my attention. "It's the princess."

A boy no older than me with strawberry-blond hair stood in full Eirian uniform next to another his age. That one had hair clipped tight to his head—a tactic to incite fear in those he fought, but on someone so young it looked strange. Their expressions teetered between confusion and anxiety as they glanced between me and their king.

I once protected boys like these from the harassment of the higher-ranking elite that enjoyed sending out fresh faces to the scars of battle. They were both too young to be safeguarding the king of Eira and too new in the ranks to know how my uncle abused me, how much contempt he held for me. Only those the king kept closest to him understood.

Three more guards flanked my uncle. Even though I couldn't see their faces, I knew their shadowed eyes watched me, derision thick upon their brows.

Screams from beyond Meyrion's walls rent the air, causing the hairs on the back of my neck to stand on end. Sounds of a battle racked across the inside of my brain.

"What have you done, Uncle?" I asked, my strained voice an octave too high. I needed to be fighting with the people of Anolyn.

His eyes narrowed, and he drew closer to a nearby stained window. He gestured to it. "Would you like to take a look? The kingdom of Anolyn will burn tonight because of you."

My stomach dropped. "These people didn't do anything to deserve your anger."

"Perhaps not, but they will be punished for *your* transgressions."

My jaw tightened. "And what have I done against you?"

"You didn't send a maniac to kill me in my sleep?" he asked, his hushed voice hollow in the cavernous room "To kill your lady's maid—a woman that's taken care of you as if you were her own?"

"No," I said, but he didn't appear to hear me.

Johan sauntered to Riaan's throne, trailing a fat finger on the back of the seat before he plopped down in it. He draped one leg lazily over the armrest—a perfect image of ease, and so vastly different from the one that truly claimed it. His guards circled him, glaring their discomfort.

Johan stifled a yawn. "If Lucan hadn't woken me, your plot may have succeeded."

The wraith shrugged, his composed actions so Lucan-like it worried me. "I thought it was the princess."

"Why would the princess want to kill her uncle?" the strawberry-blond guard said, earning a glare from one of the senior guards.

Johan huffed a laugh, ignoring the youth. His head turned to inspect me. "So tell me, who's the assassin? She looked familiar."

"I didn't send any assassin after you. Believe me, if I wanted you dead, I would do the honor myself."

His eyes narrowed. Did he hear the promise in my voice?

He answered my threat with a shrug. "You're a liar and a coward, but it doesn't matter. My men will find her,

and when they do, I'll rip out her heart and feed it to you."
He sat up straight to peer at me down the length of his
nose. "When my army brings me the heads of Riaan and
your intended, maybe then you'll feel the full effect of your
treachery."

"And why aren't you fighting with your men?" I asked,
my words braver than I felt.

One of the boys inhaled a sharp breath.

Anger and shock twisted Johan's face. "You'll pay for
that comment as well, Niece."

Another wail, wild and guttural, rang from outside
and filled me with dread. My lungs seized to the cries of
citizens' voices tearing through the night. What was
happening to the Anolynians? To a people I had grown
to love?

I pulled one of the daggers Siana gave me and held it
ready. Keeping my gaze trained on my uncle, I moved to
the wraith at the doors. "Step aside."

The corner of his mouth twitched up, but he did not
move. What game was he playing?

"You're not going anywhere, except with me," Johan
said, his eyes narrowed. "If you refuse, I'll have you killed
for being the traitor you are."

I spun. "I've never been a traitor, but I'm not going
back with you."

He jutted forward, ejecting from the throne. "How
dare you."

Faster than he looked, he lunged, reaching to grab me
by the hair again. I leaped back and slashed upward to cut
into his arm.

He gaped at the thin laceration. Then with a roar, he charged. I dashed away from his assault. I couldn't allow him to get too close. If he got the chance, he would take me to the ground where I was the weakest. If he got me there, I was as good as dead.

He spun and glared at me, heaving great breaths. His size was one problem, but my uncle also didn't train. He was once a powerful youth; now he relied on the memory of his former self and his height and girth to do the work for him.

I drew the assassin's second blade and held it low, readying for his next attack.

The corner of his mouth lifted. "Do you remember the last time you attacked me, girl?" His gaze slid to the scar on my neck.

A croak of a voice interrupted. "Your Majesty, that's—"

"What?" Johan snapped, glaring at the boy.

He shrank, but not enough. "That's the princess."

With a smile, Johan suddenly changed tactics. He sighed, holding out a hand. "The soldier's right. This is not what I wanted, my Lilipad. Come, Niece. This is all— this is all very unnecessary. Please, come with me and I'll call off the assault. Come with me now and the rest will be spared. I never wanted it to happen this way. We can still have peace."

I breathed a feverish laugh. "Peace will come, but not by you."

Johan's eyes narrowed, and he nodded. I barely dodged as three of his men attacked from behind. I whirled and blocked a sword from the first guard with both blades then knocked the second away with a frontal kick to his stomach. I rotated my knives, easily disarming my original opponent, and stabbed him through the ribcage. He slumped to the stone floor.

I ripped my weapon from his flesh and like the strike of a snake, flung it into the heart of the second guard.

Another rushed me, but before he could lift his sword, I flicked my wrist and Siana's second dagger imbedded into his throat. He dropped to his knees, his eyes wide and his breath gurgled.

A massive fist backhanded me across the face. I whirled at the impact and my vision sparked, then blackened as I collided with the ground. A groan bubbled past swollen lips and I tasted blood. My neck muscles threatened to snap when Johan pulled my hair back.

Why didn't you use your magic on your uncle? Castiel's words echoed agonizingly inside my brain. Even as I thought it, magic pulsed in my veins.

I would never give my uncle what he wanted. I couldn't.

"You treacherous cow," he said, his voice low.

My words rasped heavily in my throat. "You threaten my life and don't expect me to respond to that threat?"

"As your king—"

I laughed, and the sound echoed inside my brain. "You are no king of mine. Not anymore."

Johan raised his hand to strike, but suddenly the wraith had him by the wrist. "She'll be impossible to transport if she's unconscious, Your Majesty." Was that a touch of worry in his tone? "Our escape route is too narrow, and I cannot carry her. We must leave."

Johan jerked from his grip and glared, then he lowered his face to mine. "You've learned some nasty behaviors here, Lilipad," he said, his words echoing painfully in my ears. "I look forward to correcting them when we return home."

Voices drew the king's attention. Lucan ran and opened the doors to the throne room. "They found her," the wraith called out.

Johan released me with a hard shove. "Bring her here and bind the princess." He towered over me but before he walked away, he jerked to a halt and spun. His hand whipped me across the face, the sound of his slap reverberating in my ears and off the walls. I fell forward, a violent cough rattling my lungs. Cold and annoyed, I pushed against the ground, rising partway.

I closed my eyes as past memories matched and mingled with the present.

The two younger guards quickly came forward, their expressions pale. Pain laced my neck and face. I groaned as they lifted me to my knees. Something warm leaked from both nostrils. I jerked away from them to carelessly wiped at the blood with the back of my hand, but then they seized me again and tied my wrists behind me with a cord. Agony raced up my arms when they tied it too tight and it cut terribly into the veins.

"I'm sorry," the strawberry blond said, realizing his mistake but too afraid to fix it. When they finished, they stood over me, waiting for their next command.

I closed my eyes and focused. A few seconds later and my magic loosened the binds enough to ease the pain, but I couldn't escape them completely. Not yet.

Through blurred vision I witnessed three more of Johan's men drag in Deylah and dump her to the floor. The newcomers' eyes widened at their killed comrades, but they didn't ask what had transpired.

Deylah moaned and coughed and her captors backed away, keeping their weapons trained on her. Lucan turned his head, unwilling to view the pryor.

Her hair was mottled and halfway hanging from its tie. Her body shook violently. Blood dripped from a slash on her lips. Red coated her hands and much of her dress, except for a large, black patch of filth at the hemline. When her eyes found mine, they pled for me to help. My heart swelled. The magic within me grew, but more noticeable—more *accessible*—was the Demon Daughter pacing in her cage, ready to be set free.

Johan wiped the perspiration from his brow and sauntered toward the quaking woman. Stopping several yards away, he crouched down, angling his head to get a better look.

Deylah met his stare, the blood draining from her face.

His voice pitched low. "Her eyes…" His head jerked toward me and he glared. "Who is this woman?"

"You know exactly who she is, don't you, Uncle?" I smiled wickedly. "You know what blood runs from her veins and drips onto the floor. That's one of the Wraith Queen's pryors."

He flinched. "A pryor?"

I stood, closing my eyes as a wave of dizziness hit. The redheaded guard put his hand to my elbow to steady me, kinder than he should have been. I continued. "That's Theia's lineage. Her daughter and her cast off." And now she was barely human at all, but not by choice. "Like me." I opened my eyes in time to witness the color blanch from my uncle's face. "Say hello to my grandmother."

30

THEIA

JOHAN STRAIGHTENED, CURSING beneath his breath. My eyes narrowed at his reaction. "So you knew?"

"What?"

"You knew my true lineage?" When he didn't answer, I smiled, but my insides swirled with a torrent of emotions. "The Wraith Queen's not very happy with you is she, Uncle? I wonder why?"

Johan glared, then pointed to Deylah. "If that thing bleeds, that means the Wraith Queen has deserted her." He combed one hand through his thick hair and again moved to the window to view the ongoing battle. "Kill the woman. Sever her head and leave it as a gift for Riaan's men to—"

A deadly screeched shrilled through the night, rattling the very windows of the throne room.

My breath caught. *Ketrina*. The youngest of the falcry threw herself into the battle. Maybe now the Anolynians would have a fighting chance, but even then, fear for the mystical beast twisted my heart.

My uncle's eyes widened. "Lucan, we leave now." He turned to see that no one had yet fulfilled his instructions. "What is this?" he asked.

The soldier closest to him stepped forward, his voice lowered. "Your Majesty, we should just leave."

Johan glared. "Do as I command."

My guard with the shorn head spoke next. "But if what the princess says is true, we'll incur the wrath of the Wraith Queen. She'll kill us in our sleep. She'll kill our families."

Their leader's face deepened to an ugly shade of red. "*I'll* kill your families!"

The men glanced to each other, but still, none moved.

"Fine." Johan spat then wiped his mouth with the back of his hand. "I'll do it myself."

He crossed the distance and grabbed Deylah by the hair of her head. She screamed and flailed so frantically that he soon gave up and tossed her over his shoulder instead.

A chill settled in my bones. Fear coated my heart. She was once an innocent child—she was *still* innocent. A victim of a twisted and dark evil.

Johan moved to the throne and tossed Deylah down. Her head smacked against the seat of the chair, knocking her out cold. Her body went limp. On instinct, I grabbed the shorn guard's wrist with my bound hands and flipped him. He landed on his back with a thud. I dropped low and spun, knocking the redhead to the ground, but I didn't kill them. The Demon Daughter didn't care about them. They could keep their lives.

Fire singed the binds from my wrists as the Demon Daughter reclaimed my body. Black flames engulfed, wrapping me in a cocoon of protective warmth. She ripped both assassin's blades from the other carcasses littering the ground.

Ignoring the distraction, Johan lifted his sword to hack off the pryor's head.

My uncle had never seen the Demon Daughter. He thought it was only an absurd nickname, but it suited his needs to create a fearsome leader of a powerful army, so he promoted it. It was so much more than that. Today he would witness it. It was almost too easy to call upon her—she was ready.

The Demon Daughter took aim and threw. One dagger impaled the king of Eira at the wrist, the other his exposed side. He cried out, dropping his sword to cradle his injury.

The three remaining guards rushed the demon. She almost pitied their reckless courage—until she remembered it wasn't courage she'd seen when they watched their ruler beat an unprotected niece. They didn't deserve pity. Their blood called to her, eager for the release only she could bring. Seconds later, their bodies toppled lifeless to the ground with the others.

She looked for Cyris the wraith, but the coward had fled, the double doors of the throne room flung wide. A smile grew as she focused on her true prey, stalking forward.

Johan staggered, barely managing to keep his feet, but instead of fear, triumph lit his eyes. His lips twisted into a grin. "At last," he said, his voice smooth. He jerked the knives from him with a grunt and cupped the wound at his side, letting the blood drain freely from his arm. "My daughter has shown me her true self. Finally, you are the magician I prayed for."

Her steps slowed. Her head tipped to the side. "This is not magic you see, King of Eira, and I'm not your daughter."

He blinked. "But you *are*, Ilianna."

"And neither am I Ilianna." The Demon Daughter warmed to the shock in his eyes, but Johan didn't cower as the others did.

That wouldn't do.

"Do you speak for her?" he asked.

"I speak when Ilianna needs more than she can give," she snapped, then her head jerked toward the discarded weapons. "Pick up those blades and defend yourself. I won't kill an unarmed man, no matter how deserving he is."

"The beast is honorable?"

The Demon Daughter snarled, offended at the remark. "What do you know about honor?"

"No much, but you do, don't you Ilianna," he said, taking a step closer. He looked deep into the Demon Daughter's eyes, to *my* eyes, as if he could see straight through to my soul. "I always knew you'd be powerful, my niece. How could you not, the creation of a magician and a powerful sorcerer. You're even more beautiful than I could imagine." He checked the excitement growing in his voice. "Our kingdom needs you, Princess Ilianna."

"You speak to me, Johan," the Demon Daughter hissed, but even then, I drew away from her protection. Fought her control. "And don't pretend to do anything on behalf of the kingdom. Its citizens hate you.

"That may be true, but I have raised you—"

"I am not Ilianna! And you didn't raise her. You exploited her!"

His voice elevated to match the level of her voice. "I taught her. *Trained* her. From the fire of adversity, I forged her."

The Demon Daughter opened her arms and smiled. "And from my fire, you shall burn."

He held out his hand to stop her advance. "I made her what she is, beast. She would not have been strong enough."

"To do what?"

"To become Eira's salvation. My salvation."

Her steps halted. "What blasphemy is this, old man?" Cyris had once said something similar, but I had refused to believe it.

Johan swallowed hard. A look that could be described as pain transformed, almost softened, his features. "The Wraith Queen forced my hand. I told her I'd raise you up as her next conquest, but truly I've been raising you to submit to the will of your kingdom. I've made you a warrior to battle an evil we could never face on our own."

My breathing spiked. I reeled inside my shield, fighting the Demon Daughter's hold upon me. She wanted to take over completely, not believing I could handle his twisted reality, but even as I thought it, I knew the truth. I pressed outward, testing the powers the creature used.

The Demon Daughter held out her hand, and Siana's knife flew into her waiting fingers.

Johan's eyes grew wide.

In an instant she was there. Her fingers slid though his greasy hair and she yanked back, hovering the blade over his exposed throat. "I'm not your savior."

His breath came in gasps, his voice strange. "You don't understand. You're my only hope against the Wraith Queen. The only one who can kill her."

"Is that so?" But it wasn't the Demon Daughter's honeyed voice that spoke the words. The blood drained from Johan's face.

Deylah now sat in Riaan's throne, her chin leaning comfortably against one delicate palm. Instead of silvery-blue eyes, red ones peered back. Even as my guardian fought it, a chill coursed through to my heart. Theia watched me from the depths of her pryor, a queer smile lifting her lips too high on her cheeks. A dense pulse of dark emotions vibrated from her strange soul—an odd concoction of admiration and vexation that infected me with its energy.

"Is that your master?" the Demon Daughter asked low in Johan's ear, but his gurgled response gave no confirmation. She hissed. "You're pathetic."

Theia's gaze flicked to my uncle. "Indeed, he is," she said, her smoky words soft and much too high. "I'm disappointed, Johan, that you plotted against me this whole time. But not shocked, mind you. Despite your treachery, I'm vastly grateful. She *is* powerful." She paused to scrutinize me. Her dark, disheveled hair framed her pale skin and devilish eyes. She hummed a bizarre tune and sat up taller, rolling her neck as if it pained her. Her gaze trailed the length of my body. "Ilianna. How I've longed to see you." She hesitated when I still didn't respond. "Oh, that's right. I'm not addressing my daughter, am I? Then who are you? Can you offer me a name?"

Elyn, it answered inside my head, shocking me, but outwardly the Demon Daughter only smiled.

"Nothing?" Theia's gaze narrowed. "How fascinating. I sense my blood flowing through you, but something more. Something protects you. From me. In that way alone, you are far more powerful than *all* my children."

"And I sense *nothing* coming from *you*," the Demon Daughter said. No additional strength. No magic. The entity was weak and not worth her time. "And nothing to stop me from killing you now, or your counterpart." She held Johan closer, pressing her blade against his skin.

His breath caught.

Theia shrugged. "You're correct. In Deylah, I am limited in my powers and the time I can spend within her frame. But you'd not be killing me. Her blood would be on your hands. As for *him*"—she flicked her fingers—"kill him. What do I care for the king of Eira? His death would have come soon enough."

Johan grumbled beneath my steel. "We had a deal."

She ignored him, turning to the sound of combat in the distance. She laughed out loud, one short burst that ricocheted off the walls. "It sounds as if Anolyn might fall without any assistance from me."

Trepidation burned at my conscience. I didn't have time for this. The Demon Daughter—*Elyn*—she wasn't what I needed.

Locating that point where I paced inside my own consciousness, I focused on regaining control. Shock coursed through my guardian, but before she could react, I locked her away. The heat from her blaze cooled, leaving goosebumps trailing in her wake.

Johan's weight fatigued my strength. He dropped from my grip, folding to the ground. A wet cough rattled as his breath hissed through his lungs.

The Wraith Queen purred. "Hello, Ilianna. So nice to see you," she said. Her white teeth flashed in the darkened room.

"Anolyn will not fall," I said, my voice stronger than I felt. "I'll make sure of that."

"But it will, *because* of you. Your *uncle* made sure of that."

Johan stirred to his knees, and I pointed my knife to him. "Move from there and I'll cut your throat."

He jerked back as if shocked. His eyes searched mine for some understanding I couldn't give. "She—" He glanced from me to the Wraith Queen, then back again. His words rambled on a bloated sob. "You don't understand. She was never going to stop until she got what she wanted."

My face twisted in disgust. I choked on a foul word; the muscles in my neck twitched. "So you thought you'd serve it to her on a silver platter?"

Theia cleared her throat, regaining my attention. "He said he could give me a child, a magician like me. A two-hundred-year lifespan is very tempting—I do so hate having to change out of my host frames as often as I do. And your father was *very* handsome. The men I've taken in the past were only the ones that ever came my way, or ones my servants could procure."

I straightened, peering down at the Wraith Queen. "You mean your slaves?"

Theia smiled. "No, *servants.* I keep no slaves."

My brows tipped high. "Deylah?"

She tsked. "My older daughters are no longer my hosts and therefore not consigned to my fate. They may come and go as they please. It just so happens that my will is their will."

"And my father's will?"

A giggle escaped her lips. "Your father freely and quite *eagerly* came."

"Liar."

This time, her melodic laughter rang through the room. My hands clenched into fists.

She tipped her head to the side. "It took very little seduction to convince him he was madly in love with me. In fact, we only met once, but your uncle had already persuaded him I was the perfect match. We were married the next day and left for our honeymoon that afternoon. I took him to my home.

"After *that*, it was harder to convince him to stay. Ardenya is not the land it once was, so we did have to keep him locked up until you were born. Then, we slipped

you into a bassinet and sent you home with my Pala."
Her eyes flicked about the room. "And where is she, that
darling girl?"

"She's dead. And you're next."

She grimaced. "My child, you can't kill me."

"Yes, she can," Johan said. He lifted his hands, as if in
surrender, and rose to his knees. "Come with me, my
Ilianna. Come home. Together we will prepare our armies
against this whore. We can repair the damage done to our
neighbor country. I can protect you from this monster."

"He's lying, Ilianna." Riaan's voice sent a wave of relief
coursing over me.

The king of Anolyn entered the throne room carrying
a torch, flanked by a dozen soldiers bringing additional
light. The flames cast evil shadows upon the walls and
sent a chill up my spine. His men were armed with swords,
spears, and crossbows. All were soiled and some even
bloody, but relatively uninjured. They fanned out to the
left and right of their leader, with three taking a defensive
stance directly in front of him. Riaan's gaze traveled my
face, landing at the dagger in my hand, but his attention
snapped to the creature who occupied his throne.

The archers aimed their crossbows at the Wraith
Queen and the fallen leader of Eira, who still kneeled in
front of me.

I peered past the king for his brother, but Castiel
didn't follow and my heart dropped. Others were missing
too. I swallowed, barely able to form the word. "Castiel?"

Riaan's gaze snapped to mine. He passed his torch to
the closest guard. "He went to find you. Although, why he

assumed you'd be where he left you, I have no idea." He extended a hand. "Why don't you come with me, Princess Ilianna?"

But I still couldn't bring myself to move. "And Melia?"

"She had to subdue Ketrina."

I nodded. The bones in my legs creaked and I staggered on the first step, but I forced myself forward. When I was nearly there, Riaan motioned to his men.

"Archers. Kill the Wraith Queen."

I froze when his men lifted their crossbows, aiming it at the entity on his throne.

My voice shrilled from my lungs. "Stop! It's not the Wraith Queen!"

"What?" Shock infused Riaan's features and his men paused.

I took a deep breath to calm my overexcited heart, but it didn't work. "You wouldn't be killing the Wraith Queen. She only infests the ambassador. You'd be killing an innocent."

He half-smiled, one brow raised. "Is a pryor an innocent?"

I swallowed, taking a cautious step forward. I controlled the hysteria in my voice. "A pryor is my fate, is it not? And is it the life *I* would choose, good king?"

Riaan's eyes narrowed as he searched my face. "Hold your fire until I command otherwise."

A laugh carried across the room, raising the hairs on the back of my neck. "Well done, Ilianna. And as much as I'd love to witness this ending, I see I'm out numbered. I believe I should take my leave."

At the head of the line of soldiers, Riaan prowled forward, stopping midway. "Lady Theia."

She smiled, her head cocked to the side. "Yes, King of Anolyn?"

He smiled in return. "Tell me, why did you send your messenger to my kingdom if only to flee? Why not deliver the message yourself?"

"Oh, I do not flee," she said, her voice sickly-sweet. "And I never meant to send a message. I only wanted to see what there was to see, and you were most accommodating."

Next to me, I could sense the tension rippling from him. "And what was that?" Riaan asked.

She examined her nails. "I received word from my Pala that my daughter had run away. I came to find her—to see her myself. But if you want a message, I shall give you one." She jerked forward, leaning out of Riaan's throne. "Beware, King of Anolyn. Your kingdom only survived because I did not have an heir."

"And you still don't."

At Castiel's voice, my heart leaped within my chest. I scanned his frame for any signs of injury but found none. His dark locks were mussed. Dirt smudged his cheeks and blood coated his knuckles and stained his steel, but the strong warrior was whole and tensed for battle. His heavenly blue eyes caught mine before he stepped in front of me, both blades drawn for an attack. I swallowed the emotion that gathered painfully in my throat and mirrored him as adrenaline throbbed through my veins.

Theia smiled, taking the time to examine him head to foot. She hummed her approval. "You look like him—your father. More so than your elder brother, but it seems he's as big of a fool. I once offered the Great King Cassius a chance at life, but he refused."

"And you will get the same refusal from us," Castiel said through a clenched jaw, shielding me from her line of sight. "We don't want anything you have to offer."

Her red eyes narrowed. She tipped her head to the side. "Oh, no. You don't get the same gift. I only offer a suggestion. Leave. Leave before I return and destroy you, your family, and your kingdom."

"We're not afraid of you, witch," Riaan said, pointing the tip of his knife her direction. "We know the curse by which you are bound. You have no power here."

She leaned back in the throne. Was that a look of surprise? "Ah. Can it be that my once good friend Cyris has whispered in your ear? Is he here now?"

But Riaan did not answer her.

"Foolish king. It's true there's not much I can physically do here, but that does not mean I won't send my armies and hellfire to rip your land apart. I have followers not of my kingdom and not bound by such a curse, and they will inflict your citizen's souls, haunt their children until they beg for reprieve. And when they do, I will be only too happy to give it to them. Ilianna comes of age soon. None of my heirs has ever ignored my call, and neither will she. She is my daughter and therefore my property."

My blood pulsed through my veins as I stepped around Castiel's body shield. Anger deepened my voice. I tapped into the Demon Daughter's force. "I'm not your daughter, and I'm no one's property." Power flowed through me, wild and ready. I clenched my hands and flames erupted, enveloping me, but it didn't burn. Instead, it cocooned, protected me. Whether or not it was real, I didn't know, but the fire wasn't the Demon Daughter's. It wasn't Elyn's. It was mine. All mine.

I opened my arms, savoring the sensation.

Theia smiled condescendingly. "That's cute. But you're not the only one who can start a fire, little girl."

An explosion caused me to spin, extinguishing my magic. From the flares the soldiers held, six men were ablaze, their cries echoing in my ears. They threw down their torches, but it was too late. The magical bonfire consumed them.

And several things happened at once. Castiel jumped to put out the flames of his men, but they wildly flailed their arms, encouraging the fire. The other guards surrounded their king, shoving him back through the double doors to protect him. Riaan's voice shouted above the din. "Now!"

"No!" But my cry was not heard.

While backing out of the room with his king, an archer took his aim and released his bow.

In slow motion I watched the arrow find its mark in the chest of the monster.

It wasn't the Wraith Queen's eyes that stared out from a shocked face.

I bolted, pumping my legs hard and launched myself forward, barely catching Deylah before she plummeted to the ground. I fell to my knees, holding the woman in my arms, her skin already cold.

The arrow had hit high on her right side, just below the collar bone. Deylah's silvery-blue eyes searched mine, her mouth opening and closing like a fish.

"You'll be alright," I said, praying my words weren't a lie. Carefully, I propped her up against the throne, then ripped fabric from the bottom of her skirt. From the corner of my eyes, movement caused my heart to seize. Johan leaped from the ground, a knife in hand. He ran at the nearest guard, stabbing him in the chest, then bolted toward the door. A distracted Castiel stood directly in his path.

A scream stuck in my throat. I dropped the fabric and fell forward, splaying my fingers upon the smooth granite floor. Through my touch, I desperately sent my magic outward. Despite the chaos, my uncle's essence was easy to recognize. I wrapped my mental connection around his energy and pulled hard. Johan groaned.

Castiel put out the flames of one man and turned in time to witness his enemy crumple to the floor in a heap. His shocked line of sight traveled to me. A combination of comprehension and amazement flashed across his features before he tucked it away and yelled for aid. He ran to me.

Johan's brute strength fought against my magic, battling to be free, but I clenched on the connection. Sweat beaded upon my brow and dripped down the line of my nose. The power that flowed through me was more than I had ever felt in all my life and stronger than what came from the Demon Daughter because it was *mine.*

Finally, Castiel was at my side. I relished the sound of his voice even if I didn't understand the words. His hands covered mine, prying my fingers from the ground as Riaan's guards subdued the king of Eira. They shackled him while I kept him pinned, then surrounded him, swords drawn.

Something dark within me dared me to keep my hold upon Johan. It begged me to increase the pain and make him suffer as he had made me suffer.

"It's alright, Ilianna," Castiel said, his soothing tone breaking through my mental fog. "You did it. They've got him."

Despite the tempting thought that ate at the barriers of my mind, I let go. I lifted my hands from the floor, shaking. Tremors racked my body and sent my teeth chattering. Castiel tried to gather me in his arms, but I pulled away. "Deylah," I said through numbing lips. Ignoring his pained expression, I crawled to her.

She was still alive but fading in and out of consciousness. Castiel picked up the torn fabric I had dropped and gently pressed it against the wound. Deylah's eyes doubled in size and she groaned.

Castiel pointed to a nearby soldier. "Find the healer."

"But she is the Wraith Queen's servant," Riaan said, suddenly before us. "You saw what she did, what the Wraith Queen is capable of doing through her."

"She didn't have a choice," I said. "See this?" I gestured to the place on her dress where a black substance stained the fabric. "Melora's potion worked. The only reason Theia was able to get to her was because it was wiped away."

"And *she* wiped it."

"She was scared!" I hadn't meant it to come out as a yell, but anger flooded my face and heated my tone. "Like me. Can't you see that?"

Riaan closed his eyes and cursed beneath his breath. "Very well. Find the healer." The soldier nodded, running from the room. "But I can't make any promises, Princess," the king said.

A crowd of citizens braved the calamity and pressed into the room. Gedeon entered, bringing with him a salve to anoint the burn victims. He handed the medicine off to those who had rolled up their sleeves to help. They administered immediate care and aid in the transport of the injured.

When Gedeon finally knelt next to Deylah, his gaze met mine. "Go," he said.

"But I want to—"

"No," he said, his expression hard. "I don't do parlor tricks, nor do I keep an audience." His fingers gripped the tip of my chin, forcing my face to the side to examine my wounds. "I'll be in to see you when I can."

"I don't need—"

But he released me with a wave of his hand. "Go, go."

I stood on weak legs when several soldiers moved Deylah's body to lay with the other injured. The king of Anolyn reclaimed his throne and gestured for Johan to be brought before him. The guards deposited him on his knees. Johan fidgeted and pulled at his iron shackles, his gaze falling to me. He pointed a finger at me. "I always knew it."

I had done it. I had shown my uncle my magic. But despite everything I had believed, he'd never take advantage of me again. Not now.

Riaan glared upon him with disgust. "Men, take him to the dungeons."

Johan jerked back as if shocked. "If you do this, Riaan Anouk, peace between our lands is over."

"You are the last one able to offer *any* kingdom peace," a familiar voice said, pushing through the ranks of Anolyn soldiers. Weylan pressed forward. His green gaze first dropped to me, then to Castiel at my side. He tipped his head in acknowledgment, his carved jawline tense. Lucan-Cyris followed in his wake.

"What is the meaning of this?" Johan yelled, twisting in his restraints. "Lucan?"

"Lucan has been working for me," Riaan said, interrupting. "His main objective tonight was to protect Princess Ilianna."

The wraith pinned me with his eyes. "As I said, my lady, you were safer here with me rather than out there."

I grunted low. When this was over, I had plenty to say to the wraith. Lucan-Cyris crossed his arms over his chest, apparently satisfied with his part he played.

Johan sputtered. "Traitor! I—I demand to be returned to my kingdom."

Weylan's brows shot upward as he glared at the king with derision. "You have no kingdom. Resistors from Eira followed you here, Johan, and every single one of the fifty or so soldiers you managed to drag with you are dead or will be when Lucan finds the ones who have fled. Your people have rejected you, and a new king sits at the throne."

"You lie."

Riaan cleared his throat to interrupt. "King Johan, tomorrow you will be released from our care. You will be escorted to your kingdom to be tried for your crimes."

Weylan pulled a rolled parchment from his pocket. His voice raised, traveling the length of the room. People slowed in their work to hear. "If I may, Your Majesty." He addressed the growing audience. "By order of the king of Eira—"

Johan's hairy chest rose and fell like an overstuffed walrus. "Excuse me?"

"—I, General Weylan Laphel, am commanded to return Johan Drakara to the kingdom of Eira to be tried by the people." A murmur erupted through the crowd. "If there be any damages sustained to the people or property within the kingdom of Anolyn due to the criminal Drakara, the good king of Anolyn may send any representatives he chooses and add those witnesses for or against the fallen king."

"How dare you." Johan's mouth opened and closed as his eyes flashed about the witnesses in the room. He pointed a finger to the recently promoted Weylan. "And just who is this new leader of Eira? Who steals my crown?"

Weylan's eyes shot to me and an apology crossed his features. "Toma Drakara."

The throne room erupted with gasps and a rumble of voices, growing in number. Anolyn's citizens buzzed, their excitement mingled with confusion and fear. Their gawking eyes turned to glimpse my reaction.

But I had already hardened into a mask of control. Inside was another story entirely. Nausea threatened my composure when my heart dropped to the pit of my stomach.

"What madness is this?" my uncle asked. His hand gripped the material at his chest. "My younger brother was murdered by that beast you just witnessed, and yet you say he is resurrected?" But even as he spoke, I could hear the deceit he masked with hysteria. He lied.

"Oh, no, Johan. We found where you stashed him and freed him. Your brother Toma is very much alive. But you already knew that, didn't you?"

Rebellion gleamed within Johan's eyes.

My head spun, my claustrophobic thoughts suffocating the life from me. I swallowed against the anxiety lodged deep within my throat.

Three months ago, I was a bastard child and an orphan. I always had been. But if what Weylan said was true...

Castiel's fingers touched my wrist, grounding me to reality.

Again, Weylan's eyes found mine. "I'm sorry."

"Take him," Riaan said.

My emotional barriers cracked. I closed my eyes and allowed Castiel to guide me to him. He wrapped me in his arms, eager to soothe, and I allowed it.

"Stop her!"

My eyes flew open.

Surprisingly fast, a healed Deylah broke through the gawking crowd and rushed toward Johan. Light glinted from the steel in her hands. Before anyone could think to react, she jammed the knife between his shoulder blades then ripped it from his flesh. Johan howled in pain, rearing back. In another fatal movement, the pryor threaded her hand past his arms and sliced his exposed throat.

Light exploded inside my mind, my breath ripped from my lungs. Castiel lunged forward, but he was too late.

The king of Eira fell to his knees, the air bubbling from his sliced windpipe.

Deylah dropped the knife. It clattered to the ground before its victim followed suit.

A smile tipped one corner of her lips. She appeared almost at ease when the guards wrestled her to the floor and cuffed her bloodied arms. Amid the chaos, my grandmother's head turned to me, her silvery-blue eyes finding mine. A single word blew past her paling lips.

"Evil."

31
NEW REGIME

SMOKE FROM A DYING FIRE WAFTED my direction. I coughed against its attack.

"Are you alright there, Princess?"

I ignored Siana's annoyed question and continued rolling up our canvas tent. It was relatively small, but big enough to fit me and my new lady's maid.

"It's just amazing," she continued, sighing dramatically. "The further we get into your county, the uglier and colder it becomes." Every moment that passed, the assassin's attitude became increasingly foul.

Not that I blamed her. I wasn't that far behind.

I bundled my chin down into my thick wool cloak that did little to protect against a chill. *Nothing* was pretty in the Varian Forest. It was an excruciating six-day trek from Anolyn's Castle to my home in Eira—excruciating not because of the distance or the hardship of traveling with barely any rest, but because of what we marched toward. How often had I told myself I would never go back?

A pair of black boots stopped in the dirt next to me. "Need help?" Castiel asked.

"Of course not," I snapped.

He helped anyway, which only made me feel guiltier. My hostility was to Riaan's assassin, not my betrothed. Or was he my betrothed still? I didn't have the courage to ask.

"The princess is just taking her time," Siana said, her breath a visible cloud. "Basking in her good fortune."

My jaw tensed. "And what good fortune would that be?"

She hummed. "Good point." Her smile vexed. She stood to claim the finished product from Castiel. "I'll take care of the rest, Your Greatness." She spun on her heel and went to the waiting horses to pack.

I wiped the dirt from my hands on my pants, mumbling. "At this point, I'd take the seer's company over the assassin's."

Castiel's fingers clasped mine, sending a jolt of electricity through my frozen core. Our contact had been minimal since before our departure from Anolyn, but there had been little time between burying the dead and readying for the next week's travel. Captain Mikael, Reese, Siana, a procession of two hundred armed soldiers of Anolyn, and another hundred from Eira's resistance followed General Weylan, me, and my uncle's carriage to my motherland. King Riaan and his future bride stayed behind to calm their people, prepare their nuptials, and plan for the Wraith Queen's next attack.

Siana would bear my trials of a new family with me but was irritated about being discarded as the king's assassin. I had a feeling her reassignment had more to do with her less-than-friendly relationship with Riaan's fiancée, but the king said he wanted a spy within Toma's home.

The prince drew me away from my fire and the hosts of soldiers readying for travel, but we didn't go far. I peered to the boughs of the trees, searching for the falcry that had followed us into the forest before disappearing.

"Have you seen Ketrina?" I asked.

Tension rippled from him. "Not since yesterday."

"I'm worried about her."

"I'd be more worried if she followed us from the protection of the forest. She'll be fine."

He pulled me behind a tree whose trunk was wider than three people. Gently he coaxed me closer to him, forcing my gaze—not that I minded. He was resplendent in lower-ranking military garb and a plain wool cloak to match those of his soldiers. Although, he'd be resplendent in just about anything.

His thick black hair was already combed, and he smelled of campfire, soap, and leather. "Remember, you had a choice." His deep voice was a soothing balm to my internal wounds. My heart melted to his concern.

My fingers caressed his chiseled jaw, tracing a line to the tip of his chin. "And anger the new king of Eira?" I asked with raised brows.

His expression darkened. Penetrating blue eyes examined my face, ending at the scar on my neck. He tipped his head forward, resting it against mine, his lips so close I could almost taste them. I froze, allowing the momentary comfort, my insides a cauldron of emotions.

His hands slid up my arms and I closed my eyes, breathing in his essence and enjoying the sensation that was all him.

Heat followed his touch over my shoulders and up my neck. Cautiously his thumbs traced my cheeks, his breath warm against my mouth, but nothing more. I opened my eyes to the intensity of his as he watched me, hesitation deep within him. Then I realized what that hesitation was. He waited for me.

I slid my arms around him and raised on tiptoes, bringing my lips to his. Soft at first, I reveled in the sensation. His calloused hands—the hands of a powerful leader—cupped my face with such a gentle touch that it caused tears to prick the back of my eyes. With a muffled groan, I tightened my grip on him and deepened the kiss.

He responded with more than gratifying eagerness, his desperation matching my frantic feeling. There was nothing soft about how his mouth moved against mine, or how he held me to him, but that only made it all that much better. Would I ever feel this again?

Castiel broke away first, wrapping me in his stable arms. His heavy breath matched the beating of our combined hearts. His voice was hoarse when he spoke. "You don't have to return, Ilianna. You don't owe that to anyone. You can stay—"

I shook my head, hating the words before they even left my mouth. "I have to find out… see him for myself. If this king is truly my father—"

"He's your father, Ilianna." Weylan's voice crashed down on me, dousing my moment with the prince like a cold bucket of water. He led my horse behind him, with a sour expression and no apology for the interruption. "And he wishes to see you."

My spine straightened as I glared at the interloper.

"And it has to be *you* that takes me to him?"

His chin lifted as his eyes narrowed. "It was his wish."

My attention caught upon additional movement. Only yards away, a demon took shape. Its dark silhouette peeked from beyond the trunk of a tree, watching our interaction. Its red eyes smiled at me. Another wafted into view behind the first, but it only hovered a moment before disappearing. If I searched, I would find more than just the two. Hundreds surrounded us. I had seen them.

We have one in our midst more cursed than they, Melora had said.

Perhaps they stayed away because of my presence, or they waited for the commands of their cursed leader. Either way, it didn't matter.

I took a step back from Castiel, loathed the forced distance, and scowled at Weylan. "You could have told me my father was alive."

I snatched the reins from his grip and mounted.

Castiel stepped between us.

Weylan heaved a heavy sigh. "We've discussed this. We weren't sure he was even alive, only hoped he was. Until then, our resistance pressed forward with fighting against Johan, eager to gain your and Anolyn's support." His pointed gaze rested on Castiel and his borrowed clothing. "This charade of yours is unnecessary, Prince. I should have announced your coming in the missive. You have nothing to fear. My liege will welcome his daughter with open arms, as will his followers."

Castiel hummed a noncommittal sound. "I will discover that for myself. You may pretend ignorance, if you wish." He checked the straps to my saddle and tucked my boot into the stirrup. "Support will come to the new king when Toma proves to me he deserves it."

Weylan grumbled something unintelligible.

"Whether the princess chooses to stay is up to her, General." Castiel's eyes met mine. "A storm is coming, but if we hurry, we can reach Hartsevain before nightfall."

I nodded, a lump lodging in my throat as I watched him go to claim his horse.

Weylan moved to me. "Eira deserves a new beginning, Ilianna. She deserves to heal."

"So do I." I kicked my horse forward to follow my prince. "And stay away from me."

Anger and frustration battled over control of my senses. Eira was not mine to support and I couldn't make a promise I didn't intend to keep. As soon as I could, I would return to my new home.

But even as the thought came, unease quickly followed. *How could I abandon my people?*

Johan had not only abused me, but he had abused his countrymen and his role as king. And paid dearly for it.

Instead of being tried for his crimes, he would be returned to his brother to be buried in the catacombs of the king, or to be burned as a traitor by fire, his ashes discarded from the cliffs into the sea.

Tensions were high as we pressed forward. Wind blew through the trees and conducted an eerie song upon their leaves, racking my body with yet another chill. Castiel ran the line of soldiers with Captain Mikael, searching for signs of attack from the Wraith Queen or any of Johan's remaining supporters.

Thunder rumbled in warning before the air burst into a torrential rainstorm. Water leaked through the patchy canopy of leaves and, despite our cloaks and leathers, drenched us through to the bone. Our muddied path slowed our march and irritated our horses, but finally beams of grayed light filtered from a clearing in the trees. A wave of tangible energy passed over the line of soldiers as we neared the end of the forest. Our speed increased. I pushed my horse, sprinting her to the open air.

I breathed in Eira and all her glory and lifted my face to the sky, the hood of my cloak falling back. Heavy rain pelted my face; the cold water washed the grime from my cheeks and neck.

The harsher climate of our land was the original king of Eira's reason for settling there so long ago. The natural elements would slow down invaders, and it was impossible for anyone to enter the kingdom from the north. The oceans to the east and west and the Varian Forest were easy enough to watch for enemies. Hartsevain Castle stood tall above the hills and trees, regal upon its mountainous ledge. Six stories high, it was built to intimidate newcomers and to shield the people of Eira—at least that was what it used to be.

"I'll protect you from Toma and even the Wraith Queen," Siana said, bringing me back to the present. Her voice was thick with derision. "But I can do nothing against a cold. Cover your head, you little fool."

"There," I said, flipping the hood back in place. "Do you feel better? On or off, we're still drenched."

We pressed forward over large rocks, smoothed by centuries of the unforgiving elements. Scanning the familiar landscape of yellowed grass bent low to the abuse of the sky, I grew hopeful of witnessing the bright green sprigs of growth among the dead, promising a hopeful future. I guided our procession around the towns that separated us from our destination to avoid any additional problems our presence might cause. Eirians were suspicious of strangers.

Even still, the news of our presence would spread like wildfire, and an armed detail would march to meet us.

Within the hour, a line of soldiers appeared on the horizon. Our men halted their progress and formed into ranks of twenty. Siana tightened her cloak around her face and ducked back behind the first row. General Weylan, Captain Mikael, Lucan-Cyris, Castiel, and I led our horses to meet the small Eirian convoy.

Castiel took a position to my right. His guard was up, and no warmth emanated from him. He was as stone cold as the first moment I met him, and I shivered against the memory. How long ago that felt now.

We left the protection of our company.

Five from the other side met us, all cloaked and armed.

The middle-most man came forward. His face was thin; his long gray beard revealed an older man, pressing into his seventies. His voice carried the distance between us. "Why do you bring an army to our walls?"

"General Losso." I smiled. "I'm shocked to see you. You retired over ten years ago."

Weylan cleared his throat. "As you can see, General, we come to escort Princess Ilianna safely home."

Losso's eyes did a quick inspection of me and our remaining company. "And you, General Weylan, could not do that yourself?"

"We thought it best after Johan's attack on Anolyn."

Losso's gaze grew wide.

"An attack that was quickly followed by an appearance from the Wraith Queen herself," Weylan finished.

The others of Losso's group murmured behind him. One brow ticked high on the old man's face. "The Wraith Queen?"

Weylan nodded. "She has returned and promises quick retribution."

Losso's chin tipped higher. "I see. And where is Johan?"

"He's dead," I said, my voice harsher than I intended.

Weylan cast me a sharp look, then addressed his audience. "His casket lies in that carriage."

"King Toma will not be happy to hear that." Again, Losso scanned the line of soldiers, falling to me. "Princess Ilianna, I'm grateful for your safe return. Your father awaits you. Come with me, if you please. Your men are no longer needed."

"Sir." Mikael spoke loudly to capture his attention. "I am Captain Mikael of the king's army. In the missive to King Riaan, King Toma expressed the desire of our continued peace and allowed for our kingdom to send representatives with the return of Johan Drakara to voice our abuse of Johan's rule."

A smirk began in the corner of Losso's lips. "And since the man is *dead*, don't you think that a little unnecessary?"

"Perhaps, but my king wishes to pass on a message to the new king of Eira."

"Very well. You may bring a dozen of your men, but the rest must camp here to wait your return."

Mikael nodded. "Thank you, General."

Castiel signaled for Mikael to select additional men to follow our collection of players and to give instructions to those we left behind. Siana retook her position at my side, and together, we were quickly escorted to Hartsevain Castle through the middle of the city of Kurreg.

The rain stopped long enough for the sun to shine through a break in the clouds. I cast down the hood of my cloak to enjoy what I could of it. Citizens watched us from their cottages and shops, some brave enough to come out and inspect us closer. I nodded to those who did and kept pace with the others. Almost at the gates, a woman ran from her home in a mad dash to our line.

"Halt, madam," Losso cried, and the woman did as she was commanded.

Mikael had partly drawn his sword before Castiel stopped him with a hand to his wrist.

Mud coated the woman's shoes and her blonde hair fell from the tie that bound it. She drew a flower from inside her cloak and lifted it to me. I recovered from my shock enough to take it. She ran back inside before I could thank her.

"See," Weylan said, moving to my side. "Your people have missed you."

Ignoring the guilt that rose in my throat, I thrust the flower to my assassin-maid... but she was no longer there. Cyris received it instead. He leaned to tuck the bloom into my belt, discretely scanning the streets for any sign of her, but there was none.

If I knew Siana at all, I would be seeing her soon enough.

The roads steepened and our horses climbed higher. Hartsevain loomed before us, its stone fortifications bright against a sodden, gray backdrop of the Kurreg Mountains. Carved sentinels—statues of the great kings of old, and generals fallen in battle—eyed our coming from their great walls. Black moss crawled the towers, turrets, and lookouts. A heavy bell tolled the hour.

And my insides turned to mush. Voices screamed from within my brain. Warnings shouted from my memories. The blood leached from my face, and my hands and feet tingled.

"Breathe, Ilianna," Castiel said, pulling up beside me. But I wasn't sure I could. It was so familiar and foreign, all at the same time.

We came to the main gate as the rain returned in sheets. As if in recognition, a metallic groan sounded, and the doors opened to us. Beneath the cover of the first wall, the others removed their hoods, their eyes scanning their surroundings. I coughed against the familiar smell of mud and dank mildew. We were commanded to dismount and give up our weapons.

After several attendants disappeared toward the stables with our horses, Losso clapped his hands for our attention. "The king will first desire a private audience with his daughter. Everyone else must wait for their return."

"Perhaps somewhere we can get warm?" Weylan asked.

Losso's brows lifted high. "Of course, *you* may, General Weylan—"

"But—"

"—*After* meeting with your king," Losso finished.

Weylan flinched to his cold reception.

A warning triggered inside my brain and I gripped Castiel's fingers. "Something's not right." I said to him.

"Nonsense, Princess Ilianna," Losso soothed. "Come with me."

My muscles stiffened. "I will not meet my father without an attendant."

His gaze narrowed. "Very well. You may take *one* with you."

There was no question who. Castiel kept close. Almost in a daydreamer's haze, we walked with Toma's men toward the open courtyard, its expanse big enough to hold hundreds of its citizens. It spread beneath the balcony that led from the king's private suites.

Rain pelted my head and face and leaked down my back, but I barely felt the cold. I swallowed against my throat-closing anxiety. The Demon Daughter sensed my unease and perked up, listening for the cause of my reaction.

I pressed her down the best I could.

Four guards lined beneath the grand balcony—again, none that I recognized—but upon our arrival, they moved for us to take the center-most stance. They joined the others as Losso and his guards surrounded us. I eyed Castiel nervously.

Losso cleared his throat. "Great King Toma, may I present Princess Ilianna Drakara."

A head appeared from the ledge, three stories up. Only his eyes were visible as he cast his gaze upon his small audience. Then more of him appeared and my heart seized.

Dark, curly locks framed a pale face. Black eyes set beneath thick, bushy brows, and a full beard reminded me more of the bears that dwelled upon our northern ranges. My heart dropped. King Toma was a younger, thinner version of Johan. He leaned over the balustrade, his head angled to the side.

Toma scanned the line of men and our circling guard before landing upon me. His dispassionate gaze scrutinized me from my boots and sodden leathers, to my hair braided long down my back. Something dark flashed within his eyes.

"I don't know this girl." He straightened and with a wave of his hand, he turned to leave. Before he disappeared, his voice called over his shoulder. "Kill her."

I sputtered, shocked. "Wh-what?"

My prince was in front of me in a heartbeat. The sound of steel cut through the air as all around us, weapons were drawn. I pressed my back to Castiel's.

"King Toma!" Castiel yelled. His words vibrated me to my core. Thunder rumbled. "I am Castiel Anouk of Anolyn. I demand you retract your men." But there was no response from the balcony.

Losso laughed, gaining our attention. "Is Anolyn so poor that they cannot properly clothe the son of kings?" He smirked and crouched low. "If that's really who you are, step aside, Prince, or die with the impostor."

I growled at the threat. "I am no impostor, and neither is the prince. But if the king will not claim me as his, I will happily leave."

Castiel raised his hands. "We are on the brink of war with the Wraith Queen. We should not be shedding each other's blood."

Losso grinned, rain dripping from his lashes. "Then *don't.* Step aside, *Prince,* or die."

"I don't think so." Castiel's magic vibrated through the air as he gathered power to him. With a convincing jolt, a wave of energy flashed outward, sending the circle of Eirians stumbling back. "This is your last warning!"

Smile gone, Losso glared. "No, this is yours."

Anger choked the breath from my lungs. The Demon Daughter laughed inside my head, writhing to break free. *Elyn,* she reminded me. *Her name was Elyn.*

I tried to control her, tried to focus on my magic instead, but her flames already combined with mine, enveloping me in her fire. Red coated my vision.

"Ilianna." Castiel's voice broke through my trance, but it was too much. All of it.

To run away from the abuse of an uncle, only for an unknown father to deny me? I screamed through the rejection, my blood boiling. Toma's guards stepped back, fear reflecting within their eyes.

Another scream rent the air, causing my heart to beat painfully against my chest. Ketrina landed before me with a thud that shook the earth and rattled my teeth.

The Demon Daughter fell to the ground, receding with a jolt.

The falcry spun, her black wings outstretched, felling any soldier close to her. Toma's soldiers cried out in fear, bolting away from the mystical creature who screamed again, puffing her armored feathers. Her razor-sharp talons broke the cobblestone floor beneath her, scraping through to earth. Castiel raced in front of her, his arms outstretched to halt any additional attack.

Fear coated my heart. From my periphery, two more soldiers entered the scene, bows at the ready.

Castiel and Ketrina would die protecting me.

The archers took aim.

With a scream, I thrust my hands to the ground. Power erupted from my touch, raking like a plow, heaping the earth as it raced to its targets. An explosion of cobblestone and dirt blew back the archers.

Sheets of rain muffled the surrounding cries of confusion. I peered up to see Weylan and Mikael standing over me, their back to me as protective shields, swords drawn. Ketrina screamed and snapped her beak. Then for a moment, all was silent.

"Enough!" A slow clap reverberated from the shadows of the courtyard. Toma emerged. A black cloak and hood enclosed him, but as he came closer, his features became more distinguishable. A scar traveled the right side of his face from his hairline to his jaw. Black bruised the skin beneath his eyes and deep shadows lined his gaunt cheeks.

"I demand to know the meaning of this," Weylan shouted above the rain.

King Toma stilled. "I don't have to explain myself to anyone." Then he smiled, his black eyes finding mine. "Welcome home, my daughter."

Slowly I stood, my fingers twitching. I smiled back, baring my teeth. "You, too."

You bastard.

THE END

ACKNOWLEDGMENTS

ಒಗ

As always, this book would not
have been possible without several key people:

To my critique group, the stalwart and
never-failing Jill Burgoyne and Kate Stradling.
You are my light in the dark and
terrifying world of writing.

To Jenny Zemanek @seedlingsdesignstudio,
for taking my limited (and rather pathetic) design ideas
and transforming them into something
beautiful and unique.

To my husband, Dan, for always believing
in my abilities despite my constant insecurities,
and to my boys, Kyle and Micah, for your
never-ending love and insight.

And to my beta-readers and
proof readers (listed alphabetically):
To Donna Robinson, Marjie Mattison, Morgan Stradling,
Rohndia Bretz, Sarah Goit, and Tamara Goodman.
Your contribution is indispensable.

THANK YOU!

HERE'S A SNEAK PEEK AT
THE SEQUEL TO OF BLOOD AND DECEIT

CURSED BY BLOOD

For updates on its progress follow Rachel at
www.rachelcollett.com

಄

1

A NEW HELL

COLD AS A WRAITH'S HELL, EIRA seeped into my skin and trailed up my arms on spikes. My muscles ached from fatigue, and my eyes burned from lack of sleep, but I ignored the pain as I hustled through the frigid castle hallways. The guards posed outside my door—children, really—looked straight ahead, their expressions impassive.

"At ease, gentlemen," I said, in my usual mock tone, but they didn't respond.

The blond—I never asked their names—produced a keychain from his pocket, unlocked the door, and opened it. He didn't bother to search my room for intruders, and why would he? No one here wanted me dead, unless you counted my father.

I pressed the door shut, leaning my forehead against its chilled wood and closed my eyes.

Icy fingers clapped down on my mouth, muffling my cry. Something sharp pierced through the thicker material of my gray dress and pricked the skin at my side.

"If I were an assassin, you'd be dead, *Princess*." The intruder's warm breath assaulted my cheek. "Oh, wait. I am."

I jerked to the side and rammed my elbow back, but Siana coolly skirted away from my assault. Her hips swayed beneath a resplendent gown too beautiful for a lady's maid. *She* was too beautiful to be a lady's maid, yet the farce had been successful.

"Did I trigger your *friend*?" Siana asked, offhandedly. Her knife clattered unceremoniously to the stone floor.

I rotated my neck to ease the sudden tension in my shoulders. *Elyn*. The Demon Daughter, my ever-constant, internal companion, had a name. Why had I been so foolish as to tell the assassin?

I ignored Siana's question with one of my own. "Borrowed another one of my dresses, did you?"

"It's not like you're using them," she said, sprawling on my gigantic bed among the heavy blankets of lilac and ivory. Her hair draped over the edge, her slender fingers combing her long, black tresses.

I moved to my windows that towered to the ceiling and placed my palm against the cold glass. A door led out to a private balcony—a door that had always before been barred, but not any longer. I unbolted the lock and threw it wide. Eira's early spring wafted past me on a cold breeze and into my stuffy room.

Gardens sprawled out beneath my balcony in a mesmerizing labyrinth. A beautiful fountain tinkled in the center. Marble effigies of fairies and goblins, stallions and warriors, dotted the maze. Benches and gazebos welcomed those that lost their way and needed to rest. It was still too cold to draw many visitors, but when the temperature warmed, the gallantry would roam the grounds for hours, losing themselves in the maze.

The smell of rain soothed my nerves. I took a deep breath, savoring it

"Did you enjoy your afternoon with the peasants?" Siana asked.

I rolled my eyes, hating the assassin's dig. I turned from the view and reentered my room, shutting the door behind me. "You're Anolynian. You shouldn't call them that."

Her upside-down smile irritated. "But I'm in character, and in Eira, peasants abound."

"Which is why you should have been helping instead of sulking," I snapped, heat rising to my cheeks.

"If the king of Eira does nothing to rid his lands of such huge disparities in social classes, how much can a single lady's maid truly do?"

I heaved a sigh and sat at my vanity, another recently added piece of furniture to my once sparse bedroom. A washcloth and warm bowl of water sat in the center of the table.

I dunked the cloth then wrung it out. "If the king—"

"You mean your *father*?" Siana smiled at me like the cat she was. "Such unfriendliness, Ilianna. And after he's been so kind to you."

My father.

Toma had seen to the refurbishing of my room. What once was an empty space with merely a cot and a single chest of drawers was now filled with a bed as big as the one I had in Anolyn, a plush purple lounge chair I never touched, and two matching armoires stocked with dresses.

A porcelain tub waited in the corner of the room behind a screen of ivory drapes that cascaded from vaulted ceilings. My vanity table sat next to the fireplace that I was at one time never allowed to use. It roared with a warm fire and was the only change I really appreciated. The rest oddly made the room feel empty and cold.

Siana flipped over and watched me through her onyx eyes. "You're still doing your best to ignore him, I gather."

I didn't answer. Instead, I washed the grime from my cheeks. Toma had ordered my execution upon first arrival—an order cast to test my reaction.

She hummed. "And just how long do you think you can get away with that?"

"If he continues to disregard the prince of Anolyn, then I will continue to disregard him."

It had been almost a month since our arrival in Eira. Toma rejected meeting with Castiel time and time again, pretending to be busy with the preparations of Johan's burial and the troubles of a torn kingdom on the rebound as it passed from a one torrential leader to another. Instead the prince was sent with a small group of soldiers and retired generals on tour across our extensive countryside to Eira's most treasured sights. I rarely saw him. Castiel had been patient with the new leader, but every day that passed grated on my nerves. The sooner I could leave this new hell of mine, the better.

Leaning her chin against her palm, Siana smiled. "Your father has commanded me to fetch you to him the moment you return. Since you've rejected every other summons he's made, I told him you might need an incentive."

I growled a warning, but her smile only increased.

"You'll be interested to know that Castiel will be present during your meeting with your father. I'm sure you'll want to look presentable for you *betrothed*. You should scrub off all that peasant."

My breath caught in my lungs and I turned in my seat, not willing to show the assassin my sudden excitement. "Very well. Can you please do my hair?"

"Do it yourself."

Again, I sighed, ignoring my pathetic lady's maid/assassin protector. I couldn't be too mad at her. Life in Eira was vastly different from life in Anolyn. Not much had change with the new king, except that the princess was more available to her people and Toma was not as visibly corrupt as Johan. But Toma was no better. His works were done in the shadows.

I missed Sameen and her kindness. I missed her soft hands and her brown eyes. She was always far too good to me. Swallowing, I yanked out my pathetic braid to quickly draw a brush over my hair, ripping through the tangles.

Siana scoffed in disgust and came to me. "Let go," she said, slapping my hand away. Tsking, she worked through the knots, starting at the bottom, moving her way up.

"Where did you learn to do hair?" I asked.

One side of her mouth tipped up. "In my line of work, you have to be adept at most occupations if you want to... blend in." But she didn't give any additional information. "The back of your neck is still dirty."

I obeyed her silent command and washed as she deftly plaited my dark brown hair into an eccentric braid that fell down my back. When she finished, she gathered the basin of water and cloth, setting it outside my door to be collected, then climbed back in bed.

She grabbed a book from my nightstand and held it over her head, pretending to be instantly immersed. "You should change before you go. You look so drab in gray."

From the horde of dresses in my armoire I selected a lilac gown with a low-slung belt of silver and slippers to match. There were none of my favorite leather ensembles in the selection of outfits. None of my old armor.

Irritation flashed through me. I wasn't allowed to train with my armies, not with sword or hand to hand combat. Any magic was expressly forbidden until further notice from the king. Not that I listened to these orders.

Siana would exercise with me whenever she was in a more pleasant mood, and I didn't need anyone's help to practice my magic. If I wasn't out with the commoners, I was in my room, moving furniture or directing my control past the walls. Unsuspecting passersby suddenly had the urge to procure me food with pretend orders from the king. This enabled me to miss meals with him. Thus far, no one had been the wiser and Toma hadn't pushed.

From the pockets of my discarded dress, I pulled a small dagger and leather bands. The weapon was a cast-iron hilt masterpiece. Eirian leather knot-work weaved from the pommel to the guard. Etchings of vines cascaded down the stainless-steel blade to the razor-sharp tip.

"Where did you get that?" Siana asked, suddenly attentive. "I don't think your father knows about any weapons you have."

"And he won't," I warned with a pointed glace. I strapped the blade to my calf, lowering my gown over it. One of the gifts my father had given was a drawer full of jewelry—only small pieces and nothing too grand, but a single gold chain was more than enough to buy what I needed.

Siana shrugged. "I was just curious."

"What will you do while I'm gone?" I asked, changing the subject.

She flicked a hand in dismissal. "What I always do, my lady. Wait for you to come back."

I huffed, then pushed open the door

The guards stopped me just outside. "The king has requested your presence," the blond said.

I grinned stupidly. "You don't say?" With the wave of my hand, I displayed my gown—an abnormality for my usual selection of attire. "Why do you think I got all ready?"

The guard scanned my appearance. "Where's your lady's maid? She must accompany you."

I flinched, my brows pinching together. "Since when? I've never been accompanied in my own home."

He stood taller, crossing his arms over his chest. "Thing are different now, Princess. Your father demands you travel with accompaniment."

"What's your name, soldier?"

"Han, from his majesty's ninth regiment."

"Ninth? I didn't know there was a ninth. I don't recognize you." In fact, I didn't recognize any of them. "Why is that?"

Han peered at a spot over my head. "Your highness never came to train with the newer recruits."

"I was never *told* to train with the newer recruits. Surely you must know that. I was only ever, and still am, a humble servant of the crown." Could he hear the derision in my voice?

"Of course, Princess Ilianna."

I turned to the second guard, who hadn't made a sound or even moved during our whole conversation, and I liked him even more because of it. "Why don't you escort me," I said to him, but he only looked away.

Han answered. "We are commanded to stay vigilant at your door."

"And they are unnecessary." Siana appeared behind me as she finished fastening her plaited hair in an elegant bun at the back of her head. "Your humble servant is ready to accompany you."

I pinned her with a glare before spinning on the spot. "Fine."

Siana kept by my side as we marched the corridors that led to King Toma's throne room. The walk was so familiar to me, but somehow, I almost felt lost.

Hartsevain was six flights high, constructed of stone and marble and surrounded by an impenetrable wall. It was impressive alone, towering on the crag of the first low mountain peak of Kurreg, its white walls blended into the snowcapped mounts and clouded heavens. To the east our views overlooked a rambling crystal lake and to the west more trees until the ocean.

"Whoever designed this castle should be stoned to death," Siana said beneath her breath.

"Actually, he was."

She never blinked. "Lovely."

Inside, Hartsevain, it was a labyrinth of oddly designed passageways and un-connecting stairwells. The kings and queens of old loved this unique design of their home, as it often confused visiting dignitaries and put them at a disadvantage for figuring out the lay.

I found it annoying and I missed the simplicity of Meyrion even more. My room was on the fourth floor, just above my father's room one level lower. Guards were spackled throughout the castle and waited at each level of the split stair cases, watching me with dispassionate eyes. I led the way to the first set of disjointed stairs. "Alright," I said through a tensed jaw "If Toma's anything like my uncle, you'll need to know a few things. Be as invisible as possible—"

"King Toma's much more aware of the goings on of his castle than you think. He makes it a point to meet with *me*."

"I see."

As if reading my mind, she answered. "He seeks information on your whereabouts and also desires my help in soothing your irritation towards him."

My jaw tensed. Siana started down the stairs and I followed close behind. My uncle had used my old lady's maid, Pala to report on me and my interactions with others, and now Toma applied the same method to spy. Unfortunately for both Johan and Toma, Pala's true devoted was to the Wraith Queen, while Siana's devotion was to King Riaan and the Kingdom of Anolyn.

She continued. "I told him I didn't know you well enough to pressure you into any intimate relationship with an unknown father, but I'd do my best."

I bit back a nasty response as we exited on to the third floor and into the Hartsevain gallery. Empty chairs and a cold fireplace set the tone of the dark room where rows of portraits lined the walls. One rarely came to gaze upon the Drakara bloodline unless the king requested it, but those important enough to reside in the upper floors of the castle had to pass through it every day. Rich tapestries designed especially for each heir draped from vaulted ceilings. A gallery of marble effigies and pallid busts from famous Eirian artists watched our movements, their cold eyes condemning.

We passed the hallway that led to my father's private suites, completely blocked by four heavily armored guards and I shivered, quickening my steps. The echo of footfalls caught my attention. From the opposite end of the gallery, and near the second set of stairs, General Lasso came forward.

He had recently trimmed his long gray beard, clipping it closer to his skin. The fresher look gave him a more youthful appearance even though he pressed headlong into his early seventies. The once retired General was spryer that I initially gave him credit for. I used to think him as kind but upon my first reception to my father, he had stood ready to kill me at the order of his king.

I lifted my head higher as we drew near. "General."

He bowed low. "Your Highness. Just the person I was looking for. I was sent to fetch you for your father."

"Indeed?"

He nodded, offering his arm. "Come, I will escort you."

Obediently, Siana dropped back, allowing the General

to take her place at my side. She followed close behind, her hands clasped—ever the perfect picture of humility.

I hesitantly took his proffered arm. "Apparently, I'm in high demand."

As we passed more soldiers standing guard, General Lasso nodded to them.

"General, where are all my men?" I asked. "I've searched for them in every town I've entered."

"Ah, yes. You've been a very busy woman. I must say that your aid in Kurreg has not been overlooked. Word of your charity is spreading like the frost from the north peaks to the oceans." His gaze searched my face. "Your father has been impressed by your good deeds. Your stay in Anolyn did much for you."

I looked away, not missing his attempt to influence this conversation, and heavens knew I would much rather talk of my Anolyn than Eira any day, but I would not be swayed.

"Anolyn does much for their people. I'd like to integrate some of their traditions into ours, if possible, but it's a difficult task when I come home to strangers."

He tsked. "Am I a stranger, child?"

"I have not seen you since I was a girl of eight. Where are my men General?"

He cleared his throat. "Princess Ilianna, everyone that had anything to do with your... training has been reassigned.

"Why?"

He paused before the next flight of stairs. "Do you really not know?" This stairwell was too narrow to walk up in pairs. Losso swept out his hand for me to take the lead.

I glided down quickly and came out onto the second floor. Losso and Siana emerged behind. This level was a network of hallways with more rooms for visiting guests, nobles and high-ranking elite. Its white paneled walls opened to the large upper deck of the great hall. Luxurious, gold-colored settees and couches lined the room for resting. The marble floors reflected one of the three sprawling candelabras. An immense set of marble white stairs opened wide, descending to the bottom floor and the remainder of the great hall where the usual show of simpering nobility and self-important military lounged and conversed one with another. *Them* I recognized. Their shocked voices, whispered behind gloved hands and delicate fans, traveled up to me.

I ignored them and their watchful gazes. "You were saying, General?"

Losso cleared his throat. "Your treatment by King Johan was not overlooked by many, but anyone who argued in your behalf was either put to death, reassigned, or retired by him."

Weylan had said as much, but I didn't believe him—still didn't believe him. A chill flashed through my chest and the blood drained from my face.

"King Toma wished to make an example of all involved in your abuse by reassigning or retiring those that were once in your command."

"You and your men attacked me on my first day here. How is that any different?"

"Your father had to see for himself how the daughter of the Wraith Queen would respond to an attack. He had no desire to actually hurt you, but he was Theia's captive for all of your life. He had to see for himself."

Sickness stole my breath, although I wasn't sure why. I had never been intimate or even friendly with anyone I commanded. Johan would've never allowed it. But for them to be punished for things they had no control over...

I held to the rail and followed down the grand staircase. "This is ridiculous, General," I said, my mouth suddenly dry. "They didn't lift a finger to hurt me."

"No, but they were cowards for not fighting the ones that did."

"I didn't need them to," I said, barely recognizing my own voice.

He stopped so sharply that I juddered to a halt. He lowered his head to stare me straight in the eyes. The emotion in his stole my breath. "Didn't you?"

Without another word, the General pressed forward, leaving me to trail behind him. Siana reclaimed her place at my side as Losso called to two soldiers who stood at attention before the throne room. They quickly responded by throwing the doors wide.

My feet froze above the threshold but Losso marched down the long hall to his king. The two soldiers moved behind, and their presence pressed against me, blocking any escape.

Siana took two steps forward, then paused. Her questioning gaze turned to me. "Princess Ilianna?"

I ignored her.

Hartsevain's throne room was twice the size of Meyrion's. Two flights of stairs separated the king on his dais from those that dared to see him. Lancet windows and stained glass drew gazes upward to lofty pointed arches and snow-white vaulted ceilings with golden ribbing. Two additional candelabras hung here, matching the one above the second story hall. Golden beams from an afternoon sun shone through the windows, haloing the King of Eira in angelic light, but he was far from celestial.

Toma's curly, dark brown hair had been tamed and pulled to a tail at the back of his head. Still much thinner than Johan, a month worth of Eirian food had diminished some of the shallowed lines of his face. He was only twenty when he left with his new bride, Theia, the Wraith Queen, which meant he was now thirty-eight or nine. Like his brother, he too wore the thick gold chain and royal medallion of the Drakara bloodline, and the heavy leathers and furs. The similarities did wonders for my anxiety, causing my heart pounded out an irregular rhythm.

Next to Toma stood General Weylan Laphel. He stared at me from his elevated position, his arms crossed over the expanse of his chest. The second son to the Duke of Vaneira, and third cousin to Johan and Toma Drakara, Weylan had raised to one of the ten Generals of his Majesty's army, and the king's trusted advisors, climbing the noble ladder with apparent ease. Eira's star pupil finally had the pomp and prestige he'd always desired. He had recently cut his sandy blonde hair to match Castiel's style—cropped short on the sides, longer at the top. Whether he did it to mimic the prince on purpose, or not, it still seemed pathetic. He would never come close to the man Castiel was, try as he may.

An audience stretched out in a line before Toma, their backs towards me.

But where was Castiel?

About the Author

RACHEL COLLETT is a genuine Jill-of-all-trades. Born in Mesa, Arizona, she was never satisfied with staying in one place, working in one profession, or even pursuing one degree at a time. As a student for life, Rachel has loved learning in a multitude of disciplines, but in 2009, writing became her true passion

ALMOST TWO YEARS AGO, Rachel wondered if she had another book in her. OF BLOOD AND DECEIT was an answer to that question and since then it has become an obsession. To learn more about what other projects are in the mix, check out her website www.rachelcollett.com, or follow her on Facebook, Instagram, or Twitter.

PHOTO CREDIT: Elisha J. Schabel with Elle J. Photography

Made in the USA
Columbia, SC
30 March 2019